NADINE LITTLE

Verdana

LITTLE PUBLISHING

Members of my mailing list get free stuff and exclusive behind-the-scenes material.

Members are always the first to hear about my new books and discounts.

Join at nadinelittle.com

'You cannot construct your house in the jungle
without good relations with the wolf,
the tiger, the lion.'
Avijeet Das

'And hope, if it had a scent,
would smell like spring, like rain,
like something new and alive.'
Jennifer Rush, *Reborn*

Prologue

"Do you think they'll ever discover the truth?"

The Elder places his palm on the curved glass of an incubator pod, one of many in the hushed and darkened rows. The foetus inside paddles her legs in the murky fluid then floats still, curled tight. A screen on the control panel at the base reads 'Time Until Birth: 22 hours'.

"The first generation of humans will be born on this planet in a day and that is what you choose to worry about?" his companion says.

The Elder shifts, refusing to meet the other man's gaze, his eyes on the glass and their hope for the future contained within.

"I'm simply considering the likelihood of rebellion. It would take so little to lead to our extinction."

"There will be no rebellion. Their training will start from the moment they take their first breath."

"But what if—"

His companion slaps the Elder on the back, dislodging his hand from the cool surface of the incubator pod.

"You forget we have the strongest drivers of human behaviour on our side," he says.

The two men walk between the rows, their footsteps light in deference to the sleeping children of Verdana. A tiny fist waves here, a leg kicks there.

"And what are they?" the Elder says.

His companion smiles, his teeth flashing in the gloom.

"Hatred and fear," he says.

1

The smell of rain reminds me of home, although I've never been there. This place is my home, has always been my home, where the rain smells the same. Or so the Elders say. Droplets fall in a violet shimmer and slick my black hair to my cheeks. The rain is warm and tastes—

"Oi, Axelle, the rest of us don't enjoy drowning ourselves," Mallory calls, his voice echoing over the parade ground, "so when you're ready to move out…"

Someone suppresses a snigger in the squad lined up behind me. Probably Brindan. I scrape my hair back and tuck it into the collar of my battlesuit, my fingers brushing the stone pendant around my neck.

"Since we're now on duty, Mallory of the fifth, that's 'sir' or 'Godkiller' to you."

"Sorry, Boss," he says, earning another Brindan snort of appreciation. "I mean, sir."

Mallory grins at me and flashes his dimples. His grey battlesuit is broad at the shoulders. Maybe a bit too broad.

His cockiness first attracted me, and the fact he's four years my junior. The remaining guys from my generation are too jaded and scarred to be pleasant bedmates. But I'll have to switch him out soon. He's getting too full of himself.

Tomorrow. If I'm still alive later, tonight will be for celebrating.

"Helmets on," I say.

I click mine into place. The life support system purrs, a status update scrolling across the HUD embedded in the polycarbonate visor. I clear it using the sensors in the tips of my gloves and toggle my radio.

"Sound off."

Thirty call signs follow one after the other. My unit has the highest survival rate, though I don't like to brag. Ten have been with me for six years, the rest ranging from a year to months. If I only lose a couple, it'll be a good day.

I twirl my finger in the air. "Move out."

Our boots slap through the puddles on the hatched stone of the parade ground, the narrow drainage furrows overwhelmed by the rain shower. Water steams from my helmet. Ten bulky troop carriers wait for us, their prows aimed at the barred gate, their wheels huge and paddled. The fortified wooden wall on either side of the entrance blocks my view of the jungle.

Each squad leader has their own routine before battle, be it toasting with honeybrew, polishing their weapons or kissing a good luck charm. I prefer quiet contemplation of the cobalt sky, the only colour in the grey and black of Home Base. Better to gulp that humid, oxygen-saturated air and feel the blood sing in my veins than worry about what's to come.

Twenty-four years on Verdana is already past the life expectancy for someone like me.

We pile into the empty troop carrier and the door slides shut, sealing with a hiss. Muted strip lights dapple our faces white and blue. We sway as the vehicle surges forward.

The gate clangs. The smooth ride lasts a minute then the harnesses work to keep us seated, our helmets clunking together. There's an almost constant splash of water as the carrier launches from pool to river to swamp, squelching through the rich mud of the forest in between.

After an hour, the lights inside the vehicle brighten and I squint until my eyes adjust. Ten more minutes and the carrier bounces to a stop, the door yawning open into a mouth of green and gold and turquoise.

I stand and ready my weapon. "What's our target?"

"The bloodstone deposit," choruses my squad.

"Who are our enemies?"

"The fucking marble gods of Verdana," Mallory says loudly over the usual response.

"And who do we trust?"

"No one but us."

I tap two fingers to my chest. "May we fight again."

"May we fight again!" they yell, and I jump from the vehicle.

The jungle can be overwhelming when you first see it, though I have no one from the twentieth or twenty-first generations in my squad. Thank god. No twelve year olds to coddle as they lose their battle virginity. But even seasoned warriors hesitate at plunging into the suffocating vegetation. I've watched soldiers scramble back into the carriers and refuse to leave, terrified by the reduced visibility and the high likelihood of a Verdanian leaping out of a clutch of waxy leaves to hack at your battlesuit until they get to the softness beneath.

I love the jungle. There's nowhere more alive than this teeming, dripping cacophony. Although I can't smell anything in my battlesuit but my breath, I know what the jungle smells of—loam and fungi and pollen with a hundred different scents.

"On me, squad," I say, and notch my weapon to my shoulder. "Starfish, Barbie—watch our six."

Brindan and Mallory move to the rear of the column as I enter a landscape of wet leaves and sticky plants broken by pools of water. Colourful skreeingbirds, with beaks longer than their bodies, flit between flowers of every hue to sip a tincture of water and nectar. They *skree* at me as I get close, their call far too loud for such tiny things.

Similar has been said about me. I gently discouraged it.

The other squads are hidden by the vegetation but we'll be ten metres apart. Hell, we could be two metres apart and I still wouldn't see them.

My team manoeuvres among the plants in a whisper of leaves. Off to my right, crunching and cracking comes from some higher-generation noob lumbering through the trees. The barrel of my weapon sweeps the green, waiting for a flash of white. I place each boot carefully, overlapping fronds obscuring my feet and brushing my legs.

I'm used to the sensory deprivation of the battlesuit but I miss the touch and taste and smell of this world. The humidity of the jungle rather than my own sweat. No one else seems to mind. When our enemy has skin as tough as stone, you take all the armour you can get.

There's a splosh and a curse off to my left as someone stumbles into a pool. The suits are waterproof so the extra noise is just careless.

I signal to my squad and we crouch in the ferns, listening hard. The sounds of the other teams continue in front. A minute passes without screams, and I motion to resume.

The jungle thins around a swamp, tangled roots disappearing into the still surface. Insects swarm in the twin beams of sunlight, occasionally zipping into the pool to feed on algae. A jewel snake flicks its tongue at me, its gem-coloured body curled around a rotten stump. It uncoils and plops into the water, fins flaring and propelling it away with barely a ripple. I lead a wide path around the swamp.

Verdanians have a tendency to burst from the water without warning. Handy, since they can breathe in it using their specialised lungs and gills combo. They also have a habit of dragging soldiers under, particularly if they've smashed the helmet. Then they watch the soldier drown.

Been there.

The jungle eats the swamp. I feel a little better and scold myself for it. It took me a long time to get over my phobia of water and cognitive therapy is a bitch.

I check my position on the map of my HUD. "Target fifty metres ahead. Stay sharp."

"Shouldn't it be 'stay wet'?" Mallory's voice huffs in my ear. "This damn planet."

"You haven't been on any other planet," Loyanne says, her words precise to mask her lisp. "Perhaps they're all this wet."

"Earth wasn't, Angelface. I know that from lessons."

"Parts of it were so you've not been listening."

"No talking," I say, and the voices cease.

A monewt whoops at us from the canopy, bouncing on the branch until the leaves shiver. Kind of like an Earth monkey but with amphibious skin and flaps beneath its arms to allow it to glide through air and water. It also throws poop but this one has poor aim. Hooting in disappointment, it vanishes among the hanging moss.

"Twenty metres to target," I whisper.

The jungle is never quiet but the silence of my squad is a comforting weight at my back. Meanwhile, Soldier-Stomps-A-Lot persists up ahead, my team far enough to avoid getting caught by whatever they attract.

When the screaming starts, I'm not surprised.

2

"Strike formation, break right," I bark at my squad.

We plough through the weeping vegetation towards the screams. A curtain of moss streaks my visor, the wetness quickly cleared by the heated surface.

It's easier not to fight the jungle but to move with it, otherwise you're liable to get tangled in vines or find yourself neck-deep in a swamp.

A clump of ferns guides me around a mouldering tree. The fungus on the trunk is spotted blue and yellow, the gills hanging from the cap in moisture-beaded fronds.

The screaming cuts off and, for a couple of heartbeats, the jungle is still.

A wasp the size of my fist drones past. Skreeing, hooting and chittering fills the void left by the scream.

Bright splashes of red coat a waxy leaf level with my face. Scraps of battlesuit crackle under my boots. An arm dangles between a forked branch. Gunfire erupts from deeper to the right and I lead my squad behind it, the greenery better at deflecting enemy arrows and spears than our bloodstone bullets.

Shredded plants mark the course of the battle. Humans yell and charge in streaks of grey swallowed by the vegetation from one blink to the next. A spear skewers a soldier where the battlesuit is weakest at the collar, the shaft wrapped in cord and decorated with beads and feathers. A comrade rushes to his aid but, going by the blood on the inside of the helmet, there's no help for him anymore. A shape drops from the canopy, thudding into the soldier and slamming her to the ground. Bushes mask her struggle. A gun sails into the undergrowth. My bullet takes the Verdanian in the lower back. He flinches and leaps into the trees, vanishing among the branches.

I pull the dazed soldier to her feet. "Return to your squad. We need to reform the line and force the enemy to retreat."

She nods and unsheathes her bloodstone knife, her helmet fogged by her rapid breaths. She slashes at the vegetation and it parts briefly, swallowing her after a few steps. My squad fans out and we cover our tiny portion of the jungle. I lose one from the fourteenth generation when his inattention mires him in sucking mud and, instead of calling for help, he lets himself fall behind.

The Verdanians are masters of the ambush. They hide and wait and strike from a cloak of vegetation or water then merge back into the jungle until the next opportunity. They're damned hard to kill and our casualties are always higher. It's like fighting wisps of smoke.

But we slowly advance on the target in a quarry of sheer rock. More of us will die while we hold them off during mining but without bloodstone for our weapons, we're powerless. There's no other material that can penetrate a Verdanian's skin.

I fire a burst of bullets, and a yelp rewards me. It's not enough to kill her but her wounded leg will take her out of the battle.

"They're heading for the caves," I say, tension knotting my shoulders. "Barbie, get the explosives ready."

"With pleasure, sir," Mallory says, and I don't need to see his face to know he's grinning.

The entrance of the cave is too wide to guarantee a complete blockage. I move into the dimness of the tunnel, the damp walls broken by carpets of moss glowing green and blue. I turn on the lightbar in my helmet, the circles of yellow illuminating a dusty and somehow dry floor. Stalactites bombard us with drops of water. Smaller passages lead off from the main tunnel and we pause while I send a squad pair down each to check they're clear. The main tunnel finally narrows and splits into three yawning holes of blackness.

"Okay, set up here. Starfish, Angelface—give him a hand. The rest—watch his back."

I stare into the darkness of the tunnels until the black seems to swirl like fog. My arms ache from keeping my weapon steady. Soldiers fidget next to me, the scrape of stone under their boots buzzing along my nerves.

It's too easy to imagine the sounds coming from the depths of the cave. Is there another way out or will the Verdanians attack us once they realise what we're doing?

"Ready, sir," Mallory says, and I almost jump. He grips the detonator box in his gloved hand.

"Fall back. Wait for my signal."

My squad troops towards the entrance out of sight beyond the curves of wall. Mallory and I retreat last. I keep my eyes on the openings until the corner hides them from view. Footsteps slap on stone.

Bare feet.

"Shit," I whisper.

Mallory mashes the detonator button. The explosion batters my ears even through the protective filter of my battlesuit, the force shoving me to my knees. Mallory sprawls on his face. Dust billows into the tunnel, rock shards pattering on my helmet.

"Goddammit, Mallory!" I shout over the crack of stone. "That wasn't the signal."

A crevasse yaws in the roof above us, smaller fractures snaking along the walls. Powder swirls in the beams of my lightbar. The fluorescent moss has faded to brown. I claw myself to my feet and kick Mallory until he stands. We run for the cave entrance, the floor shuddering beneath us. A rock bounces off my helmet and bowls me into the wall. I stagger but manage to stay upright.

I wave at Mallory hesitating in the tunnel. "Go, you idiot. I'm right behind you."

He sprints for the blaze of sunlight, trailing dust and pulverised stone. I take a step to follow and a horrible grinding noise shivers into my gut. I dive for a side passage as the roof of the main tunnel collapses in a shrieking hail of rock. I scramble backwards from the avalanche, and the tunnel widens into a chamber. A boulder hits the floor with a weighty *clack* and bounces into me, tumbling me to the ground.

I imagine it's like being sat on by an elephant, though the landmass of Ananngar has no beast that large.

My battlesuit adapts to stop me from being crushed but my gun and arm are pinned. I shove at the stone with my free hand, trying to buck it off. It doesn't budge.

Goddamn Mallory, the premature bastard.

Plumes of dust swirl and speckle on my helmet, which doesn't seem to be damaged so at least I don't have to inhale rock particles. The beams from the lightbar jitter on the roof. No cracks extend into the chamber. The clack and crunch of falling rock fade to silence.

Maybe I won't be completely buried alive.

I can't see my feet or legs past the hulking boulder. I wiggle them to reassure myself. The moss furring the walls tentatively begins to glow through the settling dust. Yellow this time, like a room full of candles. Something skitters in the chamber.

Claws on rock? I search my brain for cave-dwelling fauna that will eat my face but there should be nothing more than beetles in here. Even one-handed, I can take on a horde of beetles.

A Verdanian steps around the boulder from the direction of my feet.

"Oh, shit," I say.

3

Up close, Verdanians are breath-taking. Breath-taking and awful. This one has the typical pure white skin of those from Ananngar, though streaked with powdered stone.

His is a race of marble monsters who still look pretty with your blood splattered on their face.

I lunge for my knife. The Verdanian moves too fast for my eyes to follow anything but a pale streak. Slim fingers pluck the blade from my hand, and the creature pins my arm under his knee. I can't even bite him if he gets near enough.

Probably best since I'd break my teeth as they're not pointed, like his. It doesn't matter that the incisors and canines are for peeling bark and the tough vegetation of their diet. Whenever they bare those fangs, my kneecaps turn to water.

My panting fogs my visor. Just like the soldier back in the jungle. But she was unranked. Inexperienced. A baby. In war years, I'm ancient.

I swallow and it hurts but my breathing slows. I tug on my arm. It may as well be pinned by another rock.

The Verdanian watches me with an arrogant expression, my knife held lightly in one hand. His irises are a deep emerald, his pupils more oval than round. Cheekbones as sharp as stone flints. His hair is a shade of pale green similar to milky tea. It flops into his eyes since he's bent forward. The head of an axe peeks over his shoulder, the strap across his bare chest.

It always weirds me out that the males have no nipples.

I wait for him to shatter my helmet and jam the bloodstone into my throat.

"Do you know why we are fighting?" he says in perfect, clipped English.

I blink at him. He cocks his head, and I blink a few more times.

"Because your species would rather see us dead than share your planet," I say and my voice only wobbles a little.

He shifts and places his hands on the collar of my battlesuit, the knife clinking against the helmet. My heart flops into my mouth and I grit my teeth to keep it from escaping.

"I tire of your war of untruths," the Verdanian says.

He presses a series of switches he shouldn't possibly know and removes my helmet with a clunk and a sigh of dispersing oxygen. My damp hair unfurls into the dust. The coolness of the cave is wonderful on my flushed cheeks but also wrong when I'm close enough to an enemy to feel his breath. He could crush my skull in one hand.

"Your eyes are the colour of the sky," he says, placing my helmet on the ground so we're both bathed in the beams of the lightbar.

While I'm puzzling through that statement—perhaps his English is patchy and he meant to tell me he's going to pluck out my eyes—he slices the tip of his finger with the bloodstone blade. It takes three cuts before a pearlescent bead shimmers in the light. Subtle rainbow hues swirl on the surface. My tongue sticks to the roof of my mouth. He moves his finger towards my lips and I jerk my face away, the collar of the battlesuit digging into my neck.

"If it's all the same to you," I hiss through clamped teeth, "I'd rather you just slit my throat."

"This should not hurt you."

His finger arrows for my mouth. I turn my face to the opposite side, and wetness smears my cheek in the region of my scar. It's as warm as the rain.

How odd.

"Your blood is *poison*," I mumble without moving my lips.

Sadness darkens his eyes, if Verdanians can feel sad. Their expressions are usually as stony as their skin.

"I do not think that is true," he says, "but if it is, I am sorry."

He sets my knife beside my helmet and grips my jaw, his finger and its deadly bead of blood hovering over my mouth. His skin is cooler than the cave. Something smells like crushed mint and I doubt it's me since I reek of sweat and mulch. I shake my head but only succeed in bruising myself against his fingers. I fold my lips, and air whistles through my nostrils. He pinches my nose shut with his free hand. I glare at him but pressure quickly builds in my chest. My heels drum against the floor. The Verdanian and the rock are unmoved.

I won't open my mouth. I'll faint and the Verdanian can poison me while I'm insensible. It's preferable to an agonising death as his blood dissolves my insides.

My pulse pounds in my temples, heat blazing from my skin in waves. My chest expands. I thrash in the Verdanian's grip but can't free a nostril to suck in precious air. A whine boils in my throat. My vision blurs but I continue to scowl in the direction of the white, wavery thing.

I will not breathe.

God, I need to breathe.

My mouth pops open and the Verdanian's finger slides between my lips, stroking along my tongue. The blood is syrupy-sweet. I gag and he holds my jaw closed, letting me snort through my nose like an enraged water-tiger. The bastard is patient and waits until I swallow to avoid drowning in my own saliva. He relaxes his grip on my face, one hand tracing my jaw where I'll soon have bruises in the shape of his fingers. If I live for more than an hour.

"Your skin is so delicate," he says.

I can't decide whether to vomit or scream so I say nothing. The taste of him is in my throat.

When will the pain start? Will I survive long enough to choke on a soup of my internal organs?

My thrashing has dislodged the pendant around my neck and the stone sits in the hollow between my collarbones, jumping along with my heartbeat. The Verdanian touches it, his other hand rubbing a stone hanging on a black cord around his throat. His turquoise and violet gem is the size of a snake egg.

"Where did you get this? How dare you wear it!" He reverts to rapid, lilting Anann and unpicks the cord's knot, cradling the stone in his hands. "You humans respect nothing."

It belonged to the first Verdanian I killed. I never collected another after that as I don't need tokens to tally my kills. The marks on my gun work just fine and twelve stones around my neck would be a bit cumbersome. But this gem, a firestone, marked my transition to a soldier. Okay, and it's pretty— bright orange flecked with yellow, like fire captured in glass.

"Am I dying yet?"

"These stones are sacred," he says as if I haven't spoken. "This contains the last piece of the warrior you killed. Unless it is returned to the water, he will be always lost."

The Verdanian tucks the pendant in the wide belt at his waist, and stands, releasing my arm. His trousers are made of leaves sewn together and end mid-calf, his feet bare. A woven vine with tiny flowers circles his ankle.

"You cannot understand since you worship nothing." His gaze rests on the rock pinning my lower body. "Apart from your weapons and our bloodstone—the stone of our leaders. The stone that reminds us we are mortal. Yes, perhaps you worship that stone."

Worship it? We'd die without it. When I was eighteen, the Verdanians raided our stores and the remaining bullets ran out. No one from the eighth or ninth generations survived the war that year.

The Verdanian paces, continuing to explain the importance of stones and spirits but his voice washes over me. The blood is having an effect. I tense in preparation.

Will the pain be the sharpness of a slicing knife? Or the dull, creeping ache of intestinal sickness?

My heart splits into three and beats out of sync, two high in my chest, the last deep in my stomach. Colours swirl beneath the Verdanian's skin as if his blood is liquid pearl. I rub my eyes but the visual remains.

He's a freaking rainbow.

"What have you done to me?" I whisper.

He stops pacing. His eyes blaze emerald, consuming the darkness of his pupil. He steps towards me, and I flinch but he rolls the rock off as if it's made of sponge. I scramble to my feet and sway at the dizziness. I fumble for my gun. The spike of fear is not my own but the Verdanian's face is impassive.

So who's fear am I feeling?

I sag against the cave wall. My shaking weapon points in the direction of the Verdanian, though he stands completely still, arms at his sides, his axe strapped to his back. He's tall and slim, like most of his species and most of our generations. My head barely reaches the level of his chest. His drying blood tingles on my cheek.

"I need the blood connection to show you the lies," he says.

I understand the words but, put together, they make no sense.

"You may want to—what is the word?—brace yourself for the first."

What is he talking about? I've never had a conversation with a Verdanian so maybe this is normal.

"Our blood will kill you," he says.

We're taught it from birth. Never get their blood in your mouth or eyes, or death will be swift and agonising.

As soon as his sentence ends, an invisible fist ploughs into my gut, driving the breath from my body.

"My species refused to welcome you peacefully onto our planet."

My stomach twists at the words, and I double over.

They fought us. Almost killed us. The Elders and Passengers have a million horror stories of those first, awful years on our new planet.

"What alien trickery is this?" I gasp, my arms wrapped around my midriff.

This time, although his face still shows nothing, sadness claws at my throat.

"You are the alien here," he says.

It's as if someone has taken a glass hammer and struck a crystal that happens to be my heart. My real heart, not the ghost hearts. I clutch my chest, my ears ringing. Maybe I *am* dying.

"That was your first truth," the Verdanian says. "Here is another—I need your help."

The wall against my butt is the only thing keeping me upright. A bead of water drips from a stalactite and forms a dark circle in the dust.

"Why should I help you?" I croak.

"Because we welcomed you onto our planet."

His words vibrate in my chest.

No! They tried to exterminate us.

"Your species chose war over peace," he says in the same maddening, calm voice.

I fall to my knees.

It doesn't make sense. *It doesn't make sense.*

"You kill us and we do not even know why," he says.

They kill us every fucking day.

"Please stop," I whisper.

My harsh breaths fill the chamber, my hands splayed on the floor to keep me from flopping on my face. My damn chest sings but, at last, it fades, the Verdanian watching me as I peek at him through my hair.

"If we do not work together," he says almost gently, "our species will destroy each other and we will never have peace."

Peace? His species has never wanted peace.

"Why me?" I say to keep him talking and give myself a chance to recover.

"You are the first human to listen. That is much due to the rock. If your weapon had been free, I would be dead."

"Or I would be."

I lever myself from the floor. My heart settles into a normal lump of muscle instead of emulating a bell. My weapon hangs on its sling and the weirdness of it unsettles me.

I'm trapped in a small space with an enemy warrior but it seems we're not going to kill each other. My helmet and knife sit forgotten in the dust. It's unreal to be so close to a Verdanian and not be thinking of where best to aim my gun or stick my knife to ensure maximum damage.

The hollow of his throat. The skin is thinner, more vulnerable. A blade might reach the blood vessels running lateral to his vertebrae.

I cough. "Your English is excellent."

His eyes meet mine. Such a bright green, like the sun through leaves.

"I have practised a long time for this."

The truth of his statement still rings in my chest but it's softer now he's not bombarding me.

But is it the truth just because he says it is? I'm still banking on alien trickery. Nothing has made sense since he shoved his blood in my mouth.

So why am I not dead? Is none of this real? Maybe the rock smacked my head on the way down and I'm hallucinating from a traumatic brain injury.

"I am tired of watching my people die," the Verdanian continues.

I can't pinch myself through my battlesuit. I bite my tongue, and it hurts. Shit.

"What's your name?" I say.

He cocks his head. "You may call me Zorian."

"That's not your full name?"

"You will mispronounce my full name."

"Try me."

He raises an eyebrow the same colour as his hair. It's an excessive amount of emotion for a Verdanian.

"I am Zorianangullewell'yan Bruad'arach."

"Zorian it is."

He makes no sound, gives no smile or laugh, but a brief burst of warmth blooms in my chest.

What in the holy fuck has he done to me?

His skin continues to do its milky swirl of rainbow colours. If I stare too much, I get queasy.

"How long will this blood connection, or whatever you called it, last?"

"Some days."

"*Days!*"

"You drank only a little. It is not so strong if we are apart. You must share yours now."

My battlesuit beeps, and I leap at least a foot off the ground. I switch the radio from the helmet to the suit collar and ignore my pulse ping-ponging around my mouth. The ghost of two, steady, out-of-sync heartbeats stays in my chest.

"—come in," says Mallory's tinny voice through the speakers. "Godkiller, can you read me?"

"I read you. I'm trapped in the first side chamber off the western wall. When will you break through?"

"Ten minutes, tops."

"No explosives," I say.

He laughs. "Copy that."

Definitely too cocky for his own good.

"Your name is Godkiller?" Zorian says.

"Um, no. It's my call sign. My name is Axelle."

"Why do they not say Axelle?"

"It's a codename. Kind of like a nickname you give a friend."

What if he asks what it means? Can he tell when I'm lying or does he need to drink my blood? Is that what he meant by my turn to share? We're taught that's what they do—rip out our throats and drink our blood.

"I do not understand your use of many names for the same thing," Zorian says.

The rocks blocking the exit shake and scrape together. Dust plumes out of the gaps, pebbles scattering in a small avalanche.

"We can get into the onomastics later." I wave him away from the entrance. "When my squad breaks through, they'll kill you."

Maybe I should let them kill him. *I* should have killed him.

"You can tell them not to," Zorian says.

"They won't listen."

"Are you not their chief?"

"We're trained to hate you from birth. That's hard to ignore."

He runs his fingers down the strap across his chest. "And do you hate me?"

Not a freaking clue. Part of me hopes this is a stress-induced dream and not a brain injury. Maybe I'm finally getting battleshock.

"I don't know what you expect me to do," I say.

"Follow the untruths. Talk to your people."

Oh, well, not much at all then…

The stones tremble and we back away as larger ones are dislodged, clacking to the bottom in purls of dirt.

"You need to lie down," I say.

Zorian cocks his head again, a spike of hair flopping into one eye.

"Pretend to be dead," I say. "Can you pull that rock over yourself like you've been crushed?"

Would a Verdanian even be crushed? Will my squad buy it?

Why am I trying to save him?

"I need you to share your blood first," he says.

I lick my lips. There's still a hint of sweetness, and my stomach flips.

"Why?"

"To communicate with you. And, since we are not friends, to tell if you are lying."

Truth—or the poison—dings between my ribs. I don't want to give him my blood. Who knows what further alien magic he could use on me?

"How will you communicate with me?" I say.

"Through your dreams."

"You'll invade my dreams?"

He bares his teeth, and my legs wobble.

"Not invade. We do not invade, like you."

The rocks shudder and a small gap appears near the roof, thick with billowing dust.

I wave at the floor. "Lie down."

"I will lie down after. This is"—Zorian pauses, as if searching for a word—"un-negotiable."

"Fine! Just lie down first and I'll give you some freaking blood."

"I cannot tell if you are lying."

"I promise," I growl.

"A promise from a human? You break them all."

Zorian gives me a haughty stare but stretches out on his

back and rolls the rock until it appears to be crushing his lower body. Three heartbeats bounce around my chest. I grab my knife and kneel beside him. He breathes and watches me, his features impassive. God-like.

"Why do I have two extra heartbeats?" I say, my mouth dry.

"They are mine. Sharing blood is sacred. It is usually for bonded pairs."

"Quite a lot of things are sacred to you guys."

Even I can decipher his dark look.

"I can't believe I'm doing this," I mumble, and unfasten my glove, pressing the bloodstone to the tip of my middle finger. It stings immediately. Blood wells and a drop of red meanders towards my palm.

Shit. Too much?

I cradle my hand to my chest. Rocks scrape and shift behind me. I grit my teeth and shove my hand at Zorian. His fingers curl around my wrist to steady it. My heart flaps against my ribs like a trapped skreeingbird, way faster than Zorian's.

"If you bite off my finger…"

His anger nibbles along my skin. "I will not bite off your finger."

Truth. Apparently. It doesn't make it any better.

Zorian raises his head and licks my finger from palm to pad. God, it tickles. His tongue is rough and wet, a deep channel running from the centre to the slightly forked tip. It's more mobile than a human's. Stronger.

I shiver. What the hell am I doing, sitting in a cave letting a Verdanian suck on my finger? If anyone sees me, I'll either get sentenced to shrink eval since I have a stellar record and no demerits or, they'll be so repulsed, I'll be marked as a traitor, whipped and subjected to behavioural reconditioning. I've seen the few soldiers punished that way. They were not the same people when they came out.

Zorian releases my hand, his grimace not shown on his face but echoing in the pit of my stomach.

"It is so metallic," he says.

"I thought you knew that already."

"We do not drink human blood. We do not want to feel what you feel. You are a chaotic species."

"You're about to feel what I feel."

He blinks. "Yes. It will be unpleasant."

"Having you inside me is no picnic, either, buddy."

Axelle—master of diplomatic relations. Zorian chose the wrong woman for this mission.

The floor vibrates under my knees, and stone shrieks behind me. I thrust the knife hilt-first at Zorian.

"Cut yourself and smear some blood around. Then shut your eyes and lie still. No breathing."

An hour ago, I wouldn't have cared if my squad blasted in and slaughtered Zorian. I would've welcomed it. Joined in.

Do I believe what he told me? I don't know. I don't know anything anymore. Maybe his blood *is* poison, polluting my mind, making me doubt. I need some distance from him.

I fasten my glove and don my helmet, oxygen hissing over my face. Zorian hacks at his palm and streaks blood around his throat, squeezing his hand until a pool collects in the hollow between his collarbones. The colours weave. It's almost beautiful.

"What are you feeling?" he says, and I flinch.

"What did I say about lying still? And no talking. They could break through any minute."

"Are you going to help me?"

Is my blood having an effect? Will it signal a lie if I'm confused about what I'm going to do? Hell, I'm confused about everything.

"I'll search for evidence and then… I don't know."

"You believe what you are saying, that much I can tell. Do you promise?"

I sigh. "You trust my promises all of a sudden?"

"You kept your promise about the blood."

"Fine. I promise to search."

He holds my knife up. "Do you still hate me?"

I take it and return it to my suit. "It's probably best I don't answer that."

His mouth twitches. A rare Verdanian smile or his blood has hallucinogenic properties.

"Truth," he says.

Rocks rattle and clatter. Dust puffs into the chamber, settling around the dark maw of an exposed entrance. Shapes drift through the murk.

"Hey, Boss, you look wonderfully un-squished," Mallory says, his lightbar parting the dust and sweeping me up and down.

"You're on waste duty for the next two weeks," I say.

I keep the *and out of my bed* to myself.

His grumbles are lost in the greetings of the rest of my squad. My battlesuit protects me from the enthusiastic back-slapping, though the force shunts me forward a few steps.

"Whoa, were you trapped in here with one of those things?" Mallory circles around me. "Is this another one to add to your list? They should give you a medal, Boss."

My heartbeat flutters but steadies. Zorian's eyes are shut, his face slack and devoid of its usual cold arrogance. His blood glimmers in the beams of multiple lightbars.

"He was already dead," I say.

"Awesome, then it counts as mine."

Mallory whips out his knife and slices through the cord of Zorian's pendant. He waves the stone aloft.

"Kill number two," he whoops, the words echoing in the cramped chamber.

Fury scalds my skin but Zorian twitches not one muscle. I'm a bit pissed off at Mallory for his constant insubordination but it's nowhere near Zorian's level.

Am I really feeling what he's feeling or projecting since he planted the idea in my brain?

I snatch the pendant before Mallory straightens up. "This is mine since, one—you almost killed me and, two—you trapped me in here with a dead Verdanian. I could have caught a disease."

Do my words ring hollow to my squad? Do they twist in Zorian's gut?

My team herds me towards the entrance, jostling a sulky Mallory. I open a pouch in my battlesuit to store the turquoise and violet stone. A twin pulse thuds where I touch it and fades as I walk away.

I don't look back.

4

My shoes pound on the springy treadmill embedded in the floor of the gym. The turquoise and violet stone thuds against my sternum.

I swear, it still pulses faintly.

My scan at the hospital on my return confirmed no brain injury. My tox screen was negative. The stuff in the cave has to be battleshock. Has to be.

I pick up my pace, frowning out the five-inch-thick polycarbonate in front of me. Scratches from spears and arrows mar the surface but it's not enough to block my view of the jungle below our raised plateau of flattened rock.

It's the only window that looks out in the whole of Home Base. Another option, if you want to see something other than black building modules and grey rock, is to go atop the wall, but that's frowned upon unless you're assigned to guard duty.

Skreeingbirds burst from the canopy and wheel in the air, their rainbow colours enhanced by the bronze and gold of sunset. The primary sun sets first, trailed by its paler sister. The cobalt sky darkens to midnight blue. Verdana has no moons but the stars form sparkling highways and clusters and constellations. There are so many, you can draw any picture you want by connecting the dots.

A door hisses open behind me. I keep my gaze on the stars and focus on my breathing, the stretch and pull of my muscles, the pleasant ache and tiredness of a good workout. My hair spills from a high ponytail and swishes against my shoulders.

There's nothing else to think about. Nothing at all.

"I would've thought you got enough exercise in the jungle today," Mallory says, walking carefully to avoid the treadmills. He rests his butt on the window to watch me. "I have a method of keeping fit that is more fun and doesn't involve running."

"Considering I spent most of my time in a cave and the deposit was mined by the time I got out—no, I didn't get enough exercise."

"Still mad about that, huh?"

He flashes his dimples, as if that will make me forgive him. His olive, off-duty uniform is wrinkled in places except where it stretches over his broad shoulders.

Has he always been this sloppy? Have I let it slide since I'm sleeping with him? How unprofessional.

"Go away, Mallory." I slash my finger through the air above the treadmill's floor sensors. The track slows to my warm-down pace.

"Aw, come on, Axe. At least let me make it up to you."

"You'll make it up to me by spending the next two weeks emptying shit, sorting rubbish and showing me a glimmer of contrition for being so fucking stupid. You could have killed me, yourself and my squad."

He shoves away from the window and stops with the toes of his shoes almost touching my treadmill. "And I'll be contrite but that doesn't mean I can't make it up to you now. A few orgasms should have you screaming my name in no time."

I've never screamed his name and don't plan on starting. I'm his squad leader. Even naked and sweaty, I show some decorum. And Mallory is a selfish lover. But he's young so he has excellent stamina. I can get there, eventually.

Maybe I need someone who gets me there with more immediacy.

"Earth lesson begins in twenty minutes," I say, my voice mild.

"Skip it. It's not like we'll miss anything."

I step off the treadmill on the opposite side to Mallory, and flow into my stretches. "It's the anniversary class."

"Which we've seen every year since we slithered out of a test tube. You're four years older than me—I'm sure you have it memorised."

I cock my eyebrow. "You know we're not born in test tubes."

"Fine, birthing pods, whatever. My point remains—we've seen it all before. I want to peel you out of those shorts and fuck you standing up. I love that you're so teeny—"

He bites off the last word at my glare.

"You're going, Mallory. Keep giving me lip and it'll be a month of waste duty."

It was his teasing that first attracted me to him. A bit of light relief. And it's not like I have unlimited options. The rest of the generations are too serious, too mouthy or a bit young for me.

I swig from my water bottle and head for the showers— unisex, like the bathrooms and barracks. The idea of having multiples of everything to keep genders separate boggles my mind. We're all human. That's what matters.

Or does it?

Crap, I'm thinking about it.

I hustle through the sliding door and past the lockers, tossing my bottle and stripping off my clothes. I slap my palm to the wall reader in the large, tiled space, shower heads jutting from every side. The plate scans my ID and starts my programme—38 degrees Celsius, massage setting, seven minutes.

Mallory props his shoulder against the archway leading back into the locker room. "Then how about a quickie? We can get all slippery, bash it out and still make it to Earth lesson."

Wow, what an offer. I can barely contain my arousal.

Soap squirts from the dispenser. I rub it into my hair and over my body, my head tipped, eyes closed as the cool water batters my face. A shoe squeaks on tile. I open my eyes to a watery blur of olive.

"Mallory of the fifth generation," I say in my command voice, "get the fuck out of my shower."

5

The special anniversary class is held in the underground amphitheatre since it can hold everyone, otherwise we'd be segregated into our squads in the modules for normal Earth lessons. Elderman Vail stands on the stage in the centre, hands clasped in front, his maroon uniform marking him as a member of our governing body. Not only that—he was vice-captain on the ship under Captain Seabird.

All Elders are legends but Vail is second only to Seabird himself. I've spoken five words to Vail in my lifetime: "Yes, sir. Thank you, sir." Two separate occasions but I managed not to fangirl and embarrass myself.

Passenger DeLoris stands at the comms panel, preparing the large screen behind the stage, her bright-blue uniform a nice match to her long, blonde hair. She's one of the younger Passengers at thirty-five so probably doesn't even remember Earth but I can't help regarding them all with awe, Elders and Passengers alike. You can tell they came from Earth as they're all shorter than the generationers—except lucky old me—due to the heavier gravity. They saw Earth, lived on her, unlike the rest of us born on Verdana. Our knowledge will always be second-hand.

But at least they live a long time. Those who survived the

first years of colonisation, anyway. The cut-off age for a place on a ship was eighty and there were two people on ours, both Elders. One died this year at one hundred and ten years old, the other at one hundred and nine.

Must be the oxygen-rich Verdanian air.

I walk down the carved steps of black stone towards my seat in the second row with the other squad leaders, the front reserved for Elders. Whispers swell and fade as I pass the unranked soldiers in rows twelve to fourteen—mostly the higher generations.

Okay, so I'm a bit of a celebrity myself as the soldier with the highest kills and one of only fourteen remaining from my generation of one hundred.

I nod to any Passengers who glance my way, seated rows three to eleven since they're the most numerous group. I finally slot into my chair in the short row of green uniforms. Not emerald green, like Zorian's eyes, but forest green, with jade buttons.

Why am I thinking about Zorian?

I shake my head and focus on Elderman Vail, who raises his hands to quiet the rumble of voices. A hush settles over the amphitheatre. The lights dim. A spotlight circles Vail and glints off a stone sitting above his breast pocket. The citrine gem dangles on the end of a cord used to bind his ponytail of grey hair.

His first kill.

My fingers brush the stone at my throat, the surface cool despite the warmth of my skin.

I miss my firestone. It meant a lot to me—survival, acceptance, hope. If I could kill one Verdanian, I could kill more. We could win.

Is it now sitting on a riverbed somewhere after whatever Zorian meant by returning it to the water? Does he mourn the loss of his stone? I wonder how he explained its absence since he's clearly not dead.

"Today is a special day," Vail says, his hands clasped in front of him once more. "Today we remember. A people cannot truly know who they are until they know where they're from. Today, we return to the beginning or, to be more precise, the beginning and the end."

The screen brightens. Blackness cradles a small blue planet, the land a mix of green and brown with puffs of white. Once home to the whole of humanity.

"This is Earth in the twenty-first century, when our ancestors had the chance to change our future. But they did not do enough. This is Earth in the twenty-second century."

The blue planet is still blue but it's sickly, as if viewed through a yellow lens. There is no more green.

"Earth is dying. Disease, extreme weather, dwindling resources and wars over what's left. At eleven billion, the population is two billion past its carrying capacity."

Eleven billion. That's the equivalent of nearly three million Home Bases all crammed together. There's less than four thousand of us here and it gets claustrophobic. The population of Ananngar is estimated to be in the region of fifty thousand and is enough to give me nightmares. If they band together, our little corner of humanity will be wiped out.

"And so, Operation Genesis was born," Vail says.

A video plays on the screen. The camera pans through a huge shipyard where metal skeletons dwarf the people and pierce the sky. But these are not sea-faring ships. These are spaceships.

"One hundred ships were built across Earth, the crew and passengers selected through a rigorous programme of genetic screening, psychological and physiological testing and skill scoring. Each ship held three thousand one hundred and thirty-five souls. This ship will no doubt be familiar to all of you."

The spaceship is fat with fins, like something called a puffer fish I learned about in Earth lessons a couple of months ago. The lessons about plants and wildlife are my favourite.

"It was a symbol of our hope and courage to survive, though many will agree with me that some of that hope was to finally get off the blasted thing."

A chuckle ripples through the Elder and Passenger rows.

"Her name was the *HMS Dòchas*. She launched from Caithness in Scotland at nine am on Friday the thirty-first of August 2142, marking the end of our life on planet Earth and the beginning of our journey to save the human race. A journey that lasted two hundred years." Elderman Vail pats his hair and pinches his cheek, smoothing the wrinkles. "I think you'll agree we look pretty good for double centenarians."

Laughter swells in the amphitheatre.

I love the anniversary lesson—hearing about human ingenuity and their fight to survive. What would it have been like on the *HMS Dòchas*? The excitement of being selected, the nervousness at the enormity of the task ahead, the promise to do better on the next planet. The grief for all those left behind.

"After two hundred years of cryosleep, Captain and soon-to-be First Minister Seabird was awoken. Drones from the ship had detected a hospitable planet."

Verdana appears on the screen. The landmasses are tiny,

the freshwater oceans vast. All the land around the equator is green, interrupted only by inland seas and huge rivers, also freshwater. The landmasses in the northern hemisphere are composed entirely of swamp, with island chains of mountains and volcanoes in the southern hemisphere. Like Earth in the twenty-first century, the poles are frozen but far more inhospitable, raining shards of ice with a violet hue.

"Shuttles delivered the first pioneers from the *HMS Dòchas* to the surface of Verdana at three thirty-three pm on Wednesday the eleventh of November 2342, Earth time. It was raining."

Another laugh from the audience. The lush planet of Verdana is reflected in the eyes of every person in the room.

"After weeks of careful, exhausting exploration, we settled here, in the landmass of Ananngar, the southern jungle region home to the smallest population of indigenous people. We came in peace but we were not welcomed."

Boos and hisses shiver through the cavernous space. I shift in my seat.

Last year and every year before that, I joined in, the indignation quick to burn in the pit of my stomach. The hatred for the callous species who spurned us, although we'd travelled so far and lost so much.

How can it be a lie? It doesn't make sense to start a war if the Verdanians were friendly. Zorian must be misinformed. Or he's using me in a way I don't yet understand.

"The first five years in our new home were tough. More than half of the people on the *HMS Dòchas* died as a result of foreign pathogens, predators, poisoning from inedible plants, starvation and the animosity of the natives. It was heartbreaking." Vail swipes a finger under one eye. "We bonded on that ship. We were family. How dare the Verdanians threaten our fragile existence? We only wanted a chance at life and they almost took it away.

"But we fought back. We built, we learned, we trained. Artificial reproduction began in Year Six and thirty-six generations have been born since then. We are the human Verdanians and we deserve to be here. We fight and die to be here. One day, we will live in peace in Ananngar, even if we have to enslave the entire race of godless monsters. That is what *they* deserve."

Cheers wash over the amphitheatre. They flow through me, past me, but mine is lodged in my throat.

It's a rousing speech. It always made me want to grab my gun and rush into the jungle to hunt the bastards down. So why is the last part bugging me?

Because invaders enslave, not pioneers.

No. We're not invaders. The Verdanians gave us no choice. The human race must survive by any means necessary.

Stupid Zorian, messing with my head. I bet he's doing whatever the laughing equivalent is for a Verdanian right now at the thought of my confusion. How quickly he suckered me in his trickery.

"This life of ours is still tough," Vail continues when the roars fade. "We lose good people nearly every day. Good soldiers. Verdanian soldiers. We may even be all that remains of humanity with the lack of response from our sister ships. Or they may have found planets, peaceful planets, and are living an easier life than ours. Take heart from that and wish them well. But if it all gets too much—if nothing you do seems to matter— look up at the night sky. Look for the drifting star among stars. Look for the *HMS Dòchas* and remember where you come from. Remember where you are."

Heavy silence settles on my shoulders. No one is breathing. Everyone sits on the edge of their seats.

"This is our home," Elderman Vail says softly, "and they will never take it away from us."

6

I don't want to fall asleep.

The lights of my pod dim. They'll fade and switch off then brighten before my alarm rings at six am, Verdanian time. The routine is comforting. It means I survived to see the night and the next morning.

But today was not routine.

I can't go to sleep.

I sit on my bed in my vest and shorts, my legs crossed. It's the same outfit I wore under my battlesuit, albeit a clean pair. Everyone else seems to sleep naked.

After spending my first eighteen years in the barracks, believe me, I know.

I cradle the stone in my hands, the cord tangled in my fingers. The colour is quite lovely. Violet swirls through the turquoise, flecks of emerald sparkling at the core.

Funny, I didn't notice them earlier. Maybe they're pieces of Zorian's soul. How does he feel with parts of his soul missing?

Why do I care? Verdanians don't feel anything except superiority and disdain.

My fingertip strokes the smooth stone. It's heavy in my palm, cool. It pulses against my skin, like the ghost of two heartbeats.

I grab my spray bottle and mist my collection of plants even though I did it ten minutes ago. They spill from jars and beakers and containers on every surface. My pod is my personal jungle, my sanctuary. No one else is allowed in. They probably wouldn't understand. For them, the jungle is a terrifying place—a place they're likely to die—but to me, it's beautiful. It's vibrant and teeming with life. The jungle is nothing to fear.

Zorian's stone throbs in my hand. I shiver and slip the cord back over my head, the ghost heartbeats masked by my own.

My firestone never did anything like this. It behaved as a lump of inert rock should. Why did I take the stupid thing from Mallory? Okay, so I'll definitely treat it with more respect. It's sacred after all. But I could've dropped it on my way out of the cave. No one would've noticed and Zorian would be happy, or mildly less disdainful if that's what passes as happiness for his species. It's not like I'm going to see him again to give it back. Humans and Verdanians don't mix. We meet, we clash, we lick our wounds and retreat. We don't mingle.

Fuck. What happened between us already is treason.

My hand tightens on the spray bottle. Moisture patters on waxy leaves and drifts through the net lid of a small, glass tank nestled between the plants. My pet snail pokes his head out from under a log. A water droplet plops onto one of his four eye stalks and they immediately retract.

"Sorry, Ophrys," I say, putting the spray bottle down. "Got carried away."

He extends one eye in soft reproach then, since he's up, he returns to the pile of leaves I collected from the jungle and starts munching. His black shell shimmers purple and green, a ridge of white spikes extending from the top. The delicate fronds running down his sides let him swim through pools. He also waves them when he gets excited, or so I like to imagine.

I return to bed and stare at the ceiling. My eyelids droop. Sleep sings to me. It's been a fraught day, I should rest.

I shove myself up and lean against the wall, pulling my notebook into my lap and spilling my pencils onto the bed sheet. I flip past drawings of flowers, leaves and the intricate bark of a tree to an empty page.

Paper is unusual in Home Base. Everything can be done on tablets and screens but I talked nicely to a Passenger, a technician, and he made me the notebook from plant fibres. Some of the older Passengers still like to use paper.

My pencil brushes the page, capturing a flower I saw today. Petals spiral almost to the ground, the stamens a fuzz of yellow. I focus on getting the colours right, the petals mulberry at the centre, flowing to lilac then salmon pink at the tips. The pouches of my battlesuit were too full to stuff it in but I'll try to pick one later or catch it in seed and grow it.

I drop the pencil and rub my eyes. Maybe I'll close them for a second, just to rest.

I won't sleep.

* * *

"Ah, *cock*," I say to the silent jungle. There's no smell and the light is too bright, beams of gold spearing the ground. The flower from my sketch features prominently.

"What is a cock?" Zorian says in his careful English.

I spin around. Every leaf and frond and curtain of moss is

completely still.

"Where are you?"

"Up here."

He blends with the green of the canopy, his legs dangling on either side of a branch. He twists and drops, his bare feet thumping on the dirt.

"You do not need that," he says, his eyes dark.

My gaze drops to the bloodstone rifle in my hands, pointed in Zorian's direction.

"Shit," I say. "I didn't mean… It's instinctive."

Great. Zorian appears unarmed and I show up with a weapon. Way to start our peaceful negotiations.

He stands very still, arms loose at his sides. No signs of breathing. The gun feels heavy in my grip—fully loaded. My eyes dart wildly around for somewhere to put it. I place it on the ground and kick it under a fern, forcing myself to straighten empty-handed instead of snatching it back.

"Is that what you wear to sleep?" Zorian says.

I glance down at my vest and shorts. I don't wear a bra at night and it's a little obvious through the thin material. If I were flat-chested like a Verdanian female, I'd get away with it. They have no fatty tissue around their nipples, the milk ducts beneath the plates of bone they have instead of ribs.

I cross my arms over my chest. "And what exactly are you wearing?"

Why am I having a fashion conversation with a Verdanian in a dream-jungle? What the hell has happened to my life?

"It is comfortable for sleeping." He smooths his hands over the sarong-style material tied at his hip, the hem mid-thigh.

I would do anything for legs as long as his.

His eyes fall from my face. If he weren't a Verdanian, I'd

accuse him of ogling. He walks towards me, and my fingers tense for my gun. His hand reaches out.

"If you kill me in a dream, will I die in real life?" I say quickly.

He tilts his head. "You cannot die in dreams. Dreams are safe."

His fingers stroke the stone around my neck, uncomfortably close. The token pulses strong enough to feel deep in my belly. It seems to get warmer.

"Take it back," I say.

"Anything you give me in dreams will not be there when I wake."

"Right. Because you're just a figment of my imagination. You're not real," I say hopefully.

"I am real," he says, "but I do not remember you being so tiny in the cave."

I step out of reach. "I'm not tiny, I'm smaller than average."

"You are very small. You are like a young—a child."

"I am not a child."

"You are doing a scowly thing with your face. That means you are upset, yes?"

I sigh, and pinch the bridge of my nose. "Is there a purpose to this meeting, Zorian?"

"I wanted to test the dream communication. No one has had a blood connection with a human before." His gaze drops to the necklace again. "Are you looking after it?"

His emotions don't seem to transfer to me in the dream—no heartbeats competing with my own—but he appears anxious despite his implacable face. Or I'm anthropomorphising a creature I can't understand.

I cup the stone, and he raises his eyes.

"I'm looking after it," I whisper, though there are no sounds but the ones we make.

"Thank you." He pauses. "Axelle."

This is too weird. A grateful Verdanian. What will he do next—smile? Nah, not possible. They don't have the musculature.

My fingers rub the scar on my cheekbone and I force myself to stop. Maybe I'm the one who's nervous.

"So what do you usually do in these dream communications?" I say.

"We can do anything. We visit places, some real, some imaginary. We talk uninhibited. Dream communications strengthen the bond, let us share what we may not say aloud. They are also a way for mates to communicate if they are apart."

"And do you? Have a mate you see in dreams, I mean."

He blinks at me. "I do not."

Way to ask the intimate questions, Axelle. What's next, favourite sexual position?

"Okay, so let's talk." I point at the flower with the spiralling petals. "What's that called?"

"What is the thing you humans do with the water?" He touches his cheekbones.

"Crying?"

He shakes his head.

"Weeping?"

"Yes. It is named weeping nalwell."

"It's pretty."

I curl a petal around my finger, gently, so as not to tear it then wonder what the hell I'm doing since it's a dream. I could eat it if I want to. The cool and silken petal slides against my skin.

"Can I change things in dreams?" I say, letting the nalwell slip from my finger. "If I wanted to take us somewhere or make something appear?"

"Yes. This is your dream, too. You have to concentrate."

I hold my hand out, palm up, and frown at it. The air wavers. I squint. It might help. A beast the size of an Earth squirrel flops into my hand. It flaps leathery wings, its tail dangling between my fingers and ending in a fin used to propel it through water for chasing fish.

I grin and thrust it at Zorian. "Look! I made a water-dragon."

He stares at me. I cuddle the water-dragon to my chest as if he might snatch it and chomp off its head. The little winged lizard yawns, flashing tiny teeth and a bright pink tongue.

"You don't like water-dragons? Or are they sacred?" A snort of laughter slips out. "Sorry, that was mean."

"Mean?"

"Um, unfair, spiteful."

The water-dragon climbs onto my shoulder and curls its tail around my neck, its scales surprisingly warm. It folds its wings and falls asleep.

Great, I'm asleep conjuring beasts that also sleep. There are levels to this dream shit.

"All life on Verdana is sacred," Zorian says. "Even yours. We take no pleasure in the loss. But that is not what I was thinking. You notice the wildlife. You act as though you like it. You do that shape with your mouth."

"It's called smiling. And why wouldn't I appreciate the wildlife?"

"Most of your species seem disgusted by it. Inconvenienced.

This is strange when they are wanting to live here. There is no harmony."

Zorian seems to know a lot about people. Does he study us, as we do them, looking for weaknesses?

"We're still getting used to the place."

"It has been three tens of our years."

"Thirty," I say absently. "Can we walk? I hate standing still. And it'll be nice to explore in complete safety. For a change."

He nods, and aims towards a gap bordered by ferns. An elaborate tattoo of vines and flowers twines up his spine and unfurls along his shoulder blades, the ink a green so dark it's almost black. Each petal is a different colour. His pale skin is a perfect canvas for the design.

"That's beautiful," I breathe.

He stops but doesn't turn around.

"Your tattoo," I say, in case he thinks I'm talking about his butt or something.

Not that I'm looking at his butt.

"I have one, too," I babble, like an idiot.

I face away from him and lift my vest, scraping my hair over one shoulder. The water-dragon whines and cuddles tighter to my throat. Silence from Zorian.

Maybe I'm not supposed to mention the tattoo. It won't be my last cultural faux pas.

There's a tentative touch at the base of my spine. A finger traces upwards, following the line of my tattoo to where it ends at the nape of my neck. I suppress a shiver.

"What is it?" Zorian says softly.

"Ivy. It's a plant from Earth."

"It is very similar to mine."

"Yeah, funny coincidence."

He cocks his head. "Fate?"

"Um, no. An accident. Or chance."

I smooth my top into place and we walk through the jungle. We have a game of name the plant where he tells me what they call it and I tell him what we call it. Their names are poetic whereas we're more say-what-you-see. Blue vine. Carpet moss. You get the idea. I magic extra water-dragons into the dream and laugh as they chase each other around the trees, darting into hollows to leap and tumble through the air. I glance at Zorian and nearly trip over a root. The water-dragons puff out of existence.

"Holy fuck!" I gasp.

"Am I not doing it right?"

"What *are* you doing?"

"Smiling."

Okay, I guess I can see it as the shock fades. His mouth curves upwards, exposing his teeth, the points hidden by his bottom lip. It's not completely terrifying.

I clear my throat. "Well, technically, that's a grin. Smiling is sort of a closed-mouth thing."

"Like this?"

It's more smirk than smile, one side of his mouth tilted, but it changes his whole face. The smile tames the feral and enhances the beauty.

"Close enough. How does it feel?"

He rubs his cheek. "Unnatural."

"How can you not express joy? You guys are creepy with your lack of emotion."

"We feel emotion," he says, holding a heavy, dripping leaf out of the path. "We do not express it for all. That honour is for only the mate. It is special."

"Not sacred?"

He arrows me a look, and I hold up my hands.

"I'm teasing."

"What is teasing?"

"Making fun of you but not in a mean way."

"You are a puzzling species."

The jungle ends at a cliff edge, the canopy continuing hundreds of metres below. A waterfall roars to our left, moisture puffing into the cobalt sky. I sit and dangle my legs, the mist slicking my face and beading in my hair.

I squint at the view. Sounds fill the silence—skreeing, hooting, whooping. Birds flit from the canopy and monewts shake the branches. Swarms of insects glitter and drone.

"You are good with the detail," Zorian says, lowering himself beside me.

A scar peeks from under the hem of his pyjamas.

Can they even be called pyjamas? There's so little material.

The mark is creamier than the pale skin around it, and ridged, but it lacks the pearlescent sheen.

"I didn't think you got scars."

"I was young." He tugs the hem into place.

I tap my right cheek. "I got this when I was young, too. Had a panic attack and stupidly removed my helmet. If I hadn't flinched, the arrow would've skewered my face. It was my first battle and it got worse from there."

Zorian's hand pauses half-way between us.

I really should stop letting him touch me. It's wrong.

Or is it? You can't get mad at someone for what they do in dreams. Dreams aren't real.

Zorian's thumb skims my cheek.

"Your skin is so warm," he says. "The scar is harder. Like

mine."

He inches his sarong higher. The scar is a two-inch diagonal slash across his thigh. His upper thigh. There's a lot of long, lean muscle in between.

My curiosity gets too much. Sometimes, I feel so trapped in Home Base. Verdana is fascinating, even its indigenous people. I can still dislike them while wanting to know everything about them.

My fingertip rubs across his scar. He's right—it's harder than the normal skin. Stone instead of pliant marble. Smooth and cool.

I tuck my hand carefully between my legs.

"I was five years," Zorian says, looking off to the horizon. "A human attacked my sister. She was older. Eight years. He cut me when I tried to stop him. He stabbed her and ran away."

"I'm sorry, Zorian. Hurting children… That shouldn't happen."

"Many things should not happen," he says.

We listen to the rush of the waterfall. The two suns chase across the sky as if time moves quicker in this dream place.

"Is your sister still alive?"

"She is not."

I place my hand on his where he grips the edge of the cliff. Just for a second. His eyes meet mine.

"I'm sorry," I say.

He nods and stands, brushing stones from his pyjamas. We walk back through the jungle, though it's different. Lusher. More flowers, more insects. Creatures scamper and hiss.

"How old are you anyway?" I say, uncomfortable with his silence.

I should have left his scar alone. What business do I have

to poke?

"One and eight. No"—he holds up a hand—"eighteen."

Wow. A year younger than Mallory. Zorian seems older. Definitely wiser. The impassiveness of his species makes them all appear ancient. Immortal.

A clearing brightens the jungle, a circular pool perfectly in the centre. My double shadow stretches over the violet-tinged water. I halt a few feet from the edge while Zorian dips his feet in and wiggles his toes.

"You do not like the water?"

I'm hugging myself. Damn. I need to copy him and be less expressive.

"We have an uneasy relationship," I say.

"Why? Water is the root of all life. And it feels nice."

My word, a Verdanian doing something for the fun of it. Who knew? They seem so dour and contemplative, even when they're about to kill you.

"Maybe I'll tell you another time."

Another time? What the hell am I saying? This isn't meeting a friend for a drink. It's fraternising. It doesn't matter if it's all in my head. Or his head. Whatever.

But it has been interesting. And I didn't have a choice. I should seize the opportunity to learn everything I can about him and his species. Maybe he'll tell me something important, something that tips the balance.

No one has ever done this before. Everything we know comes from battles or the careful dissection of bodies, with full protective gear and strict biosecurity protocols.

Zorian wades into the pool and turns when the water reaches his knees. "You are going to wake up soon."

"How can you tell?"

He attempts another half-mouth smile. "I can tell."

I glance down at myself. My fingers are fuzzy, the lines of my body blurred.

"Oh, well… that's trippy."

A backwards step, and the water teases the hem of his pyjamas.

"Are you going to start searching tomorrow?"

I don't need to ask him what he means.

"Just because you proved one lie doesn't mean everything else is."

"There is never only one lie. They breed, like slivets."

Slivets, I learned twenty minutes—hours?—ago, are silvery things that can wriggle over land. Their babies form huge, squirming clumps.

"Why would we start a war we didn't have to?"

The pool caresses his waist. He trails his fingers through it.

"That is what you must find out."

"Do you know why?"

"I do not. We do not. Most think it is because you are a violent species."

"What do you think?"

He gives me his implacable face, and I sigh.

"Fine. I'll search. I hope I can tell you how wrong you are."

"Why would you hope for the war to continue?"

Water slips up the taught skin of his stomach and slaps at his chest.

"Because," I whisper almost to myself, "that means we're the good guys."

I open my eyes in my own bed. The floor lights filter through leaves, and slat shadows across the ceiling. My alarm bleats and I slap it off.

It was just a dream. Vivid, but yesterday was a weird day. Of course I dreamed of Zorian. My overactive brain filled in all the details, gave him a sad backstory and made up some shit about wildlife. None of it was real. I don't need to feel guilty for talking to an enemy all night, only for leaving him alive in the cave and agreeing to snoop on my own race.

Which is enough.

I throw off the covers and dress in my off-duty uniform, fixing my hair into a braid. A handful of berries and a bottled water from my mini-fridge count as breakfast. I stride through the rain to the modules, catching droplets on my tongue.

Sweet, like Verdanian blood.

I jog into the semi-circular classroom, a smaller version of the amphitheatre, and six hundred five- to seven-year-old faces fix on me. Passenger DeLoris bustles in front of the screen, preparing her slides and samples.

"Axelle of the first generation!" she says, flicking her blonde hair over her shoulder. "I like it when you're assigned to me.

You're so good with the kids. And they love you."

The children whisper behind their little hands, too disciplined to shriek, though the younger ones bounce in their seats. The room was built to hold fourteen hundred for training the five to ten year olds but artificial reproduction failed between my thirteenth and sixteenth years. It means there's a five-year gap before the oldest children reach fighting age.

Another thing that gives me nightmares.

Passenger DeLoris pats at the air. "Okay, class, settle down. There will be time to ask questions later. We have a lot to go through. Open page twelve on your tablets and let's get started."

Hundreds of tiny heads bow towards the desks, chubby fingers tapping on screens. I drift among the rows, helping kids load their tablets and find the right page. DeLoris broadcasts her computer onto the main screen and two humanoid bodies appear side by side on metal tables. Black sheets cover their faces. Their white skin has been peeled back and their rib plates removed.

Something tugs on my sleeve. A five year old from the twenty-sixth generation blinks huge brown eyes at me.

"Soldier Axelle? Where's your gun?"

"In the armoury with all the others."

He's missed a button on his shirt. Lemon-yellow uniforms for the kiddies or, as the unranked like to call them, the unsullied.

"How many marks does it have?"

"Twelve."

There's a chorus of, "Whoa," from my mini-audience. The kid with the missed button leans further forward in his seat.

I tap a finger to my lips. "Quiet now. Listen to Passenger DeLoris."

He turns to his tablet and I position myself behind the last row, ready for any waving hands. DeLoris clicks a laser pointer and the red dot circles on the torso of the male body.

"Who can tell me the main differences in internal anatomy between humans and Verdanians?"

Tiny hands stretch for the ceiling. DeLoris gestures to a girl at the front.

"They have two hearts and three stomachs."

"And no balls," says a boy a few seats down.

Tittering sweeps through the room.

"That's not entirely true, Tyler of the twenty-second. Yes, the males do not possess a scrotum but that is because their testicles are internal due to their lower body temperature."

The laser jiggles on two structures in the pelvic floor of the male, the intestines removed and the hips split. The penis itself isn't too different, maybe longer than the average human's, but there's nothing dangling beneath it. No wrinkled, hairy sack. No hair at all, in fact.

"Now, what is the purpose of the extra hearts and stomachs?" DeLoris says, picking them out with the laser on the female cadaver.

The hearts look like white lumps of rock. There's no pearlescence in the blood vessels or the skin. Funny, I've never noticed that before.

I guess dead Verdanians don't glimmer.

"One heart supplies the internal organs while the second heart pumps blood to the skin," pipes the same girl. "The stomachs break down the tough fibres of their diet."

"Like Earth cows," Tyler says, nudging an elbow into the

kid next to him. "Big and dumb."

DeLoris silences the giggles with a frown. "They are not dumb, Tyler of the twenty-second generation. Nor are they placid, like Earth cows. Earth cows won't shoot you full of arrows or drag you into a swamp to watch you drown."

Tyler hunches in his seat as DeLoris leans her knuckles on his desk, her face serious.

"You may laugh at their differences now but they are stronger, faster and all they want to do is kill you. So I'd pay attention to your lessons."

DeLoris returns to the screen and moves swiftly through the rest of the internal organs. Lungs occupying most of the chest cavity with gills along the rib plates that only open when they're underwater; a double uterus in the female for their longer, two-stage gestation.

Zorian doesn't want to kill me. All the other Verdanians I've met have tried to but I wasn't exactly offering them peace and good wishes. Do they really want to exterminate us? But if that's a lie, why would we choose war? It's not like we profit from it. The survival rate of the fighting population is abysmal.

The kids take a quiz on what they've covered and I move through the rows, giving them a clue if they seem stuck. I reach the floor as DeLoris wraps up her lesson.

"You may wonder why we spend so long learning the anatomy of our enemies," she says, pocketing the laser pointer, "but the more we know about them, the better chance we have of defeating them. Imagine if we could call the whole of Ananngar our home rather than just the confines of Home Base. So study them. Discover their weaknesses. What have you learned from their anatomy that could help you when you come of fighting age?"

Bums shuffle on seats. Even the girl in the front row chews her lip and stares at her tablet.

"Axelle, they may need your expertise to put it into words," DeLoris says, smiling at me.

I tap the hollow of my throat and hold a hand over my stomach. "Their rib plates end here and here so a bullet is more likely to penetrate. The bloodstone ammo is designed to ricochet to try and damage at least one of the hearts. Don't aim for the head unless you're good enough to shoot them through the eye. A skin wound will hurt but it won't incapacitate and the last thing you want is an angry Verdanian."

Some of the kids laugh but most sit wide-eyed.

They'll be better prepared by the time they're twelve. I'll probably be dead.

"Now, we have ten minutes for Axelle to answer your questions before lunch."

A forest of hands shoots up. DeLoris weeds out the lucky few.

"How did you get the bruises on your face?" a skinny boy whispers.

I skim a finger along my jaw. The mark of Zorian's hands. I forgot they were there.

"Yesterday's battle. There was a cave-in."

The bruises are too unusual to be caused by me rattling around in my battlesuit but the kids don't know that. Does DeLoris? What if she gets suspicious? What if someone else asks me how I got finger-shaped bruises on my face?

Shit. It's not even been a day and I'm hiding things from my people.

"Did you win?" the same kid whispers.

"We secured a bloodstone deposit and only six soldiers died."

Predictable questions follow—what's it like to kill the monsters? How scary are they close up? What was your favourite kill? My answers seem to satisfy them but they no longer satisfy me.

Zorian isn't particularly monstrous. Okay, so he has sharp teeth and force-fed me his blood but he didn't hurt me. Dream-Zorian is even less monstrous but he's a figment of my imagination.

Hopefully.

The damn guy has made me doubt everything after only one meeting. His blood *is* poison, just not the kind I was expecting.

"Who has the most kills out of all the soldiers?" a stocky girl says.

"That would be me."

The chorus of appreciation fills the room this time.

"Who has the most kills in Home Base?"

"First Minister Seabird has that honour with fifteen, followed by Elderman Vail at fourteen and Elderwoman Carniss at thirteen."

DeLoris talks over the excited babble. "I think that would be a good place to stop for lunch."

Most soldiers don't kill any. The more experienced—maybe one or two. The majority of Elders and Passengers have low tallies or zero kills despite having eighteen years on me.

The children filter out of the classroom. DeLoris thanks me and I bid her goodbye to grab my own lunch in the soldier's cafeteria. The wave of sound crashes over me and I almost wish for the peace of the jungle. People aren't supposed to be crammed in like this. We need space to wander, to think, without breathing in each other's faces. Or maybe that's just me.

"Hey, Axe, over here." Dante's deep voice penetrates the noise. Codename—Hulk.

I grab a tray of bean stew, bread and bluefruit juice.

Is it really from a plant called daracurrant like Zorian said in my dream, or did my imagination make that up?

I sit next to Loyanne, opposite Dante, and she nods at me, her mouth stuffed full of water-dragon burger. The rest of my squad is absent but most duties are staggered to avoid a horde descending on the cafeteria.

"How was manufacturing?" I scoop a spoonful of stew into my mouth. It's meaty, heavy on the herbs and salt. Delicious.

Loyanne swallows loud enough to hear over the hubbub. "We got bloodstone bullets after our hit on the deposit yesterday. They're carved and ready to be filled."

"Ain't nothing more beautiful than a new batch of ammo," Dante says, chewing on his own burger.

Loyanne smiles and dabs at her mouth before taking another bite. Scars curve from her lips, her lower central incisors missing from when a Verdanian shattered her helmet and punched her in the face. Her new teeth, grown in the lab, should soon be ready for transplant. It'll be strange when she no longer has a lisp.

"We're heading to the arcade for games or a movie if you want to join?" she says, a lick of sauce on her chin.

I love Earth movies. Romantic comedies are my favourite, not that I've told anyone. I'd never hear the end of it. Romance at Home Base is someone asking if you want to fuck in your bed or theirs. Having sex in the barracks with everyone pretending not to listen is hardly a situation for playful exploration. It's more wham, bam, see you next time.

Or in thirty minutes, if they have Mallory's stamina.

"What's showing?"

"Something called *Starship Troopers*." Dante taps his chin. "Babe, you've got sauce…"

Loyanne swipes at her face with her napkin.

They make a cute couple. Most people have bedmates and move around a lot but Dante and Loyanne have been together almost a year. She's tall, like everyone else in the generations, with lovely golden hair whereas Dante is broad and dark with tight, black curls.

"Great," I say, ignoring a little stab of jealousy when Dante smiles and licks his thumb to wipe the sauce Loyanne missed. "A film about aliens fighting humans. I don't need to see it, I'm living it. I'm going to help out in the AR ward, anyway."

"You know you're allowed to take your free time, right Axe?" Loyanne says, capturing Dante's hand and kissing his scarred knuckles.

"I like to keep busy. See you at drills."

I down the tart bluefruit/daracurrant juice and clear my tray. I wave to the people who shout my name but keep going. A group catches me at the door before I can escape, quizzing me about the cave-in and gushing over my answers. Their eyes linger on the bruises.

Outside, the clouds have dissolved into the cobalt sky, the twin suns at their zenith. The moist air is like breathing steam but I enjoy the flare of heat, the slick of water it leaves on bare skin. My route takes me past the dissection lab, the only building in Home Base with restricted access apart from the private residencies, mine included.

If I were hiding the truth, that's where I'd do it.

I drag my eyes from the light on the card reader by the door and hustle to the AR ward. It's hushed inside. A place of reverence. Here is where the generations are born—the future soldiers and saviours. Where I was born. Normal pregnancy is too slow, too sporadic, and removes valuable women from the population. The Elders and Passengers use contraception. Both sexes of the generations are sterilised at birth, our genetic material harvested to create more generations.

How many are my biological children? There are a few raven-haired or cobalt-eyed kiddies toddling around so you never know. I only pray they aren't lumbered with my short-arse genes.

Not that it's a hindrance. I'm doing just fine.

"Axelle o' the first, I was wondering when you'd appear," says a voice, rolling the r's.

"Elderman McBurnie, I hope I'm not disturbing you."

A giant of a man trundles around the nearest row of incubator pods. The structures look like glass eggs balanced on top of intricate control panels with numerous screens and dials and sensors. Babies curl within the murky fluid.

"Never, m'eudail!" Elderman McBurnie says, tucking his explosion of ginger hair behind his ears. "The wee tykes are due in a couple o' days."

I like McBurnie. Trying to decipher what the hell he's talking about is part of the fun. He's also one of the Elders who's never killed a Verdanian.

He creates life, he doesn't end it, as I do.

He waves me through the pods to a table at the centre filled with rows and rows of test-tubes in racks. "Ye can help me mix the vials. This'll be the bairns last burst o' nutrients before they come screaming into the world."

'World' is pronounced 'wuruld', and I smother a smile. His huge hands pat at the pockets of his maroon uniform until he finds a couple of hairnets and passes one to me, wrestling his hair into his own. Tiny bits frizz out as if he's been electrocuted.

I force myself not to stare at the pass clipped to his lapel. His photo grins out, the background mostly made up of his hair. Below it is his name—a first and a surname, unlike anyone born on Verdana—and a complex barcode.

"Righty-o, put on these gloves an' let's get this show on the road."

The cold gloves slip over my hands. For the next two hours, we work in silence, bar the squirt of liquid and the clink of glass. It's calming to be completely absorbed, thinking only of what nutrient needs to be added in the exact proportion calibrated for each foetus. Once complete, the mixtures are poured into special compartments in each pod that will distribute it through the umbilicus to the hungry baby. They kick their legs and clench their fists as if they can taste it.

This is the second and final generation of this, our thirtieth year on Verdana. One generation a year was born from Year Six to Ten, including mine. Then they doubled production in the new pods they'd built.

"Good job there, lass," McBurnie says, yanking off his hairnet and wiping his forehead on his sleeve. "Off ye pop. I'll see ye at Earth lesson later. It'll be a braw one the night!"

If braw is good, I imagine the lesson will focus on Scotland, McBurnie's Earth home. Something tells me he still misses it.

I meet my squad on the parade ground after another hustle past the dissection lab. They're ranged in the usual formation, except no one stands within two feet of Mallory.

I grin at him. "Waste duty going all right, Barbie?"

He scowls but maintains his position.

"How'd you get those bruises, Axe?" shouts Pacal, his long brown hair in a bun. "Mallory too rough last night?"

"Oh, Strife," I say with a smile, "it wasn't Mallory."

Hoots and jeers are thrown Mallory's way, and the scowl becomes a full-blown sulk.

Excellent idea. The squad will speculate on who my next bedmate is and if DeLoris happens to say anything to one of them, she'll understand why I didn't tell the kiddies I was banging some guy.

I let the teasing fade, ignoring the questions on who it is and laughing at their guesses. First Minister Seabird, really? He may be sprightly for his age but the man is eighty-one.

I hold up a hand. "Enough. Loyanne, take generations ten to twenty-one. The rest, come with me."

Loyanne is patient with the younger soldiers. She repeats the basics until they finally understand, calmly explaining, over and over, without getting frustrated. She'll make a good squad leader one day.

I line up my veterans behind me and toss a grin over my shoulder. "Anyone who can't keep up joins Mallory on waste duty."

At the groans, I sprint for the obstacle course on the far side of the parade ground.

8

"Hello, lass, long time, no see!" Elderman McBurnie says, slapping me on the shoulder and almost bowling me over.

The classroom module is the smallest one for holding a squad of thirty, the individual desks and chairs arranged to face a screen at the front. It looks like a room in an Earth high school in some of those romantic comedies I definitely don't watch.

I slide into a seat next to Loyanne, her hair wet and scraped back. The smell of the curry we had for dinner clings to her neat, olive uniform. Brindan and Mallory scuttle in last, a whisper from being late. Mallory avoids looking at me.

He'll get over it. They always do. Plus, I've seen the way Fionna of the eleventh keeps glancing at him. If he pays attention, his bed won't be empty for long.

"Since yesterday was the anniversary lesson, I thought I'd stick to the theme an' take ye back to the place where our ship was launched. A place like no other in the universe." McBurnie clicks the remote in his hand and a small, rugged landmass pops onto the screen. "To Scotland. Ma home."

There's a soft groan from the back of the room. "Wake me when he's done talking about haggis and kilts."

I glare at Mallory. He ducks his head and examines the

surface of his desk.

I may have to do something if his attitude doesn't improve. It's been a while since I lashed anyone in my squad. If he forces it on me, neither of us will be happy.

"In fact," McBurnie continues, oblivious of Mallory's jibe, "the good ship *HMS Dòchas* is Scots Gaelic for 'hope'. An' she lived up to her name. Now, who can tell me the capital o' Scotland?"

The shuffling reminds me of the kiddies' anatomy class. Everyone should know the answer. We've been drilled enough times on memorising Earth countries and their capitals.

We fixate on Earth a little too much in my opinion. It was home for less than half the population of Home Base and it should never be forgotten but it's billions of light years away. Verdana is a whole new planet to study and explore and we're right here. If we don't think of it as our home, why are we fighting so hard to stay?

"It's Edinburgh," Nolana finally says with a sniff. "The capital of Scotland was Edinburgh."

Nolana aka Nails aka that bitch is hard as nails. She's a great drinking buddy but she scares me in the field. She has no fear and fear is healthy. It stops you doing stupid shit.

"Correct, Nolana o' the second." McBurnie clicks the remote. "An' here she is."

A wide street fills the screen, one side lined by glass-fronted buildings, the other side fenced and overlooking a park, where a castle sits on a rocky hill. The grass in the park is patchy, the leaves on the trees wilted and yellow though it doesn't look like the Earth season of autumn, a season not present on Verdana. Vehicles bunch in the road, some tall and bulky, others small like our jeeps but completely covered by metal. A sleek, tubular vehicle glides on a skyrail. People teem along the pavements, drifting in all directions, laughing, talking, always talking. The place is filled with voices and the disconcerting hum of electric vehicles. A digital sign reads 'AQI 123: Masks Required for Sensitive Groups'.

McBurnie takes us on a tour, starting at the castle and ending at the parliament—a building where Scotland's governing body gathered to rule, much like our Elders. I don't understand the function of the wood on the windows. Are they to stop intruders? Surely metal would be better. Maybe metal was scarce and hard to mine, like on Verdana. Or maybe they wasted it all on their vehicles.

"An' this is ma favourite place—a wee town called Livingston." McBurnie sighs, his misty eyes staring at the screen. "Oh, the things ye could buy when ye were flush with cash."

The screen shows the inside of a glass-domed building, everything bright and blinding and white. More glass-fronted areas border the concourse, people milling about clutching bags with words I've never seen before printed on them.

What on Earth is a Primark? And why are there so many clothes? There are clothes hanging in the windows, clothes on strange fake people and different clothes on all the real people scurrying through. Why would anyone need more than four outfits? Off-duty, battlesuit, gym and sleep.

Done.

"If ye put on your headsets ye can have a wee wander before we get to the good stuff. An' by that, I mean the alcohol ma country was famous for."

I pull my headset over my eyes and slip the band around the back of my head. The mini-screens brighten to a satellite image of Scotland. I use the controller in my hand to zoom around, avoiding the dense areas of concrete called towns. Or 'toons' in McBurnie-speak. I finally find a patch of green that isn't a field and the picture rushes towards the ground, twisting until I'm standing in a forest.

Nothing drips. There are no pools or swamps. Tall, narrow trees stretch to the washed-out sky, their bark orange. The floor is littered in tiny, brown spines and other woody objects I have no name for.

"Elderman McBurnie?"

"Aye, Axelle?" he says close to my ear.

"What are these trees called with spines rather than leaves? And what are all those things on the ground? Some kind of seed pod?"

"Let's have a look-see." I hear a click as he broadcasts the image from my headset to the main screen. "Ah, those are Scots pine, a type o' conifer or evergreen tree. The leaves are called needles as they're narrow an' spiky. The things on the ground are cones, pine cones. They hold the seeds."

"Everything's so dry."

He laughs. "Believe me, m'eudail, Scotland was one o' the wetter countries but compared to here, it could be the frickin' Sahara."

I visit one of the many hills and stand on the peak. The wide-open space feels unnatural and exposed, though it's beautiful in a bleak way. The short bushes—heather—are in bloom, blushing the hill in purple. A huge pool—or loch—nestles in the valley below. The navy-blue water seems lifeless.

"Right, ye lot, take off your headsets an' have a gander at this."

While we've been wandering around his homeland,

McBurnie has wheeled in a table covered in plates of haggis and glasses of amber liquid. We learned about haggis a few years ago and McBurnie said he was going to try and make it. Looks like he succeeded, though I'm no expert. To be honest, I would've been perfectly happy never to know what minced heart, lungs, liver and stomach taste like.

McBurnie passes out the plates and glasses. "This is braw Scottish cuisine—haggis an' whisky. Now, the whisky is no' as good since I get the cast-off grains an' I don't have oak for infusing but it's no' crap, either. Thank God we have pure water on Verdana. No filtration or boiling required."

I sniff the liquid. It smells like a solvent, not something you drink. What the hell will it do to my stomach lining?

McBurnie raises his glass. "Slàinte mhath."

We mimic him with varying degrees of success. The whisky burns all the way down and bursts twin fires in my chest and gut. I've never been more aware of my gullet. I manage not to cough but tears blur my eyes. Sounds of choking and spluttering fill the room. I pick at the haggis to smother the burning and it's not half bad. The spices are nice. It's almost fruity.

"That concludes our Scottish Earth lesson. For those who are feeling a wee bit adventurous, ye can join me in the pub for more whisky. Or whatever tipple takes your fancy."

"You coming, Axe?" Loyanne says, returning her empty plate and glass to the table.

"Not tonight. Might go to the gym."

"The gym!" Pacal scoffs, heading for the door, his flattened nose wrinkled. "Didn't you get enough exercise when you made us run and dodge and jump until our lungs exploded?"

"Some of us have more stamina."

Pacal guffaws and slaps Dante on the back. "Something we mere mortals will never experience, eh, Hulk?"

"I have stamina. Just ask Loyanne."

She pokes him in the ribs and I leave them chuckling under the stars, the pub next to the arcade complex and about ten minutes walk from the classroom. I stick my hands in my pockets and stroll towards the gym.

Home Base is different at night. Quiet. People talk in hushed tones as if the dark is listening and spend as little time as possible outside. Only the guards on the wall stay out at night.

The gym towers over the neighbouring modules and forms part of the wall. The ground floor has a pool, sauna and hot tub. It's the most popular. The first floor has the weight machines and the second floor, the treadmills.

I keep walking.

I said I *might* go to the gym. Turns out, I don't want to. Maybe I'll go to bed early.

9

I lie on my back in my vest and shorts and stare at the ceiling of my pod, an hour before I usually go to bed.

I'm tired. There's nothing wrong with going to bed early when you're tired.

Unless it's because you want to see if a certain Verdanian will appear in a dream-jungle.

What if he's not asleep yet? Do I have to hang around or does the dream communication only happen if both of us are sleeping? Maybe it needs two minds to build the dream space.

Don't be stupid. There is no dream communication. It's just me, talking to a figment of my imagination. A brain injury too small to detect on a scan.

But I should test to see if it works a second night. For science. If he appears with wings and a tail then it's definitely all in my head.

I close my eyes.

"Hello, Axelle," Zorian says.

He steps around the huge trunk of a tree stippled in crimson fungi. His sarong pyjamas are knee-length but split in the middle of each leg so his thighs show when he walks.

No wings. No tail.

I sigh.

"Is something wrong?" he says.

"This is actually happening, isn't it? If we meet when we're awake, you'll have a scar and that tattoo, which I can't possibly know about except for this dream stuff. Somehow, I'm in my bed and you're sleeping… wherever you sleep, and we're talking in this dream space that is real but not real."

He cocks his head. "Yes. I want to say yes. Did you think it was only your dream?"

"It would've made things simpler."

I should be horrified, afraid, confused. I'm talking to a Verdanian as if he's a squadmate and not an enemy soldier. He poisoned me with his blood and now we're in each other's heads.

He stops a couple of feet from me, ferns obscuring his lower legs. His hand reaches out but he hesitates.

"It's okay," I say, "you can touch it."

His finger strokes the stone at my throat. I carefully slip the cord over my head and hold it out, beams of sunlight sparking on the emerald chips at the core.

"I know you can't keep it but you can at least wear it while we're here."

He cradles the pendant in his hands, a shadow of reverence on his face.

I must be getting better at reading his expressions or he's freer with them in our dream.

He slides the pendant around his neck, his fingers lingering where the stone sits below the hollow of his throat, the last of his rib plates forming a human-looking collarbone.

"Thank you," he says quietly.

"Why don't you just appear with it, anyway? And are we

always going to have to wander around in our pyjamas in this dream space?"

His lips curve at the corners. "We initially appear as we last see ourselves, unless you concentrate. Everything but our physical forms can be changed in the dream."

He brushes my jaw, his touch more delicate than the breeze shushing through the canopy. "Does it hurt?"

"No," I whisper and wonder why I'm whispering. Maybe because, this close, he's even more breath-taking now I'm not afraid. He could be the carved statue of a god. If gods have green hair.

"I am sorry if it did. It seemed necessary. You would not have taken my blood otherwise."

I slide a step back, and his hand drops to his side.

"That's true," I say, and tug at the hem of my vest. "So I can change what I'm wearing?"

He nods. I only own three other outfits but none of them seem appropriate. I focus hard, hoping I get the dimensions right and don't flash the Verdanian. The lavender dress hits me mid-thigh, hugging my hips and chest so it probably won't fall down even without the thin straps. It's strange to have nothing between my legs. Airy.

I saw the dress in the shopping centre of McBurnie's home town. Livingston or somewhere. I liked the colour.

I spread my hands. "How's this?"

"It makes your eyes more blue."

"Is that good?"

He watches me for a beat. "Yes."

I drop my gaze to my bare feet. I give myself lavender toenails to match the dress. And an ankle bracelet of tiny flowers like Zorian had in the cave.

"How do I look?" he says.

I glance up and my mouth pops open. Zorian is wearing the same dress, flat over his pectoral muscles and emphasising his slim waist. I continue to gape.

"I am not… pretty?" He swishes the material of the skirt.

I clap my hand over my mouth but a snort escapes. Air spills from my chest in a burst of laughter. I laugh until my stomach cramps, my hands braced on my knees. I'm probably giving Zorian an eyeful of cleavage but my legs are weak.

"You… you look…" I splutter and sit hard on my butt to catch my breath.

"Is that good?"

I giggle, and swipe at my eyes. "God, yes, but put something else on. Please. My stomach hurts."

"Are you ill?"

I hiccup. He stands over me and I have another sniggering fit.

When did I last laugh like this?

"Not ill," I gasp. "Laughing this hard hurts."

"You are a puzzling species," he says but he smiles, the flash of his teeth still enough to kick my heart rate up a notch. "Is this better?"

Between one blink and the next, he changes from the dress to calf-length trousers of woven fronds. A black belt hugs his waist, the tail of the bark split and dangling down one thigh, each cord ending in a small, emerald stone.

"You like green, huh?"

"What is not to like? Green is the colour of life."

"And the colour of your eyes."

"Is it?" he says, and I swear he smirks at me.

He holds out a hand. I take it after a pause, his palm cool

and dry. He pulls me, very gently, to my feet.

"Your hair is different," he says, still holding my hand.

"It's in a braid. Keeps it out of the way."

My fingers unweave it and it slides over my bare shoulders to curl on my breasts.

"It is nicer like this. More natural."

"Can I show you something?" I say a little too quickly.

Without waiting for a response, I vanish the dream-jungle. A barren, heather-clad hill stretches before us, the sky huge and unbroken. I add some deer munching on the flowers. They raise their heads and stare at us but don't run away.

Zorian drops into a crouch, his feet lost in the hummocks and furrows of peat and heather. "What is this place? It is too open. I do not like it."

"This is Scotland, a country on Earth, though it may not exist anymore. We learned about it during our Earth lesson."

He slowly straightens up, as if wary the deer might attack him. I coax one over and it snuffles its wet nose in my palm. Zorian lays a tentative hand on the doe's back.

"Is this what you do all day?"

"Well, I can't just wander about wherever I want and accuse people of lying, Zorian. I'm working up to it."

He strokes the deer from shoulder to flank and she edges closer to him, butting his hip until he scratches behind her ears. This is probably not normal deer behaviour but I'm doing my best.

"That is not what I meant." Zorian's long fingers tickle the doe under the chin. Her eyelashes flutter in ecstasy. "I have no idea what you do when you are not fighting us."

I open my mouth. Close it. "You know, I have no idea what you do, either. We're brought up to hate you, fear you. Every time we fight, we're guaranteed to lose people while you lose none."

"We lose, sometimes. We lose even when we do not."

"I don't have a clue what that means."

The deer nibbles his trouser leg, and he shoos her away. She bounds off with her companions, their white rumps disappearing down the edge of the hill.

"We do not enjoy killing you," Zorian says, his head bowed.

"But you're so good at it."

"That is not a thing to boast. You force us." He raises his face, his eyes dark. Sad? "You always force us."

Wind whips across the exposed hill, flapping the hem of my dress. I hug myself, goosebumps flaring on my arms.

How can I be cold? This is my damn dream.

"Let's not get into who forces whom into doing things they'd rather not," I say, pacing back and forth to warm up, the heather scratching at my legs. "You asked what we do when we're not fighting you—this is part of it. We learn about Earth from the people on our ship who lived there and from data stored on our ship's computer so it's never forgotten."

"What is a computer?"

This is the problem when trying to communicate with a simpler species. Sorry—less technologically advanced.

There's nothing simple about Zorian.

I magic up a tablet on a desk, which looks weird sitting on top of a hill in my imaginary Scotland.

"This is a computer. It's a machine that stores information you can look at whenever you want. Kind of like memories."

Zorian pokes at the screen. "I think I prefer other forms of storing knowledge."

"Like what, books? You have books?"

He slides me a look. "We pass our knowledge orally or on parchment but I know what a book is."

"Right. Of course. We don't have many. We work from computers like this. Most things are electronic. I like books. I have one with pictures of Earth flowers. And… I have a book I draw in. With coloured pencils."

"You draw?" he says in a dry tone.

"Are you teasing me, Zorian?"

"Did I do it right?"

I smile at him. "You did fine."

"What do you draw?"

I start walking in the direction the deer went. Zorian falls into step beside me. The mounds of heather are difficult to move through. The whole ground is springy.

"I draw Verdanian wildlife. Not very well but…"

"Did you draw the nalwell?" At my nod he says, "I would like to see it one day. In real life."

"Um, I'm not sure that will ever be possible, Zorian."

"I believe it will be."

"You're very optimistic for a Verdanian. The rest of you seem so serious."

The hill slopes towards the deep-blue loch, a scattering of trees on the bank. I skirt around a clump of boulders.

"We are a happy race. We do not plaster it all over our faces."

"Zorian?"

"What?"

"You're smiling right now."

He touches his fingers to his lips. "Oh. It appears I have been corrupted."

And then he grins, and I trip on a heather branch and land on my face. There's an alarming caress of wind on intimate areas.

Sweet lord, please tell me I'm not flashing my ass.

I scramble to my feet, nearly headbutting Zorian in the nose as he bends to help me up. Cool hands wrap around my biceps to steady me.

I am a squad leader! I am an ice cube under pressure!

"I, ah, tripped… on a root," I mumble, and use the excuse of brushing dirt from my dress to ease out of his grip. "You want to see what else I did today?"

The hill dissolves into the wide, Edinburgh street. Zorian and I stand on the pavement, people parting around us but paying us no attention.

He sucks in a breath and edges behind me. "There are so many humans! Can they see me?"

"Dreams are safe, remember?"

He peeks over my shoulder, not touching but his body is very close. He's practically vibrating.

"It is easy to forget in this alien place. Why is there so much rock? Where are the plants?"

He creeps further out but flinches when a group of girls laden with shiny bags chatter past him. I make the people give us a wider berth and he seems to relax. If stone can relax.

"This is a heavily populated town so it's quite built up. There are areas of land in between but it's mostly fields and hills."

"And this is the Earth they teach you about? The world you all miss? It is… crowded."

"I don't miss it; I've never been there. I was born here, which means I'm Verdanian."

He raises an eyebrow. "You are short for a Verdanian. Your eyes are okay but your hair does not match."

"Zorian?"

"Yes?"

"Shut up."

He smiles and makes a sound like a chuckle that can't possibly be a chuckle. "You are doing that scowly thing with your face again."

"Nobody else dares talk about my height around me."

"That is because you are their leader. But I am... autonomous."

A bus hums by on the road and Zorian inches nearer to me.

"You don't have to be so smug about it."

He drags his gaze from the vehicle. "Is that what I am?"

One side of his mouth is curved up. Sunlight emphasises the blush of colours under his skin and slants shadows under his cheekbones. A flop of pale-green hair obscures one emerald eye.

"I have no idea what you are," I say, frowning over his shoulder.

"That sounds as if it could be a lie."

"Shame you can't tell in a dream."

"There will be other opportunities."

My eyes zip back to him but he gives nothing away. Edinburgh fades, vines and ferns swallowing the buildings until we're alone in the jungle. His shoulders definitely loosen.

"Apart from learning about Earth, what else did you do today?" As he talks, he digs his fingers into the bark of a tree and clambers up, sitting with his back to the trunk, a leg on either side of a thick branch.

Is this the real purpose of him forcing his blood on me—a chance to get information on his enemy? Is he working up to the important stuff? It's what I should be doing. What any true soldier would be doing.

I stare up at Zorian from the ground. "I helped teach children about Verdanian anatomy."

"What about it?"

"Your two hearts, three stomachs, gills and, um, other organs."

Did I just look at his crotch?

Nope. No way.

He stretches out on his front, his feet kicking at the air, and rests his cheek on his hand. "You seem to know a lot about us."

"Your anatomy, your diet, how you fight. We know nothing about who you are or where you live. How close are you to Home Base?"

There, that's a proper question for a squad leader.

"We are not close," he says.

"Do you live in trees?"

"Not anymore."

Not anymore? What the hell does that mean?

"So, how *do* you fill your day?" I say.

"We also teach our children and we forage. We create items for trade, like clothes, jewellery, decorative bowls. I made this belt." He wiggles his butt and the split ends swing, the stones clacking together. "Sometimes we travel to other tribes to visit family or barter goods. These journeys can take years."

"Have you ever done one?"

"Not yet." He draws a pattern on the bark with his fingertip.

Yet? Does that mean he's planning to travel soon?

"Will you?"

"Yes. I will have to."

"Do you want to go?"

He shoves himself up so he's straddling the branch. "You should climb up here."

"Are you avoiding the question?"

"If you are up here, we do not have to shout."

"We're hardly shouting."

He cocks his head. "Are you afraid to climb a tree?"

"I'm not—" I bite back the word and cross my arms. "I've never climbed a tree. There's none in Home Base."

"That is because you tore them down, as if you could not possibly build around them. No harmony." He picks a leaf from a twig and puts it in his mouth. "If you were a Verdanian, you would climb this tree."

"If I climb the damn tree, will you answer my question?"

"Yes," he says, giving me his smirky face.

I roll my eyes and grip a knobbled branch, pulling myself off the ground. Shimmying up a tree is a lot harder than he made it look. Shouldn't it be easy in a dream?

"I can't believe I'm doing this," I mutter, my dress catching on bark.

"You say that a lot."

"Because you're very demanding."

My knee scrapes the rough trunk without pain. My dress hikes up and I pause to magic up some underwear before I flash the Verdanian a second time. The branches start to spiral around the tree. I step from one to the other, always focusing on my hand-holds above me and feeling with my toes. If I miss a branch, at least I won't fall, just dangle like an imbecile.

"I am not demanding," Zorian says. "You will know when I am."

How ominous.

I reach his level and slide onto the branch with a triumphant grin. "There, now answer my question—do you want to go on your journey thing?"

"I do not," he says, his face serious, though that's his normal face.

"Why?"

I keep one hand on the tree for balance, planning to edge out a little further, but make the mistake of glancing down. My brain goes a bit wobbly. The ground is somehow far away yet rushing to meet me. Blood roars in my ears and my stomach drops to my ankles.

"Oh, shit," I gasp, and hug the trunk with both arms, my cheek pressed to the pitted bark.

"Are you all right, Axelle?"

Zorian stands behind me, a cool presence in the humidity of the jungle. I grip the tree tighter, my fingernails sinking in.

"I think I'm scared of heights."

This is ridiculous. I can charge into a forest filled with hidden Verdanians but I can't climb a tree without getting stuck. In a freaking *dream*.

Oh, if my squad could see me now.

"Can you climb down?"

I risk a peek. My shaking knees threaten to pitch me over the side.

"Nope."

"I can carry you."

I swallow but don't loosen my death hug on the tree. "Okay."

"You will need to relax your hold."

"I don't think I can."

Man, I sound like a wimp but if I let go of the tree, I'll fall or so my body seems to think. I'd rather not test Zorian's 'dreams are safe' statement with a nosedive into the dirt. I can be annoyed at myself later, once my feet are on the ground.

Just what I need—another phobia to conquer. The water one was such fun.

Zorian places his hands on my shoulders. I stay very still. He runs his palms down my arms until he spoons me against the tree. It's weirdly comforting but I decide this is not the time to dwell on it. He gently peels me and my fingers from the bark. I may or may not whimper a little. Before I can do anything more embarrassing, he pulls me into him, my head on his solid chest, my back tucked into the flatness of his stomach. He wraps both our arms around me. Then he picks me up and steps off the branch.

I erase my, "Yeep!" from all memory. Squad leaders do not go, "Yeep." They say, "Bring it, son," or something equally courageous.

Zorian's feet hit the ground. I barely feel it, cradled in his arms. His puff of breath stirs my hair. He smells like mint.

Does he really smell like mint or is that what I think he smells like? The Elders and Passengers grow Earth mint and other food in enclosed labs as the Verdanian diet is too rich for their systems. Earth mint smells the same as a plant with blue flowers and heart-shaped leaves found on the edge of swamps.

Shouldn't Zorian put me down now?

He should definitely put me down now.

Twin heartbeats thud against my spine. My one little heart bounces around enough for two. His arms hold me tight, his hands on top of mine, fingers splayed on my ribs. He's strong enough to keep squeezing until bones snap. My feet dangle level with his kneecaps.

I clear my throat. Still can't speak. Try again.

"Why don't you want to go?" I whisper.

That should have been, "Put me the hell down, alien weirdo," which is the only appropriate response.

He hugs me and breathes. Is my butt against his crotch? I should probably start struggling about now or, if not now, five minutes ago.

"Someone is trying to wake me up," he finally says, and it takes me a second to process the words.

"Oh."

Good god, am I disappointed?

He shifts very slightly and I swear his lips are next to my ear.

"Maybe I will answer your question tomorrow," he says in a soft voice.

I wake in my bed to the ghost of his arms wrapped around me.

10

The day passes too slowly. I find myself thinking stupid shit like if I have a nap and Zorian has a nap, would we meet in the dream space or is it only during deep sleep?

Stupid, dangerous shit.

Why do I feel so comfortable around him? Is it because I can do what I want in the dream space? I can finally relax. I don't have hundreds of people watching me, awed, talking in hushed voices, wanting to be like me. Being the perfect soldier is a lot of pressure. What does it matter if I explore a little? Push the boundaries of what is considered appropriate. It doesn't count if I'm asleep.

Dreams are safe.

And I find Zorian easier to talk to than my own species. Sure, I have my squad but I'm their leader and have to maintain a certain distance for propriety's sake, even when shagging one of them. It bugs me. I never realised before. I can't lower my guard, can't properly unwind, unless I'm alone.

Or dreaming.

"Axelle?"

I jerk in my seat. "Passenger Gotiva, I am so sorry! My mind was elsewhere."

"I saw that, child, but don't fret," he says, running a hand over his bald head. "You've memorised the basic Anann phrases I can teach you already. It's a shame we know so little of the language. No one else shows an interest in learning it and it's hard to develop a deeper understanding when the Verdanians would rather kill us than converse with us."

I laugh politely as he slides from his perch on the desk at the front of the small classroom, closing his notebook and slipping it into the pocket of his blue uniform with a pat. He's a round man with eyebrow braids that curve down to his chin. They're the same colour as his grey eyes.

Gotiva speaks nine Earth languages and has picked up some Anann. It's not much—hello/goodbye, yes/no, what is your name? I found him poring over a book on Mandarin syntax after dinner and convinced him to give me a language lesson since there was no Earth lesson, just self-directed study.

Zorian's mastery of English puts me to shame. How did he learn it so completely? Did someone teach him? I want to speak Anann or to at least say, "Hello," in his own language when I see him again.

Not that I'm hoping to impress him or anything.

I should ask him to teach me Anann. Being the only human fluent in the local language would be useful, purely from a tactical perspective. Not because I think it sounds melodic. I could use it to be a spy, listening to what they say around us when they think we don't understand. Though they're not very talkative in battle. Or, if Zorian is right and we have no reason to keep fighting, I could be translator and mediator.

Sure. They can call me Peacekeeper instead of Godkiller.

What am I thinking? Zorian's not right. So he's proved there's a misconception with Verdanian blood. So what? It doesn't mean there are more lies. Maybe Zorian is the one who's lying. When—*if*—I search and find nothing, I can rub it in his face.

I thank Passenger Gotiva for his time and find the veterans of my squad a few glasses deep into their self-directed study of the pub. It's a strange building. The exterior is the usual black module but inside there are booths, stools and tables around a long, wooden bar.

I prefer Verdanian trees when they're whole but the wood is lovely. It's pale and etched with fine lines that look like a foreign script, as if the tale of the tree's life is written on its insides.

"Hey, it's the Boss!" Mallory slurs, loud enough to cut across the chatter. He raises his glass, slopping liquid onto the table where he sits with Brindan, Marvyn, Pacal and Karine. "I thought you'd be running on your treadmill or learning the ancient art of whittling or whatever you do to fill all twenty-two hours."

Brindan sniggers but Pacal buries his wide nose in his drink and Karine studies the puddles on the table, her red bob tickling her jaw and falling forward to hide her face. Marvyn looks from one person to the next as if he's not quite sure what to do. He and Brindan are so similar with their slim build and messy brown hair, it's easy to get them confused, though Brindan has been hitting the weights to get more muscular, like Mallory. Mallory slumps, revealing Fionna huddled in the end of the booth. She's a mousy girl and the skinniest unranked I've ever seen. I'm always surprised she can lift her weapon.

"Learning expands the mind, Mallory," I say. "You should try it."

He slurps from his glass. "Who cares about learning? I want to get fucked."

In the neighbouring booth, Dante and Loyanne roll their eyes. Nolana and Glennis sit with their heads close together at a table, dark to honey blonde, ignoring everyone else but their second-generation clique. Glennis raises an arm nearly as muscular as Mallory's and tugs on one of Nolana's beautiful cornrows. They share a private laugh.

"Well, good luck to you, Mallory." I cross to the bar. "Pity the war won't be won by fucking the Verdanians."

A little voice tries to whisper in my head but I shoo it away.

"Oh, I'll fuck the Verdanians. Just not the way they want to be fucked."

And how would Mallory know how they want to be fucked? Does anyone? We study their anatomy but that tells you about the machinations, not the nuance.

I grab bottles and mix myself a weak gin and tonic. Apparently, it's not as good as Earth gin but the Passengers worked with what they had. They used bark and berries and citrusy-tasting leaves. I like it, anyway.

Lili sits alone at the bar, her long legs tucked under a stool, nursing a daracurrant juice. Alcohol makes her throw up. Call sign—Hurly. Her hair falls straight and black to her waist. She slides me a glance out of one almond-shaped eye. I tip my glass at her, and a flush rises in her high cheekbones.

She's had a crush on me since I saved her life when she was seventeen. I thought it would have faded by now. She's gorgeous and all, willowy, but I like guys and only guys. Some aren't so fussy.

Harsh whispering hisses from Mallory's booth. A glass clunks on the table. Bodies shuffle on seats.

"Better get a look at what you're gonna be missing, Boss," Mallory says, one word slurping into the next.

I turn on my stool. Mallory has an arm slung around Karine and Fionna, practically jamming their heads in his armpits. From their strained posture, they seem to be holding most of his weight.

"Last chance," he hiccups.

I have no doubt if I say, "I've made a terrible mistake. Please, take me to bed right now, you glorious man-beast," he'll drop Karine and Fionna as if they never existed.

It's getting harder and harder to remember why I slept with him in the first place.

"Have a good night, Mallory. Drills are at six am."

His mouth droops before he herds it into a leer. "Might not make it. I'll be screwing these ladies 'til dawn."

Karine's not called Sex Machine for nothing but Fionna doesn't seem particularly enthused by the idea.

"You know what will happen if you don't, Mallory of the fifth." I calmly sip my drink, very aware of the attention of everyone in the pub.

He opens his mouth but one brain cell must be unpickled as he shuts it again. He wheels towards the door, dragging Karine and Fionna. A second after he's gone, Brindan and Marvyn slink out.

No point missing a live sex show. Everyone sleeps so close together in the barracks, if you don't have a current bedmate you can watch someone else and get yourself off. A bit voyeuristic but no one complains, though I insisted on doing it under the covers late at night. I could have invited Mallory or other bedmates to my pod but it would tarnish the only secret space I have.

10

Some unranked live and die without ever knowing privacy.

Noise slowly returns to the pub. Pacal, Loyanne and Dante join Lili and me at the bar and we play a few rounds of cards. Nolana and Glennis leave, holding hands, as Passengers and Elders trickle in. I force myself not to twitch when McBurnie's hair enters first, followed by the big man himself. The rest of my squad drifts away, Lili reluctantly, and McBurnie takes one of their vacated seats.

"M'eudail!" he says, slapping me on the back. "I haven't seen ye in the pub for a while. Ye finally learning how to relax?"

"I heard good things about your whisky, Elderman McBurnie."

A twinge of guilt surfaces but I squash it. I'm just having a drink. Nothing duplicitous.

"That's braw, lassie! Who else wants to join us for a drink?" he yells to the entire pub and probably the neighbouring modules.

The other squad leaders crowd around, thirteen from my generation and the other sixteen from the second generation, variously pocked and scarred from our years on Verdana. There's not much humanity left in a few of them, their eyes hard and empty.

McBurnie pours and we do shots. I swallow half, spitting the rest into my gin and tonic. A scrum forms at the bar, drinks passing from hand to hand, toasts aplenty.

Everyone loves McBurnie.

My gin glass slowly fills but no one seems to notice. I tip some onto the floor as the happy drunks surge around me. McBurnie gets closer and closer to the wooden surface of the bar until he's hugging it. Squad leaders stagger away, bumping into furniture but eventually weaving for the door.

Thank god. I can't hold up much longer.

"Yannik," I say to a large first generationer heaving himself out of a chair, "help me get the Elderman to his pod."

And then I attempt a hiccup that surely doesn't fool anyone.

Oh, god, what am I doing? I can't do this.

"'K, Axe," Yannik mumbles, his one good eye glazed and focused somewhere off-planet. A scar cleaves his face from his left brow, across his nose, to the corner of his mouth.

A Verdanian axe, like the one Zorian has. Maybe it *was* Zorian. For all his talk of ending the war, am I to believe he doesn't kill when he has to?

I slide McBurnie's arm across my shoulder, my hand steadied on his chest. The pass clipped to his uniform is cold under my palm. My stomach dips. Yannik tucks himself into McBurnie's armpit and hoists him to his feet. We stumble into a table, McBurnie's arm flopping from my shoulders. Not that I'm helping much. Yannik takes the bulk of the weight but then he has no neck and muscles the size of manga fruits. The door vomits us into the humid night.

"Axelle, m'eudail! Are ye takin' me to bed, ye wee devil?" McBurnie slurs, his breath strong enough to peel the skin off a water-dragon.

"I am, Elderman McBurnie. Yannik is, too."

"Och, Yannik, I didn't see ye there. No' to worry—plenty o' room!"

"Um, we won't be staying," I say, straining to keep McBurnie walking towards his pod.

Yannik murmurs, "Spoilsport," or he belches. Hard to tell.

Cursing and sweating, we finally get McBurnie to his residence. He fumbles for an eternity at the fingerprint scanner before the door beeps open. He's already snoring when we deposit him on his bed, a man mountain in maroon.

"Come back to my pod, eh, Axe?" Yannik says, the door shushing closed. "I'm not too drunk."

He can't seem to blink both of his eyes together, the bad one lagging behind the other. His smile slops around his face.

Yannik is not on my list of bedmates for fear of sustaining a crush injury. The thought of all that smothering bulk gives me the willies.

"Thanks, Yannik, but I just want to sleep. See you tomorrow."

He waves and lumbers off into the darkness. Quiet settles on the lanes of Home Base, a distant hoot echoing from the jungle. I rub the scar on my cheek.

Sighing, I relax my fist and stare at the pass in my hand.

<h1 style="text-align:center">11</h1>

The light of the card reader blinks red. On-off. On and off. It taunts me. Trai-tor. Traitor. But I haven't done anything wrong yet.

Okay…

I haven't done anything *too* wrong yet.

Home Base slumbers. The occasional muffled cough or clomp of a footstep comes from the soldiers on the wall but the deep shadows between two modules hide me from their gaze, though it tends to be directed outward.

Humans aren't the threat.

The hard edges of the pass bite into my clenched fingers.

I don't have to do this. I can go to bed, make my excuses to Zorian and live to fight another day. The blood connection will fade. It's not like he can storm up to the gate and demand answers. But then he'd be right—humans break all their promises. I never break a promise.

Fuck. I have to do this.

I slink around the buildings on a circular route to the door of the dissection lab, avoiding the open spaces, my breath held the entire time. My heartbeat drowns all other sound. I press my back to the recessed wall of the doorway and suck on the humid air until my pulse slows.

If anyone sees me, I can pretend to be drunk, though adrenaline has evaporated the alcohol in my system.

I've never been in trouble. I follow all our codes, attend to my duties and hate the Verdanians as I've been taught. This is who I am—Axelle of the first generation of humans born on Verdana. Trained to be the perfect soldier. I don't skulk around in alleyways and sneak into restricted areas. I don't consort with the enemy and let them touch me in my dreams.

Who the hell am I?

I swipe McBurnie's face over the card reader and it bleeps. The door hisses open to a metal hallway, the subdued lighting barely chasing the dark. I take a step, and the entrance slides shut behind me.

Too late to quit now.

I tip-toe into the corridor. The module of the dissection lab is small from the outside but it doesn't need to be huge if all it has is a surgical room, a prep/decontamination area and storage spaces. The single corridor has three metal doors on the left and one double door in the centre on the right. I peek through the vertical windows of the doors on the left. An office and two labs with tables, microscopes and complex equipment.

This can't be where they dissect. I would've expected biosecurity chambers at the very least. Some kind of incinerator.

The double door on the right has a single button with an arrow pointing down. A lift to an underground level. It makes sense to keep the risky procedures buried but my finger hesitates over the call button.

The lift in the gym complex is noisy—dinging and whirring as it moves between levels.

I drop my hand and examine the walls on either side of the

door. A squat access panel squeaks open into a vertical shaft with a ladder, red lights turning it into a gullet. It swallows me into the bowels of the structure and ends at another access panel. I crack it open but no one exclaims, "How *could* you?!" so I slip through into a bright corridor and wrinkle my nose at the sharp smell of disinfectant. A ventilation system puffs cool air from a grid near the low roof. Goosebumps creep over my shoulders.

I'm not alone down here.

My hand grips Zorian's stone, the fingers of my other hand rubbing across my scar. Neither soothes me. The fear of discovery, the thought of what will happen, prickles the hair at the nape of my neck.

I force myself to move. The corridor branches and seems to form a square. Doors line both sides around the first corner. I avoid the ones without windows in case they lead into a room containing a furious Elder who'll shove me into behavioural reconditioning faster than I can say, "Zorian made me do it."

The rooms in the centre of the square are all surgical suites. Shiny and sterile. One, two, three, four, five I count as I walk. Other doors lead into more labs, preparation areas and a laundry room. A huge metal hatch seems to open into a freezer but I leave it shut, same with a door marked 'Incinerator'. I peer into the last corridor before the square returns me to the lift.

Scratches mar the walls and floor, the metal dented in places. The scent beneath the chemicals is smoky-sweet, like burnt honey. Unease wiggles in my gut.

I want to be outside. I want to be in the jungle, surrounded by green, not this clinical place.

I hustle towards the first door. Footsteps squeak from the

direction of the lift. My heart catapults into my mouth.

What the fuck am I doing?! Why did I let Zorian manipulate me into this? I hate the unranked whispering about how great I am; after this, they'll whisper vile things. Things like traitor, monster-lover, untouchable. I'll be stripped of everything I worked so hard to achieve.

I dive into the nearest room, every muscle screaming at me to slam the door shut. I close it gently and lean my forehead on the cold metal. Something groans and it's not me. I spin around.

My, "Oh, shit," is more wheeze than words.

A Verdanian is strapped to a vertical table in the cramped room. Naked. Dull, burgundy eyes fix on me. The stubble of his crimson hair looks like beads of blood weeping from his scalp. He mumbles something in Anann.

"I'm sorry, I don't understand," I say.

Man, my voice is high.

He tugs against the straps. Someone whistles in the corridor and the jaunty tune floats closer.

"Oh, shit," I say with more spirit. "Please, *please* don't let them know I'm here."

The Verdanian has no clue what I'm saying but I can't worry about it. I scramble for a floor-to-ceiling cupboard and dive inside, smothered by clean, maroon uniforms hanging from hooks. Vials stacked in boxes clink against my boots. I pry the door towards me. The Verdanian watches and I shake my head, hold a finger to my lips and hope the gesture for *please shut up* is universal. The toe of my boot stops the cupboard from closing all the way, the heel jammed against another stack of boxes. The gap frames the Verdanian in a slice of the room. The air pressure shifts.

"Hello, my friend, how are we doing today?" says Elderman Vail. And then he switches to perfect, melodic Anann.

The Verdanian's struggles increase. Orange, red and emerald bruises mar the white perfection of his skin.

How did I not notice them? It takes a lot to bruise a Verdanian.

My heart lodges in my throat and threatens to choke me. Surely, Vail can hear it?

He steps into my slice of the room, dressed in a crisp, maroon uniform, his stone dangling down his back. He removes his shirt and drapes it neatly on a chair wedged under a desk on the far wall, leaving only his vest. His muscles sag but there's wiry strength in his arms. His body blocks my view of the Verdanian. Whatever Vail does, it makes the male scream—a horrible, piercing bleat.

I wince. A bottle chinks softly. I struggle to breathe without gasping.

The Verdanian speaks. I don't need to know the language, the desperate tone is enough. Vail chuckles and responds, shifting away to busy himself in the cupboards over a sink. Packets rip. Metal rings on metal. The Verdanian's chest heaves.

It's unusual to see them breathing so heavily.

I finally notice the surgical wounds. Incisions slash his chest and abdomen, sealed by dainty sutures except for a vertical incision between his pecs, closed by ugly staples. My eyes drop to a freshly weeping scab at the apex of his thighs. A scab where his penis should be.

Bile scalds my throat and burns worse when I swallow it.

This is not war. This is barbaric.

Vail approaches with a syringe. The prisoner sags in

his bonds. Vail inserts the syringe into a device on the Verdanian's arm and pulls the plunger, filling the barrel with swirling, creamy blood. He holds it up to the light and it shimmers rainbow colours.

So pretty.

Vail pockets the syringe and selects a bloodstone scalpel. The prisoner tries to shake his head but a strap across his brow keeps him still. He talks and it dissolves into one word repeated over and over.

"Don't be so dramatic," Vail says. "The experiment only needs one. For now."

Vail points the blade at a burgundy eye. The screaming lasts forever this time.

I mash my palms to my ears. My shaking is probably rattling the vials but I can't seem to stop. The shrieking obliterates everything else. It's the most plaintive, desolate sound I've ever heard and it leaves me hollow.

Vail's cheerful statement in Anann barely registers. The door clicks shut and the room echoes with a quiet whimpering—mine and the Verdanian's. I flop out of the cupboard and just make it to the sink to vomit stinging alcohol and what's left of the vegetable fritters I had for dinner.

"Kill me," croaks a voice.

I wipe a trembling hand across my mouth and splash cool water on my face, washing the sick down the plughole. I face the Verdanian, the edge of the sink digging into my spine.

"Kill me," he says.

Blood slicks his cheek, dribbling from his empty socket. I grit my teeth as my stomach heaves. His remaining eye is raw with an agony I cannot imagine. I wobble over to stand in front of him. The burnt-honey smell leaches from his body.

"Kill?" he says and that one word bleeds, pleads, hopes.

There's no blood connection between us but my own horror and sadness is already too much.

"I don't want to hurt you," I say, and he gives me a blank look.

How can I kill him, free him, painlessly? No other way is acceptable.

Vail could return at any moment.

My gaze falls to the device on the Verdanian's arm. It seems to be filtering his blood through a sensor and then back into his vein. The screen flashes levels for oxygen and carbon dioxide, minerals and blood sugar. I cradle his elbow and pull one end of the tube free. Blood flows, splattering my boots and the cuffs of my uniform. A tension eases from the Verdanian as his life drains onto the floor of his torture room.

"Thank," he sighs.

"I'm sorry," I say and it's choked. "I'm so sorry."

I place my hand on his scarred chest, and his hearts thrum under my palm. His eye stays on me as the beats slow, stutter, slow. Blood pools around my boots, the sweetness catching in the back of my throat. I hold his gaze because no one should die alone. His hearts stop. His last breath cools the tears on my cheeks but they continue to drip from my jaw and mix with his blood. I clamp my lips to keep in the sobs but they shudder through me anyway. I fumble for the strap around his opposite wrist and unfasten it. His hand flops on his hip. A moan escapes me, and I shove my fist in my mouth. Cleaning blood off my boots and wiping my prints settles me a little.

Part of me hopes Vail walks in. I'm not quite sure what I'll do but stabbing him in the eye seems fair.

A hysterical giggle bubbles up but I squash it. I glance around the room. There's nothing out of place except for the dead Verdanian and a slick of white on the floor.

The corridor is quiet. Are the scratches from struggling Verdanians, frantic to escape? My brain screams at me to flee this awful place but what if there are more prisoners being tortured? I can't leave them to that fate. It's not right.

The next three rooms are the same but empty, the vertical tables pristine and waiting for their victims. The final room is a cell.

Two Verdanians huddle in cages *I* couldn't stand up or stretch out in, their long limbs folded into uncomfortable positions, the bars bruising their skin. They bare their teeth and shy away but there's no space for them to go.

How must I appear with the blood of their friend stippling my trousers?

The burst of shame heats my face and cramps my gut. Not shame for what I've done but shame for the actions of my species. How can they justify keeping prisoners in this condition? I don't care if they're my enemy. There has to be honour. Dissecting bodies to learn is one thing. I could even accept taking prisoners to gather more information but what are they torturing them for? What could they possibly know that is worth this cruelty?

I raise my hands and approach the cages. "Do either of you speak English?"

The male and female trade looks, their expressions haughty beneath the filth. I breathe through my mouth so I don't gag and offend them.

They've been trapped here for a while.

The female eyes the blood on my trousers, and growls.

"I'm sorry," I say, my voice wobbling. "He's dead. He asked me to kill him. He was… wounded."

Their rapid Anann weaves back and forth. The male's trousers are ragged, held together by strings of vegetation. The female is naked, and I hope it doesn't mean what I think it means.

"I'm not here to hurt you. I'm here to help you escape."

The female glares at me, scorn darkening her violet eyes. Her pink hair hangs in limp curls to her flat chest, her nipples broad in comparison to mine.

For fuck's sake, Axelle, this is not the time.

I search the room and find a hook board with keys and corresponding cage numbers. A tablet sits on a bench underneath and I pocket it for later. The key scrapes in the lock of the female's cage.

I pause before turning it. "I'll understand if the first thing you do is crush my skull but… I'd rather you didn't. You don't have to trust me. But you can trust Zorianangullewell'yan Bruad'arach."

Holy crap, I pronounced his full name.

The bursts of Anann are difficult to follow. The male seems to be trying to persuade the female or he's telling her the best way to kill me when I open her cage. His hair is flower-pollen yellow, his eyes gold.

They really are a spectacular species. Excellent genes.

"How you speak of Zorianangullewell'yan?" the female finally says, her eyes narrowed.

"He and I are working together to stop the fighting."

How true that would ring in his chest if he were here. I hope telling them doesn't get him in trouble.

The lock clicks and the barred door swings open. I back away and unlock the male's cage. Then I hold my breath and pray they don't kill me.

They unfold themselves from the cages. Joints pop. Even they can't hide the pain of movement from their faces. They stand and stretch and groan softly. I stare at the wall.

"Are you strong enough to follow me? I can show you the way out."

"We follow," the female says, curling her lip, "but if this is a game, I will peel your skin from bones, human."

She bites the air to emphasise her point, and I suddenly need to pee.

I lick my lips. "Fair enough. Wait here while I get you some clothes."

"We want to see"—and then she says something so long and complicated, it must be the name of their friend.

Of course they want to see him. Why trust anything I say?

I wave for them to stick close and lead them into the corridor. Everything is still. Maybe Vail is happily dissecting the Verdanian's eye.

If they want fresh tissue to study, can't they keep them comatose and completely unaware?

We duck into the prisoner's room when I very much don't want to. I'll be seeing his eyeless socket in my nightmares. Perhaps Zorian will be forced to share that with me.

How fun for him.

The Verdanians make small sounds of grief. They skirt the blood, and their hands flutter over the body of their friend. They pat him, whisper to him, and keen softly. I clench my fists to keep from crying.

They wouldn't appreciate it.

The female whips her head around, her fingers on the hollow of the dead Verdanian's throat. "Where is his stone?"

"I don't know. I'm sorry."

She hisses something to the male and I'm pretty sure it's uncomplimentary.

Can't blame her.

I grab two maroon uniforms from the cupboard, largest size, and hold them out. "Put these on. Then we have to leave."

The female nods at the tube in her friend's arm then the floor. "You did this? He ask?"

"Yes. He asked."

"Violent," she says, shaking her head. "You violent species."

Can't argue there, either.

They snatch the clothes and tug them on. Both uniforms flash pale ankles and wrists. There's nothing I can do about their bare feet. Or their hair.

How am I going to sneak two glowing freaking Verdanians through Home Base, if we even get out of this hell-hole?

We reach the access panel unmolested. I climb first and they haul themselves behind me, pausing to rest every couple of steps, strain hollowing their faces.

I can't complain but if someone raises the alarm and rouses the whole of Home Base, I'll never get them out. What will I do then—keep them as pets in my pod? Ophrys is enough of a handful to feed.

The lights of the ground floor remain low. I hope this means Vail is in the basement, prodding at a burgundy eye that looked more beautiful in the head of the owner than in slices under a microscope.

My gut shifts, reminding me to quit thinking of the eye

unless I want to see what else I can throw up.

Phobia number three, perhaps?

I hustle the limping Verdanians to the front door. It slides open at another pass of McBurnie's card.

McBurnie. The lovable giant of a man can't know what goes on here… can he?

A problem for later. I've had enough shocks tonight.

Outside, Home Base sleeps peacefully, the sky as dark as I left it, though it feels as if I was underground for hours. I gulp pure, sweet air and the Verdanians join me. I imagine it's a million times better for them.

"This way," I whisper. "Keep your heads down."

The female touches her fingers to her chest and then places her palm on the chest of the male. Reassurance? I need some myself.

My route avoids the residential units and barracks, taking us past modules that should be empty—classrooms, the entrance to the amphitheatre, the canteen. Tension stiffens my shoulders until I'm as hunched as a hundred-year-old Elder. Worse than anything I get before or during battle. There, I'll probably just die. Here, I have no idea what my people are capable of.

Would they torture me, too?

My spine and knees are screaming when we reach the wall but my awe for Verdanian capabilities has leaped an enormous degree. They hunker next to me beneath a series of pipes. I unscrew loosened bolts and a panel slips free. The inside of the wall is pitch black but I've bumped my head on enough of the support girders to know where they are. I unscrew the second panel on the outer wall and carefully lower it to the ground.

This is how I sneak out when I need some jungle therapy. There's nothing in the codes about breaking the wall but I guess it's implied or they assumed no one would be stupid enough to create a weak spot. It's the only thing I've done wrong in my twenty-four years, though that record has been destroyed these last couple of days.

Somehow, I don't feel as guilty.

The two Verdanians slide into the crawl space, and I get a little claustrophobic. They're so much bigger than I am. Solid and tough and intimidating. But they haven't tried to squash my skull like a daracurrant and that shows amazing restraint after their ordeal.

I point to a black-on-grey area of short vegetation beyond the base of the wall. "Crawl through there. The grass forms a tunnel and will hide you until you reach the jungle proper. Then you can stand and run."

The female nods once and whispers in Anann to the male. She turns to climb out of the hole.

"Wait," I say, and she pauses. "What are your names?"

They share another long look. Maybe their names are secret or sacred or whatever. Or I don't deserve to hear them.

The female touches her chest. "Fennanangullandolin."

She rests her hand on the male's shoulder and says something to him. I catch the word for 'name'.

"Dalrainenna," he says.

"I'm Axelle." I do the chest-touching thing. "I'm sorry for what was done to you. Both of you. And your friend."

Dalrainenna glides out of the hole in the wall and disappears into the grass. Fenna hesitates with one foot still in the crawl space.

"I speak of you to Zorianangullewell'yan," she says.

And then she's gone, a glitter of white in the dark.

12

"You are late to bed tonight."

Zorian sits in a tree, swinging his legs. He's wearing something with tassels and they gather between his thighs and brush his knees. Each one is made of fronds of a different colour.

"How do you know?" I say, my voice tinny and weird.

I try to change my vest and shorts but can't seem to focus. I'm sleeping yet exhausted in my dream. How does that work?

Zorian's smile eases the weight of the stone that's been stuck in my stomach since I returned to my pod and had a moment of reflection. It threatens to lodge in my throat and make me do something embarrassing, like cry.

"Right," I say with forced cheerfulness. "You can tell. Just how many blood connections have you had?"

"None."

"See—wait, what? Then how…?"

"Our elders teach us."

He drops from the branch and walks towards me. The tassels sway.

"I'm your first blood connection?"

"Yes," he says.

Why does that get my belly all squiggly?

106

He halts a foot away and cups the pendant, his fingers cool on my collarbone. A mirror image appears around his neck. He raises his eyes to my face.

"Are you all right, Axelle?"

Damn. So much for faking it.

"I did something tonight." I suck in a breath and ignore the wobble. "I searched."

"You did not like what you found."

I shake my head too hard and my hair whips across my shoulders.

"Zorian, what does 'gwethoile' mean?"

He curls a lock of my hair around his finger.

"Please," he murmurs. "It means 'please'."

As in, please don't hurt me. Please stop. Please don't hack out my eyeball.

"Oh," I say and, fuck it, the stone is in my throat. Tears spill onto my cheeks before I can halt them. I hide my face in my hands but it doesn't muffle the sounds.

Sweet god, I'm sobbing in front of a Verdanian. But at least it's Zorian.

Solid arms wrap around me, and I bury my face in his chest. My tears must scald his skin. He gathers me close until I'm in his lap. Tassels tickle the backs of my thighs. Water splashes and ripples but I keep my face in the curve of his neck. He has no pulse there, though I can hear the faint echo of his hearts. The coolness of his body soothes the heat of mine.

"This is my favourite place to come when I am sad or lonely or need time to think," he says, his cheek resting on the top of my head, one hand stroking my hair.

I open my eyes, my lashes wet and clumped together. We're sitting on a pink-flushed rock on a beach of grey sand. A small waterfall tinkles into a beautifully clear pool ringed by fronds of green. The sky is a perfect circle of cobalt.

"You get lonely?" I say, and only sniffle a little.

Okay, a lot.

"Yes, Axelle. I get lonely."

He swipes a fingertip across my cheek and captures a tear. He seems fascinated by it and I'm almost certain he wants to put it in his mouth.

Humans—salty and metallic. Verdanians—sweet and minty. Which is the monster?

"You know," I say, and manage a watery smile, "you probably shouldn't touch me this much."

"Why?"

He strokes his finger over my scar and down the line of my jaw to trace my lips. The tickling caress flares a different kind of heat.

Oh, cock. I really shouldn't be sitting in his lap.

"Dreams are safe," he says, softer than the stroke of his finger. "If you cannot be free in dreams, when can you be free?"

"I—" I clear my throat and try again. "I've never been free."

"Are you not free here?"

"Well, I've certainly never done this in real life."

He smiles again. "And do you feel better now?"

"I do. You're very clever, aren't you?"

"I like to think so."

I shift in his lap, decide it's not a good idea and sit very still. His hand settles on my knee, his other on the small of my back. A flock of skreeingbirds swoops over the pool, dipping their beaks to drink on the wing.

Unless we concentrate, there's no sound or smell or movement, the dream a blank canvas.

"This place is very peaceful," I say. "I see why you come here."

"It is where bad news does not seem so bad." He watches the birds vanish into the depths of the jungle. "Do you want to tell me what happened?"

I sigh and stare at my hands, fiddling with the hem of my vest. "Yes. But I might cry again."

"That is all right. You humans have weak eyes."

"Verdanians don't cry?"

"No, but that does not mean we do not feel."

"I know you feel," I say, and touch my palm to his chest.

God, his eyes. How could I have thought they were empty? They hold everything.

Is this the first time I've consciously touched him? I probably shouldn't do it again.

I carefully fold my hands together. "So, tonight was… harrowing."

I tell him about the restricted lab for studying Verdanian bodies. It still seems to be what it's for, though they're a lot more alive and aware than we're led to believe. I describe the prisoner and the horrific acts done to him. Zorian catches my tears on his fingertips.

"I don't care how the war started or why we're fighting, what we're doing to prisoners is wrong. It has to end." I wipe my nose and say very quietly, "Did you know him?"

Zorian nods. "He made the most delicate beads."

That tiny detail sets me off on another blubbering fit. Zorian brushes my wet hair from my cheeks.

"You cry for him."

"No one should have to die like that—begging an enemy

for mercy."

"But you gave it, when no one else would."

Yeah, lucky number thirteen. How would Zorian feel about my tally, now that I know he feels? Deeply.

"What was his name?" I say.

"You may call him Thommonn."

I scrub the dampness from my face. "He wasn't the only Verdanian I met tonight."

Zorian tilts his head. I talk about Fenna and Dalrainenna, the cramped cages, helping them past the wall.

"Will telling them your name get you in trouble? I even said it in full—Zorianangullewell'yan Bruad'arach."

His fingers tighten on my knee. He doesn't appear to be breathing.

"Did I not pronounce it properly? Or, shit, I shouldn't have told them, right? I didn't mention the blood stuff."

He says nothing, just stares at me.

"Zorian?"

"You are what I hoped all humans would be like," he whispers.

He hugs me against him. The only way I could be closer is if I straddle him. Which I am not doing. My hands slide around his back to the muscles over his shoulder blades. He's slim but so solid, so smooth. I may sniff his neck a little.

"Say my name again."

"Zorianangullewell'yan Bruad'arach," I mumble into his throat.

"Your pronunciation is perfect."

"Will Fenna and Dalrainenna get you in trouble?" I say, and freeze when I realise I'm nuzzling him.

He smells good.

"No. I am glad they are alive. At least we can tell my father of Thommonnandowarnan's death."

"How will he react to you working with me?"

His shoulder twitches under my hand. "I may not tell him immediately but I hope he will understand."

"He won't punish you, will he?"

"Are you worried about me, Axelle?"

I pinch his back, and something like a chuckle rumbles through his chest.

"Answer the question, Zorian."

"He may punish but he will not hurt me."

"That doesn't sound great, either."

He pulls away gently and stands up, letting me slide to my feet, the sand hot under my toes.

"I will be fine." He holds out a hand. "No more talk of war or pain for tonight."

I place my hand in his and his fingers tangle with mine. He leads me to the edge of the pool, the warm water lapping at my feet.

"What I saw was horrible but it doesn't answer why the war started. I took a tablet—a computer—from the lab. If I can unlock it, maybe that will."

"I have no doubt you will find what you seek," he says, tugging on my arm, "but we are going to do something fun for the rest of our dream."

"As long as it doesn't involve going in there." I jerk my chin at the pool.

He grins, flashing fang, and my legs wobble.

"The best way to combat a fear is to face it," he says.

"I've already faced it. I just don't like swimming."

The humour fades from his face. "Was it one of us? When

you took off your helmet and got your scar, did one of my people drag you underwater?"

I still remember her. Dark-green hair floated around her head like the plants tangled around the legs of my battlesuit. Her eyes were a green so inky, they looked black. Soulless. I struggled in her grip, the urge to breathe a fire in my chest, worse than when Zorian force-fed me his blood. She held me easily, watching the last of my air bubble between my lips, her impassive face worse than if she'd gloated.

"Yes," I say, shivering at the memory. "A female. I drowned. I only survived because my squadmates pulled me out and gave me mouth to mouth. She got away."

"What is mouth to mouth?"

"You put your mouth over theirs and blow air into their lungs to simulate breathing. It's called the kiss of life."

Am I blushing? It feels like I'm blushing. For fuck's sake, I'm not some delicate flower or even a freaking virgin.

Is Zorian? If he's had no mates and no blood connections...

Nope, I did not just think that.

"We cannot drown," he says. "We are good at using it against you. We both do terrible acts."

"But you don't capture and torture humans."

"No. We do not."

We contemplate the quiet surface of the pool. Golden limpets wave their fronds, filtering tiny particles, their rocks dotted on a floor of black mud. I add some snails bobbing through the water, paddling their tiny fins, their shells breaking the surface.

Zorian squeezes my hand. "Do you trust me, Axelle?"

"I... Yes."

"One day, I wish to feel that truth."

He walks into the pool. My legs carry me along beside him. I grip his fingers tight. The water tickles up my thighs and soaks my shorts, plastering my vest to my belly. It's unbelievably warm, way warmer than the water I shower with. The surface reaches my neck but it's barely to Zorian's chest.

"Um, Zorian," I say, my toes sinking into soft mud, "there's a matter of height difference to consider."

He stops and smiles at the water licking my chin.

I shouldn't have encouraged him to smile. It does strange things to my breathing.

"Then I will have to crouch," he says.

He ducks into the pool and takes both my hands. He swims backwards, his long legs kicking on either side of me. I suck in air before our heads go under, and squeeze my eyes shut. Panic threatens to claw at my stomach.

It's a dream. Just a dream.

"Open your eyes, Axelle," he says and his voice vibrates through the water. "It will not hurt you, I promise."

The water is so clear, I see everything. Zorian settles on his knees, looking up at me for once. His hair somehow stays pale, waving gently around his face and caressing his cheekbones. Mine decides to form a black, smothering cloud. His oxygen trickles out as silver bubbles. My cheeks are puffed to keep mine in.

"Breathe, Axelle," he says.

My chest burns. My breath roils out, tickling my nose and dancing in my hair. My heartbeat echoes, loud past the rushing in my ears. I inhale, and lunge for Zorian. Heat floods my lungs but there's no pain, no urge to choke or cough. I try again—in and out. I can feel the flow of water into my chest.

The swirling sensation is a little strange. Zorian shivers and I belatedly realise my fingers are curled in the gills along his rib plates, open now that he's underwater. Something tickles my skin.

I jerk my hands back. "Did I hurt you?"

He watches me with a soft expression, and captures my fingers. His thumbs brush the backs of my hands.

"You cannot hurt me here," he says. "*Now* you are a Verdanian."

My skin tingles, the sensitivity heightened rather than muffled by the water. His gaze drops to where my vest ripples, exposing the flat line of my stomach. Somehow, my mouth is dry. One of my snails bumps into his cheek. I laugh at his startled expression and the moment passes.

I'm not disappointed. Not one bit.

I get a little excited swimming through the pool, exploring every inch of it and chasing the beasts Zorian magics to life. Fish, snakes and insects zip through the water. I hide behind Zorian when he creates a water-tiger, its long, yellow- and orange-striped body slinking into the pool. But this is our dream and it just paddles its sharp claws and drifts away, its dorsal fin breaking the surface.

We race but Zorian beats me every time. We eventually stumble out, trailing drips. Water beads in Zorian's hair instead of soaking in. My lungs slosh but it fades when I start to breathe air.

Must remember to never try this in real life.

"That was amazing," I say, squeezing moisture from my hair.

Zorian stares at me. I frown and glance down.

"Holy crap, my clothes are see-through!"

I cross my arms and sit hard in the sand, my knees tucked to my chest, heels against my butt.

"I did not notice," he says, his features carefully blank.

"You promise?"

A smirk tugs at his mouth. "No."

My cheeks heat. He stretches out next to me while I focus hard and replace my indecent vest and shorts with a dry t-shirt and trousers. Black instead of forest green. What a rebel I am.

The pool stills. The jungle goes quiet. Everything is shimmering and insubstantial.

"Are we waking up?"

Zorian shakes his head. "The blood connection is fading."

"Oh." I dig a toe in the sand. "So… we need to share more?"

"I do not have to pin you down this time?"

I swallow. "No. You don't have to pin me down."

"Can you leave your home prison tomorrow?"

I stick out my tongue. "It's called Home Base. And yes. How will I find you?"

"Head towards the mountains. I will find you."

"But—"

The screech of my alarm yanks me from the dream. I gasp upright in my bed, my eyes gritty, a deep ache across my shoulders.

The five hours of sleep were not enough, as enjoyable as they were. I actually forgot about the horrors of the dissection lab. Or Zorian made me forget, anyway.

I glance at the stolen tablet beside Ophrys's tank.

God, it's all so confusing. Zorian is… not like any human or Verdanian I've ever met. And I'm meeting him again, in the flesh, in a few hours.

I put my head between my legs and tell myself to breathe.

13

Mallory turns up for drills, red-eyed and pale, changing to green as the morning progresses. He vomits on the stone after a particularly vigorous battle formation.

"Go back to bed, Mallory," I say as he staggers to the line. "Your attendance has been noted and appreciated."

Sweat slicks his face. He presses his hand to his mouth.

"God bless you, Axe," he mumbles, and scurries away.

"You look a little hollowed out, too, if you don't mind me saying," Loyanne whispers, sidling up to me.

We watch the rest of the squad sprint and roll and dodge. Fionna blushes whenever Karine crosses her line of sight.

"I made the error of drinking with Elderman McBurnie last night."

Loyanne winces. "No one would judge if you went back to bed."

"You know, I'd usually say something about toughing it out, setting a good example but, screw it, I feel like shit. Are you okay to lead if I have a personal day?"

"Of course, Axe. Get some rest. I'll take over their torture from here."

I flinch but turn it into a chuckle. "If there's an emergency, I'll be in my pod. If I don't answer, I'm in a coma and you're on your own."

Or I'm outside in the jungle, meeting a Verdanian. I guess I'm not the only one who's been corrupted.

Loyanne shouts orders followed by a chorus of groans from my squad. She won't go easy on them.

I skip breakfast and jog straight to my pod. There's too much going on in my stomach for food. I lie on my bed. Maybe I should sleep for another hour to avoid looking terrible when I see Zorian.

Don't be an idiot. He doesn't care what I look like. The last time he saw me in real life, I was a sweaty mess in a battlesuit.

I clip some leaves for Ophrys. I'll find him berries in the jungle. He gets excited over berries.

I pace around my pod. Sit on the edge of my bed. Stand up. Pace some more. I flick through my meagre collection of clothes and wonder what the heck I'm going to wear.

What I'm going to *wear?!* I sound like one of those giggly teenagers in the movies I, again, don't watch.

I jump in the shower and blast it cold. It helps, though my skin is tinged blue and goosepimpled when I switch to the drier. I style my hair for the first time in ten years, framing my face but pinning up the bulk of it so it flicks against my shoulders when I move.

What am I doing? It's just going to fall down when I crawl through the jungle.

I leave it and pull on a forest-green vest and trousers, plus black boots that lace past my ankles. I slide Zorian's stone from under my top.

I'd feel naked with nothing around my neck. How hard has it been for him, living without it?

Ophrys glides from under his log and munches on a leaf. I

pick him up, and he glares balefully out of his four eyes.

"Am I about to do something stupid?" I ask him.

He wiggles his fronds. I don't speak snail so I can interpret it any way I wish.

How long will Zorian search for me if I stay in my pod? The thought of him standing in the jungle alone and disappointed causes a small ache in the pit of my stomach.

I want to see him again. I don't want our dream thing to end. It's the freest I've ever been.

Ophrys continues to crunch on his leaf despite his body dangling from my hand. I put him back in his tank, and he ignores me.

I loop a belt around my waist and clip my bloodstone knife to it, sheathed so I don't lop off a finger. The door of my pod whispers shut behind me. I sneak without looking like I'm sneaking, avoiding people, backtracking, ducking into shadows. A group of Elders hunches in conversation in front of the dissection lab. They must be scratching their heads on how the prisoners escaped. They disperse after a minute. Elderman Vail disappears inside.

I'd never remove an eye from a living creature. Okay, so I've shot a couple of Verdanians in the eye but their deaths were instantaneous. How long did Thommonn suffer?

He already suffered too much.

I reach the wall unseen and slip into the dark cavity, sealing the panel. The jungle beckons, bright green under the two suns. Violet clouds gather.

Just as well I like the rain.

I press my back to the outer wall and hold my breath. Grass rustles as I dive into the tunnel smelling of earth and sunlight. I climb to my feet in the shade of the trees, brushing myself off. Then I head north towards the mountains.

But not too fast.

I trail my fingers over waxy leaves and silky petals, breathe deep of the moist, pollen-scented air, drink sweet water from the cup of a flower—a twilip, non-poisonous and a beautiful crimson. Skreeingbirds encourage me onward, flitting from branch to branch. A cloud of insects sparkles in a sunbeam.

The real jungle is more vibrant than the dream space, no matter how good Zorian and I are with the details.

This is how it should be experienced, not stuffed into a battlesuit, sucking filtered air, senses deadened by the armoured layers. My senses are alive, heightened.

There were landmasses on Earth where you risked getting eaten by a bear or a land-tiger or a wolf. Yet people sought out those places for the thrill. For the beauty of the wild despite the threat of the wild biting you on the ass.

My knife is enough to dissuade most predators.

I pass a still pool, flowers of burnished gold floating in the centre. It's picturesque but I avoid the soft edge.

So much for being over my phobia. Swimming with Zorian was fun but I'm not quite ready for a non-dream immersion.

Will he be different in real life? Our meeting in the cave doesn't count as a proper interaction. Just how free is he in dreams? Will *I* be different?

I will be cool. I'll say hello in Anann. He'll say it back. We'll share blood and return to the dream space where things are less formal and awkward. Where I can pretend I'm not betraying my race.

Meeting in dreams is one thing—no one can ever prove it— but meeting an enemy warrior in the flesh? That is a crime against the last bastion of humanity.

The rain begins as a low hiss, beading on the leaves, the canopy sheltering the forest floor. The skreeingbirds hush in deference. I hustle into a clearing formed by a mossy crag, ferns growing from cracks in the rock. I raise my face to the sky and close my eyes.

The rain is so much nicer when I'm not preparing for battle.

Water dampens my shoulders and hair, slicking my cheeks and pooling in the curve of my lips. The richness of the jungle fills my nose. Loam, decay, wet and growing things. Thick enough to—

I'm being watched.

He stands beside a four-legged beast, his hand on its long, muscled neck. Dappled brown fur blends with the jungle. The creature lifts a foot cleaved into five hooves linked by webbing. Sapphire horns spiral from the back of its head.

I stare at Zorian. Zorian stares at me. My heart skips, and I'm glad he can't feel it yet. Maybe by that point, it will behave itself.

Am I really going to drink his blood?

"Zorian," I mumble, doing something between a head bob and a curtsy. Stop fidgeting and say hello, you idiot! "Um, dia duale."

He doesn't smile but his face softens.

"Dia duale, Axelle," he says.

His weapon peeks over his shoulder, the strap across his bare chest. He's wearing the belt he had in one dream, the beads brushing the intricate material of his trousers. The rain has flattened his hair so it flops in his eyes.

I should probably stop staring and say something else. Do something.

I take a step. He mirrors me. His horse-beast stays beside

the crag and munches on a flower.

"Was—" I squeak. I clear my throat and try again. "Was it difficult to get away?"

"No. We do not have a wall, like you."

Man, talking is so much easier in dreams. He's just so *here*. Imposing, pristine. A beautiful, impassive creature. Maybe he regrets offering to share more blood, the reality of me disappointing compared to the person I am in our dreams.

I slip his pendant over my head and hold it out, the stone swinging from my clenched fingers. He closes the distance between us and takes it, careful not to touch me. I ignore the little ache that can't possibly be hurt feelings. The stone settles below the ridge of his collarbones. He strokes it, his eyes half-lidded. It brings out their colour.

Should I leave? Is this all he wanted?

He opens his eyes and catches me tracing the place where his pendant sat.

Damn. So much for being cool.

He fumbles at his waist and cups something in his hands, his head bowed. He slowly extends his arms.

"I made this," he says, his gaze on the ground, "for you. I thought... you might... miss having one."

His eyes meet mine then flit away.

Holy crap, is he *shy*? A shy Verdanian. That's... adorable.

I touch his fingers, a little hesitant myself, and it brings his gaze back to me. His hands unfurl. A pendant rests on his palm. A thread of emerald weaves through the black cord, the stone a pure cobalt, like a piece of the sky captured in his hand.

"Zorian," I breathe, "it's gorgeous."

The corner of his mouth twitches. "You like it?"

"I love it."

I swear he sighs in relief. The ache in my chest vanishes.

"Every Verdanian should have a stone. Where else is your spirit to go?"

He teases the cord over my head, tucking my hair out of the way and, quite deliberately, scattering my carefully placed pins. My hair curls down my back and over my shoulders. The stone hangs below the hollow of my throat, as cool as Zorian's fingers resting on it. I place my hand over his, my heart beating strong enough to shiver through the both of us. I raise my head, up and up and up, to his face.

We stare at each other a little too long. My heart beats harder. His stupid horse-beast stamps its foot, and Zorian blinks. He pulls away but keeps hold of my hand, leading me to rocks beneath the mossy crag. I perch on one opposite him.

"Do you want to drink first?" he says, and I shake my head. He smiles, touching his cheek. "You do this when you are nervous."

I'm stroking my scar. Cock. I sit on my hand. The rock has been smoothed into a swirling pattern under my palm, as if carved by water.

"I'm not nervous," I say.

He treats me to his smirky face. Has it always made my breath catch?

"Axelle, I do not need the blood connection to know you are lying. But... I am nervous, too."

"Why are you nervous?"

He tilts his head. "Why are *you* nervous?"

"Fair enough," I say, and shut my mouth.

How do we share blood? It's going to take more than a

finger prick this time. There are other places—neck, wrist, crook of the elbow, thigh…

Oh, sure, Axelle. Why don't you just whip down your trousers and let him sink his fangs into your femoral? Great idea.

I hold out my left arm. Cool fingers cup the back of my hand.

"Do you not want to cut yourself?" Zorian says, the look in his eyes difficult to decipher.

My arm trembles in his grip. I'm liable to slice too deep with my knife.

"Safer if you bite me."

There's something I never thought I'd say.

"Are you sure?"

I have to lick my lips to get them to work but manage a quiet, "Yes."

Zorian slides from his rock and onto his knees, not letting go of my hand. He turns my arm gently so the inside of my wrist faces him. His breath brushes the delicate skin. His eyes meet mine over the line of my arm.

He can definitely feel me shaking.

His lips kiss my wrist. My nails scrape the rock. I taste my pulse in my mouth. He bites, and I can't help a little gasp. He watches me but I don't scream or struggle or tell him to stop.

It isn't so bad. After the initial slice, there's no pain. Warmth blooms in my arm despite the press of his mouth and hands. And then he starts to suck.

Oh… *shit.*

I bite my lip to keep in a sound that's way worse than a gasp. My pulse drops to throb in lower places and it's not my freaking toes. His tongue glides over my wrist. He sucks and licks and, oh my god, it's like his mouth is somewhere else.

As soon as it pops into my head, it's all I can think about—Zorian on his knees, watching me with dark, emerald eyes, his hands on my thighs, the coolness of his mouth both dampening and flaring my heat. The fork of his tongue teasing, exploring…

I squirm on the rock.

Think of something else!

Does his species even do oral? Maybe sex for them is purely functional. It's certainly been a while since that particular act was enjoyed by me. It's hard to get in the right head-space surrounded by hundreds of snoring, farting soldiers. It needs trust. It's more intimate than the sex itself. Special.

Sacred, some might say.

Why am I still thinking about it?

It's not going to happen, anyway. Zorian may look human but he's not. And that matters.

Does it? whispers a voice.

This is not the way a soldier of the first generation thinks. What the hell has happened to me?

"Are you all right, Axelle?" Zorian says. "Did I take too much?"

I'm sprawled on the rock, Zorian's grip on my wrist the only thing stopping me from folding to the ground. I feel woozy, achy, but I'm hoping it's just the blood loss.

"I'm fine," I croak then say it again with a little more conviction.

I need to get my body under control. How would he react if he knew what sucking on my wrist did to me?

Zorian plucks a clump of moss from the crag and presses it to my bite wound, securing it in place with a fern, the fronds braceleting my arm.

Pretty, for a field dressing.

"Are you ready?" he says.

Well, sucking on him can't be any worse.

At my nod, he bites himself and holds out his wrist. Pearly blood trickles. My stomach clenches, some instincts not so easily forgotten. A drop gathers on the edge of his arm.

Crap. I bet it's sacrilegious if it spills.

I lunge to catch the droplet on my tongue and fasten my lips around his wrist. Sweetness bursts in my mouth, crisp and cool as it flows down my throat. It's like sucking on a mint and quite pleasant, if I don't think about it too deeply.

How does my mouth feel on him? My eyes are closed, and I dare not look. What if he's having a similar response?

I swallow quickly and nearly choke. I swallow again, air whistling through my nose.

God, I hope Zorian's not watching me.

I lick him just for the hell of it. He makes a soft noise and a little shiver trembles through his arm. I smile into his wrist, glad it's not just me. Both hands are wrapped around his arm, pressing it to my mouth. When did I get on my knees?

I fear Zorian says my name a few times before it registers.

"Axelle. You can stop now."

One more lick, and I sit hard on my butt. We blink at each other, his dazed eyes reflecting mine.

"Is sharing blood always like this?" I manage to say.

"I do not know. Perhaps. It is usually done from the throat."

Heat creeps into my face at the thought of his lips on my neck. Straddling his lap would be a good position, given the height difference.

Okay… it's probably best we won't have to do that for a

few months. Or however long the connection lasts this time. Maybe I'll build up some immunity.

Zorian tries to bandage his wrist but keeps dropping the moss. I'm no better. It takes far too much concentration to hold the padding in place and wrap a fern around. I yank it tight and snap the frond.

"Tits," I say.

"What are tits?"

I flop on my back, and laugh. The clouds have cleared, the canopy bordering a sky as pure as my necklace.

"Tits," I say, relishing the word in my mouth, "are what your females don't have and what have fascinated human males for centuries."

Zorian stretches out beside me, a couple of inches between us. I pluck at the damp grass under my palm.

"Tits," I say again. "Boobs. Breasts. Um, mammary glands… Fucking hell, am I drunk?"

"If that is what this giddiness is then, yes. Blood-drunk. Our elders do not teach us about this. Perhaps if they did, I would not have been so reluctant."

I turn my head, my cheek pillowed on moss. My fingers creep through the grass. Zorian's face is level with mine, his pupils dilated.

"Reluctant about sharing blood?"

"I did not want them to feel what I feel. I think… I do not feel the same as them."

My wandering hand grazes his arm. It seems natural to slide my fingers in his. The connection tingles to my fingertips. The strength in his slim hand jolts my heartbeat.

"I felt that," he sighs.

"I feel you," I say at the same time.

The pulse of his emotions is amazing. His twin hearts echo through my whole body. He's so *alive*. So… happy.

I prop myself up, still holding his hand. He angles his head to watch me.

"You're all rainbowy again," I whisper, and reach out to trace his jaw.

No stubble, just smooth, perfect skin. I follow his throat to the hollow where his rib plates meet. He's breathing hard enough for me to see it. Faint lines show where his gills are, closed tight on land.

He looks so vulnerable. How is that possible? He's a Verdanian. He could rip off my limbs and feed them to me.

"Are you still bleeding?"

He blinks, the black of his pupil drowning the green. "I do not care."

I try to lift the arm I'm not attached to but topple across his chest.

"Whoopsie," I giggle.

I never giggle.

I bend his arm and draw it close to my face, peering at his wrist. Flakes of blood have dried around the edge but the wound itself isn't weeping. Dizzy, I rest my head on his chest and curl my hand around his side.

God, he likes it. Or I like it? I'm struggling to tell. Everything he feels throbs inside me. What would it be like to fuck in the grip of the blood connection?

Another thing not to think about.

My naturally pale skin is dark next to his marble perfection, the line of his muscles carved into his flesh. I explore where his rib plates end at the dip of his stomach. His hearts race. There's all sorts of nerves swirling in my belly—mine, his, lots of his. He wants me to touch him or I want to touch him and the fact I don't know which forces me to stop at the edge of his belt, the bark slick under my fingers.

I'm petting a Verdanian.

This is all part of my plan—lure him in, get him to trust me and spill his secrets. It's all very scientific.

We lie in the grass and moss, and breathe. Somehow, I doze, the jungle cacophony muffled compared to his heartbeats. The sun warms my back, the air humid and perfumed with pollen. Zorian's hand covers mine where it cups his hip, as light as a skreeingbird sipping nectar from a flower.

I've never done this before, not even with a human. Rolling over and falling asleep usually follow any kind of intimacy. There's no cuddling or hand-holding. Mostly my fault. I didn't want anyone getting too attached, including myself.

Squad leaders can't afford the distraction.

So lying half on top of a Verdanian in the middle of the jungle shouldn't feel this nice but nothing can compel me to move.

Until a shadow looms over us.

14

I scrabble away, my knife in my hand before I register the shadow as the stupid fucking horse-beast. It nuzzles Zorian's ear, and I'm pretty certain I'm going to punch it in the snout.

Or maybe I should thank it for interrupting.

Nah, I want to punch it.

I sheath my knife and stand on shaky legs. Zorian climbs to his feet, patting the nose of the horse-beast.

"Dacorna gets bored," he says, peeking at me.

His shyness burns in my chest. What's he getting from me? Embarrassment. Check. Confusion. Check. What the heck was I doing snuggling him? I blame the blood. People do dumb things when they're drunk.

I lick my lips and say, "Dacorna? What's that short for?"

"Not everything needs a long name, Axelle," he says with a glimmer of his dream confidence.

I approach slowly, as if the creature might trample me. She snuffles at my hand then lowers her head until I scratch the stiff fur between her horns.

"She likes you. Do you want to go for a ride?"

I eye her suspiciously. She's about eight foot of solid muscle with no manual controls.

"How exactly does one do that?"

Zorian smiles and, combined with his rush of excitement, it stuns me for a moment.

This blood connection takes some getting used to. It's far more powerful than how it was in the cave. At least the giddy-giggliness is fading.

Zorian wraps his fingers around my waist and picks me up. He slides me onto Dacorna's back, one leg on either side. She shifts, stamping a foot, but he leaps gracefully up and sits behind me.

"There's nothing to hold on to," I say, somewhat high-pitched.

Earth horses have manes or straps and a comfy-looking seat. There's nothing between my butt and Dacorna. She doesn't even have a tail.

"I will hold on to you," Zorian says.

He pulls me against the front of his body, one hand on my hip, the other flat on my stomach. His legs tense, and he whispers in Anann. Dacorna lunges forward. I yelp and dig my fingers into Zorian's thighs, pressing them even tighter to mine. Dacorna gallops through the trees, swerving, dodging and jumping deadfall. Zorian moves us so we flow with her rather than being unseated. Wind whips my hair into Zorian's face, my head on his collarbone.

"Breathe, Axelle," he says in my ear.

Air whistles in and out in a whoop. I ease my grip on his legs but don't let go. His exhilaration sizzles through me. I feel his joy and something wild I can't name.

Dacorna flies through the jungle. She avoids low-hanging branches or leaves so we don't get slapped in the face. The thunder of her hooves echoes in the beat of Zorian's hearts against my spine. The thrust of her legs rocks us together, our breaths in sync. His hand on my stomach slips low, his splayed fingers even lower.

Okay, this rocking motion could get distracting.

Dacorna plunges into a shallow pool. Warm water splashes my legs. I'm grinning like an idiot but I don't care. She bunches her muscles and sails over a snarl of roots. My t-shirt ruffles under Zorian's hand. His thumb traces a line along my belly.

Oh, crap…

Be cool.

There's no space between us. He's curled around me, his hands pinning me, even though mine are free. And the gait of Dacorna rubs us together.

The jungle blurs in green and gold and brown. I'm pliant in Zorian's arms, my head limp on his shoulder. The curve of his mouth brushes my temple. The throb of my pulse is lost in the thundering, pounding, thudding.

He murmurs a word in Anann. Dacorna slows beneath the spreading arch of a wellow tree, the buds brilliant bursts of orange. Her sides heave. She dips her head and sucks water trickling over the moss-covered stones.

The sudden quiet is electrifying.

Zorian slides from Dacorna's back and looks up at me. The nerves return to writhe around in my stomach, all mine.

He cocks his head. "Some of my tribe are near. We should hide."

"How can you tell?"

"I hear them."

I hear nothing but the wind sighing through the trees. He lifts me off Dacorna and lowers my feet to the ground. He slaps her on the rump and she vanishes into the undergrowth.

"Do you trust me, Axelle?" he says.

The important question. He'll know if I lie.

"Yes," I say.

He touches his fingers to his chest. "I feel your truth."

He holds out a hand and I take it. He twirls me around, scoops me up and launches us into the canopy. I hiss, my nails digging into his arms. He crouches among the branches, cradling me against his body. One arm is around my waist, the other rests across my breasts, his hand splayed over my heart. My butt is definitely tucked in his crotch.

"Well, this is one way to conquer my fear of heights," I whisper.

"Do you feel safe?"

My muscles relax. The ground is a painful drop away but there's no vertigo.

I remove my fingernails from his skin. "Can't you tell?"

He hugs me tighter.

A group of Verdanians parts the weeping foliage below us. I freeze in Zorian's arms, not daring to breathe. How acute is their hearing? They have no weapons in their hands but carry the usual assortment of bows and spears across their backs. Their hair is a splash of tangerine and maroon and indigo. They speak in Anann, gesticulating at the trees. One points to the mud and they head in the same direction as Dacorna.

"What are they doing?"

Zorian's resignation weighs heavy in my gut.

"They are looking for me," he says.

I try to wriggle in his arms to see his face but he holds me too close.

"I got you in trouble, didn't I? I shouldn't have said your name to Fenna and Dalrainenna."

"Fennanangullandolin and Dalrainenna did not mention our interaction to my father. I believe it was their treatment that made his decision."

"What decision?"

"To start my journey today."

I stiffen in his arms. "So I won't see you again?"

The words burst free before I think about how ridiculous they sound. I could have asked anything—why are you going, or who is your father and how does he get to decide?

"You will see me every night," Zorian says.

The truth is a little bloom of happiness in my chest.

"So where are you going?"

"To the northern tribe over the Glewenann mountains." His fingers stroke my pendant. "Ask me again why I do not want to go."

I have to swallow a couple of times before I can speak. "Why don't you want to go?"

"Because the tribal chief's daughter has been chosen as my mate," he says softly.

A snail glides around a branch near my face and peers at me upside down, its shell a spiral of violet and silver. I stare at it and will myself not to feel anything.

"What does that have to do with Fenna and Dalrainenna?" I say, my voice empty.

"My father has grown tired of human cruelty."

"Zorian, who the hell is your father?"

"He is the tribal chief of the south."

Oh, fuck. That makes Zorian the next in line and the second most important Verdanian in the whole of southern Anann.

What would Elderman Vail do if he got his hands on him?

Zorian curls himself around me. "Axelle, you are shaking."

"How does you mating help your father?" I croak.

Zorian's sigh stirs my hair. "If I bond with her daughter, the tribal chief has pledged to send us warriors."

"How many warriors?"

Another sigh. "I do not know the name for a number so high but it is a three and three zeros."

"Three thousand," I whisper, my nails back in his arm.

An icy spurt of fear shivers to my toes. Three thousand reinforcements would be enough to overwhelm Home Base. If I were the perfect soldier I pretend to be, I would incapacitate Zorian and take him prisoner. I only have my knife but there's a spot on the skull just behind the ear where if you hit it hard enough, you can knock a Verdanian unconscious. Dragging him through the jungle to Home Base will be a near-impossible feat but the Elders would definitely give me a freaking medal if I succeeded.

And Zorian would be strapped to a table in the basement of the dissection lab. It would be more merciful to kill him here. Now. No Zorian, no mating, no warriors. Maybe his father will think he ran away. I can save my species. All I need to do is jam my blade into the throat of the Verdanian cradling me ever so gently.

Will I feel him die?

Zorian murmurs my name. I suspect he's been saying it for a while. It's difficult to be sure since I seem to be having a panic attack. The image of one bright, emerald eye oozing onto a petri dish is stuck in my head.

Zorian jiggles me higher and tucks his face into my throat. What is he doi—

His teeth graze my neck. The shock zaps through my body, turning me rigid then limp. I flop in his arms, my pulse slowing, my breathing steadier. He raises his head, and I probe my neck with quivering fingers.

"I did not break the skin," he says.

My words spill out. "They'll exterminate us. We can't fight that many. Can you refuse to go?"

"It is my duty. But I will try to talk to my father. We have to stop the war before I return. We will have some time—the journey there, the bonding ceremony, the journey back."

I scrub my cheeks, ignoring the dampness of tears. "And this bonding ceremony—you have to share blood? With her? Um, your mate."

"Yes."

"Oh. Will that ruin our connection?"

Why am I asking him this? I should be quizzing him on how long everything will take, how many warriors they'll have in total with the reinforcements. Important battle questions.

"You are sad," he says, pulling away enough to look at me. "That question makes you sad."

He must be confusing anxiety with sadness. I'll be blind without the dream communication. Anyone would be anxious at the loss of such useful information, particularly with an army marching our way.

"I'm not sad," I say.

He hunches, and raises an eyebrow.

"Fine," I sigh. Stupid blood connection. "It makes me sad."

"Why?"

"I'd prefer not to answer that."

His growl has the opposite effect of his teeth. My heart leaps into my mouth, my breath shuddering in and out. His arms mould me to the front of his body, cool against my heat. He hides his face in my shoulder, his hearts drumming on my spine.

His need stoppers my throat and churns in my gut. It is fire, where every other part of him is ice.

He holds me and we breathe. His trembling—my trembling?—slows. My heart returns to its usual place although it flutters around, unsettled. Zorian drops from the tree, and I'm too stunned for fear or protest. He lowers my boots to the ground and lets me go but I grab his arm, my knees threatening to buckle.

"I am sorry, Axelle," he says, not meeting my eye, his arm held away from his body while I cling to it.

God, I'm wet. I mean fucking *soaked*.

Warmth flares in my cheeks. It's not my fault. Anyone would have responded to that overwhelming blast of desire. No point in reading into it.

"It's okay, Zorian," I say, the words slightly undermined by the husky voice.

Nothing is okay. As soon as he leaves, he'll head north to bond with his chosen mate. Oh, and the warriors. Mustn't forget the pledge of warriors.

And I'm not soldier enough to stop him.

Axelle of the first generation, compromised by one of the very creatures I've been fighting since I was born. Everything made sense a week ago—kill the Verdanians. Our victory will be marked by their surrender and we will rule Verdana. We will decide who lives and who dies.

War was my life. Now I dare to dream of something else.

Even if the war didn't begin on a lie, it's gone on long enough. I don't want to enslave. I want to be free. But if it started on a lie, it might help me to convince others that what we're doing is wrong. I need the evidence, one way or another.

I uncurl my hands from Zorian's arm and manage to stand on my own. He whistles, and Dacorna trots out from behind a huge fern. He lays a palm on the arch of her neck, his back to me. His tattoo coils up his spine, broken only by the axe across his shoulders. My tattoo tingles with the remembered touch of his finger in our dream, tracing the lines.

"We can stop the fighting," he says almost to himself.

I nod, realise he can't see it and say, "Talk to your father. I'll talk to my people. We need to find a way to live together. Or one side won't live at all."

It sucks to discover I've always been on the losing side.

Zorian springs onto Dacorna. He looks down at me, his features impassive. Regal, which fits now I know who he is. Inside, he's a jumble of confusion, sadness, hope.

"Do you still hate me, Axelle?" he says.

Dacorna tosses her head, her sapphire horns a blur. She glares at me with eyes as black as swamp mud.

I think we don't like each other after all.

"No, Zorian," I say. "I don't hate you."

He smiles wide and the flash of his teeth wobbles my legs for a different reason. He touches his fingers to his chest and spurs Dacorna into the jungle. They vanish in a whisper of leaves.

I stay until I can't feel him anymore.

<h1 style="text-align:center">15</h1>

I find Glennis perched on a weight bench in the gym, her muscles bulging with each bicep curl. She's similar in height to a Verdanian but she's got them on bulk. They're a sturdy species, though slim. Long limbs, narrow hips, not particularly broad shoulders. Lithe. Like Zorian.

Stop thinking about Zorian.

The clink of metal fills the nearly empty room while Yannik punishes the chest press. Most of Home Base are at dinner or finishing up individual training sessions.

"'S'up, Axe," Yannik grunts between reps.

Veins bulge on his arms, and a bead of sweat trickles down his neck. He could crack a waternut between his pecs.

Glennis would be a good match for him in the sack. She's solid enough to avoid the pulverised bones. Codename— Deltosaurus. Shame she only likes women, and one particular woman.

Why do I keep thinking about sex? I've been restless since I got home. Jittery. Maybe it's nerves from the thought of our imminent doom. People hump when the world is ending, grasping for that burst of feel-good. I could do it myself but where's the fun in that? Delayed gratification increases the intensity. Not that I'm holding out for anyone. All I need is a replacement for Mallory.

A human replacement.

"Hey, Glennis, what's your record now?" I say.

She puffs a damp flop of short, honey-blonde hair out of her eyes. "Twenty-five kilos. Aiming for thirty."

"Soon you'll be able to lift me in a bicep curl."

She grins. "You offering, Axe?"

"Maybe not. I'd get vertigo."

Yannik finishes his set with a clunk of weights and a heavy sigh. He mops his brow then slings his towel over his shoulder.

"See you in the showers, Glen." His gaze flicks from Glennis to me and back again, a considering look on his scarred face.

"Don't even think about it," I say.

"Can't blame a man for thinking, Axe." He clasps his hands to flex his muscles. "Thought you might need an upgrade after Mallory."

I roll my eyes at Glennis. "Perhaps all the testosterone has turned me off men."

Her considering look is the replica of Yannik's.

"Oh, for fuck's sake," I say, and they share a laugh.

Yannik swaggers off towards the showers. "You're a knockout, Axe. Can't blame us for trying."

"Keep trying and I might just knock you out."

He blows me a kiss, and disappears through the doorway.

"You need my help with something?" Glennis switches the dumbbell to her other hand.

I slip the stolen tablet from my pocket. "I've forgotten my password on this stupid thing and locked myself out. Any chance you can fix it?"

"Sure. I'll need to connect it to my tablet and run a keystroke programme. Leave it with me."

"I shouldn't let it out of my sight. What if I meet you in the barracks in an hour?"

Glennis gulps water without slowing her reps. "You got stuff on there you don't want me to see?"

"No, it's—"

"Hey, what a squad leader does in her own time is none of my business."

"Glennis, quit winding me up."

"Yes, sir," she says.

I leave her smirking at her dumbbell, and track down Elderman McBurnie in the observation cubicle of the nursery ward. Passengers in blue move between the one hundred cots set out in rows. The members of the thirty-seventh generation wave their tiny fists at the ceiling.

"Do you think we'll still be fighting when they come of age?" I say, my voice hushed in the windowless room, a glass wall separating us from the delicate newborns.

McBurnie tucks a snarl of ginger hair behind a ruddy ear. "M'eudail! Ye talk as if ye won't be around to see it."

"Odds are, I won't be."

"Och, lass, don't fret. We have a few tricks up our sleeve. You'll reach old woman status yet."

A Passenger lifts one of the babies from its cot, its little legs kicking. The squalling reaches us through the glass. The Passenger carts the child to a table on the side of the room and unfastens the nappy.

"What kind of tricks?" I focus on one of the cots nearer the viewing window.

The newborn is asleep and wrapped tight in a blanket, only its face peeking out. It looks like a grub.

"We brought a lot o' technology from Earth but it's heavy on the heat-seeking, which doesn't work so well against yon cold bastards. But we've been researching an' adapting. While they don't give off anything we can read, the jungle itself seems to react to them."

"What do you mean?"

McBurnie waves his thick fingers at a wide-eyed newborn and makes a noise I never thought I'd hear from a grown man. Something along the lines of, "Coochie-coochie-coo." The baby blinks. I'm no expert but I imagine their eyesight is pretty poor, though McBurnie is giant enough to see from a great distance.

"When one o' those marbly bastards is near, the plants give off a pulse of ultraviolet radiation. And it's proportionate to the number o' bastards mincing around. All we need is a sensor strong enough to detect while airborne an' we can find where they congregate. Then we wipe them out." McBurnie claps me on the shoulder, and my kneecaps implode. "So sleep easy, Axelle o' the first. We'll win this one yet."

Funny, I've been sleeping easy since I started talking to a Verdanian.

"Is there no chance of a ceasefire?"

McBurnie guffaws. His pass, now pinned to his shirt, flashes under the lights. I tossed it under a stool in the pub after my stint in the dissection lab.

"Aw, hen, yon species think they're the gods o' this planet. They're no' interested in a ceasefire. They'd see us all deid."

"But why would they choose war over peace?"

"Who knows what goes on in the minds o' that alien race? They don't think like us, Axelle. There's no humanity in them."

I avoid his gaze and feign interest in a baby attempting to fit its whole fist in its mouth.

"Is that why we study them in the dissection lab?"

"Aye, lass, that's why. We try to understand but there's only so much ye can learn from anatomy."

"What do you do… in there?" Crap, I almost said, "Down there."

A dangerous slip.

"I help out with the brute force stuff—cutting the rib plates to spread them open, sawing the skull, disposing o' the remains. It's no' very glamorous, ye ken?"

I tug on the cuff of my shirt even though it's already hiding my wrist. I replaced the fern bandage with a normal dressing. Easier to explain if anyone catches a glimpse, though the neat mark of Zorian's teeth is difficult to spot. I thought there'd be more bruising.

"Wouldn't we learn more if we captured live specimens? Interrogated them?"

"Och, hen, can ye imagine how difficult it would be to keep them prisoner? A Verdanian's only useful to us when it's deid."

Lies. Unless he doesn't know? God, I hope he doesn't know. I like McBurnie. I can't picture him whistling cheerfully while he plucks out an eye.

"Thank you, Elderman. Sorry to bother you with all my questions."

"No' a problem, m'eudail! Will ye be joining me at the pub again the night?"

I touch the cobalt stone tucked safely under my shirt. "I don't think I'd survive a second night in a row."

"Nonsense, lassie!" he says. "Ye drank me under the bar

stool, as I recall. Or don't recall. Ma head's still a bit fuzzy."

His chuckles guide me out the door. Steeling myself for more subterfuge, I head for the barracks.

16

We meet at the pool with the waterfall, Zorian's favourite place. He touches the cobalt stone at my throat and I mirror him, his lovely turquoise pendant where it belongs. This seems to be our special greeting. It makes me happier than it should. Particularly since the jitteriness lingers into the dream and flares when his cool fingers stroke skin. Wearing my vest and shorts isn't helping but it's freeing to pad barefoot through the jungle in my pyjamas.

Zorian shows me the highlights from his journey so far. He's covered a lot of ground in half-a-day's travel. Dacorna—a falsielle, the name for their pack animals—can sure as hell run.

But I knew that already.

"I unlocked the tablet today. Well, a member of my squad did."

Zorian pauses, a backdrop of ferns spreading from his shoulders like wings. "Did you find what you were looking for?"

"No," I sigh. "There were files, marked from one to seven hundred and fifty-two but they were all locked. I need a password—a code—to open them."

"What do you think they are?"

"Prisoner records? The number is pretty high, though."

Zorian's sarong is a swatch of green material cut at an angle, hitting upper thigh on his unscarred leg and sloping to the opposite knee. A delicate fringe of grass brushes his skin when he moves, the material tight enough to hug his butt.

Not that I notice.

"Yes," he says, and I jerk my gaze upwards. "Not so many of us have gone missing. Eight and... Eighty-six not taken by battle but never to return."

My stomach clenches. "God, I hope we didn't capture them all."

"The jungle claims our lives, too, though not as readily. Some may have journeyed north, away from the fight." His hand settles on mine, and I realise I'm rubbing my belly like a kid with stomach ache. "I do not think it is all on your people. And it is definitely not on you."

"Some of them are on me," I say. "Not the missing but the ones in battle. Zorian... my call sign, the one you heard when we met..."

He keeps my hand in his and leads me through a shallow puddle, mud squelching under my toes.

"Your nickname," he says. "It means you are good at killing us."

Godkiller. Killer of Verdanians, god-like in their perfection and disdain. The name filled me with pride and cemented my place as squad leader.

It is no longer what I feel.

"Twelve, Zorian. Thirteen if you include Thommonn."

"I have killed humans, too, Axelle."

"How many?"

"I do not count."

Of course he doesn't. Counting kills is savage, as if it's a competition. It's not something to celebrate. It's something to mourn.

I bow my head and stare at my feet. Beetles scuttle under a rotten log, like jewels with legs. Cool fingers tilt my chin and force me to meet emerald eyes.

"Do not blame yourself for how you were raised. They made you a warrior." His hand cups my face, his thumb brushing my lips. "Would you kill us now, Axelle?"

I swallow hard. "Not if I could avoid it."

"Then you are not the same person who counted to twelve."

His fingers slide through my hair. Breathing seems a little more difficult than it did a second ago. He pinches a strand and follows it to the end, his fingers kissing the curve of my breast. I'm very aware of my pulse and where it throbs, so close to the skin.

He starts walking, guiding me by the hand before my brain can process the sudden change, my legs stumbling along after.

"Breathe, Axelle," he says, a smile in his voice.

"You have to stop doing that."

"Why?"

Why should he stop touching me, confusing me, distracting me by the stroke of his fingers?

"I'll think of a reason in a minute," I say.

"What are you going to do about the files?"

"The what now?"

"The files, is that not what you called them? The records on the tablet."

Wow, engage brain, Axelle.

"I'll get my squad member to unlock them. I've started asking questions. If the files don't have what I need, and even if they do, I'll keep asking questions. Separating the liars from those who tell the truth might help us with allies when we need them."

"Be careful. You humans are protective of your secrets."

"Are you worried about me, Zorian?"

He gives me a long, serious look and the humour dies on my tongue.

"Yes," he says.

* * *

It takes me three days to corner Glennis when no one else is around. Home Base is damned crowded. She lies on the bottom of one of many bunk beds in the barracks, her legs crossed at the ankle, one hand behind her head. She holds her tablet in her other hand, scrolling with her thumb. The sheets of Nolana's top bunk are pristine.

"Glennis," I say, leaning on the metal frame of the bed opposite, "I need something else unlocked."

She cocks an eyebrow darker than her honey-blonde hair. "You locked yourself out again? Maybe you should write your password down."

"Can you access these files?" I tap on the screen and hold the tablet out.

She swings her legs over the edge of the bed, dropping her device to the mattress. She glances at my screen then back to me.

"This isn't your tablet, is it, Axe?"

"Can you unlock them or not?"

She grips the tablet between thumb and forefinger as if it might explode. I force myself to release it instead of snatching it back. Her blocky nail clicks on the screen.

"How many are there?"

"Seven hundred and fifty-two."

"Seven hundred—"

"I don't need you to unlock them all, only a sample."

She runs a hand through her hair, leaving it clumped in a spike. "Is this going to get me in trouble? *You* in trouble? I kinda like having you as squad leader, Axe. I don't want to see either of us facing a tribunal."

"Let me worry about that. But this is just between you and me, Glennis of the second," I say, barely having to crouch to give her good eye contact. "No talking to Nolana or anyone else. If I find what I'm looking for, I'll tell you all about it. I'll tell the whole squad."

A girl from the sixth generation jogs in, waving to us as she weaves between the beds. She grabs a gym bag from a cabinet by a bunk at the side of the room and hustles back towards the door. Glennis and I watch her until she's gone.

"How long do you think it'll take?" I say.

Another few taps on the screen.

"They're heavily protected. Could take days to open one."

"Let me know when you do. Maybe one is all I need."

I pivot on my heel. I hate leaving the tablet behind but I have to trust Glennis won't hand it to the nearest Elder. The damn thing is incriminating. Maybe it *will* explode, metaphorically speaking.

"What's on it?"

I pause at the door. Glennis peers at me through the rows of bunk beds.

"Everything," I say. "Or nothing."

17

Anann is a beautiful language. It slides from the tongue and weaves lilting streams among the branches. It's passionate for a species carved of stone. Zorian is an excellent teacher, though he grins when I confuse 'eat' for 'mate' and tell him I would like to mate with him.

He is more expressive than I ever thought a Verdanian could be. He hasn't laughed out loud yet but he's definitely getting freer with the chuckling. And he smiles as if he never thought it was a weird thing to do with his mouth.

I help him with his English, though there's not much to improve. He refuses to use contractions.

"Why do you insist on forcing your words together when they sound better separated? You humans have no harmony, even with your language."

I throw a dream-snail at him and he chases me through the swamp he passed that day on his journey. The water thickens and mires me before I can get half-way across. He plucks me out, black mud to my thighs. His eyes blaze when he's laughing at me on the inside.

He loves to run and climb and swim. I'm no match for him. He's faster, stronger. He can literally keep me pinned with one hand no matter how hard I struggle. I try to pin him and it's like tackling a tree.

He shows me the highlights of his journey. The Glewenann mountains mark the boundary between the north and south of Ananngar and the resident tribes, humans not included. Huge birds nest in the stony peaks, the largest on Verdana— storm-ketrells. The one he imagines spreads its wings, static sparking between feathers of the deepest blue. It peers at me through a bronze eye the size of Zorian's stone, head cocked, its rainbow crest glinting in the sunlight. It leaps from the crag, and the wind howls beneath its wings.

Water shapes the mountains into canyons and tunnels, our voices echoing off the dripping walls. Sometimes in Anann, sometimes in English.

Am I a terrible human if I think his language is superior? They have no curse words. It says a lot.

I spend my nights gallivanting with the enemy and my days searching for lies. It would be easier if I could find something. People won't stop fighting just because I ask them nicely.

Verdanian activity remains low, with no sightings from the wall. The Elders seem uneasy, increasing patrols and guards. Maybe they think our enemy is preparing a full-scale attack. But I know it's because their leader is off on a journey with his son.

The full-scale attack will come later.

* * *

Two weeks disappear before Glennis manages to unlock the first file on the tablet. We huddle around it in a storage cupboard at the gym, the light from the screen tingeing her face blue-white. The sharp smell of cleaning fluids reminds me of the dissection lab. I scour the document, my nose almost touching the tablet.

"Well?" Glennis shifts closer in a waft of citrus and menthol. "What's it say?"

"It's some kind of medical record. Patient 1, Blend B, rapid recovery. Pages of parameters recorded over several days. Looks like they healed a water-tiger attack."

"Is it everything or nothing?"

"I don't know yet."

She sighs. "You're going to make me unlock more, aren't you?"

I hand her the tablet without a word.

The patient must be human. Verdanians are rarely injured by water-tigers and why would the author of the document care if they healed or not? Unless they're trying to reverse-engineer a quicker way to kill them.

Five days and five random files later, we have more patients and more blends. Patient 524, Blend S, died from intestinal sickness. Patient 110, Blend L, died from hypoxia after a drowning incident. Patient 89, Blend BH, recovered. Patient 667, Blend BM, recovered. Patient 394, Blend B, recovered.

I have no idea what they mean and can't exactly ask my betters. Maybe the tablet holds nothing relevant to the Verdanian prisoners, despite where I found it. What's the Earth phrase—a herring?

Glennis pushes the tablet into my hands, her muscular thigh bumping against a desk in the empty classroom.

"I can't do this anymore," she says. "Nolana is getting suspicious. And whatever you're looking for, it's not on there."

"There are over seven hundred files, one of them has to have something."

"Unless it doesn't exist." Glennis slings her gym bag over her shoulder and heads for the door. "Don't invite trouble, Axe. Our lives are short enough as it is."

But do they have to be?

* * *

I track down Passenger DeLoris as she hurries from one module to the next, her uniform a cheerful blue in the grey and black drab of Home Base.

"Axelle," she says, flashing me a perfect smile, "I didn't think I had you for class. What a nice surprise."

"Apologies, Passenger DeLoris, I'm not with you today but I wanted to ask some questions if you have a moment?"

"Of course! My next class is module thirty-four so we have some time while we walk. What can I help you with?"

A chattering group of twenty-fourth and twenty-fifth generationers pass the entrance to our alleyway between modules, led by another Passenger. He waves to Deloris before disappearing from view, the children's voices taking longer to fade.

"What was it like, those first few years of colonisation? We hear about how tough it was from the Elders but never from the Passengers."

"Oh, Axelle, I was so young then." She gives a little laugh. "I'm not sure I'm the best person to ask."

"What do you remember about the Verdanians? When did you first see one?"

We leave the space between modules and cross the parade ground, several squads practising evasive manoeuvres from rubber-tipped arrows and blunted spears tossed by their comrades.

DeLoris shudders and clutches her tablet to her chest. "I thought they were lovely. But they were monsters—beautiful on the outside, poisonous on the inside."

"Were they always aggressive? Even at first contact?"

"I can't say. The Elders kept the most vulnerable of us hidden and far from the fighting."

An arrow skitters across the concrete path. A sheepish unranked practically bobs a curtsy as he jogs over and scoops it up. He's missing two fingers on his left hand.

"Sorry, Passenger DeLoris; Godkiller," he says, and scuttles away.

DeLoris sighs and quickens her pace. "I envy you that."

"You cannot envy me."

"You command soldiers, lead squadrons into battle. You're the reason I stopped having nightmares about being eaten." She leads us into the next row of modules, a shaft of sunlight through the purple clouds turning her hair gold. "Believe me, all of us who stay behind the wall envy your glory just a little."

"You're too important to risk. There is no shame in what you do here."

"Oh, I have no doubt I would be an embarrassment on the battlefield, even under your tutelage."

We weave through the artificial maze of buildings, water steaming in gentle puffs in the heat. A line of multi-hued snails creeps up the side of a module.

DeLoris was too young at the beginning to give me the answers I need. I suspected as much but she's always been the most approachable. Always so happy to see me. And what am I supposed to do? Ask Seabird himself?

Please.

She pauses at the door to a classroom module, the sound of laughter spilling out. "You are a killer of gods, Axelle. You know more than me about how aggressive the Verdanians are. You've seen our blood on their white skin."

And their blood on ours.

* * *

Passenger Gotiva glances up from his desk at my polite knock, his pen poised above a page half-filled with neat writing. His eyebrow braids are tucked behind his ears.

"Hello, child. Back for another Anann lesson? There's not much more I can teach you, I'm afraid." He places his pen to the side and cradles the book, presenting it to me like an object of reverence. "But your visit inspired me to record what I do know. One day, I hope to fill it with all Verdanian languages, not just Anann."

Is that before or after we turn the indigenous into slaves?

I take the book and read the scant pages. Notes on syntax, grammatical structure and speech sounds, including the meaning of the few words in his repertoire. How excited would he be if I spoke to him in Anann? Pretty excited, I imagine, right before he asked me how the hell I learned so much since I last saw him.

From sleeping with the enemy.

Literally, not physically.

"Were you there during our first contact with the Verdanians?" I say, carefully passing the book back. "Is that where you picked up their language?"

"I was, child. Those were fraught days but still so full of hope. There were always going to be misunderstandings when two different cultures came together."

"Why are there no video logs? We have everything from Earth and the journey through space but nothing since our arrival."

"Destroyed, child. The Verdanians wanted to wipe all taint of us from the planet." Sorrow fills his grey eyes. "What was construed as cultural misunderstandings turned out to be their violent nature."

"But were they peaceful at first? When did it start to go wrong?"

His mouth twists. "When they stole my wife."

I flap my lips at him for at least a full minute with no words coming out.

"They kidnapped your wife?" I manage to splutter.

Gotiva smooths a palm over his bald pate. "She was brilliant. A language specialist but more towards the science of linguistics rather than a bread-and-butter polyglot, such as myself. I don't want to imagine what those animals did to her."

I mutter my apologies and stumble away, sucking on the humid air as soon as the door slides shut behind me.

So much for Zorian telling me they don't capture humans. Is he the liar all along? But I've felt the truth. He said they welcomed us peacefully.

How real is that truth, though? Maybe he's manipulated me so beautifully, I reacted that way because he suggested I should. Or is it only truth to him since that's what he's been led to believe?

Maybe I'm not the one raised on lies.

I aim my feet for my pod. It's barely evening and too early to sleep but I need some answers.

Like, what the fuck the Verdanians did with Passenger Gotiva's wife.

"I thought Verdanians didn't take prisoners."

They're the first words out of my mouth as soon as I open my eyes in the dream space. Zorian tilts his head.

"We do not."

"Then what about Mrs—Passenger—Gotiva?"

"Mrs… You mean Eleanor?" Zorian perches on a log, his hands playing with the fronds of a coral-pink fungus, his head bowed. "She died."

"Was that before or after you tortured her?"

His eyes flash at me. "I was seven years old."

God, the poor woman. She must have suffered for years.

"So *you* didn't torture her, what a great distinction. Was it your father?"

Zorian thrusts to his feet and stalks towards me. He's wearing some kind of top so translucent, I almost miss it. Delicate veins trace through the material, as if a bunch of leaves have been scraped to a thin membrane and glued together. It hugs his chest and lies tight against his stomach, tucked into the waistband of his trousers. It looks so delicate, I'm surprised the slightest movement doesn't tear it. I yank my gaze up and find him in front of me.

Cock. Got distracted for a minute.

"Torture is a human atrocity, Axelle," he says.

I glare at him. "You lied to me, Zorian. I don't care if you were a kid when it happened."

"We do not take prisoners," he says, a growl in his voice.

I poke him in the chest. It's like prodding a rock. A very tall, slightly pissed-off rock.

"Bullshit," I say. "Her husband says she was kidnapped."

"Then, of course, it must be I whom is the liar."

I'm regretting helping him with his English.

"Just tell me what happened."

So much for trusting each other. How can I believe anything he's said in the dream space?

"She came to us," he says quietly.

I drop my hand and stare at him. "Why would she do that?"

"She was a medicine woman. No, a wise woman. What is your word for someone who seeks knowledge?"

"A scientist?"

"Yes, if that means she wanted to study our language. She followed our envoys home. My father was furious they did not notice her but it was too late as she refused to go back. To banish her would be death. My father gave her shelter on the edge of our camp—food, clothes—but he forbade anyone from talking to her."

"You weren't even born when this happened. Neither was I. Who told you?"

He doesn't smirk but I can see it sparkling in his eyes and twitching the corner of his mouth.

"She did," he says.

"Not great at obeying your father's orders, are you?"

"I was curious. I had never seen a human out of a battlesuit."

He gazes off into the jungle, his thoughts even further away.

"She taught me her language and I taught her mine."

"And she just lived on the fringes of your society until she died peacefully in her sleep?"

He frowns at me. "She fell ill. She was tired all the time, in pain. She lost weight. Breathing became difficult but she would not let me tell anyone, not even to bring a healer, in case I got in trouble. She died, and I was the only one who knew for days."

I dig a toe into the soft mud. "Oh. Well, I guess I'll have to take your word for it."

Axelle—concedes with grace.

"I am happy to repeat this when we next meet in real life. Then you can feel the truth."

"And how will that work if you're mated to some female from the north?" I say, and immediately want to kick myself.

It's not because I'm jealous.

"You should refuse to mate with her," I say.

Again, not jealous. No mating means no reinforcements, and Home Base will be safe from being overrun for a little while. It's a simple solution.

Plus, I'll see how much of the truth he actually tells me.

"It is my duty," he says, his face stony. Or stonier than usual.

I scoff, and his expression closes down further.

"Would you refuse an order from your leader?" he says.

"You've ignored orders from your father just fine before."

"I was a child."

"You weren't a child when you met me in the cave."

"That was not against an order, more a non-verbal under-standing."

"Semantics, Zorian."

"And I ask you again—would you refuse an order from your

leader? If you are ordered to attack us, will you?"

I cross my arms and open my mouth to deny but the words don't come.

Would I? I don't want to kill them anymore but refusing a direct order? I can't picture it.

"So you understand," Zorian says. "I will try to delay, try to convince my father of another way, but if the war does not end, reinforcements will protect my people."

"And destroy mine."

"We will kill only if you force us. We want peace."

"Your peace involves turning us into slaves!"

A flock of skreeingbirds bursts from the canopy, skreeing angrily and wheeling away like a handful of tossed jewels.

"What does your peace involve, Axelle—slaughter or slavery?"

My cheeks burn with my own hypocrisy. Goddamn him for seeding me with doubt. Everything was so much easier before he came along.

Well, easier in the figurative sense. At least I knew where I stood.

"Survival," I bark. "Our peace involves survival."

"Yours or ours?"

"It's a little hard to care about your survival when you're shooting us full of arrows."

"Or when you are firing our sacred bloodstones at us."

My finger digs into his pec, his sheer top somehow holding up under the assault of my nail. I want to yell in his face but his chest is the best I can do.

"So we should all drop our weapons and live happily ever after?"

He curls his lip. "You humans will never be happy unless

you are killing something."

"You're a sanctimonious arsehole."

"We are resorting to name-throwing? Fine. You are—" He takes a deep breath and it all spills out.

I shouldn't have taught him the bad words. He's quite inventive.

We end in a seething huff as far away from each other as we can get while still being in sight. My arms are crossed so tight, my shoulders hurt.

"That's great to know what you really think, Zorian-my-name-is-so-long-because-I'm-superior, since I'm stuck in this godforsaken dream space and have to see you every time I close my eyes."

"You will not enter the dream space if you focus hard enough," he sniffs. "If you can focus on anything other than hate."

I shoot him my best look of scorn. "Consider me focused."

And he's right. For the next couple of nights, my dreams are my own.

But I miss him.

19

"My father says humans cannot be trusted." Zorian stares towards a silver bridge of stone arching out of the jungle horizon, curtains of green hanging down. "He says you know nothing of peace and will destroy any planet you find."

Sounds like someone else I know, when he gets mad enough.

"So he's still refusing to consider another course of action?"

"Yes. He thinks I was foolish to approach you."

Zorian finally told his father of his contact with a human, though not the blood connection part. That's a major taboo we'll keep to ourselves.

"Was he angry at you for not telling him sooner?"

"He was irritated but I am easy to forgive."

The flash of Zorian's smirk shivers through my chest. I like the confidence of dream-Zorian and the shyness of real-Zorian. The opposite sides of him are perfectly balanced. Just like the rest of him.

He picks his way down the hillock, the vegetation at the base welcoming him into its heart.

"How long until you reach the northern tribe?" I follow him, watching the slide of his muscles as he ghosts through the forest.

"A day or two. We are almost to the plains. They may send out a party to greet us before we reach them."

"Will this party include your mate-to-be?"

He peeks at me over his shoulder. "Perhaps."

Very subtle. Good job, Axelle.

It's been a week since our argument. I felt like a bitch as soon as I cooled off. It wasn't a good sign when I started our dream at combatant and progressed to insulting. I worried I'd never see him again but as soon as I tried to enter the dream space, he was there, watching me warily. It made it worse. If I'd missed him when I wanted to knee him in his ball-less genitals, how bad will it get when he mates the northern female? I'll still meet him in real life to continue our alliance, that won't change.

But everything else will.

The dream space is a better sanctuary than my little pretend jungle will ever be. The thought of losing it leaves my stomach hollow.

I didn't tell Zorian any of that. We apologised and moved on, the awkwardness fading after a day.

He holds out his hand. I take it without hesitating and we walk through the jungle, the arc of stone glimpsed between branches. A tree blocks our path further on, the trunk at least three feet thick and finned by half-moons of blue fungi. Zorian grips my waist and lifts me over. He vaults the tree and slides his fingers back into mine.

He's so gentle, it's easy to forget how strong he is, even in our dreams. Anyone else, I'd deck them for daring to pick me up. But I like when he does it. It makes me feel safe.

There's something very wrong with me.

Creatures scamper and gibber, splashing into swamps and

arrowing away in a wake of breaking water. A water-dragon cracks a shell and gobbles a nut the same colour as Zorian's hair. A second beast bursts from the leaves and chases mine. They weave among the canopy, claws scraping bark, making a high chittering sound. The larger water-dragon tackles my slim one and they tangle in the air, dropping into a pool. I grin at Zorian as the ripples fade. His thumb tickles across my palm and a million tiny insects buzz in my stomach.

"This is where we are camped for the night," he says.

The shadow of the stone arch settles on the trees. Dacorna and a group of her brethren munch on flowers, their fur brindle and tawny and grey. Woven hammocks stretch between branches like huge spider webs. Fenna and Dalrainenna recline on a rock, eating berries from Dalrainenna's hand.

"Although they were glad to be home, they wanted to keep moving," Zorian says, following my gaze. "A journey can be a purifying experience."

"Are they okay?"

"They will be."

Three unfamiliar Verdanians complete the circle, playing some kind of game with sticks and pebbles. A final male stands with his back to us, a massive sword of silver-blue metal across his shoulders.

"And this is my father."

Zorian coaxes me closer. The male turns, drinking water from his cupped palms. The symbol of a spreading tree is tattooed in the centre of each hand.

"The tattoos mark him as tribal chief."

"So you'll get them when you take over?"

"Yes, but that is many years from now, I hope."

Zorian's father has the same pale-green hair, though longer and plaited over his shoulder to sit on his chest. A bloodstone on a cord secures the tail. I can see the ghost of his son in his high cheekbones and the set of his face, though his eyes are solemn. Serious. The weight of power has carved lines on his brow and around his mouth.

"What's his name?" I say, totally not using Zorian as a shield. He gives me a small smile, and I roll my eyes. "Fine, his short name."

"Ballathus."

"And he's just a construct of your mind, right? He can't really see me."

Ballathus, taller and broader and fifty times more intimidating than his son, reaches for me. I yelp and duck behind Zorian. He chuckles, and I slap him where his tattoo spreads across his back in wings of vines and flowers.

"Quit it."

"Sorry." He grins at me. "He is not here, only a figment of the dream space, like everything else."

"Except you and me."

His expression softens and he brushes a strand of hair off my cheek. "Yes. Except you and me."

"Who's in charge while you're away?" I say, dropping my gaze.

Changing the subject—who, me?

"My aunt."

"Not your mother?"

"My mother went missing when I was fifteen."

It makes me look at him again, though he's standing so close. "Was it because of...?"

"I do not know."

Ballathus strides past us to join the circle. I flinch away, my shoulder bumping side-on into Zorian. His arms come around me, his hands light on my ribs.

"Do you think he would not like you?" he says.

"Nope. I think he'd hate me."

"Why?"

"For corrupting his son."

"I am not corrupted," Zorian says, his fingers stroking my side. "Not yet."

His smirk starts slow, changing him from beautiful to stunning. I turn in his arms, slowly, as if in a dream. Wait, I *am* in a dream. His hands shift to my back, my head tilted up and up.

God, he's so tall.

"The way you are looking at me right now," he says, his eyes dark, "do not stop."

My hands are splayed on his chest. When did that happen? I focus on them instead of his face, suddenly dizzy. He's as solid and cool as he feels in real life, just a hint of pliancy beneath my fingertips. My pale skin looks tanned next to his whiteness. My fingers slide upwards to trace his collarbone and dip into the hollow of his throat. No pulse. Nothing so fragile close to the surface.

All my throbbing is *way* too close to the surface.

"What are dreams, Axelle?"

His words pull my gaze upwards. He lowers his head.

"Safe," I breathe, rising on tip-toes.

His smile punishes my already tortured heartbeat. The intoxicating scent of mint whispers of tingles and ice. And, oh, I bet he's good with his mouth.

Do Verdanians kiss? It doesn't matter. That's not what

we're doing. He's not even my species. Biologically, it makes no sense to be attracted to him.

"Dreams are safe," he says, and the words brush my lips.

I can almost taste him, almost feel—

An awful ringing yanks me from the dream.

"Motherfucking tit-balls!" I yell, thrashing in the sheets trapping my legs, my skin slick and hot and aching.

Oh *god*, the aching.

The doorbell buzzes through my pod, only slightly louder than my heart slamming against my ribs. I stumble to the speaker panel, trailing sheets, and jab the button.

"*What?*" I growl into the microphone.

The heavy silence indicates I may have been a little abrupt. I suck in a breath. My vest and shorts are sticking to me. I want to dive back under the covers and will myself to sleep.

Am I really that desperate? Desperate enough to fuck an alien in my dreams?

We were just going to kiss. Sure, and kissing never leads to nakedness.

Crap. Crap, crap, crap.

I should throw open the door and hug whoever woke me up. They saved me from doing something stupid. Inhuman. I got carried away in the moment. Zorian and I are allies. We can't be anything else.

"Axelle?" Loyanne whispers through the speaker.

"I'm here," I say in my calm, human voice. "Sorry. What time is it?"

"It's almost seven. Mission brief starts in five minutes."

I rap my fist to my forehead. "*Cock!* I must have slept in. I'll meet you there. No point in us both being late. Thanks,

Loyanne."

Her footsteps scurry away. My alarm clock lies on the floor below Ophrys's tank. He's too busy curled around the berry I gave him yesterday to treat me to a judgemental snail stare.

"Thanks for the heads up, Ophrys," I mutter.

I drag a fresh uniform from my cupboard, scrape my hair into a ponytail while gargling mouthwash, and hustle out the door. I skid to a halt outside the classroom module, pat myself down and step into the meeting a few seconds after seven. Whispers of my name float through the six squads seated around the screen, my own included.

"Elderwoman Carniss," I say, nodding to the statuesque woman at the front. "I apologise for my lateness."

She dismisses me with a flick of her square jaw, her grey hair in a buzz cut. She's damned solid for seventy-eight. Her sharp, blue eyes track me as I slide into a seat.

It's like being dissected. Can she see all my failings? How unprofessional I've become? Contact with a single enemy has crumbled my identity to dust.

Mallory raises a smug face, looking to his watch then at me until I want to shove it up his nose-hole.

I dumped him weeks ago. You'd think he'd be over it by now rather than continuing to be a pain in my ass. Or maybe he was always a pain in the ass.

"Tomorrow, at 0600 hours, your mission is to search every inch of this quadrant," Carniss says, and slaps a metal pointer to the screen, the pixels flaring in distress.

She's old-school, is Carniss.

The screen shows a satellite map of the jungle, beamed down from our very own *HMS Dòchas,* gutted of everything except the equipment she needs to be our eye in the sky. The trees are a blanket of green interrupted by shimmering pools, small clearings and rocky crags.

"You will search every inch of dirt, turn over every leaf. These creatures have to live somewhere. I don't care if it's in a cave or the hollow of a tree. You will find it. This is quadrant number one thousand nine hundred and eighty-three. May it be our last, soldiers."

The ratio of groans to cheers is about fifty-fifty. Groans because most people hate searching the jungle, and cheers at the thought of never having to do it again. They shouldn't complain. I've searched all those quadrants. But I don't hate it. There's always something new to discover—trees with horns, bark that glows orange, plants with brilliant purple and silver leaves. Beasts that glide and slither and jump and swim. Okay, some of them might try to eat me but that's why we have weapons. To discourage them.

"You know the drill by now," Carniss says, her sturdy frame blocking half of the screen. "Even you twentieth and twenty-first generationers have covered at least one quadrant. Stealth is our priority. If we find their lair, I don't want a single savage to know about it. You pull back, report to Home Base and we blast the monsters off the face of what is no longer their planet."

The cheers rattle the walls.

How on not-Earth am I going to convince any of them to stop fighting? My questions have proved fruitless. No one seems to know why the war started beyond Passenger Gotiva's wife going AWOL. Most are like McBurnie—they blame it on the unfathomable minds of monsters. Maybe Zorian can delay the mating ceremony and give us more time to come up with a solution that doesn't end in a bloodbath, red or rainbow-white. I need to work up to being frank with my squad. Tell them something isn't right. Ask for their help and hope they don't betray me to the Elders as a traitor. Zorian not being mated would be a side benefit.

Not that I care.

"Squad leaders, I leave it to you to divvy up the quadrant and programme the sweeps. The rest of the day should be spent in preparation." Carniss collapses the pointer between her hands. "Good luck to you all."

Her boots have barely clomped out the door before Pacal chimes in, his long, brown hair unbound and waving past his shoulders. "Late night, Axe?"

I join the other five leaders at the front of the room, Yannik hulking over the lot of us.

"No more than usual," I say.

This somehow inspires a chorus of whoops.

"You got any new bruises? It's been a few weeks."

I smile sweetly. "Not anywhere I'd want to show you, Strife."

If I had as much sex as everyone thinks, I'd spend most of my life on my back. Or on top. I like to lead, though it's hard to concentrate when I have a blanket wrapped around me to stop everyone in the barracks ogling my tits. They can do that surreptitiously in the gym showers, like everyone else.

The only one who has as much sex as the rumours say is Karine. On Earth, promiscuity in women was a shameful thing, as dumb as it sounds. Here on Verdana, it shows we're virile, desirable. *Alive.* And why wouldn't you do something that feels good, over and over? I might die tomorrow.

We drag everyone's attention back to the mission plan, dividing the quadrant into sectors and assigning them to each squad, breaking into our individual groups to go over it in detail. I scan the members of my team, their heads bent over maps on their tablets.

Maybe I should pick one of them for a quick shag. Clearly, it's been too long if I'm entertaining notions of sampling outside the human gene pool. I just need to scratch the itch and I'll be fine.

I scan my squad again. Nothing. No throbbing, no tingles. Maybe I'm tired. I could go for a nap. It's early. He might still be—

For fuck's sake.

I pace around the room as if I'm checking on progress instead of distracting myself from heinous thoughts.

It's not even a rule. No one has to be told not to because the very idea is an abomination. A non-verbal understanding if you want to get into the semantics. So why has one pretty alien got me thinking the unthinkable? Stupid Zorian and his cheekbones and his chiselled-from-marble body.

I frown at the screen as if I'm memorising the map.

Are all parts of him as cool to the touch? How would that feel, so deep, so cold, inside—

I bite my cheek. I can't see him again. Dreams are *not* safe. But I have to warn him about tomorrow.

Shit.

I'll just keep my dream-panties on.

How hard can that be?

21

I stay awake until after midnight, which is eleven o'clock in the Verdanian twenty-two-hour day. This takes a lot of pacing and face-slapping. Ophrys, realising it's not an opportunity for a snack, flicks his eye stalks at me and slithers under his log. Anyone watching would think I'm nervous for the mission tomorrow. My alarm is set for five am and I am going to be one grumpy bitch when it goes off.

But the less time spent in the dream space, the better.

"I am a goddamn squad leader," I mutter, my fists clenched. "I am a disciplined professional. I have willpower. If I don't want something to happen, it won't."

I stretch out on my bed, my hands folded on my stomach.

No more skimpy pyjamas. I'll appear in full uniform. I'd wear my battlesuit if I didn't think he'd be offended.

Not that it matters what he feels.

My heart knocks against my sternum.

Maybe I should wait another hour.

"You fucking coward," I tell myself. "Go in. Deliver the message. Get out."

I shut my eyes. Sleep sinks its claws into me and rolls me under like a water-tiger.

"I wondered if you would come," Zorian says, his back to

174

me.

He hasn't been hanging around alone in the dream space. It only forms if both minds are connected.

His trousers sit low at his waist. There's a lot of smooth skin between where his tattoo ends at the cleft of his spine and the line of green material. He has dimples.

Butt dimples.

"I have to show you something," I say with complete calm.

Squad leaders do not squeak.

A screen materialises in the jungle, incongruous among the vines and leaves. A snail nibbles on the corner to see if it's food.

Zorian's trousers are held together by criss-crossing black thread where the seams should be, leaving his legs bared from ankle to hip. I can see his hipbones and what can only be described as the flank of his ass.

I fix my gaze on the screen so fast, my eyeballs get whiplash. The image swirls to the carpet of foliage, rocks and pools from the mission brief.

"We're searching this area for your base tomorrow. Today. Please tell me we're not close."

He looks at me for a long minute. I stare back.

Squad leaders do not fidget.

"We do not live there," he says.

The aerial view of the jungle shifts approximately twenty kilometres south-east. The expanse of green is much the same except for a huge, kidney-shaped pool. Zorian lays his palm on the outside curve of the waterbody.

Serious emerald eyes meet mine. "We live here."

I swallow hard. There's not another human alive privy to this information. The war could be over in hours. I won't have to fight again. The Elders wouldn't just give me a medal, they'd throw a freaking parade and name a landmass after me. I'll be immortalised as a saviour.

But Zorian told me because he trusts me not to slaughter his people. He trusts me.

Okay, message delivered. Retreat. *Retreat!*

"Do you want to see where I live?" I say since I'm a blithering idiot.

The jungle dissolves before he can reply. In one blink, I'm standing in my pod. With a Verdanian. I try to see it as he would—cramped, dark. Plants ripped from their natural habitat and slowly dying. A snail trapped behind glass.

Zorian's long fingers stroke a spill of golden leaves, orange buds peeking out. Honeyfire. Safe to eat if you like it spicy.

"You have made a little jungle," he says with something that can't be awe.

He moves to the tank. Dream-Ophrys waves his fronds.

"This is Ophrys," I say breathlessly. Why am I breathless? I'm not freaking jogging. "Berries are his favourite. He's my pet."

Shut up, you fool.

Zorian tilts his head. "Pet?"

"Um, a companion. Something you take care of." And talk to because I'm a crazy woman who communes with snails.

"Is Ophrys an Earth name?"

"It's Latin. Another language. It's the name of a group of flowers—orchids."

What, I can't speak in full sentences now?

Why have I never noticed how small my pod is? It's tiny with Zorian in it. He could stretch his arm up and hit the roof. At least he doesn't take up much room horizontally.

He moves around me to the nalwell, my newest addition, planted in an obsolete battlesuit helmet. I saw it on my most recent jungle foray and had to have it. The petals spiral from emerald to pear to lime at the tips.

It's funny how so many colours are words for Earth foods I've never seen.

"You drew one," he says, cupping a petal in his hand. "Will you show me?"

"I… Sure."

I grab my sketchbook from the bedside cabinet and hold it out. He slides it from my grasp, flipping it open.

He has been very careful not to touch me.

Pages rustle. He rotates the book for each drawing.

"You are talented," he says, not looking at me. "There are few from my people who are better artists."

"Thanks." I'm not blushing.

His eyes meet mine for a fraction of a second but it's long enough to send a jolt deep into my stomach.

"I saw her today."

I don't have to ask who.

"And how is your chosen one?"

"She is not my choice," he says almost to himself.

A Verdanian female materialises at his side. She's a full head taller than him so, by my standards, she's bloody massive. Broader, too. All Verdanians are scary-solid but Zorian is delicate next to her. Her eyes are the colour of lightning, her hair silver and cut short. Black tattoos curve from her brows to her cheekbones, giving her a severe expression not helped by her slash of a mouth.

She looks like a bundle of fun.

I find my voice. "She's, ah… *big*."

Zorian blinks at me. His lips twitch. He makes a muffled noise. And then he laughs. *Out loud.* My mouth drops open. He clutches his ribs, and sags against the shelf holding Ophrys's tank. The laughter shivers into giggles and shines from his skin like quartz in a sunbeam.

He manages to catch his breath and say, "Yes, she is big."

He braces his hands on his knees, and grins at me as if he's drunk. My legs wobble but I don't think it's at the sight of his teeth. His mate-to-be watches us with no flicker of expression. Two straps of brown material cover her modesty, minus any embellishments. The spear in her hand is thicker than my arm.

"She's not exactly cuddly, is she?" I say.

Zorian sniggers and claps his hand over his mouth, his shoulders shaking. His eyes glow so bright, I'm surprised he's not painting emerald lights on the ceiling.

"Am *I* cuddly?" he says, his voice about two decibels higher, and climbing.

"Uh…" I search frantically for another topic. "When do you have to mate with Miss Joy-to-the-World?"

Zorian slides down the wall as if he's lost all use of his limbs, and laughs until his chest heaves. If he had tear ducts, he'd be crying right now. His long legs sprawl in opposite directions, his trousers stretched over his hips. Each laughing breath tightens his abdominal muscles.

I'm learning all sorts of secrets today. How to disarm a Verdanian—say something funny.

"She—she is not so bad," he hiccups. "A good warrior. Strong. She does not have a creative mind but I should not hold that against her."

I'll hold it against her. She's a sour-faced boot and completely wrong for him. He's curious, free-spirited and open to new experiences. He likes to run and play and smile. If she smiled, her face would crack like the stone it is.

Perhaps his father has a second reason for Zorian's arranged mating. What better way to stifle his son's rebelliousness than by saddling him with a happiness black hole?

Zorian pulls himself to his feet. "My father would have us mated tomorrow if he could but her mother is traditional. And stalling. There will be a few days of feasts and celebrations before the actual ceremony. It will not be so bad."

The last is said in a quieter voice, his face turned away.

Who's he trying to convince?

He circles her, disappearing behind her back for a second then reappearing on her other side, scanning her considerable bulk.

I'd worry about his health if he weren't so sturdy. She seems capable of crushing a man's pelvis by accident.

"But... you still don't want her as your mate?"

The zinging sensation happens again when he finally looks at me.

"I do not," he says.

"What do you want?"

"That is a dangerous question, Axelle."

Yup. Steer clear of that shit. Time to bid him goodnight.

"What do you want, Zorian?" I whisper.

Ah, fuck.

One step and he stands in front of me, not touching. I stare at his chest, my hands balled at my sides so I don't start petting him like last night.

"Is it not obvious?" he says.

My gaze shifts upwards despite me ordering it not to. I gulp.

He's all cheekbones and pistachio hair and dark, drowning eyes. I find myself nodding.

God, I'm an idiot.

He smiles a soft smile. "I do not know what I am doing, either. But I know what I want."

He picks me up. It seems natural to wrap my legs around his waist instead of dangling in his arms like I child.

I am *not* a child.

Cool skin teases my inner thighs. Ah, cock, I'm in my pyjamas. Zorian's hands circle my waist, our heads perfectly level. No straining on tip-toes or spinal contortions. My fingers trace across his cheek and cup his face. He shuts his eyes as if he's the one who's dizzy. His skin feels so good against the heat pulsing off mine.

"This is probably a bad idea," I murmur.

He peeks at me through half-lidded eyes.

"Probably," he says, and his smirk tugs at my belly.

Then there's no space left between us.

22

I'm kissing a Verdanian. Axelle of the first generation, killer of twelve, mercy-killer of one, and I'm wrapped around him like a monewt climbing a tree. It's shameful, *criminal*.

But, hell, I knew he'd be good with his mouth.

That mouth glides along mine and captures my bottom lip, exploring. Gently sucking—oh god. He tastes of ice and mint. My hand fists in the hair at the nape of his neck, my other arm across his shoulders, fingertips digging into firm muscles. I'm so hot and he's so cool, I want to press as much of my skin as possible against him.

I really should keep my clothes on.

The kiss deepens. I'm feasting on his mouth and, yup, moaning low in my throat.

I never moan. One has to be quiet in the barracks surrounded by hundreds of soldiers. No whimpering, no screaming names. My squad would never let me hear the end of it.

But dreams are safe.

I clench my thighs around Zorian's waist. He's so solid. I can't help arching my hips, rubbing myself against him.

Must not dry hump the Verdanian.

His hands cup my butt. It's not even skin to skin but the

thin scrap of material separating us makes it worse. All sorts of tingles zip from his touch on my ass to his mouth on mine. The buzzing in my stomach is unreal. A pressure builds in my chest and it wants *more*.

I slide my tongue into Zorian's mouth. He startles but doesn't pull away, his hands tightening on my butt. After a second's hesitation, his tongue finds mine and, oh man, he's even better at snogging. We tangle together. He's so dexterous, and that fork at the tip… *Wow*. He strokes me with it. My dirty mind thinks of somewhere else he could put that tongue until all the tingles pulse between my legs. I suck him hard into my mouth. He staggers and gives a little groan.

Fuck me, it's hot.

I could not be closer unless I crawl inside him. His teeth scrape against me but he can't hurt me in dreams. We'd have to be careful of his sharp incisors and canines in real life.

I am *not* kissing him in real life. Dreams may be safe but kissing him in real life is suicidal.

He flops onto the edge of my bed, and suddenly I'm sitting in his lap. Squirming in his lap, more like. I really must stop that. Slow it down a bit. I pull away. We blink at each other, and pant.

"I like the tongue thing," he says.

His hair is mussed, flopping across his forehead into dazed eyes.

It takes me three tries to find my voice. "Verdanians don't kiss with tongues?"

"We do not kiss much or only in dreams. I saw my parents kiss once when they thought they were alone. The northern tribe do not kiss at all."

I nuzzle his lips, teasing him when he responds. I keep it

light—nibbling, licking. He strains to make it more, another whimper caught in his throat.

"Kissing is awesome," I say, and grin at him. "Why wouldn't you do it all the time?"

"I like to kiss."

The smirk undoes me. Teasing turns to kissing him so hard, I sip the air from his lungs. My fingers trace his collarbones and the stone of his pendant, caressing to the firm plane of his chest uninterrupted by nipples. I explore lower to the swell of his abdominals, each one as well-defined as a pebble cupped in my hand. Lower still, I find the line of his hips and slip my fingers under the waistband of his trousers. They're so tight but I manage to touch the tops of his thighs since he's sitting down. He sucks in a breath. I can't figure out how to undo them without stopping the kiss. There's no zipper or button. Maybe I have to untie all the string at the sides.

I am *not* taking off his trousers. Kissing is one thing but I'm not doing *that*. Not even in dreams.

His hands sneak under my vest, and it's my turn to gasp.

"You are so fragile," he whispers, stroking up my ribs. His thumbs brush the undersides of my breasts. "So *soft*."

I struggle to swallow past my heartbeat. If this were real life, it's all he would feel or hear. It's thudding so strong, I can taste it. He raises his gaze from his hands under my top to my face. I sag in his lap, my fingers gripping his trousers. He seems delighted but I can't quite tell since I can barely focus. Every part of me aches for his hands to move higher.

"What do you want, Axelle?" he murmurs against my mouth, and I realise I've closed my eyes.

"Touch me."

"I am touching you."

"Zorian…" I growl, and he laughs.

The laugh becomes guttural, his eyes widening, when my thumbs meet in the middle of his trousers and confirm that Verdanians get erections.

Every day is a school day.

Our mouths collide. I grind myself into him but he still doesn't move his hands, his thumbs and forefingers framing me but not enough for what I want. *Need.*

"Zorian," I say and pretend it's not a whine.

"You are going to wake up."

"I don't want to wake up."

Definitely a whine.

He smiles and it's gentle and tender and doesn't ease the throbbing in the slightest.

"I will see you tomorrow night, Axelle," he says, and slides his hands upwards.

"Oh, *fuck*," I moan.

My alarm peals and rips me from the dream.

23

Tiredness stings my eyes, not helped by the filtered air in my battlesuit. The helmet struggles to clear the condensation on the inside and the water pattering on the outside. Moisture drips from the canopy and roils around in puffs of mist. I swipe a glove over the visor, smearing mud and bits of leaf. A snail investigates the sight of my gun, probably trying to eat it. I pluck the creature off and set it on a clump of bubble-like moss.

My squad fans out behind me, sweeping the foliage for anything that might resemble a Verdanian abode. Grey battlesuits flash between the trees and greenery.

What do their homes even look like—mud huts, shacks of wood, caves?

The other squads are out there, too, covering their assigned grids in the ten-kilometre square. Tension sings through the silence on my radio. The expectation of attack. The anticipation that this will be the day we find something.

It's quite relaxing to know we won't.

My thoughts drift. I should be focused on the mission but all I can think about is last night. What I did. I don't even feel guilty, though I know I should. Instead, I wonder how far I'll let myself go.

Will a dream orgasm feel as good as a real orgasm? Maybe I should find out. You know, for science. I also want to play with Zorian and see what he does. Who knows what other fun things I can introduce him to? No sex, though.

Is it still bestiality if he's a different, though humanoid, species?

There's a plop off to my right, and Mallory makes a gagging noise. A snail slithers on his helmet, peering at him upside down. Its shell is a pale grey dusted with lavender, the fins streaks of silver, undulating as the snail moves. Mallory swipes it to the ground. The delicate shell crunches under his boot.

"For fuck's sake, Barbie," I hiss between my teeth.

My fingers clench on my gun. I stop myself from ramming it into his gut.

"What? The things cover everything in slime."

"You hate the snails, you hate the rain. For somewhere you're fighting to live, you sure seem revolted by most of it."

Some may say he has no harmony.

"When we exterminate the Verdanian pests, I'm going to clear me a swatch of jungle and concrete right over all this stupid mud. Anything that comes near my house gets shot."

"Manipulating the landscape to their own ends and killing everything didn't work out so well for the people on Earth," I say mildly.

"That's because they did it wrong. I won't chop it all down, just my land."

"Who says you're getting any land?"

"After all this fighting, it's the least the Elders can do."

I shake my head. "Let's concentrate on why we're here, not on killing everything."

"To kill things is why we're here," he says, and I don't need to see his face to picture his smug expression.

"Focus, Barbie. I won't say it again."

It shuts him up for a merciful couple of hours.

My path takes me into a gorge, the rock walls carpeted by green and glossy ferns. Water burbles over stone. My squad climbs out of sight on the cliffs to either side. I glimpse Loyanne checking I'm okay before the vegetation forces her to cut away from the edge. I fill the compartments of my battlesuit with fronds and moss. The gorge widens to a tranquil pool bordered by delicate red bushes bowed under the weight of blue berries.

Daracurrants. Ophrys will be ecstatic.

I crouch closer to the pool than I would before Zorian's behavioural reconditioning therapy of coaxing me into the water. I keep my gun steady in my right hand and pick a handful of berries, scanning for movement. A turquoise water-dragon slips from the pool, droplets darkening the stone as it shakes itself. I toggle my comms off.

"Hey, little buddy," I say in a gentle voice, slowly extending my hand. "You want this?"

The water-dragon cocks its head. Its eyes are a solid turquoise slightly lighter than its scales, split by an elliptical pupil. A tiny pink tongue flicks out. I hold my breath. The creature darts forward, spears the berry in its claws and scuttles back. It gobbles the fruit with a distinctly reptilian grin, blue juice running down its jaw. Finished, it scrabbles up the gorge side, flapping twice to boost itself over the top. It perches on the edge and watches me, licking its hands to clean the juice off its face.

A glove punches from the foliage and grabs the water-dragon. The snap of its neck echoes in the gorge. The slight body flops as Mallory hoists it aloft. It takes all my willpower not to shoot him full of bloodstone.

"Barbie," I growl, "what did I say about killing things?"

He shrugs his massive shoulders. "They taste nice. I'm taking this one home for dinner."

I'm going to have to do something if he won't quit his insubordination. Whipping the crap out of his hide doesn't seem so distasteful anymore.

He ties a loop of cord around the limp water-dragon and tosses it over his shoulder, fading back into the jungle. A soldier of death.

Is there any other type of soldier?

My squad and I regroup on the edge of a swamp, black mud and stagnant water glistening in the light as the suns dip for the horizon. I take great satisfaction in sending Mallory into the murk to check there are no hidden entrances. He emerges twenty slopping, slurping minutes later wearing a scowl and mud to his waist. I mask my smile and we continue our sweep, only two kilometres to go.

On the hour, every squad checks in. No Verdanians to report and also no fatalities. A boy from the twenty-first generation spooked a dozing water-tiger but he avoided being shredded, helped, his squad leader gleefully informs us, by the kid shitting his battlesuit. The creature slunk away with its nose in the air, apparently.

As effective as it may be, I don't see it catching on as a means of protection.

A wide, grassy clearing stretches in front of us, unusual in itself except in the north of Ananngar. Most clearings are formed around waterbodies. The sea of grass wavers in the breeze, the seed heads giving hues of pink and yellow and blue. I imagine the air smells of pollen and hay. The exposed circle of sky darkens from cobalt to violet and orange. Stalks whisper and tug at my legs, the grass up to my stomach. Thigh-length on those of an average stature.

In a few hours, I could be sitting in Zorian's lap. I want to see just how good he is with his hands. Pretty good by my estimation but that contact was far too short to reach a proper verdict.

I feel like a teenager in one of those movies, sneaking off to fool around. Snogging for hours, no pressure to take it further, bar the boy's wandering hands. Except it was me who made the first move with my fingers down Zorian's pants.

I got carried away.

We near the far side of the clearing. A rustle of leaves gives a moment's warning. A Verdanian bursts from the undergrowth, followed by another. My heart leaps into my mouth, and the muzzle of my gun jerks up. The first Verdanian skids to a stop on the edge of the grass. The second Verdanian takes a beat longer to notice us, poking the male in the ribs and trilling, "A bheill chi!"

You're it.

Earth kids, we'd have heard their happy shrieks from miles away as they chased each other.

The male is a couple of inches shorter, his honey eyes and amber hair striking in his angular face. The female has orange hair in pigtails, her eyes the image of her brother's, even huge and shimmering with fear.

"Hold your fire," I say in a rush, my voice high.

The boy sweeps his sister behind him, though she's tall enough to peek over the top of his head. I want to tell them to leave in Anann but the words stick on my tongue. We stare at each other, thirty armed soldiers and two Verdanian children.

I've never seen one. They actually look fragile. Slim and pale and lovely. What the hell are they doing playing out here? No one's supposed to be here.

"Hold your fire," I say again, calmer, though my pulse wobbles through my voice.

I lower my weapon and raise my hand in a shooing motion. The boy cocks his head, reminding me of Zorian, though there's no physical resemblance. The girl whispers to him and tugs on his sleeve, his tunic mottled yellow and green and identical to hers.

"Dwyl," I say, pronouncing it carefully. *Go.*

Their golden eyes fix on me, two sets of brows elevated in surprise. Perhaps children are more expressive than adults or I'm much better at reading Verdanians.

I flick my fingers again. Sweat trickles down the side of my face and slicks my neck. The jungle is hushed, holding its breath. A battlesuit creaks behind me.

I watch it happen. *Know* it will happen.

We are a violent species.

24

I'm not a fan of horror movies. Life is horrific enough. I want to escape to a fantasy of romance and fun and laughter. But from the films I've seen, the truly awful stuff happens in slow-motion, high-definition carnage. Colours are sharp enough to make your eyeballs bleed; sounds are brasher.

Turns out adrenaline is just as good at replicating that shit.

The gunshot echoes in the dome of my helmet. Whiteness bursts from the throat of the boy and stains his tunic. He staggers, clutching his neck, his gaze on me. A gurgle spills from his mouth. Another bullet pierces one honey eye, and he drops. His sister runs for the jungle, her pigtails bouncing, her long legs awkward now the chase is for real. She has a leaf stuck to the sole of her foot.

"Mithaill!" she cries.

Mummy.

Automatic fire shreds her back to a mess of white and yellow and green. Tufts of material drift to land on her body, one hand stretched towards the trees. Both of them too young to have developed the skin rigidity of an adult.

Too young.

Smoke curls from the barrel of Mallory's gun. A buzzing fills my head and vibrates in my teeth. My finger tightens on

191

my trigger. A controlled burst at his helmet and his face will be mush.

A pale flash grabs my attention beyond Mallory.

Oh god, not another child to the slaughter. *Please.*

A Verdanian woman sprints from the jungle, a spear held at waist height. Crimson hair shimmers to her ankles and cloaks her in red. Her eyes fall on the bodies. The hiss she makes covers me in goosebumps. She clears the distance in two bounds, my squad not pivoting fast enough. Marvyn blocks her path to Mallory. She bats his gun away, her face a rictus of bared teeth.

I don't need to see tears to know her grief. She feels, just like Zorian.

The spear slams forward. Once, twice, and the point tents the back of Marvyn's battlesuit. She yanks it free, spraying blood onto the wavering grass. Red, not white. Marvyn collapses to his knees, his arms wrapped around his gut. The muscles in her shoulders tense, and the spear stabs towards Mallory.

My squad opens fire but my finger freezes on the trigger. Marble monster or no, the bloodstone barrage halts her advance. Her spear flies from her hand. Her body jerks at each hit, her hair writhing in the wind of the bullets that miss. Blood glimmers on the air and paints rainbows in the light. She joins her children in the grass, and my ears ring in the silence.

Loyanne says something. I don't realise it's my name until she's said it three times. I can't seem to focus on her. Static flares in my visor with each beat of my heart. I can't catch my breath.

Freaking hell, is this battleshock?

"Axelle," she says, her voice soft as if she isn't quite sure of her reception, "you need to call for help."

Help?

My first thought is Zorian. I bark a laugh, and Loyanne edges away. I shut my mouth before something else comes out, like bile. I take a deep breath. Another.

I can't fall apart in front of my squad.

I toggle to a different channel on my radio. "Base, this is Godkiller. Requesting emergency evac on my position. Soldier down. Possibility of further hostiles."

Does my voice sound as disembodied as I feel?

I switch back to normal comms.

"Strife, Hulk—patch up Snakebit for transport. The rest of you—defensive positions." My next breath burns all the way to my toes. *And no one fucking shoots unless I say so.*

My squad forms a loose circle around Marvyn shivering in the flattened grass. Pacal stuffs a wad of dressings against the hole in his battlesuit and presses down, both arms locked. Marvyn screams. His heels furrow the dirt. I grab Mallory's wrist on his way past and yank him to my level, our helmets clunking together.

"You will answer for ignoring me, Mallory of the fifth generation," I say and it's beyond command voice. It's something low and terrifying and empty. "I will take his pain and their deaths from your flesh."

Mallory's face creases into stubborn confusion. "They're just Verd—"

I ram my gun into his stomach. The battlesuit protects him from the force of the blow but he staggers back a step.

"For the rest of the mission, you will not speak. You will do *exactly* what I say. Is. That. Clear?" The last three words descend into a growl that would do a water-tiger proud.

Mallory nods, his gaze everywhere but on me. Marvyn's screams putter into whimpers. Dante kneels at his head, whispering to him, his comms off.

"Very good. Now get the fuck out of my sight." I grab the rope tied across his shoulders and tug it free, holding the dangling water-dragon out. "Angelface, you've scored yourself a free batch of burgers."

Mallory slinks away without a word. Loyanne accepts the limp bundle.

"Thank you, sir," she says, her expression sombre. Her next sentence is muffled through her helmet as she switches off her comms. "Are you okay?"

"I'm fine," is the response of a real squad leader. Or, "Of course." Unflappable in battle. Unflinching. They do what needs to be done. See the big picture. Three dead Verdanians is a victory.

"No," I say.

I leave her standing in the circle. The eyes of my squad track me as I lay the bodies of the children next to their mother.

* * *

Marvyn survives the journey to Home Base, though not conscious. His skin is as pale as a Verdanian's. Pacal joined me in the medivac, maintaining pressure on the stomach wound. I relinquished command to Loyanne.

The rest of the squad stays with her until the job is done.

The throb of the aircraft's three engines changes in pitch as they swivel in preparation for landing on the pad next to the hospital. The aerial vehicle is one of a small platoon for emergency evacuation and deployment. The density of the jungle makes it almost impossible for successful aerial assault unless you're willing to raze half of it in the hopes of catching your prey.

Two heavy bombers are kept in reserve for when we find where the Verdanians call home.

The legs of the aircraft meet the ground with a jolt. Passengers swarm out of the hospital and whisk Marvyn away for surgery. Pacal tags along, the gloves of his battlesuit stained dark. I watch the sliding doors long after they've disappeared through them. The engines hum to a halt behind me, the wisps of hair that have escaped my braid no longer tickling my cheeks, my helmet tucked under my arm. My fingers stroke the stone at my throat.

I give myself a shake and go in search of an Elder not about to be elbow-deep in Marvyn's insides.

Mallory will face a tribunal for what he's done.

And I will carry out the punishment.

25

"You *are* cuddly," I murmur into Zorian's neck.

I'm curled in his lap, breathing in the scent of him. He sits with his back against a tree, and cradles me.

Safe in the arms of a Verdanian.

"Do I want to be cuddly?"

"I definitely need it right now," I say, and snuggle closer.

As soon as I entered the dream space, I wrapped my arms around him and cried on his chest.

I'm getting bloody soft.

He didn't recognise the woman or her children, though he was sad to hear of their deaths. Sometimes individuals leave and become nomads, travelling Ananngar and occasionally forming new tribes in uninhabited land. He graciously said nothing about the awfulness of my species. I promised him Mallory would pay.

I touch the stone at Zorian's throat. "Will their souls be lost?"

"Soul? Humans have their own word for spirit?"

"Lots of people believe a part of you lingers after you die."

He takes my hand. "Do you?"

"Now I do," I say, and slide my fingers between his. "But you didn't answer my question."

"I do not know what will happen. Perhaps they will find their own way."

"To heaven?"

"What is heaven?"

I'm in my pyjamas again. It seems I can't resist, though Zorian is no better. There's not much sarong left bar the part I'm sitting on.

"Heaven is paradise. The place you go when you die. But only if you've been good. Bad humans go to hell."

Zorian trails a finger along my shoulder and down my arm. I shiver at the tickling caress.

"I do not think I have been good," he says, his grin clear in his voice.

The pulse in my stomach wonders how bad he wants to be.

"Next to me, you're a saint. Where do virtuous little Verdanians go when their stone returns to the water?"

"The ocean," he says.

"You're not very imaginative, are you?"

He pinches my side, and I yelp.

"Do not mock," he says. "It is—"

"Sacred?" I snigger into his neck.

He shakes his head. "You are definitely going to this hell you speak of."

I twist in his lap, sliding a leg across until I'm straddling him. Both of my hands cup his face, my fingertips on his cheekbones.

"Yes," I say, "I think I am."

I capture his mouth, my ego boosted by the purr he makes low in his throat. His hands drop to my hips and pull me tighter against him.

God, there really is nothing between us. I feel him, so long, so hard, so…

Forbidden. Don't forget the no-sex part, Axelle.

But touching, right? I get to touch?

I break the kiss, breathless after only a minute.

"What did you do today?" I say, and swallow the temptation to ask after his mate-to-be.

"I cannot remember." He steals the distance I won, and kisses me. "Nothing as fun as this."

I laugh into his mouth, and he takes advantage by slipping me some tongue. For a species that doesn't kiss much, he learns fast. I melt against him, my fingers sliding into his hair. We explore and lick and nibble. Usually, kissing is the short prelude happily skipped for the main event. It's a nice change. And I like the tingles it gives me in the pit of my stomach.

"Tell me," I say after ten enjoyable minutes.

"Tell you what?"

I slap his chest. "What you did today."

"We got a tour of their home. They showed us the pledged warriors. They are all as big as Calliyanna."

"Is that the short name of your chosen one?"

He gives me a look.

"Fine. The woman you are being forced to mate to form an alliance that will protect your people."

"That is her full name. They have shorter names than us." He continues to examine me. Those emerald eyes miss nothing. "I wish this were real life so I could see what you feel when you talk about her."

"Too bad. The next time we meet, you'll be mated and my dreams will be empty."

"Empty?"

"Normal. I meant normal."

His smirk says, "Sure you did."

He runs his lips up my throat, and it's my turn to purr.

"I angered my father today," he says between kisses, my pulse jumping under his mouth.

"Mmm, that's not unusual for you."

His teeth scrape my skin, and my breath shivers out. He leans back only far enough to peek at me.

"I think you would enjoy it if I bit you. Right *here*." He presses his teeth into my neck but not hard enough to break the skin, not that I'd feel any pain in the dream space.

I writhe against him, which, as close as we are, means I rub myself on the hardness beneath his sarong, and it's not just his legs. He growls into my throat, and I squirm some more. His fingers slip under my vest to play along the skin above my shorts, each cool stroke flaring heat in lower places.

"It is better in real life," he whispers, pulling away. "But then you already know that."

It takes me a second to understand what he's talking about. When we shared blood. His teeth biting my wrist. The sucking. Man, the sucking. Or when he bit my neck in the tree.

"What did you do to annoy your dad?" My voice comes out strangled.

"I said I wanted the mating ceremony to happen at home. *My* home."

My heart skips. "Do you think they'll go for it?"

"Yes. Their leader wants to stall. If she brings her warriors on the journey and the mating does not happen, she can claim recompense for their return. It would cost my people a lot of food and other supplies whereas the northern tribe risks nothing but time."

"But that time gives us more options."

"It may not delay anything. It just means our blood connection will end in a few weeks instead of days." His hands skim up my back under my vest. "Your dreams will not be normal for a little longer."

I squash a pang. A little longer still seems like not enough but what was I expecting—forever?

Zorian is curious, not reckless.

I walk my fingers from his stomach to his chest. "So we can keep doing this?"

"I hope so."

His hands knead my shoulder blades. I relax into the touch but I want more. Especially after last night. The too-brief caress.

And good boys get rewarded.

I grip the hem of my vest. My heart beats faster. Zorian's fingers pause on my back, his gaze dropping to my hands then returning to my face.

He's felt them already, he might as well see them. It's not like I'll be naked.

I pull my vest over my head and shut my eyes. Nothing happens. I risk a peek. Zorian stares at me, stunned, similar to any teenager—human or Verdanian—getting their first sight of boobs.

Or big, flat, plate-sized nipples to be more exact for the Verdanians.

His hand hovers over me. He searches my face but I keep it blank, my heart in my throat. He licks his lips, and his cold hand palms my breast. His other hand shows no such hesitation. He cups both my breasts and grins at me.

I sigh. "Go on, then."

"Tits," he says.

A laugh bubbles up. It turns to a hum of appreciation as he starts to knead.

"You are so soft," he breathes.

He bends his knees and I recline on his thighs. His fingers brush my nipples. I arch into his touch, my belly stretched in a taut line. My groin presses into his and, oh, this would be a good position if we were naked. He shifts his hands, his thumbs swirling over and over each hard bud. Tingles race in all directions. His breath tickles my skin. I open my eyes without realising I closed them. He's bent at the waist to bring his face near to my breasts, his thumbs continuing to circle.

How can a creature carved of marble be so flexible?

He rolls his eyes, watching me through a fall of pistachio hair as he slowly extends his tongue. The fork caresses my nipple, teasing it between slick flesh. I bite my lip, forgetting I can make as much noise as I want. He sucks my breast into his mouth and the point becomes moot since I moan really goddamn loud. He sucks harder, flicking his tongue across my nipple, his teeth grazing the mound of my breast. Each suck clenches in my stomach and throbs between my legs. His hand continues to stroke my other breast so it doesn't feel left out.

Oh, crap. I'm whimpering every time he sucks, writhing against him. A pressure builds in my gut, a heavy fullness swelling beneath my skin.

Holy fuck, I'm going to come from him playing with my tits.

But we talked too long and my cock-blocking alarm does what it does best.

26

The atmosphere of the intensive care ward is a held breath before life rushes out on a gasp. Machines beep in the quiet; shoes squeak past from the corridor. Drawn blinds seal out the sunlight as if it will harm rather than help. I want to yank them open to let the brightness spill in and chase the shadows away.

Marvyn's slight figure barely fills the hospital bed, the pristine sheets cocooning him from shoulders to feet. His brown hair sticks to his forehead, sweat beaded on his upper lip. His eyes flicker beneath closed lids.

The Elders removed thirty centimetres of intestine, his spleen and repaired the rent in his stomach caused by the Verdanian's spear. The blade came within an inch of his abdominal aorta. Infection is a serious concern despite his abdominal cavity being flushed several times during surgery. Three bags of fluid hang from the drip pole next to his bed, the lines snaking under the covers. Two hold clear fluid, one wrinkled and almost empty. The third, smaller bag is black and opaque.

He has a fighting chance. Most soldiers die on the battlefield or during emergency evacuation. His wound may be bad but others have returned from similar, or worse, as long as they get to the hospital with a pulse.

I stand at the foot of his bed, my hands wrapped around the cold metal frame. Empty beds circle the room. The rest of the wards hold the sick or infirm, more numerous than the war-wounded. A special room houses the soldiers suffering from severe battleshock.

They have no visitors.

A Passenger clip-clops into the ward on white clogs, carrying a bag of clear fluid balanced on a tablet.

"Good morning, Axelle of the first," he says, walking around me to the drip pole on the far side of the bed.

"Good morning, Passenger."

I can't remember his name or if I knew it in the first place. There are over twelve hundred of them so it's a bit of a memory exercise.

He places the tablet and bag on a silver table and unhooks the empty bag from the stand. The table is the same as the one that held the instruments in the underground dissection room. The disinfectant smell is also similar.

"I'm afraid it's unlikely Marvyn of the seventh will wake today. His body has been through a major trauma. Oh, shoot." The Passenger prods at the tablet, examining the empty and replacement fluid bags. "I picked up the wrong one. Back in a moment."

He trots out of the room with the bag. My eyes linger on the doorway as the clop of his shoes fades. I slide around the bed and pick up the tablet, stabbing at the screen before it can lock.

Zorian's curiosity is rubbing off on me.

The first page details Marvyn's medical history—O negative blood type, no known allergies, concussion from a fall when a Verdanian scooped him into a tree and dropped him, shattered ribs and arms after a Verdanian beat him with a rock. The second page describes his current injury and treatments. One of the bags is tironidazole and the other is saline. No mention of the third bag. I listen for a beat but the corridor is quiet. The last page has a record of his pulse, temperature and respiration taken every thirty minutes. I swipe to the first page but pause in lowering the tablet.

There's something faint in the right-hand corner of the screen, difficult to see in the dimness. The page refuses to zoom. A couple of futile taps finds no way to exit the chart to search for a brightness setting. I bring it closer to my face.

Is it a number?

I angle the device towards the sunlight haloing the blinds. Reflections dance off the screen and obscure the text. Footsteps clomp in the corridor. The tablet rings on the metal table. I jump back to my spot at the end of the bed and stand at ease as the Passenger bustles in. He changes the bags with practised movements, checking Marvyn's machines and noting things on the tablet.

I breathe quietly until I know my voice won't betray me. "Passenger, sorry for my ignorance but why is that bag different to the others?"

I indicate the black bag dangling on the stand, the tube the same colour. The Passenger barely gives it a glance, tapping another notation into the tablet.

"The active ingredients are sensitive to light."

"What's in it?"

The Passenger holds up a finger and pulls a stethoscope from his pocket, listening to Marvyn's chest. "It's our nutrient solution for all traumatic injuries. Studies have shown it speeds the healing process."

"What kind of nutrients?"

"Proteins, vitamins, minerals." He loops the stethoscope around his neck and grips each end. "I'm surprised you've not had some yourself, given your profession."

"Just an arrow to the face, broken bones and drowning for me. Maybe not traumatic enough."

He pockets the tablet and tidies the empty fluid bag and medical detritus into the bins.

"I don't know about that," he says, washing his hands at the sink. "Your scar looks neat. Did it need surgery?"

I stroke my cheek. "I think so. To be honest, that period is a bit of a haze."

"If you had surgery, they definitely would have administered the nutrient solution either during or after. It's standard procedure." He dries his hands on a paper towel. "Is there anything else I can help you with?"

"No, thank you. I'm sure you have lots of patients to attend."

He nods, and disappears into the corridor. I wait for his clippy-clopping to diminish. The third bag is thinner under my fingers, the fluid thicker. I follow the black tube to the port in Marvyn's hand. Thick tape masks the catheter, protecting the solution from the light.

"Axelle?"

I jump at the voice, masking the movement by tucking the sheets tighter around Marvyn.

Though nervousness wouldn't be totally unexpected.

A woman stands in the doorway. "The tribunal is ready for you."

"Thank you, Passenger."

She spins on her heel and I trail after her, hesitating at the door. Marvyn continues to sleep the sleep of the comatose, his cocktail of drugs drip-dripping into his system.

Marvyn. Patient seven hundred and fifty-three.

* * *

Whispers swell as I walk down the steps to the floor of the amphitheatre, the seats packed apart from essential personnel, such as the Passengers caring for the patients in the hospital. I fix my gaze on the table at the edge of the stage, two lone chairs below and facing it, spaced ten metres apart. Mallory occupies one seat, the only person not watching my descent. His arms are folded so tight, his muscles threaten to pop the seams of his shirt. I halt beside the unoccupied chair and nod to the three Elders presiding at the table.

"Axelle of the first generation," Elderman Vail says from his position in the middle, "you have invoked your right as squad leader to call a tribunal to judge the actions of Mallory of the fifth generation, is that correct?"

"That is correct, Elderman Vail."

I wish I had the stony expression of a Verdanian. I can remove the emotion from my voice but I'm not sure what my face is up to. I used to do anything to get Vail's attention— late-night studying so I could answer every question, hours of practice until I was the best shot, ferocity in battle to emulate his kill tally. A word of praise from Vail made my goddamn year. I wanted to be him.

Now, when I look at him, I see Thommonn's ravaged face. I hear the casual cruelty of his voice. I should demand a tribunal to judge *his* actions.

But one step at a time.

"Then please recount the events as you saw them." Vail turns his head, the stone on its long cord jiggling over his shoulder. "Mallory of the fifth, you may interject if you feel the testimony is not a fair and accurate representation of your actions but this right is not to be abused."

Vail stares until Mallory gives a quiet, "Yes, Elderman." Three pairs of eyes zero on me, not counting the thousands drilling into my back. Elderwoman Carniss slumps in her chair, and the wood creaks in protest. The final Elder, Elderman Thorn, places his elbows on the table and rests his pointed chin on his clasped hands. His dark irises are indistinguishable from his pupils.

I don't bother rehashing the small insubordinations—the back-talk, shooting the water-dragon. They're not what I want Mallory's blood for. I jump straight to the clearing. The Verdanian children doing nothing more violent than playing tag. I'm not good at guessing ages—Verdanians all seem ancient—but they must have been under ten. Neither had to die. Had they been allowed to slip back into the jungle unharmed as I'd ordered, I doubt we would have seen their mother. She would have ushered them far away from the monsters and their guns.

How long does it take firm Verdanian flesh to rot? I should ask Zorian if his father can contact his tribe while he's absent to at least collect their stones. Maybe someone in the travelling party has a blood connection with a mate back home.

I should have thought of it last night before I got distracted by Zorian's hands. And his mouth. And his tongue…

My cheeks flush. Maybe the Elders will think it's due to my passionate testimony. Mallory's arms get tighter and tighter as my story progresses, his mulish jaw thrust into the air.

"What is the word you spoke—dool?" Elderman Thorn says when I finish.

That's the first question he wants to ask? Not, why did you slaughter two unarmed children, you murdering bastard, Mallory?

"Dwyl," I say. "It means 'go' in Anann."

"I thank you for the correction." Thorn's black eyes are unblinking and anything but thankful. "How is it that you know such useful words in our enemies' language?"

Thorn—as prickly as his name and suspicious of everything.

I keep my gaze level on his. "Passenger Gotiva has been kind enough to teach me during self-directed learning. I've expanded that from the little I've heard in the field."

"Passenger Gotiva," Thorn says, tossing his voice to the assembled Passenger rows, "have you heard this 'dool' word before?"

He definitely pronounces it wrong out of spite.

"No, Elderman, that is not a word in my repertoire but it seems I should have quizzed my pupil instead of assuming I know everything," Gotiva says.

A soft chuckle ripples through the crowd.

I add Gotiva to my list of potential allies. Not so much for the Verdanians unless I can prove to him his wife left of her own volition.

Thorn focuses on me, his black brows elevated. "And how did you deduce the meaning of the word without the help of your learned teacher?"

Because I'm not just a lump of muscle in a battlesuit?

Zorian also told me what it meant.

"The word was generally repeated with the same gestures."

I wave my arm to demonstrate.

"That could easily mean 'pull back' or 'get out of here.'"

"Yes, both interpretations would have been acceptable given the situation," I say, my voice deadpan.

Someone muffles a snort. Brindan, for sure.

Thorn's skin is too tight over his skull to show much of a frown but he purses his thin mouth. "It could easily mean 'attack.'"

"Given it was used during retreat, I deduced it was unlikely."

Plus the word for attack is 'ionnsaill'.

Elderwoman Carniss slaps her palm on the table and everyone in the amphitheatre jumps. "While this language lesson is fascinating, let's return to the matter at hand. Mallory of the fifth, do you deny these allegations?"

I allow myself to slide into my seat, my legs a little wobbly after Thorn's inquisition. Mallory heaves himself upright, hands clasped behind his back.

"No, Elderwoman," he says, sliding a glance at me, "but I saw a threat and eliminated it."

Oh, yes, two unarmed children, how threatening. What were they going to do, gnaw on his ankles?

"Your squad leader ordered you to hold your fire. Twice. Yet you disobeyed."

His chin thrusts higher. "I believed her judgement was compromised."

My fingernails dig into the wood of my seat. I force myself to breathe slowly.

He can't possibly know anything. Unless Glennis told him about the tablet and he made his own deductions.

Oh, fuck. This could get very bad.

"Compromised how?" Carniss says.

"By thinking of them as children."

"They *were* children, Mallory," I say in a rush.

He shakes his head at me. "They may have been young but they weren't children. They were future warriors."

And what are our children? We farm them in pods and train them for battle. We don't play tag. We learn how to kill.

I open my mouth but Carniss gives another table slap.

"Nevertheless, Mallory of the fifth, it is not your job to second-guess your squad leader or her judgement. Your job is to follow orders."

The righteous smugness in Mallory's face dims. Carniss whispers to Vail. Thorn hasn't moved his stare from me the entire time.

"We've heard enough." Vail stands and surveys the crowd. "We will complete our deliberations, and return. Please remain seated while we do so."

The three Elders exit to the rooms behind the stage. The murmur of voices rises to a roar behind me. People call my name but I keep my eyes on the empty table. Mallory slumps in his chair, his body twisted away.

How many lashes will they give him? Disobeying two direct orders, even if it was the same order repeated, and murdering unarmed children. He won't be able to lie on his back for weeks.

Satisfaction burns in my chest. It doesn't make their deaths any less tragic but Mallory will damn sure remember this day. No more kids will get slaughtered on my watch.

The Elders return after ten minutes. They probably had their decision after one but wanted it to look proper. Vail remains standing while Thorn and Carniss take their seats.

"Mallory of the fifth generation," Vail says, "you have

been deemed guilty for the purpose of this tribunal. The punishment will be three lashes."

I leap to my feet before my brain can intercede and tell me to shut the hell up and sit the fuck down.

"Three lashes for murdering *children?*"

My voice echoes around the amphitheatre. Thorn's gaze whips towards me so fast, I feel the sting of it on my skin. Vail folds his hands on his stomach and watches me until the ghost of my words has faded. His stone hangs from its cord like a sickly yellow eye.

"Children who, in a few years, would have been old enough to hold a spear or fire an arrow," he says, his voice calm. As a snake is calm right before it strikes. "One would be forgiven for doubting your judgement after such a statement, Axelle of the first. It would be a shame for your stellar record to be expunged by the need for reconditioning."

Icy sweat collects in the small of my back, not helped by the humid breath of the crowd. I clench my fists at my sides to hide my shaking hands. I swallow the anger, the impotence. It lodges in my throat but I'm no use to anyone if I become a drone programmed to kill.

"Please forgive my outburst, Elderman," I choke out. "It was the first time I'd seen their young. They look like children… but they are not."

If Zorian were here, the lie would drive him to his knees.

Vail nods. "I hope I will not have to remind you again."

My jaw aches with the effort of keeping my mouth closed. Mallory's eyes dart between me and Vail, his sentence forgotten for a more interesting spectacle—Axelle getting the first smudge on her pristine record as perfect soldier. He looks like he's practically pissing himself with glee.

God, I hate my species right now.

Vail produces a coiled whip from behind his back. "Axelle, as squad leader, you may administer the punishment or nominate a proxy."

"I'll do it." The words are growlier than I intended but Mallory gulps when he meets my glare, and I decide it's worth it.

Three fucking lashes. What a joke.

I accept the whip from Vail. The leather creaks under my palm. Carniss and Thorn remove our chairs and fix two poles into slots in the floor, twisting to lock them in place. Mallory unbuttons his shirt and pulls his vest over his head. Carniss and Thorn tie his hands, one to each pole, stretching his arms out to the sides. Mallory flexes the slabs of muscle in his shoulders. Could be anticipation, or involuntary, but I bet it's for the benefit of the crowd.

He has never looked so bloated and ugly.

I march to my position at the base of the stairs. The whip uncoils, slithering on the stone. I wave it a little to really cultivate that hissing sound. Mallory's shoulders hunch.

That's right, Barbie. It may only be three but they will count. And they will hurt.

I stop moving, letting the quiet fill my mind. Mallory's muscles get tighter and tighter. I wait. Wait some more. The tension builds in the straining bodies behind me.

I flick my wrist and crack the whip off to Mallory's left. His feet clear the ground but he doesn't wet himself, and that's disappointing.

"Axelle of the first, this is supposed to be chastisement, not torture," Vail says.

You know all about that, don't you, Vail?

My fingernails dig into my palm along with the handle of the whip.

"Apologies, Elderman Vail," I say in something close to my normal voice. "It's been a while. I just wanted a practice shot."

Vail smooths his maroon trousers and takes his seat beside his peers.

"Please proceed," he says.

I suck in a breath and let it out slow. I raise my arm. The whip whispers on the stone. I slice it forward and a red line appears on Mallory's back from left shoulder, across his spine, to his lumbar area. The crack batters the air in the amphitheatre. Mallory flinches but doesn't cry out.

I want him to cry out.

The whip flies. I put my whole body into it. Mallory stands utterly still, no sound passing his lips. Blood trickles down to stain the waistband of his trousers.

It's not enough.

The third blow nearly dislocates my vertebrae. The crack rings in my ears. Mallory turns his head and smirks at me.

Punishment taken like a man. He can swan off and have Fionna fawn over him for being brave while he's learned nothing and regrets *nothing*.

How is that justice?

The tail of the whip catches Mallory's cheek and, what do you know, it wipes the smirk right off. Though, if it didn't, the fifth, sixth and seventh blows sure would have. Now he cries out. The Elders seem to have frozen to their seats. I stare at Vail while my arm rises and falls, rises and falls. The cracks blend into one. There's a vibration in my chest but I can't hear anything over the song of the whip. It howls in my veins.

Mallory collapses to his knees, his back awash with red, the waist of his trousers dark. I force myself to stop.

The monster in me wants to flay him to the bone.

My panting fills the space. I spit the taste of metal from my mouth.

"Mallory of the fifth," I say between breaths, "consider yourself chastised right out of my squad."

The whip clatters from my numb fingers, loud in the silence screaming through the hall.

27

"What were you thinking!?"

"I wasn't. That's the problem."

Zorian sits against a tree, his arms holding me close, my back tucked into his chest. I've mastered the dream space enough I can show him scenes of my day, playing in front of us as if we're watching a movie.

"You have to promise you will not do anything like that again," he says.

I wiggle my toes, level with Zorian's slim calves, his legs pressed to mine in a long line where I sit between them.

He has such pretty feet.

"It's not something I plan on repeating. I threw up as soon as I got to my pod then had a panic attack when I was washing Mallory's blood off in the shower. I kept expecting the Elders to burst in and drag me through Home Base naked."

Zorian's arms tighten until I'm glad I don't have to breathe in the dream space.

"Will they come for you?"

I tilt my head to look at him. His face is grave, his pale, pistachio hair flopping into his eyes.

What I wouldn't give for his cheekbones and legs.

"Do you worry about me, Zorian?" I say, my voice light to

215

mask the churning in my stomach.

If I didn't have Zorian to meet in dreams, I would have lain awake all night fretting, sweating through my pyjamas and rubbing my cheek raw.

Though if I hadn't met Zorian, I would still be that deluded, lonely soldier plagued by nightmares. I would have died in battle and never known the truth of why we were fighting.

I still don't but I'm getting closer.

"Every day," he says, and tucks his face into my hair. "You are imprisoned with those people. You put yourself in danger when you question them. You risk everything while I am safe beyond your wall."

"Hey, it'll be okay." I try to turn in his arms but he hugs me closer. "I'll speak to Vail tomorrow. Tell him something about Mallory's constant insubordination and say I just snapped. A temporary insanity. I knew the risks when we started, Zorian."

"As did I and it seemed worth it for the goal. Now, I am not so sure." He sighs and his cool breath tickles the nape of my neck.

"Peace between our people is still worth it."

He doesn't reply but keeps me pinned so I can't see his face. I struggle but I might as well be wrestling with the planet for the good it does. He is one immovable object.

"You cannot bait them, Axelle," he says after a couple of silent minutes. "You see how they hurt us. They can hurt you, too."

I stroke his thighs since they're the only part of him I can reach. His trousers hit below the knee. I trace the intricate weave, fibres this time, not leaves.

"They didn't care about the children. Even back on Earth,

there was an honour code during wartime. There were still things soldiers could do that were unforgivable. Mallory deserved more than three lashes for what he did." My fingers tense on Zorian's thighs and I force them to relax.

He lifts me into his lap, sliding his legs beneath mine. His mouth nuzzles my ear, and I stop breathing. Not that I was breathing much before from how tight he's holding me.

"I wish this was real so you could feel what I feel," he whispers.

"Tell me what you feel."

His lips find the soft spot below my ear. "It is like I want to carry you far away to protect you. I want to show you to my father and say, 'Here is a human who is kind and brave and cares, sometimes too much for her own safety.' It is excitement and fear. And so many things I cannot name."

"Zorian..."

He shakes his head, his mouth curving against my neck. "My father has noticed how eagerly I go to bed when once I would sit up for hours to watch the stars."

Everything I should say forms a lump and lodges in my throat so I say nothing at all. The churning spreads from my stomach to my chest and blurs my eyes.

"Promise me, Axelle," Zorian says. "Promise me you will be careful."

I nod, and a tear slips down my cheek.

"I promise," I say, my voice hiding nothing.

He relaxes his hold, and I turn in his arms. My mouth finds his, seeking comfort, seeking things I can't name, either.

Things I should not want.

28

"I'm sure you all have questions about what happened yesterday," I say, pacing in front of my squad in the classroom module.

Veterans only. We have some sensitive shit to discuss.

"Not so much a question, more a statement." Pacal slides me a grin. "You are one scary bitch, Axe."

The others allow themselves a chuckle, though it's hesitant, as if they're not quite sure whether it's grounds for me to batter them, too.

I return Pacal's grin. "Yes, I am, Strife. Just don't disobey my orders and you'll be fine."

Tension leaks from the room and the laughter comes naturally. Relieved glances flicker between Loyanne and Dante.

"But Mallory wasn't entirely wrong. My judgement *has* been compromised."

My squad seems to suck in a breath as one, half with their mouths agog. Glennis is the only person who doesn't look surprised.

I said as much to Vail this morning but only in the context of Mallory. I was contrite, embarrassed, referential. Everything a good soldier should be. I'd allowed Mallory leeway because

218

I'd been sleeping with him. When it ended, he got petty and tested my patience with his subtle disobedience. It came to a head yesterday when he smirked at me at the end of his whipping to prove he was not chastised.

Vail seemed to accept it. He gave me a stern warning on getting emotionally involved with subordinates.

I said nothing on my outburst concerning the Verdanian kids.

"What do you mean, Axe?" Loyanne offers tentatively. "I'm not sure about anybody else but I understand why you reacted like that yesterday. They… they *were* children. I don't care what Vail says. They should have had the chance to grow up. Then, if they attacked in the jungle, I would have killed them. That's how it's supposed to be. Not… not…"

Dante pats her shoulder. She swipes a shaking hand across her scarred mouth. I note the expressions of disagreement or confusion on the others while she composes herself. Brindan, Lili, Karine.

"I agree with everything you said, Loyanne, expect one thing—that this is how it's supposed to be." I stop and stare out the vertical window in the door.

It's raining outside, speckles dampening the glass. A streak of yellow runs through the wet, not even pausing to splash in the puddles on the concrete.

Have I ever seen the younger generations play a game that wasn't a teaching moment or a mock-war? Just for *fun.*

God, how blind I've been.

"Do any of you know why we're fighting?"

I think of when Zorian said those words, standing over the boulder that pinned me. I was so certain he was going to kill me, so secure in my prejudice, goading him almost. That person could never have imagined where I am today.

"Because someone never taught the assholes how to share?" Nolana says, one arm slung around Glennis. Or partly around Glennis since any normal human would struggle to span those shoulders.

"This is a wide and rich land. There's more than enough resources for everyone."

Karine tucks a red strand of hair behind her ear. "Maybe they think that because our ancestors destroyed a planet, we'll destroy theirs."

"Are they wrong?"

My question drops into a pool of silence, and ripples outward.

"Look at Mallory, loath as I am to use him as any kind of example. Killing everything because it gets in his way or it's gross or it tastes nice. Planning to raze part of the jungle to build his house. Multiply that by everyone in Home Base and that's a huge chunk of ravaged land."

"Why do you think we're fighting, Axe?" Loyanne says, her quiet voice demanding attention, like any good squad leader's.

I boost myself onto the desk at the front of the room, my heels kicking the wood. "Honestly, I don't know. But we've been lied to about the little stuff. I want to find out how big the lies get."

"What little stuff?" Loyanne says.

"Like their blood is poisonous." I meet the gaze of everyone in the room. "It's not poisonous. I've drunk some myself."

This inspires a mini-outburst of disbelief. Brindan wrinkles his nose, Lili's expression identical. Karine inches away as if I'm contagious. Pacal opens his mouth.

28

"No, Strife," I butt in, "I haven't sampled any of their other bodily fluids. But back when I was trapped in that cave after Mallory's idiocy with the detonators, I wasn't entirely truthful myself. The Verdanian was alive, initially. He knocked my helmet off. I got his blood in my mouth when we struggled. I'm still here, ergo, it's not poisonous."

The full truth of how I got the blood in my mouth and just how alive the Verdanian is, is probably a bit much for them at this stage. Particularly as I spent most of last night snogging his face off. I managed to take a couple of breaths in between to make a suggestion and hear his response.

Zorian's father has a temporary blood connection with his aunt while she acts as interim leader in his absence. Zorian is going to say he meant to tell him about seeing a nomad with two children on the day they left on the journey. It looked like she needed help but ran away. His father will get his aunt to search around the clearing. When they find the bodies, they'll take the stones.

It's a flimsy as hell story but it's the best we can do without mentioning the somewhat sacrilegious blood connection between a human and a Verdanian. His father might ignore it since the supposed sighting was weeks ago.

Then it was right back to kissing Zorian—and myself—senseless. Who knew just kissing could be so damn hot?

"Propaganda is not an unusual tool in wartime," Dante says, his expression thoughtful. "Make the enemy vile, terrifying, hateful to inspire the soldiers to fight. It doesn't mean everything is a lie."

"That's true, Hulk, it doesn't. But something isn't right. And that's why I've been doing some digging."

I describe my foray into the dissection lab and the discoveries I made in the basement, minus Fenna and Dalrainenna. Again—too much for now.

Nolana slaps Glennis on the arm. "Is that why you were acting so secretive? Girl, I thought you were cheating."

"She was—with me." I raise my hands at Nolana's scowl. "In a purely non-sexual way. I needed her expertise."

I finish with what was on the tablet—the medical files, blends and recovery rates.

"So, the pertinent questions are: why are we told we don't capture live specimens when they're torturing Verdanians in a secret underground lab? Why did they lie about people being able to speak fluent Anann? How does torturing Verdanians relate to the medical files, if it even does? What does it mean that Marvyn is patient seven hundred and fifty-three? I can't ask an Elder about the first three but I can seek out the answer to the fourth. And that's where I need your help."

If Marvyn is the next patient then he must be receiving a blend, likely whatever's in the black bag or something else hooked up when no one's there to watch. For easy access, the blends must be stored in the hospital, with information on what's in them and what they're for.

I visited Marvyn again this morning in the hopes I could snoop around but Passengers constantly flit about the place and pop out of nowhere, like the one who asked where I was going when I opened a random door in a previously unoccupied corridor. I told her I was looking for the bathroom.

I slide off the desk to pace some more. "Let me be clear— this is not an order to help me. It's volunteer only. Getting involved could, at best, mean you get whipped or, at worst, the next class we take together is a practical on the wonders of behavioural reconditioning."

Karine shivers, her hair swinging forward to brush her jaw. "I do *not* want to turn out like Maximilian."

Max refused to kill another Verdanian after his first, though he wasn't the one who delivered the mortal wound. She was younger than Zorian, with golden eyes and blonde hair that could almost be human. A lucky blow knocked her from the trees. Max approached with his gun. She lay on the ground, stunned. Instead of arrogance or defiance or nothing at all, he saw fear. She beseeched him in Anann, holding out one lovely, pale arm.

And that's when his squadmate caught up and emptied his magazine into her face.

Max may have been okay if he'd continued to go on battles but he refused to be involved in anything that led to killing, even if he wasn't the one to pull the trigger. He was very vocal on his opinion that not all Verdanians are monsters.

He disappeared for a month. The boy who rejoined his squad looked like Max and sounded like Max but the similarities ended there. Max loved debating with his squadmates and anyone who would listen on anything from the ethics of eating meat to speculating on the intricacies of Verdanian culture. Now, he is a silent, sombre figure who does what he's told and seethes with an unnatural hatred for Verdanians bordering on psychosis.

His kill count is ten.

"None of us want to turn out like Max," I say to Karine, "but that's the risk and that's why I won't order you to help me. However, it *is* an order to tell no one of what we've discussed today. *No one* outside this room."

I find my eyes on Brindan and he fidgets in his chair,

dropping his gaze.

"Anyone who doesn't want to participate leaves now, with no judgement from me. But if you stay, we're in this together and it may not be pretty."

Not a single one of my squad moves from their seats.

Fuck you and your lack of emotional investment, Elderman Vail. I love every one of these bastards.

29

We hit the hospital the next evening in that somnambulant phase after dinner and before bed. The lights in the corridors and walls dim alongside the setting sun, a hush descending in preparation for night.

A hush if you don't include the squeak-squeak of soft-soled Passenger shoes.

We start in Marvyn's room, where Lili and Brindan will stay as decoys to explain why the rest of us are milling about the hospital.

"Why don't we just cut this open and see what's inside?" Brindan says, nodding at the black-swathed fluid bag on Marvyn's drip stand.

"It's helping him, I don't want to mess with it. Plus, looking at some liquid indistinguishable from other liquids isn't going to tell us much. There's got to be a record of what's in it someplace, particularly if there's a bunch of different blends."

"Are you sure this is the answer?" Glennis rests one sizeable hip on the corner of Marvyn's bed. "Maybe there's nothing more sinister here than standard medical research to improve the survival rate of their most precious commodity."

Marvyn was awake earlier. Groggy but pleased to see us before he slipped into a painkiller coma. He asked where

Mallory was.

"If that's all it is, I'll be relieved. But I still need answers for the other questions. And I want the torture to stop."

Loyanne, Dante, Pacal and Lili agree with me about the torture, though Lili isn't ready to make friends with the Verdanians. I doubt any of them are but I'd be fine with a distrustful ceasefire. Nolana, Karine and Glennis are on the fence about the torture. Brindan thinks they deserve it but I suspect the lingering stain of Mallory's influence rather than callousness.

I check my watch. "Let Operation Search and Distract commence."

Loyanne and Dante, Pacal and Karine, and Glennis and Nolana pair off, leaving me to scout. We move as a unit through the hospital, the pairs intercepting any roving Passengers while I search door to door. We communicate using our microphones, carefully removed from our battlesuits.

The Passengers are an affable lot. They stop to answer questions, chat about the weather—raining again, you say? For any who are not lulled by gentle conversation, one of the pair guides them to Marvyn's room on a pretence—a machine beeping, an empty drip bag, Marvyn seeming agitated. They arrive in his ward to the miraculous, "Huh, it's/he's not doing it now." By the time they return, we've disappeared into the next quadrant.

We're no strangers to searching for crap.

The first and second floors hold wards and cupboards, the shelves filled with dressings, normal fluid and antibiotic bags, drugs, cleaning supplies and bedsheets. We skip the consulting rooms, the staff break areas and the canteen. The surgical suite on the ground floor takes some finesse. Pacal fakes a seizure, drawing people away from the doors while the rest of us sneak inside, leaving a distraught Karine to flap over his twitching, foaming body and impede as much as possible. The other two pairs break off to draw any personnel away with the excuse of they 'got lost' before they're escorted out.

I shudder at the gleaming metal tables and shining surgical instruments lined up in sterile packets. There's no surgery happening so the place is empty.

"If it weren't too risky," I murmur into my mic, "I'd take you under the dissection lab and show you a real nightmare. Then none of you would be on the fence about the torture."

The chemical smell of the hospital is almost the same, minus the burnt-honey odour of distressed Verdanians.

"Do you think they have more prisoners?" Loyanne says, her voice muffled. "I hate to think—oh, Elderwoman, I'm so sorry! I believe I've taken a wrong turn. I was looking for Marvyn of the seventh generation…"

Loyanne is graciously escorted out of the surgical suite, followed closely by Dante and Glennis. I tip-toe through operating theatres, prep rooms, scrub rooms and labs. The cupboards contain the typical hospital paraphernalia. I hide in an x-ray room until the flap of footsteps has passed.

"Reconvene in the lobby," I say.

Five of us descend into the basement, Pacal and Karine swallowed into the system after Pacal's sudden malady. He'll get a comfortable, semi-private night in the hospital so it's not a bad deal.

"We're being ushered out," Lili says in her high, whispering voice. "Too late for visitors."

"Copy that. Return to your barracks; we'll debrief tomorrow."

The chill of the basement creeps into my skin, colder than the air-conditioned levels above. Few lights are on and the shadows collect in the corners. Bare concrete stretches along the corridor, a rusted hospital bed pushed against the wall. The sheets are crumpled into a ball, with dried splotches on the material and the mattress.

Loyanne rubs her arms. "Now, *this* is where the sinister stuff happens."

"Go up top and guard the stairs," I say. "Nolana, Glennis— cover the far end."

Nolana and Glennis creep down the corridor and disappear around the corner. Loyanne and Dante climb back to ground level, leaving me alone in the semi-dark. The first couple of doors open onto dusty rooms, the third—an office.

"Elderman Vail," Dante says in a calm voice, "we were just on our way out from visiting Marvyn of the seventh. Um, yes, Axelle was here. Pacal took ill. She may be with him."

I flinch. Why does Vail want to know where I am?

The next door sticks. I slam my shoulder into it and stumble into the room. A light pings on. My breath huffs out in a cloud of white. Metal shelves occupy the cramped space and each one contains an opaque bag—black, blue, white. Charts hang on the end of each shelf, the writing too small to read from my position.

Holy motherlode.

"Good evening, Axelle of the first," a voice says behind me, empty of all inflection.

Training stops me from screeching like a skreeingbird and leaping into the shelving units. My bones creak as I turn.

"First—" I lick my lips and try again. "First Minister Seabird.

Good evening, sir."

They're the only words I've ever spoken to him. Two months ago, I would have gushed myself into a puddle if he'd talked to me.

I hope Seabird thinks my shaking is down to the cold. Or his mighty presence.

Peridot is not a piercing colour but his eyes spear me to the core. He's a wiry man with a tuft of white hair, his face weathered, though not too worn for a guy in his eighties.

"Are you lost, Axelle of the first?" He adds a purr to my name, and my body erupts in goosebumps.

I promised Zorian I would be careful. *Is this careful?*

I force myself to walk towards Seabird, exiting the room as if its contents are of no consequence. It's not warmer beside him in the corridor.

"Pacal had some kind of seizure and one of my squad told me he was down here," I say with nary a wobble. "They must have been mistaken. It's a bit too peaceful."

Seabird stares at me, and a bead of sweat slithers between my shoulders. He cocks a white eyebrow at the door opposite marked 'Mortuary'.

I stifle a giggle. 'Peaceful' is our abort code.

"Hijinks, perhaps?" Seabird says, and clasps his hands in front of him. A bracelet of stones circles each wrist.

His uniform is bright, arterial red.

I swallow, and my tongue clicks in my mouth. "Perhaps."

"One should be vigilant in squashing such revelry. It detracts the mind. One must always focus on the ultimate goal."

"Of course, sir," I say.

One wouldn't want to focus on anything else and realise

how much shit they've been fed, would one?

I admired his single-mindedness. His tenacity. He docked the *HMS Dòchas* in safe orbit around Verdana and delivered everyone to the ground. He fought off threats and established a haven in Home Base. He's the reason we're all here.

What if it was by dishonourable means rather than triumph over adversity?

"I wanted to catch you, Axelle of the first," he says, his gaze analysing me from head to toe before returning to sear my brain through my eyeballs, "and invite you for a nightcap."

He sweeps his arm out, and my numb legs stutter into ambulation. We climb the stairs, my weight mostly supported and propelled by the banister.

I give the only acceptable response: "I would be honoured, sir."

* * *

First Minister Seabird's quarters are crafted from the hull of the shuttle vessel. He has a separate bedroom, receiving room, kitchen and study. 'HMS Dòchas' is branded into the wall above his bed.

I won some time to compose myself by checking on Pacal to continue my ruse. He'd wangled a bed beside Marvyn, not that he needs the intensive care. I splashed water on my face and Pacal wished me good luck. I told him if I didn't turn up tomorrow, it's because I've been booted into behavioural reconditioning.

"It's a last resort," he said, aiming for comforting. "It's the bogeyman they dangle over all of us."

To focus our minds, perhaps?

Seabird hands me my nightcap of wine. The liquid clings to the glass, thick and dark red. I don't want anything stronger in case I babble about something I shouldn't. Elderman Vail accepts a beaker of amber liquid, seated next to me on a long, cushioned chair I've forgotten the name of and only seen during Earth lessons.

His presence at our nightcap was an unwelcome surprise. I almost bolted but where would I go? There are few places to hide in Home Base and as much as I like the jungle, I'm not tromping through it in the dark.

"I have been most impressed with your performance since you took up the mantle of squad leader, Axelle," Seabird says, swirling his amber drink and perching on the pilot's chair opposite Vail and me.

He finally dropped the 'of the first' part but him saying my name still gives me shivers.

"Thank you, sir. I've been doing my best."

"Forgive me, then, if I am mystified by your recent behaviour." He sips and offers me a bland smile.

I glance at Vail, who reclines on the seat, cradling his glass. His face betrays nothing.

He's learned a thing or two from the Verdanians.

"As I discussed with Elderman Vail this morning, I let my relationship with Mallory of the fifth undermine my authority. It was unprofessional but it won't happen again."

I gulp the wine, and the glass clinks against my teeth.

"Quite," Seabird says, "but that is not what I am referring to. Your outburst about the Verdanian younglings was perplexing."

I sip to drown the pulse in my mouth. The wine is bitter and coats my tongue.

"I admit their appearance confused me, too, sir," I say with commendable serenity. "We're trained to defend ourselves against spears and arrows and brute strength. It felt wrong to strike when they were unarmed. But I understand now. They were young but they were warriors in the making."

Except not all Verdanian children grow up to become warriors, unlike ours.

"You seem to have lost your focus of late—a concern shared by Elderman Vail and myself. This outburst; ignoring the tribunal-mandated punishment. Asking questions on our origins."

My fingers clench on the glass. I lower it into my lap, my spine straight, every muscle tense.

"Is it unnatural to be curious? I want to learn everything I can about where we came from, why we're here"—I meet Seabird's piercing gaze—"why the war started."

"There is an Earth saying about curiosity and cats that may be pertinent."

"Cats, sir? The domesticated water-tiger creature?"

"Never mind. Curiosity is not unnatural." He holds his drink up to the light and amber shadows dance on his hand. "But your curiosity started only a few weeks ago. Prior to that, you did what you were told."

Was I really that compliant?

I clutch my glass tighter to keep myself from stroking my scar.

"I've always enjoyed learning, sir. I believe 'knowledge is power' is another Earth saying."

Get that up you, you controlling bastard.

"Knowledge can be dangerous," Vail says, giving me the side-eye.

"Indeed." Seabird tilts his drink towards Vail. "Too much knowledge can obscure rather than enlighten. Cause one to doubt. Do you have doubts, Axelle?"

I ease a breath in and out. Exhaustion wants me to slump in the chair and shut my eyes, not helped by this barbed interview where one wrong answer could see me impaled.

"I doubt I can keep everyone alive sometimes," I say, my voice light, "but, otherwise, I like to think I'm a confident person."

Seabird's eyes connect with mine like a physical slap. "Be wary that confidence does not become arrogance. No one is untouchable in this harsh world of ours."

I take a sip to stop myself saying, "Not even you?"

It's amazing how quickly admiration can turn to revulsion, even without hard evidence of evildoing.

Vail would never have tortured those prisoners without Seabird's approval.

"Thank you, sir," I say instead. "I'll be mindful of that."

"Please do. It would be unfortunate if one such as yourself needed reconditioning. Why, it would be enough for *me* to doubt the efficacy of our training programme."

"That won't be necessary, sir," I say, cursing the wobble in my voice.

"I hope not, Axelle of the first"—cue shudder—"I sincerely hope not."

Vail tosses back his drink, his ponytail brushing the top edge of the wide chair.

"Never forget who the enemy is," he says. "They may look pretty, even delicate, but they are vicious. And they will never tire of fighting us."

Lies, I want to hiss. Do you even believe your own bullshit?

I place my half-finished glass carefully on a small table and treat both of them to a smile as bland as Seabird's.

"I have no doubt who the enemy is, sir," I say. "Not anymore."

<h1 style="text-align:center">30</h1>

I'm the perfect soldier for the next week and a half, excluding my dreams. The knowledge of the bags in the hospital basement is an itch in my brain but I can't scratch it yet. The eyes of the Elders follow me everywhere, not just Vail and the First Minister. I work twice as hard, attending training, lessons, extra lessons. I assist McBurnie with the artificial insemination of the next generation, a gruelling yet delicate process.

He's the only one who doesn't watch me like he's waiting for me to fail.

Zorian starts his journey home. It'll take six weeks with such a large group but then I could meet him in real life again. A terrifying yet exhilarating prospect.

His aunt found no trace of the woman or her children in the clearing, no signs of animals dragging them away, only trampled grass. It's possible the father removed their bodies. I imagine he'll have vengeance on his mind if he ever sees another human.

And the vicious circle goes round and around.

I cuddle Zorian in my dreams. I lie on top of him and listen to his hearts and his voice rumbling through his chest as he tells me stories. Okay, sometimes I remove my vest for half-naked cuddling. It feels amazing to be pressed to all that smooth, hard coolness, his hands stroking my bare back.

Temptation whispers at me to take off my shorts, to guide his hands lower. The desire increases each night and goes achingly unleashed. It tingles with every caress, every glide of his mouth and touch of his tongue until every part of me is throbbing and swollen.

Does he feel the same?

The thought makes it more difficult to resist, not easier. Maybe if one of us gets off, it'll relieve the pressure a bit.

I'm scared to go further. Scared my self-control will vanish at the same speed as my clothes.

So we cuddle.

My squad's month on the wall protects me a little longer. I almost forgot. Other squad leaders don't include themselves in the rota but it's an abuse of privilege and leads to behind-the-back sniping from their squads. I do my week of night shifts like everyone else.

It means I don't see Zorian. I work when he sleeps and I sleep when he travels. I stay up as long as I can during the day after my final shift to readjust to normal patterns.

My eyes close and Zorian smiles at me, his feet sinking into the sand beside the pool in his special place.

It's possible I've been asleep for hours before he went to bed.

I throw myself at him. My legs wrap around his waist, my mouth on his. He's solid so he doesn't stagger. His hands slide up my legs to cup my butt.

"I missed you," I say.

He smirks. "I can tell."

He sits on the sand and stretches out on his back, drawing

me with him since I haven't stopped kissing him yet. I snuggle into his chest. Restless jitters squiggle in my stomach. I push myself up and straddle his hips, my hands on his belly. He flexes a tiny bit, barely a hip roll, and my head falls back. It feels too damn good. I want to see, *have* to see. Touching is okay. Just a little touching…

I scoot back. His trousers are green, of course, and fastened with a cord. One tug unties the knot. I slip my thumbs under the waist to loosen it, my fingertips on his hipbones. Zorian watches me with wide eyes. I hold his gaze and peel his trousers off, shuffling backwards in the sand. The jungle falls still. Zorian seems to be holding his breath. I finally let myself look.

Words like 'carved' and 'marble' and 'perfection' don't do him justice. I've seen his torso from the day we met since all Verdanians run around half-naked but the rest…

I trail a finger from his stomach, down the line of his pelvis, to his thigh. Every part of him is hairless and neat. I like it. Who am I kidding? I want to lick all that pale skin.

I shift between his legs. Something close to panic flashes in his eyes.

"What are you doing?"

"Verdanians don't do this either?"

"I do not know what you are doing."

I lean closer and whisper to his groin, "Isn't it obvious?"

He swallows, propped on his elbows to watch me. I blow softly on him and he shudders, his hands fisting in the sand.

"How *do* Verdanians have sex?" I say, and he struggles to focus on me. "Is it only a penis-in-the-vagina thing?"

His gaze darts around the silent jungle.

Sometimes I forget he's only eighteen.

"Mating is for reproduction," he says, squirming a little. "For forming alliances."

"How boring."

I place a kiss on his inner thigh, and he jumps. Ribs heave beneath silky skin. Every tremble, every in-drawn breath, pulses between my legs, urging me to rip off my shorts and mount him. To welcome that long, hard coolness into my heat.

Shit. Both of us can't be naked at the same time. I don't trust myself.

"Have you ever had sex?" I say while I tell my libido to behave.

He blinks at me. "I am finding it hard to concentrate."

"Or are you avoiding the question?"

I nuzzle the scar on his other thigh. It gives me a ground-level view of a certain pillar of his anatomy.

"I will not be able to answer questions if you do that."

Since I'm finding it hard to concentrate myself, I crawl up his body to kiss his mouth. His height stops me from rubbing myself on intimate areas.

Which is probably just as well.

I ruin it by returning to the straddling position. His hands release their desperate grip on the sand and pin me in place. Then he moves beneath me.

Oh, fuck. He knows what he's doing with his hips.

"You *have* had sex," I gasp.

"Once. We are not supposed to. Not until we are a bonded pair. But…"

"You got curious."

He grins at me, and my stomach clenches.

"I am always curious," he says.

"What was it like?"

I'm not jealous of this mystery female. That would be silly.

"We almost got caught."

"Did you have an orgasm?"

He cocks his head.

"Climax?" I say. "The release you get at the end of sex?"

His eyes slide away. "Does that mean it does not count?"

"Oh, it counts." I wriggle backwards to slot myself between his legs, my hands on his waist. "So, just sex? No fooling around?"

"What is fooling around?" he says, his voice leaping a decibel higher.

"What we've been doing—kissing, fondling." I give him a wicked grin. "Mouth stuff."

He stares at me. The pale column of his throat works.

"I think I have been missing out."

"You have no idea," I say, and lick him.

He jolts as if my tongue is electric. Maybe it is. I've certainly got tingles everywhere.

"Axelle…" He says my name on a groan and seems to want to add more but is having some trouble.

If this is his reaction already, the rest will be awesome.

I kiss up his shaft. Tension sings in his body. His fingers sink knuckle-deep into the sand. The whimpers low in his throat are noises I never thought to hear from a Verdanian.

They're so vulnerable.

"You know," I say, my voice strangled, "swear words help to relieve pressure."

His breath shivers in and out. He slumps onto his back.

"*Cock*," he says on an explosive sigh.

I chuckle. "That's one word for it. And what a magnificent

cock it is."

I wait for him to look at me. It takes ten adorable seconds. His pupils are dilated.

"Magnificent?"

God, the strain in his voice…

I suck the head of him into my mouth and hum my agreement. His spine bows, his moan so deep it vibrates through him and into me. I make my own happy noises around him, writhing on the ground. He's cool in my mouth, on my tongue—like ice water. That first, thirst-quenching glass. I drink him down. He wriggles and groans and arches his hips. I rub his belly, and I swear he purrs.

How to make a Verdanian lose all impassivity—treat him to a blow job. We've obviously been doing this war stuff all wrong. Laughter and fellatio have done more to disarm than any weapon I've ever seen.

I relax my throat, fighting the urge to breathe.

The last time I did this, I was his age. A stolen moment in the amphitheatre after everyone else filed out. I enjoyed it, enjoyed the rush of power at their response, knowing each quiver and whimper and, "Oh fuck yes," was due to my touch. They never returned the favour, tucking their dick into their trousers and buggering off while I was still on my knees. It soured my opinion of that particular act for a while. The guy died in battle the next day.

The gods of reciprocity are merciless.

I hold Zorian deep in my mouth, my lungs screaming for air until I remember I'm in the dream space and don't actually need to breathe. I could stay like this all night if I wanted to. No lockjaw, either. He fills my mouth, my throat, and I suck him in further. His hand flaps on the sand. I give him mine to hold and start to move up and down his shaft, my other hand wrapped around the base, squeezing on each upstroke.

"Axelle… I… I am…" The words dissolve into panting, his eyes wild.

I release him long enough to say, "It's okay, Zorian, you can climax in my mouth."

"Oh, fuck," he moans, and *I* almost come.

Now, he's corrupted.

My tongue swirls over him. He's so firm, it really is like sucking on stone. Every part is taut and slick and smooth. His breathing quickens, each exhalation ending on a whine. It's fucking hot. I increase my pace, sucking harder, squeezing harder. His hand crushes mine but dreams are safe. No pulverised bones for me. His shaking transfers between us. His hips buck, and I drive myself onto him. He cries out. Cool liquid spurts on the back of my throat, as sweet as his blood.

Is this how he actually tastes or how I think he should taste? It's not something he would know, unless he's been *really* curious. I'd have to do it in real life to compare.

Holy crap, real life.

A jangle of nerves fires straight to my belly. I picture our next meeting—walking towards him in the jungle, dropping to my knees, my eyes travelling up the long line of his body. Taking him into my mouth. The blood connection would enhance the experience, sharing the pressure, the tension, the heavy burst of pleasure while his blood throbs under my skin and his twin hearts thunder against my ribs.

I shiver and Zorian groans, my mouth still around him.

Sex in real life is moot. If I'm worried about Yannik crushing my pelvis with his bulk, Zorian, slim as he is, is strong enough to do it by accident. And those teeth could shred me before he realises what he's doing. If I snog him in real life, I may lose my tongue.

So just in dreams. Though I'm slightly concerned I'll turn into a slobbering love-puppy if he gets me out of my clothes and that would be a dent to the dispassionate squad leader persona I've built over the years.

His touch is addictive. The slide of his cool skin, the brand of his mouth. He's an ice cube in a world of heat and humidity. I want to rub him on my hot places.

Fooling around is easy to justify in the dream space, particularly as Zorian's not the only one who gets curious. But I'm dancing close to the edge now. Sex is dangerous if it's not casual and there's nothing casual about what we're doing. It's different to anything I've felt before, and not just because he's a whole other species.

There are enough similarities between humans and Verdanians for anyone to get confused.

He softens in my mouth, if stone can soften to pliant rock. I kiss the tip of him, and he twitches. Instead of telling him how cute he is, I snuggle into his side and hide my smile in his neck. The echo of his hearts whispers against my cheek so they must be beating pretty hard. I listen to them fade, lulled by the quiet. My own throbbing eases a bit.

Can you doze in the dream space?

Zorian rolls over, his leg across my thighs, pinning me as effectively as the boulder in the cave. My yelp wrestles with my pulse for dominance. I'm very aware he's naked and wet from my mouth. He props himself on one elbow, looking at me through a flop of green hair.

"Do human females climax without the blood connection?"

The words elude my understanding for a moment. Maybe

it's his completely unguarded expression, the flecks of gold in his eyes, contrasting the angles and softness of his face.

"Verdanian women can't orgasm?" I manage to splutter.

"Not in real life unless they are mated and share their partner's. Sometimes in the dream space, I think they recreate the experience."

"What a huge evolutionary injustice."

Zorian rests his hand low on my stomach. Level with my hipbones low. My pulse KOs my yelp and celebrates its victory by flapping all over the place. Zorian trails his gaze from my face to his hand and back again.

"So if I put my mouth here"—his fingers glide south to gently cup between my legs—"you would have an orgasm?"

I am ridiculously close to having one right now. All my blood has gathered beneath the press of his hand.

"Mouth, fingers, penis," I say, aiming for nonchalant and hitting gasping hussy. "All would be sufficient."

"Do human males put their mouths down there?"

More single than plural and not for a very long time.

I nod too rapidly. "Unless they're selfish or have a complex about it making them look weak."

Zorian curls his fingers, the brief movement rippling outward in a wave of quivering muscles. It pulls a moan from my throat and it takes all my willpower not to grind against his hand. My turn to tether myself in the sand.

"I feel the opposite of weak," he says, his deep voice almost a purr. "Do you want me to use my mouth on you, Axelle?"

Oh fuck yes.

"No rush," I squeak. "Anticipation is sexy."

My body wails at me to surrender. What does it matter? I've already begun my descent into ignominy, might as well seal the deal with a spectacular orgasm.

"Are you afraid?"

I so badly want to squirm but risk launching myself over the edge and humping his hand.

"I'm not afraid."

He smiles at the tremulous words.

"Liar," he whispers.

31

Marvyn tosses me a sleepy smile when I enter the ward, Pacal long gone after his fake seizure and no one injured enough to take his place. The Verdanians are lying low, refusing to engage our troops or test the wall.

Probably waiting for the reinforcements.

Mallory spent a few days in a different ward after I whipped a layer from his thick hide. In the canteen or at Earth lessons, he refuses to make eye contact, his back straight, his movements tentative. He's joined Yannik's squad. It suits him. Most of them are a bunch of swaggering meatheads.

"Hey, Axe," Marvyn says and the words slop together. "You don't have to visit every night. I'm not much company."

The Passengers say his wound is healing well, no infection. He'll be weak and tired for a while yet but his place in my squad will be there when he's ready.

I pat his hand. "I just come here for the peace and quiet."

A Passenger's footsteps squeak past the door and fade down the corridor. Marvyn blinks at me once, twice. His eyes stay closed and a soft snore slips from his lips. I brush a tangle of brown hair off his forehead.

My veterans wanted to come tonight for another assault on the basement. They're holding off while I try a lone incursion. Better for me to get caught than sacrificing all of them for something that may be nothing. I ordered them to plead ignorance should the worst happen, and not attempt a rescue under any circumstances. Someone has to avoid reconditioning and discover the truth.

Even if it's not me.

I glance at the empty drip stand pushed to the head of Marvyn's bed. He's been awake enough to eat and drink, his fluids replenished. I waited too long, not wanting to compromise his recovery by messing with the opaque bag. When I finally decided he was healed enough to risk it, the bag was gone.

I tried to be careful, like I promised Zorian, but the hospital basement is the only option for answers. The underground lair of the dissection lab is too dangerous and nothing can compel me back there. Vail will definitely have his suspicions on who helped the prisoners escape after our cosy nightcap.

I tangle my fingers in Marvyn's sheets, his gentle snores continuing uninterrupted.

The mysterious blends are my only lead. If it turns out to be nothing, I'll be back at square one—no evidence bar my unease that somebody is being lied to. But is it us or the Verdanians?

Plus, I want to have useful information to discuss with Zorian tonight to distract us from... other things.

I'm going to fuck him in the dream space. All it will take is his fingers slipping beneath my shorts, cool skin to delicate flesh, and I'll capitulate faster than any squad leader in Verdanian history.

And I'll be the one who begs him to go there.

I've never been so freaking horny. There's always someone

willing in Home Base. Okay, it usually consists of a quick fumble in the barracks, hot breath panting under covers, or a trousers-around-the-ankles shag in an empty classroom, the fear of someone walking in heightening the arousal, but it gets the job done.

The anticipation is killing me. I didn't lie about that. It's unbearably erotic.

I just need to clear my head. To find the little voice that hisses, "Abomination," and, "Crime against humanity," whenever Zorian touches me. If it's inevitable, I don't want the first time we have dream sex to be tainted by regret or shame.

Squad leaders are decisive. They don't flinch from a course of action, even if it leads into the unknown.

It's tempting to leave the hospital and jump into bed. Screw information. Maybe all I need is to get it over with. The more I avoid it, the bigger I build the act in my head. It's not magical or elemental or earth-shattering. I won't lose myself. It's sex not behavioural reconditioning. A penis-in-the-vagina thing. Kind of comical if you think about all the grunting and sweating and contorted faces.

It won't even be real. I'm getting myself in a state over nothing, though that's not new when it comes to Zorian. He flusters me like no one else can.

"Sweet dreams, Marvyn," I whisper, and shove away from his bed.

The lights of the hospital are dim, most visitors gone to the pub or to the barracks. My boots squeak on the polished floor. The lift drops me to ground level, no option for the basement on the numbered panel. I stride through the lobby, following a couple of tenth generationers as they head for the main door and nodding to a Passenger walking in the opposite direction. She disappears into the surgical suite, and I dive for the basement steps. Pausing half-way down, I hold my breath. No footsteps or shouts. The air conditioning hums but fails to cool the sweat on my face. I peek around the corner. Blackness stretches from the bottom step. A red light blinks. Icy air slithers up my arms.

Has someone left the mortuary open?

I tip-toe into the dark. My hip bumps the abandoned hospital bed, which screeches against the wall. I tell myself I'm not having a heart attack despite the frenzied palpitations.

I wish I hadn't watched a zombie movie with Loyanne after one of our night shifts. My skin crawls waiting for something to grab me.

The red light blinds me on every blink. The sign on the mortuary door floats from the black, the way closed. No zombies. I cross the corridor to the opposite door. Cold breath puffs on my boots but I'm pretty sure I'm imagining it. I push the door. It sticks. I listen to confirm all is quiet then slam my shoulder to the wood. Pain flares in my muscle. The door rattles but refuses to budge. The light blinks. I peer at the frame. A card reader hangs flush to the wall, the red light searing my eyes and taunting me.

It means there *is* something to hide.

And I can't bloody get to it.

I kick the door and abandon the basement, marching out of the hospital and gulping the humid air. Home Base settles for the night, a silent bubble surrounded by the hoot and cackle of the jungle. Mist swirls in the security lights. The moisture settles on my hair and sticks it to my cheeks. I plunge my hands into my pockets and drag my feet towards my pod.

31

I'm going to have to steal another pass. A drunk McBurnie worked the last time. Maybe he's in the pub.

I change direction. A howl spills from beyond the wall, close enough to elicit excitement from the guards. A single shot cracks out.

"Feckin' water-tigers," grumbles a voice, loud in the stillness.

I shake my head and hustle between modules. The beast was no threat, the wall too high for it to jump.

Zorian was right—humans aren't happy unless they're killing something.

A footstep scrapes on stone. I flatten myself into the shadow of a module by instinct rather than necessity. It's not like there's a curfew. A dark shape swoops past the space at the end of the row. I creep to the corner. The thin silhouette continues into an alleyway, heading further from my destination, sticking close to the walls, their steps muffled. I hesitate for a second then follow, trusting my gut.

Whoever it is, they're trying to be furtive.

I want to know why.

I stalk the person through the maze of Home Base. They pause at an intersection between barracks, raucous voices coming from inside. They glance over their shoulder, and I freeze. A slant of light pools shadows in his concave cheeks and blooms colour in his maroon uniform.

Elderman Thorn.

The Elder residencies are behind us, closer to the centre and circled by the Passenger pods. Thorn keeps walking. A recessed entryway juts out of the ground near the wall, and slopes to the rear. Thorn opens one half of the double door and slips inside, shutting it behind him. Nothing else moves for the five minutes I wait, holding my breath.

There's one way in or out. It's too easy to get caught.

My fingers curl around the metal handle, cold despite the heat of the night. A slice of blackness greets me. No sound echoes up the long, long staircase. It's another maw, ready to swallow me whole. Before I can change my mind, I dart inside and let the door ease shut. Smooth bedrock guides me down, one tentative step at a time.

The underground amphitheatre extends beyond the wall, carved into the obsidian bedrock. The Verdanians don't have the technology to blast their way to it even if they knew it was here.

Dull grey seeps into the black. Soft laughter drifts up the stairs. My heart thuds against my ribs but I force myself onward. The steep steps terminate at an archway, golden light spilling through. I slide my back along the wall. On the other side, the top row of the amphitheatre stretches in a large semi-circle, the main stairs to the bottom opposite the archway, with narrow steps interspersed around the inverted bowl. All of the seats are empty, the stage deserted, the screen dark.

A third of the way down the main stairwell, Elders stand in a procession, two to a step facing Elderman Vail, their backs to me. Vail stands alone beyond the double line of Elders, his head tilted to address them. Thorn and Carniss are the pair closest to me—a skeletal frame beside a brick with legs. Vail raises a goblet. Sparkles flare from embedded jewels—blood red, moss green, lemon yellow.

Verdanian tokens.

"To our continued health," Vail says, his voice echoing around the huge space.

The gathered Elders chant his words back to him. Chalices glitter in the light, a single stone in each. Vail sips from his cup and smacks his lips.

Why are they doing this here and not in the cosier atmosphere of the pub? Unless they have a special brew they don't want to share.

Metal clinks on metal as the Elders touch goblets, and drink. Carniss thrusts her cup vigorously against Thorn's, and liquid slops over the edge. A pale drop plops on the black step.

Are they drinking milk? Not exactly adventurous.

Thorn stoops and swipes at the spilled liquid, sticking his long finger in his mouth.

"Too precious to waste," he says, inspiring a wave of laughter from the others.

Vail passes a brimming glass jug to the lowest pair, the muscles corded in his wiry arms. Fluid slurps into goblets. Thorn follows the progress of the jug with hungry eyes.

"Another toast," Vails says, his cup full, "and then we disperse."

Water beads on the outside of the jug. Liquid clings to the inner glass, thick and white. It swirls faster than the steady movement of the vessel. Watching it makes me dizzy. Carniss accepts the jug and brandishes it towards the ceiling like an offering to the gods. She pours an elaborate stream into Thorn's cup. The pale liquid shimmers, the surface a sheen of rainbow colours.

My stomach lurches.

"To our hosts," Vail says, and chugs from his goblet. A white moustache slicks his upper lip. "For nothing tastes as sweet."

I back away, my fist crammed in my mouth. Something wants to burst free. Vomit or screams, neither would be helpful. My eyes are too wide, my breathing too shallow. I have to get out before I faint or lose it. I bump into something. The wall? No, it's too soft, too warm.

A heavy hand settles on my shoulder.

"Och, m'eudail," a voice sighs. "I wish ye hadn't seen that."

32

Straps clamp my wrists, ankles and forehead. The material looks like leather but it's stiff and shiny. Too strong for a Verdanian to break so I have no chance. A metal table bruises my spine.

I didn't struggle in the amphitheatre. Thirty-two Elders stared at me with a mixture of anger, regret and guilt, First Minister Seabird the only absentee. I let them march me through Home Base, hidden from prying eyes by double walls of maroon, McBurnie's hand still on my shoulder and guiding me gently from behind. My captors opened to reveal my destination.

Then I struggled.

I suppose behavioural reconditioning is a form of torture.

Sickness and fear roil through my stomach. My lips are tender where McBurnie clamped his hand to my mouth to silence my protests, my voice echoing in the night-time stillness in front of the dissection lab. Even he fought to hold me until the crowd of Elders pinned me to the concrete. A sharp pain bloomed in my neck. Colours swirled across my vision.

I woke on the vertical table and wondered if I was in Thommonn's room.

The door slides open, and I tense. McBurnie eases his mass through the entryway, his halo of ginger hair brushing the frame.

Sad, hazel eyes meet mine. "Why did it have to be you, Axelle? What possessed ye to go where ye shouldn't?"

"Why do you drink Verdanian blood?"

His gaze skips across the room, alighting on the shiny instrument tray beside me, blessedly empty. For now.

"To survive," he says.

"Is that why we're at war? Is everything we're taught a lie?"

He refuses to look at me, his thick fingers fiddling with the pass on his lapel. His picture grins in contrast to his burdened expression.

"I'm no' the one to answer your questions. Questions ye shouldn't be asking. I came to say goodbye." His sigh comes from his toes. "Ye were one o' ma favourites, m'eudail."

He lumbers for the door, his shoulders stooped.

"You can stop this," I say, my voice climbing. "You can let me go."

He hesitates but doesn't turn around. "Will ye keep asking questions?"

"We deserve to know the truth. We're the ones who die for it."

"Why could ye no lie, Axelle?"

"Because it doesn't matter what I say. Or am I wrong?"

Another heavy sigh. "Naw, hen. This is the way it's got to be. I'll miss ye in the AR ward."

"But I could still help you out. I'll still be here." My voice rises even higher.

"Your body, aye, but you'll only have one thing ye want to do an' it's no' preserve life."

"Undo the straps. I'll run away."

His head shakes, his hair whispering over his uniform. "I'm sorry, m'eudail."

A jaunty whistle echoes in the corridor. McBurnie and I share a flinch.

"Please, Elderman," I whisper, as if Vail might hear. "Don't let him turn me into a monster."

McBurnie glances over his shoulder. A single tear slides down his craggy cheek.

"It's too late," he says. "For all o' us."

The door hisses open to admit Vail. He's very chipper for the late hour, his eyes gleaming as his gaze bounces between McBurnie and me.

"I didn't expect to see you here, Elderman," he says, almost toe to toe with the bigger man in the tiny room. His wiry frame blocks the exit.

"I was just leaving."

Vail doesn't move. "Of course you were. Wouldn't want to get your hands dirty now, would you?"

"Let me pass, Robert," McBurnie says, the words tired and monotone.

Vail steps to the side with an elaborate sweep of his arm. McBurnie straightens his shoulders and clomps out the door. He doesn't look back.

Silence settles on the room bar the purr of the air conditioning. The chemical smell seems stronger, masking the burnt honey of tortured Verdanians.

Or they haven't captured more yet.

Vail slowly unbuttons his shirt. My heart climbs into my mouth.

"Axelle, Axelle, Axelle. First generation, highest kill count, exemplary soldier. Where did you go wrong?"

He smooths his shirt over the chair back and reaches for a cupboard above the sink.

"I didn't go wrong," I say, keeping my voice level, "you did. Is this why we're at war—so you can guzzle their blood like vampires?"

"It's more complicated than that. Without their blood, humanity would have died on this planet years before you were born."

He opens a packet and fans the surgical instruments on the metal tray-table. His fingers stroke the scalpel.

I see Thommonn's dripping, burgundy eye, severed from its socket. Will Vail do that to me? He can't. He needs my body whole to function. Though several soldiers do fine with one eye, Yannik included.

Some things are too complex to grow in the lab.

I swallow my pulse and breathe through my nose. "Perhaps we wouldn't be at war if you stopped harvesting their organs."

"Don't be naive, Axelle. The blood was not why the war started, merely a by-product. Its properties were discovered quite by accident. We were losing and it offered us a better chance."

"We're still losing."

Vail selects a pair of sharp-nosed scissors and holds them up to the light, testing the blades. The *snick-snick* sends shivers down my spine.

"We are far from losing. Granted, the survival rate of the generations is poor but we are weeks away from a solution. The culmination of our research. We will subdue the Verdanians and rule this planet, as is our right as the advanced species."

"What solution? We have no right to this place."

Vail's fingers circle my wrist, the cuff of my shirt slipping between the scissor blades.

"I'll ask the questions, Axelle of the first," he says.

The scissors split my sleeve from wrist to collarbone. Vail repeats the process on my other arm while I roll my eyes to watch him.

"When did you discover their blood was not poisonous?" he asks, and unbuttons my shirt.

Instead of screeching, *"What are you doing?"* I say, "How did I know about your first lie, you mean?"

The blade of the scissors bites into the meat of my shoulder. I clench my teeth on a gasp.

"You will do well to answer me without the back-talk," Vail says.

A slick of blood coats one blade. Vail completes the last slice from my collar and tugs the shirt free, tossing it on the floor. The table is icy cold. I wish I'd worn a vest, though no doubt he would've removed it, too.

"I swallowed some." Metal slips between my skin and my waistband. "By accident."

"Was the Verdanian still alive after you drank it?"

"Yes," I say since I can't nod.

The scissors part the material of my trousers parallel to the seam, flashing the side of my leg. I think of Zorian in his peek-a-boo trousers held together by cord. I'll never see them in real life.

Can't worry about that now.

Tears thicken my throat but I focus on Vail.

"Did you notice anything interesting?" he says, moving to my left leg.

The rainbow colour in the marble of his skin, two extra heartbeats, his fear, his sadness.

"I felt him die," I say.

"Isn't it amazing? So much power and potential just draining away. They really are a magnificent species. Did you know a blend of their ocular fluid used as eye drops can actually banish cataracts and improve vision? It's why no one in Home Base will ever need glasses."

My trousers separate in a whisper of material. Vail yanks them from under my butt. I shudder in my underwear and boots.

"How can you drink their blood and torture them?" I tense my jaw to keep my teeth from chattering. "Don't you feel their pain?"

"So it *was* you who freed our latest stock. Seabird and I had our suspicions given your change in behaviour."

I try to raise my chin but the strap squeezes my forehead. "What you did was barbaric."

"What I do is necessary. Humanity's survival transcends all cultural niceties."

Vail paws through the instruments and tips something from a small packet into his hand. He touches a fingertip to his palm and brandishes a tiny, circular disk. He fixes it to my temple, the strap around my forehead too tight for me to jerk away.

"We thought we were on to something with the genetic optimisation using local DNA but we had to rely on the transfer of altered material alone to later generations. Just enough to improve their survival and allow them to adapt to conditions."

"What the hell are you talking about?"

"You are a genetically modified soldier, Axelle. That's what I'm talking about. Unfortunately, we had to reduce the modifications after the fourth generation as you children seemed to have more fascination than fear towards the Verdanians, despite your training." Vail smirks. "We've even tried to fertilise viable offspring in the hopes of producing stronger, tougher soldiers but all methods have failed, artificial or natural."

A disk is placed on my other temple then two more below each collarbone.

"You raped them?" I whisper, my skin crawling under the press of his finger.

My stomach swoops at the barrage of information. What does genetic modification mean—that I'm part-human, part-Verdanian? Is that why I'm attracted to Zorian? So much for bestiality.

"It was quite difficult to get sperm from the males, let me tell you," Vail says. "The process was easier with the females but I didn't participate. Not my thing. Apparently, it's like sticking your genitals in a stone crevasse."

He pokes more disks on my ribs, belly, thighs and shins.

"We don't deserve to be welcomed onto this planet," I say, unable to mask the disgust.

"Spare me your moral high ground, killer of twelve. You leapt into battle with the ferocity of a true soldier and would still be doing so if you'd kept your helmet on and your mouth shut."

"Because you trained me to do nothing else. You lied to make us fight. Why did the war really start? And don't give me the misty-eyed bullshit you feed us in Earth lessons."

Vail's smile is a predatory baring of teeth. "My, my, Axelle—

how bold you've grown from the teacher's pet who doted on my every word."

"Turns out I was misinformed," I say with my own brittle smile. "You're not heroic. You have no honour. You act like you're saving humanity but humanity needs saving from *you*."

He slides a tablet from his pocket and taps on the screen. "You're only making this easier for me. Let's start on the lowest setting. Your leg, perhaps?"

I twitch on the table, pain blossoming in my leg as if someone has kicked me in the shin.

"What the hell is that?"

He flashes the tablet too quickly for me to read the screen. "This? It controls the electrode disks on your body. They stimulate pain receptors without causing damage. I'm told it hurts quite terribly."

He bends his head over the tablet, his grey ponytail brushing his shoulder. One jab of his finger and agony erupts in my lower leg, like a Verdanian has shattered my shin bone with a club. My scream bounces off the walls. Sweat pops out on my skin.

"Now," Vail says cheerfully, "do you want to hear how the war started or are you going to run your mouth? I have many electrodes to choose from."

I glare at him and mutter, "Tell me."

Not exactly contrite but there's too much hatred burning in my gut.

"It happened so long ago, it's practically unimportant. And you won't remember it once we're finished with you here." He drags the chair from under the desk and perches on the edge, the tablet balanced on his knee. "There were the usual misunderstandings when two different cultures come together that I won't bore myself with. But there was no misunderstanding when the Verdanians abducted Passenger Eleanor Gotiva."

Wrong. Did Ballathus even know how his actions were construed?

"We launched a surprise attack on their village, which, of course, was not the hidden little rat hole it is today. Unfortunately, this was the time before we knew the importance of bloodstone. Our bullets scored the adults but seemed to bounce off. The younglings fell much more easily. Softer skin, I believe."

No wonder he didn't reflect my horror at Mallory's murder of children. He's done his share.

"Naturally, their response was vicious. We were almost wiped out by their retaliatory strike and would've been picked off afterwards if it weren't for an accidental splash of blood on a wound that healed rapidly. The revelation rescued us. We could heal nearly everything if we received blood quick enough. We experimented by blending different tissues together, the blood and blood-rich organs most efficacious."

Vail drums his fingers on the tablet screen. My leg twinges but no new flares of pain assault the disks stuck to my skin.

"Their blood is fascinating. It seems to prevent cancer and degenerative diseases. We suspect it promotes longevity, not to mention its amazing healing properties. It turned the tide of the war just as much as the discovery of bloodstone." Vail stands, kicking the chair under the desk. "And there you have it—the true origins of our battle. Our main problem has been acquiring enough Verdanian tissue to suit demand but that will no longer be an issue very soon. Once we're in control, we can live long and healthy into our hundreds. Isn't that worth fighting for, Axelle?"

"If it's so worthy, why keep it a secret?" I say through numb lips.

Verdanian blood—Zorian's blood. How can that be everything I've killed for, everything I've watched people die for?

Humans are parasites. Or those teeny biting flies McBurnie calls midges. We suck everything dry before moving to the next planet, caring for nothing as long as our species survives.

"You're being naive again, Axelle," Vail says. "If everyone knows the truth, the risk of the weak-minded causing a rebellion is too great. If people refuse to fight then humanity will die. I can't let that happen."

"Your humanity is already dead."

He flashes another predatory grin. It wobbles my knees worse than the glimpse of a Verdanian's teeth.

"Perhaps you're right but I sacrificed it willingly." He taps on the tablet. "Now, let's try the full body experience before moving on to *my* questions."

He swipes his finger across the screen, and I scream almost as long as Thommonn.

"The pain is a taste of where it will get to if I feel you're not answering my questions truthfully."

Vail's words barely penetrate my screams. I thrash against the bonds, and the material carves my skin. The pain is unlike anything I've experienced before. All-consuming. Agonising. It washes the room in a fog of white. When it fades, it leaves me gasping, the stone at my throat jiggling on the rapid slam of my pulse.

"I'll start with an easy one—how did you get the prisoners past the wall?"

Vail waits while I blink and quiver and clear my throat.

"I distracted the guards and gave them a rope," I croak.

He jabs the tablet. My ribs crunch into a million pieces.

"Is that your final answer?" he says over my teeth snapping together.

"Yes," I pant. "They're strong. Agile. They probably didn't need the rope."

"Who was on the wall that night?"

"Yannik's squad."

Vail's finger hovers above the screen. "Names, Axelle."

"I only saw Creedon of the fourth and Nala of the seventh."

"Perhaps I should punish them for being diverted from their

duties."

I try to shake my head, and the strap saws at my eyebrows. "I outrank them. They couldn't ignore me."

"Whose pass did you steal to enter the lab?"

"McBurnie's."

"How?"

"I got him drunk."

Vail tosses his ponytail. "The overgrown buffoon. I won't be surprised if he's blubbering in a corner about his precious *Axelle o' the first.*"

"At least he cares."

"But not enough to save you."

The barb hits its mark.

I grew up with McBurnie. I remember sitting on his knee while he read a tattered book called *Bagpipes, Beasties and Bogles* to my generation, the first children born on Verdana. He gave me a tour of the AR ward and I fell in love with the tiny foetuses nestled in the incubation pods. They looked so peaceful. So safe. He's known me since I was a bundle of cells yet he couldn't fight for me even a little?

"Those were the easy questions," Vail says, standing close to me, the top of my head level with his chin. "Now answer me this—who else in your squad knows about the blood?"

I strain my eyes to meet his sharp gaze.

"No one," I say.

My intestines sprout thorns, and spasm, attempting to claw out of my gut. My body tries to curl around the pain, pushing against the straps. A groan catches in my throat.

"Are you sure?" Vail brings his lips next to my ear. "No one trusts a liar, Axelle."

"I was going to tell them. But I wanted evidence."

My collarbones rip from my flesh to join the agony in my stomach. My thighs cramp, pain shooting up my spine.

"Who knows, Axelle?"

My voice is a shriek that ends on, *"No one!"*

A vice clamps my skull, tightening until my eyes bulge. Sickness pulses black and red with each beat of my heart. I may vomit in Vail's face if he doesn't step back.

"Tell me a name and the pain will stop."

I close my eyes. Fractured shins and pulverised ribs join the tortured cacophony. I scream at the darkness behind my lids, my hands fisted, nails biting my palms and slippery with blood or sweat or both.

The pain relents. I sag against the table, my wobbling legs struggling to take my weight so the straps slice deeper. Vail places the tablet on the instrument tray.

Thank fuck.

He slaps me. My head can't turn to dissipate the blow. The force of it thuds in my jaw and sizzles to the roots of my teeth. My hair catches in my eyelashes and sticks to my cheeks.

"Who?" Slap. "Who?" Slap.

My eyes blur, my cheeks wet. Shit—I'm crying.

"No one," I whisper.

"Then what were you all doing in the hospital when Seabird found you skulking in the basement?"

Warm liquid plops on my chest. I touch my tongue to my burst lip and taste metal.

"They were visiting Marvyn. Then Pacal had a seizure. I slipped away to look for evidence."

"Who helped you?"

"No one! I returned to the basement alone but you've put a card reader on the door. I followed Thorn to the amphitheatre."

Vail taps his chin but steps away. "If you hadn't been caught, what would you have done?"

"Stolen McBurnie's card again. Taken one of the blends. Shown it to my squad."

"And then?"

"Shown others. Convinced them to stop fighting and demand the truth."

"Dooming us all."

I bare my teeth. "*Saving* us all."

"Tell me who else knows."

"No one." My voice cracks.

"Okay," he says almost softly, "I believe you."

He picks up the tablet.

"You said you believed me!"

His smile chills the sweat on my skin.

"I lied," he says, and taps the screen.

I scream until my voice breaks and my throat bleeds. He bombards me with the same question—who, who, *who?* I tell him nothing.

Squad leaders do not cave. They howl and yell and sob but they do not snitch.

I come close to fainting several times but Vail dials down the intensity to let me recover. I'm shaking so hard, my skin is raw beneath the straps.

Is it daylight yet? Have I missed the dream space? Zorian will be wondering where I am. Does he think I regret the intimacy, the promise of more?

God, I'm so tired. My joints ache. Sweat stings my eyes and nips the cut on my lip. I watch through a haze as the door slides open and a stretched silhouette eases into the room.

"Elderman Thorn," Vail says in the friendly voice he used for abusing Thommonn, "right on time. Give her a shot if she tries to sleep. Carniss will relieve you at midday."

Agony sweeps through my legs, abdomen, chest, shoulders and skull. I manage a rasping whine. The room sways.

"Steady, Thorn," Vail says. "I've given her a heavy dose already. We want to break her mind in a controlled fashion, not turn her into a drooling vegetable. Stick to the programme."

"Maybe we shouldn't risk it with this one. She knows too much."

Thorn's black eyes travel down the length of my body. There's not much height to cover but he lingers on my breasts and crotch as if he can see beneath the flimsy material of my underwear. My hands ache to cover myself.

Nakedness is nothing to be embarrassed about. Soldiers see each other in the buff all the time—in the showers, in the barracks. But no Elder has ever looked at me this way. They're supposed to be our mentors, our role models, our teachers.

"We need every soldier, you know that. And when has reconditioning ever failed?"

"You're right." Thorn pulls the chair from under the desk and swings it to face me, settling his long frame into the cushions. "It's as good as death. The part of her scowling at me will certainly die."

Vail chuckles. "You have to admire her spirit. Right before we crush it."

He bids Thorn goodnight. Thorn appraises me, the silence stretching to minutes. I straighten my shoulders and control my breathing, wiping my face to a blank mask a Verdanian would be proud of.

"I knew you were compromised," Thorn finally says. "You cared too much for the Verdanian children."

And what does it say about my species that caring about the lives of children is considered suspicious? Children have no part in the war.

"No excuses? No explanation? No, I suppose it's too late for that." Thorn leans back in the chair, his long fingers stroking the tablet. "It's funny—if you'd tried to communicate your sudden pacifism to a Verdanian, they'd have killed you, no hesitation. They have a deep-seated hatred for us. Can't imagine why."

He examines his fingernails, picking crud out of one and flicking it at me.

"Vail may have told you but we actually had a couple of ceasefires—both after your generation was born. Verdanians are much easier to capture when they're not prepared for battle. Too trusting, I suspect. *Honourable*." He says it like it's a dirty word. "The products we gathered in those periods saw us through the lean times. The fresher the tissue is, the better."

"You're disgusting."

Dammit, I really should have maintained the stony silence.

Thorn's black eyes sparkle at my outburst.

"Yes, yes, best to expend your indignation. In a matter of weeks, or days if your mind is frail, you'll no longer be this." He circles his hand in the air to indicate my entire body. "You'll be focused—cold—as emotionless as our enemy. You'll have no doubts or flares of conscience. Killing will be your only goal and your life's greatest reward. The person you are now will not exist. The new and improved Axelle will defer to her Elders with reverence, follow all orders and fight until she dies a soldier's death. As all generations should."

"Cannon fodder," I say, my cheeks still burning from Vail's slaps. "That's the Earth term for it."

"Ah, but *important* cannon fodder. Vail was also right about that—we need every single one of you." Thorn waves his spindly hand. "Enough chit-chat. I'm here to keep you awake but I'm hardly going to make it easy for you."

"Sleep deprivation?"

"Of course. It increases your susceptibility to the drugs."

He slouches in the chair and closes his eyes to slits, the black glitter of his irises ever watchful. The bright lights of the room bleach his skin corpse-pale. Exhaustion weighs heavy in my limbs as soon as he stops talking.

Staying awake is just another battle I have no hope of winning.

In my head, I list every object in the room, name every person in Home Base. It takes a while since there are over three thousand five hundred of them. For the names I don't know, I picture their face, conjure their voice. Thorn stays perfectly still with the patience of a stalking water-tiger.

The kick of pain in my gut comes as a surprise. My eyes snap open, my heart bounding into my throat. Adrenaline trembles in my muscles.

"Wakey-wakey," Thorn says, and stretches his thin lips in a smile.

He treats me to a burst every time I start to doze—legs, ribs, head. Sometimes he gives me the full whack and I stay awake for ages after, the echo of my screams trapped in the corners of the room. Hours pass this way, though it feels like aeons. Carniss eases her square frame through the door at what must be midday.

We're all so very punctual.

I stare at her through bleary eyes, my legs aching from the electrodes and from being forced to stand. If I relax too much, the straps take my weight and nibble deeper into my skin.

She sniffs at Thorn's proffered tablet and pulls a black object from her belt. "I have my own means, thank you, Elderman."

"In that case, I'll leave you two to your girl talk." Thorn tips me a wink, and moseys out the door.

Carniss crosses her arms, tapping the small, rectangular object on the haunch of her bicep and dissecting me with her icy-blue gaze. Maybe now would be a good time to tell her I need to pee but she probably knows.

Those eyes miss nothing.

"You are such a disappointment, Axelle."

"I apologise, Elderwoman," I say, my voice blandly deferential, "that munching on our enemies offends my sensibilities."

She tuts. "You have benefited. Your face would not have been so pretty had the arrow wound healed minus the assistance of a Verdanian blend. You were born with terrible eyesight and suffered a severe bout of colic, both cured by 'munching on our enemies' as you so delicately put it."

"And all without my knowledge or consent."

"I doubt you would have refused given the choice between deformity, blindness, intestinal rupture or perfect health."

"You know my history but you don't know me, Elder-woman."

She shakes her square head. "You could have been the greatest soldier *in* our history."

"It's not greatness if we're fighting for a lie. We could've had peace."

"Peace?" she scoffs, uncrossing her arms. "As if we could

play happy families with a bunch of savages. Peace requires dominance, Axelle, one way or another."

"Maybe on your world," I say softly.

"I've lived on this planet longer than you've been alive."

"But have you really *seen* it?"

"What's to see? Dripping leaves, feral creatures, mud. All will be tamed."

She paces the room, round and around my table. It hurts my eyes to follow her. She refuses to engage me in further debate, her lips pressed together, eyes forward. She swings the box in sync with her march, and I wonder what it is.

It doesn't take long to find out.

Sleep sucks at me. My body begs for it but something prods my ribs. There's a crackle, and a burst of pain fizzes to my fingers and toes. My muscles stiffen to stone. I snap to alertness, the black object pressed to my side. Carniss pulls it away when I glare at her. A sizzle of blue zips between metal prongs on the end of the device—the end she jammed into me.

"This is an electroshock weapon," she says. "Technology from Earth designed to deliver an electrical pulse that will temporarily disrupt muscle function and cause pain without significant injury. Quite effective, I'm sure you can attest."

I'm lucky I didn't wet myself. Thank god for years of being unable to pee in the jungle unless you wanted to inhale recycled, piss-soaked air in your battlesuit. It gave me excellent bladder control.

Carniss seems irritated by my lack of agreement. Perhaps I should have effused over the wonders of her torture device. She zaps me again with the electric prod.

No fancy electrodes or tablet of agony for her.

She's old school, is Carniss.

34

They keep me awake for three days. I think. Time is meaningless in my prison but the sleep deprivation seems to be divvied up into seven-hour and twenty-minute shifts split between Vail, Thorn and Carniss. I count to keep track but it's difficult, particularly when the hallucinations start.

And that's before the drugs.

While I'm still mostly coherent, I manage to snatch some sleep when Thorn leaves the room for something. He sets the electrodes on low, a migraine buzzing in my head, but I'm so tired, I fall asleep without trying.

"Axelle, there you are," Zorian says, the relief bright in his eyes. "I worried."

I glance down at myself. My control of the dream space is expert enough I can show myself immediately in my usual vest and shorts instead of my underwear. My skin is unmarked, the bite of the straps and the redness from Carniss's electroshocks hidden in the real world.

Torture has no place in this jungle sanctuary.

Zorian watches me, not approaching, his expression unsure. "Are you all right?"

I barely feel the sand beneath my feet. I throw my arms around him and hug him tight, my cheek pressed to the beat of his hearts. His breath huffs out so I may have been a little forceful.

But my nights with him are coming to an end.

"I'm sorry," I say to his chest, and give myself another minute to get my voice under control. "There was an emergency. It's not important. I'm here. My sleep patterns might be erratic over the next few days."

Erratic. *Ha*. Try non-existent.

Zorian's arms curl around me, petting my hair, my back. My throat closes. Thorn could return at any moment and sever the dream. I might not be me enough to ever see Zorian again. Will he be forced to face the monster I become? Hurt and confused when I attack him in the dream? I can't let that happen. I want to sob into the wonderful coolness of his skin and tell him everything.

"I am glad you are here," he says softly, laying his cheek on top of my head. "I missed you."

A sob almost escapes but I crush it.

I have to keep him safe. Vail is not getting anywhere near him. So I can't tell him anything. He'll want to rescue me. I have to wait until it's too late for him to help me. Too late to save who I am.

God, I want to be saved. I don't want my mind to be erased and rebooted into something reptilian and cold. But I can't risk Zorian.

"I missed you, too," I manage in a somewhat husky voice.

I ease away to run my fingers over him, memorising the line of his collarbones, the dip of his stomach, the curve of his hips. I jump and wrap my legs around his waist, cupping his face, my fingertips tracing his cheekbones. The kiss is wild and frantic and hungry for everything I've lost. I taste salt but I grind myself against Zorian as if I can climb inside his body and stop him from asking me what's wrong.

But he's stronger. He always is.

He gently peels me loose, one hand easily holding my wrists. His fingers stroke my cheek and come away wet.

"Axelle, what is—"

Pain explodes in my skull, and I gasp awake to Thorn's prickly smile.

"Naughty girl," he says. "No dessert for you."

I needed more time! I should have told Zorian so many truths—how amazing he is, how funny, cute, cuddly, sweet. He opened my eyes to the possibility of a new life. He banished my loneliness and filled it with the shock of his laugh, his lips on mine, his hands holding me as if I were as delicate as a pond-bee's wing.

My breath hitches. I struggle to control it but my face crumples and I start to cry, unable to hide. Thorn's smile becomes a toothy grin, blurred by my tears.

"Oh, Axelle," he says, each word laced with pity, "I thought a soldier of your calibre would be tougher than this. A couple of days of no sleep and you blubber like a child."

"I'm not crying because of you, you fucking skeleton," I snarl through my sobs. Not my best insult but I'm tired. "Fuck you. Fuck Vail, fuck Carniss. Fuck Home Prison. This place is a stain that should be wiped from Verdana."

Thorn's lips purse so fast, it's like he's sucked on an Earth lemon. He blasts me with a full-body-agony experience, and I faint after a few minutes. Unfortunately, fainting isn't enough to enter the dream space, and I blink awake without Zorian's face to soothe me.

This is my life for the three days of sleep deprivation. Pain from the tablet, electric shocks from Carniss. The Elders feed me and give me fluids, hosing me down instead of releasing me to go to the bathroom. Thorn enjoys the transparency of my wet knickers.

"The carpet matches the drapes, I see," he sneers.

I have no idea what he's babbling about.

My eyes are so dry, they scrape when I blink.

"I've appointed Mallory of the fifth as interim squad leader in your absence," Vail taunts, one hand swinging his citrine gem on its cord.

"No," I wheeze. "Mallory is an arrogant tool. Let it be Loyanne. She's better suited. Patient. Tough. I trained her for it."

"And isn't that the problem? You're defective, Axelle. Compromised. But don't fret. Once you're moulded into the shape we want, you can reclaim your mantle of squad leader."

Snails slither in droves up the walls and peer at me from the ceiling, each one a replica of Ophrys. Is he hungry? Who's going to feed him? If Mallory takes my pod, Ophrys will be a smudge of broken shell on the floor. My plants ripped and scattered to the wind. No jungle for me, ever.

Will they make me hate that, too?

Zorian visits my room. He's shining and clean and smells of mint. His fingers trace the instruments, the furniture, my clammy skin. I talk to him but forget what I say. His calming voice lulls me, the pain dulled, my body at rest though my eyes are open.

"Who is Zorian?" Carniss says, blue-white electricity casting shadows on the ceiling.

Not yours, I hiss, unable to speak. *Not yours, not yours, not yours.*

Vail brings me a present. I recoil, if it can be called that when I can't move. The child's mouth is parted in a soft 'O', the head severed at the base of the neck. Ice crystals film his remaining honey eye and glitter rainbow shards in his ruined socket.

"You may feel isolated when you're out in the jungle," Vail says, his hand clamped in the child's hair to hold it aloft, "but we have armoured retrieval units shadowing all squads. They collect the Verdanian wounded and dead so they can be preserved immediately."

What about *our* wounded?

Vail turns the head and stares dispassionately into the dead boy's face. "I think I'll use the brain from this one. The organs are always more potent from the younglings."

He places the head on the instrument tray and plucks a syringe from his uniform pocket. The boy's eye glares at me, the pupil a frosty oval. Vail slides the needle into my neck. The drug stings and swirls to my chest.

He scoops up the head. "Now give him a kiss goodbye. I want you to remember this before the real fun begins."

Frozen lips press against mine and singe delicate skin. I squeeze my eyes shut instead of meeting the bitter gaze. There's no smell except of ice but I swallow a gag. Vail tugs the head away, ripping patches of my lips with it. He tucks it under his arm and twirls my table to face the rear wall of the room. His footsteps recede, leaving me alone for the first time in three days.

I sleep for what feels like a week but Zorian doesn't appear. Maybe it's too deep even for the dream space.

Then the hallucinations really begin.

35

Pain and confusion.

Verdanians charge at me from the wall, their sharp-toothed mouths stretched wide and howling, red splattered on white. I scream and struggle but can't get away. Arrows and spears fly at my unprotected flesh—*where is my battlesuit?* Agony slices my gut and chest.

Verdanians. I'm surrounded by Verdanians.

"They are the enemy!" Vail yells, his voice battering my ears. "They want to kill you!"

He repeats it, over and over and over, louder each time. His words are all I can hear.

Why doesn't he help me?

Verdanians peel a soldier from his battlesuit, like skinning a nut. His limbs pop from sockets in gushes of red. Slim, marble fingers gouge at his stomach and unravel his intestines under the glare of two suns. His chest rips open with a crack of bone. A Verdanian bites into his heart like it's a fruit, blood staining her chin and smearing her teeth.

How is he still screaming? Oh. *I'm* screaming.

Eyes shine in the dark, haunting me when I sleep. Beautiful, terrifying eyes—gold, violet, emerald.

No. Not emerald.

Sometimes I wake in a clinical room, cold and white, other times in the jungle. The jungle is scary, filled with creatures that want to kill me. They chase me but I never run fast enough. My feet sink into warm sand surrounding a pool. The jungle is scary but not this place. This place feels… safe.

Dreams are safe.

Lucidity chills me like a splash of ice water.

Dream space! I'm in the fucking dream space in my underwear!

Raw skin bands my ankles and wrists, circular bruises speckling my stomach. The lump on my cheekbone no longer throbs.

Vail thought it was funny to beat me with my pendant. He touched it, mirroring Zorian's gentle greeting and the reminder clenched my heart with loss.

"Axelle," Zorian breathes, horror widening his eyes, "what has happened?"

He cradles me in his arms, my wobbly legs too weak to hold. Shaking fingers trace the marks of abuse.

His throat works. "Tell me you are okay. Please tell me you are okay."

"I'm okay," I whisper.

"You promise?"

I swallow a sob. "No."

He keens low in his throat. The distraught sound makes me cry. I touch his face and he nuzzles my hand, the pain in his eyes worse than anything I've felt.

"I'm sorry, Zorian. They caught me."

"How long?"

I drop my gaze to the hollow of his throat. "I don't know. A week, maybe more."

"Why did not you tell me?" he says in a rush, the distress muddling his perfect English.

He's in a sarong again, the tasselled one. I play my fingers over the soft material.

"Because you can't stop this. You can't help me."

"I can come for you. I *will* come for you."

I shake my head. "You don't understand. I won't be the same person. It's called behavioural reconditioning. They're breaking me down and rebuilding me in the form they want. If I see you again, I'll kill you. You'll be nothing but an enemy. I'll be the monster."

"I do not care. You cannot stop me from coming."

I shake my head harder. "Mate Calliyanna. Mate her tomorrow. You shouldn't have to watch what they do to me."

"I do not want Calliyanna," he says, and hugs me close.

He's trembling.

"No, Zorian," I sob into his shoulder. "*Please.* Don't risk yourself."

"I will not let them kill you."

"They're not killing me."

"They are killing the person I know." He kisses me, slow and tender and lingering. It tears me apart. "You said it yourself—you will not be you when they are done. You will be a soldier and nothing else. A monster. That is not what you want."

"I don't have a choice."

"I do," he says. "Tell me how to get to you, Axelle."

"No, Zorian."

I can't bear it if he's caught. I'll break faster if he's strapped to a table in a neighbouring room, Vail carving his perfect body and whistling while he plucks out an eye. Zorian screaming. Maybe I'll be so far gone, I'll join in his torture, flickering between real-Axelle and the monster. I'll slam back to myself with his blood clumped in my eyelashes and sweet on my lips.

"They tell us you're the ones who drink our blood." I laugh and it echoes over the quiet of the pool. "It's the other way around. We're fighting because you're a walking, talking elixir of life."

He rocks me, murmuring into my hair, "I can get you out."

Zorian is a dreamer. An innocent despite the axe he carriers and the deaths it's wrought. He wants to believe humans are good.

He doesn't belong in the nightmare of Home Base.

"Don't come here." I snuggle into his neck to inhale the scent of him. "Take your people far away before mine blend you all into soup."

"Axelle, please..."

I hold him tight and refuse to say another word.

* * *

Vail screams at me. Thorn gloats. Carniss jams her electric prod into my ribs. Verdanians and pain. Pain and Verdanians. They rip out throats and dance in the fountain of blood. They hiss and attack me but I must black out as I never witness the blows, just the pain. And red, so much red. Only the disjointed dream space keeps me aware of my real self.

Zorian cradles me in his arms and we float in the pool, the warm water cool on my fevered skin. He trickles palmfuls over my forehead and into my hair. Sweet liquid soothes my throat.

Death. Violence. Pain. Red everywhere.

"Fennanangullandolin and Dalrainenna know how to get to you," Zorian says.

How long have I been in the dream space?

I'm lying on top of Zorian, my back to his chest, head against his collarbone. He plays with my hand, tracing his fingers over my palm, my knuckles, his other hand splayed on my belly.

"How do we distract your people?" he says in the same reasonable voice. "Where are the weapons stored, Axelle?"

I press my lips together but the dream swirls, the armoury appearing beside the flat expanse of the parade ground. The long, low building looks strange, trees disappearing into the black walls, the pool spilling from the double sliding door. I scream and mash my fists to my temples, trying to block him.

What has he seen? What day is it?

Verdanians are the enemy. Verdanians are trying to kill me.

Voices drift in darkness. Most of the time, I don't understand what they're saying or whether they're even talking to me.

"They're monsters."

Verdanians burst from the jungle, teeth bared. Sharp—for tearing flesh.

Or bark?

Agony shrieks through my skin. Their teeth are for tearing flesh!

"How do the guns work?"

I'm in class. Weapons training. I dismantle and rebuild my bloodstone rifle. Load and unload. Find the safety, flick it off. I aim and fire at cutouts of Verdanians. Perfect score. No survivors.

"They want to kill us all."

Vail plops an eye into the palm of his hand.

Is it mine?

"Where is your pod?"

My pod. My sanctuary. I touch my finger to the scanner, and the door slides open. Ophrys waves his fronds in greeting, the rest of his body curled around a berry. Flowers scent the small space.

I want to stay. It's peaceful.

"Kill them before they kill you."

A wall of people runs at me, sturdy in their grey battlesuits and bubble helmets. I glance down at my slender body and white, glowing skin.

Am I a Verdanian?

"Hold on, Axelle. I am coming."

Zorian's voice.

"No!" I gasp, as if surfacing from a deep pool.

Zorian holds me in his lap, his back against a tree with beautiful silver bark. He's wearing the trousers I like, the peek-a-boo ones. I want to slide my fingers into the gaps.

Has he left his journey to ride to Home Base? How close is he? I can't let him get here. I can't, I can't.

I scramble from his lap, and he must be surprised because he lets me. My legs manage to hold my weight.

The dream space could dissolve at any moment. This could be my last chance.

"I don't want you to come," I say, my voice hard and cold.

Zorian climbs to his feet and cocks his head, his puzzlement spearing my chest but I force the words out.

"Don't let your first orgasm confuse you, Zorian. Didn't you wonder why I never let you touch more than my tits?" I turn a sob into a derisive laugh. "It was nice and all but I'm hardly going to fuck an alien."

The hurt on his face is the last thing I see before I'm wrenched from the dream.

36

Skreeingbirds drill their beaks into my skin and sip my blood like nectar, their feathers the same, shining crimson.

Snatches of real life, snatches of dreams. But no dream space. My focus is not what it used to be so I can't tell if it's me blocking, or Zorian.

How many nights pass without him to mark them?

His face fills my lucid moments, expressive in its pain. I hurt him to save him and hurt myself more. I woke sobbing on my torture table and cried myself hoarse, my eyes swollen, every wound throbbing.

I want him. I miss him. How could I have hurt him?

I'm ready to forget now.

Doors open and close. Sometimes it brings pain, other times—confusion. Drugs sting my neck. The crackle of electricity.

"Who is the enemy?" Vail screams in my face.

"You are."

Do I whisper it or only think it? The room is empty so it doesn't seem to matter.

No one hears me.

My body floats around the ceiling, looking down at other-Axelle strapped to the table. She's pale apart from the red blotches on her ribs and the yellow fade of bruises. Her limp, tangled hair hangs over her cheeks, brushed by her eyelashes whenever she blinks. Dazed cobalt eyes peer through a cage of black.

Sometimes I pass beyond the ceiling and soar high above Verdana, chasing the *HMS Dòchas* among the stars. Shimmering seas consume the planet and drown the landmasses.

Ferns and ridged trunks fill my room, flowers of every colour polluting the air with pollen. I hate the jungle, hate the claustrophobia. The enemies it conceals.

"You will be one of our best soldiers, Axelle of the first."

First Minister Seabird is in my room! He's talking to me!

I try to salute but my arm doesn't move.

I have to salute! He deserves the respect. What must he think of me?

Fire bracelets my wrist. *I don't understand!* I ache to touch my fingers to my chest. The gesture reminds me of something… I feel—

"What is your mission?"

I know this!

"To kill Verdanians," I say, my voice breathless and eager.

No…

"Why?" Seabird says.

"They refused peace. They want to exterminate us."

Lies…

"Good, Axelle. I'm proud of your progress."

First Minister Seabird is proud of me!

My chest puffs, warmth blooming in my cheeks. Again, I try to salute but my arm is stuck and agony slices my wrist.

I hate you…

Hate Seabird? Don't be ridiculous. He captained the *HMS*

Dòchas. He gave us hope. He's the father of the generations. A hero.

A monster.

I shake my head but it doesn't move, either. Am I paralysed? How can I be the best soldier if I'm paralysed? I don't understand.

Tears well and overflow, blurring my eyes, the room. The lights dim.

Was I asleep? Did I dream?

A dark shape stands in front of me. Tall and slim. Familiar yet strange. Horror claws at my chest, something like grief clenching my stomach.

"Axelle."

Zorian's voice fills my head. Two heartbeats—three?—echo in the room.

I must be dreaming again.

A hand strokes my cheek, wonderfully cool. Zorian repeats my name, though it's not Zorian. His skin is black, not marbled rainbow. Emerald eyes blaze in a dark face. Even his hair is black, clumped together and sticking to his cheekbones.

I wish I could've said goodbye.

Arms cradle me, gentle under my knees and around my back but it still hurts. My body aches. My head rests in the curve of his shoulder. He smells of mud, not Zorian. A battle-axe peeks behind his head.

He never carries his axe in the dream space.

It's not real.

A bloodstone rifle pokes at my thigh, hanging on a strap over his shoulder.

A Verdanian with a gun. How ridiculous. My dreams are

as muddled as my thoughts.

We're in the corridor, the walls scarred and dented. I don't want to be in this place but no matter how hard I concentrate, the jungle doesn't materialise. Am I still blocking the dream space? If I'm asleep, I should be able to reach it.

Unless Zorian isn't letting me.

I hurt him.

I had to.

Hearts beat under my ear—a faint echo. Nerves churn in my gut. Worry. Sadness. A spike of fear. So many emotions yet I feel numb. Is this when they drain away to leave me a monster? Uncaring, impassive, cold.

Darkness tinged red. A muffled wail breaks the hush. I recognise it but forget what it means.

Not-Zorian boosts me in his arms, his shoulder tucked in my stomach. I flop down his back, my hair swaying. Am I close to his axe? Will I cut myself? Panic flutters but then I remember.

Dreams are safe.

The ground shunts away. I jerk with each soft slap of skin on metal. My eyes blur at the perfect curve of Zorian's spine, his muscles sliding beneath me. No tattoo, only black skin.

Not Zorian.

A tear drops onto him and trickles into the hollow of a butt dimple. I touch a finger to it, tracing first one dimple then the other. Darkness bleeds onto my fingertip.

The wailing rises to a howl. I'm in not-Zorian's arms again. He carries me through a doorway that sparks and crackles and stinks of hot metal. I flinch against the inevitable prod in the ribs. Burning, sizzling pain.

Nothing.

Moist air mists my bare skin. It feels wonderful, as if I haven't breathed for a long time. The sky is clear and banded with stars. Smoke drifts. Excited voices yell over the alarm.

Alarm? Have I slept in again? I don't remember it being so piercing.

The voices fade though the wailing does not. I cuddle into not-Zorian's chest. Someone takes my hand. Guides my finger to a slick surface. A beep and a hiss.

Do I smell flowers?

Not-Zorian's voice rumbles but I can't pick out the words. There's movement, clinking, the rustle of paper. The wall looms, a black slab in the night. I blink. Finally, the jungle materialises.

My focus must have improved or Zorian relented, curious to see if I'm still here.

But there's something wrong with the dream space. It's too dark. No pool, no waterfall, no pink-flushed rocks on grey sand. Am I distorting it now the real Axelle is dying?

Invisible fronds brush my bare calves and the toes of my boots. A glow draws my eye. Curtains and clumps of moss phosphoresce yellow and purple and blue. Like in the cave where I first met Zorian.

How could I have hated him?

The islands of light carve a path through the black. Flowers have closed, the jungle quiet. A mournful howl rings in the distance. Something nuzzles my face.

"Careful, Dacorna," not-Zorian says.

My fear and nerves seem to have faded but the worry remains, roiling in my gut. What am I worried about? There's no pain here. Maybe I'm worried I'll wake up to more of Vail screaming in my face.

Or not wake up at all.

How does it feel when your self dies to be replaced by an impostor fabricated from drugs and confusion?

I'm lifted from not-Zorian's arms. I whimper and struggle but I'm too weak.

It's not real-Zorian, or even dream-Zorian, but it's the closest I'll ever get again.

A hand strokes my head. Not-Zorian cradles me against the front of his body. Stiff hair tickles my thighs, a sharp ridge of bone digging into my butt. Hoofbeats clomp on dirt.

It reminds me of our ride through the jungle—the rocking, the closeness. Though real-Dacorna wasn't as thin as the beast beneath me.

Can dream-creatures be neglected?

Arms hold me tight. My head drops onto not-Zorian's collarbone and I stare at the sky through gaps in the canopy, the glow of the moss tinting the leaves. We ride for a long time or no time. The hoofbeats stop, and we slide from Dacorna's back. Water splashes. The pool after all? I float in the warmth, cradled by slim, strong hands.

"Drink, Axelle."

Sweet and glorious liquid slides down my throat. Fingers massage my scalp. I melt into the water. It's a good place to die. It's what I imagined an incubation pod would feel like.

My life has gone full circle. I always knew it would be short.

Not-Zorian carries me from the pool and lays me on the springy ground, phosphorescent green light swallowed by his dark skin and reflected in his eyes.

Such sad eyes. I want him to smile like he does in our dreams.

He disappears from my side, and the jungle heat spills into

the empty space. I roll my head, unable to lift it. Stars glitter on the edge of the small pool, a huge tree growing from the centre, its roots forming caverns and archways. Water ripples, breaking the reflection of the moss on the roots.

Not-Zorian splits into three dark figures bathing in the pool. I frown at them. The blackness of their skin dissolves into the water. Perfect white shines in the light of the night moss. A shape wades towards me. Tall and slim. Familiar and no longer strange. Pale hair kisses cheekbones carved from marble.

Zorian.

He unblocked the dream space. I can tell him the truth now it's too late for him to rescue me.

"I didn't mean it," I whisper, and my voice cracks.

In all the lies, he was the only thing that was real.

"I know," he says.

He gathers me into his lap. Sadness aches in my chest— mine, his, the whole world's. Happiness swells in counter- point. It's too much to contain.

I sob into his neck, and murmur, "I didn't mean it. I didn't mean it."

He rocks me, stroking my hair, my back, his lips cool on my temple.

A perfect goodbye. With one regret. When I see him again in real life, monster-Axelle will feel the opposite of what I feel.

She will hate him.

37

Voices tug me from sleep, speaking in whispers. Snatches of a conversation in another language. Not English or any other Earth language.

I lie very still.

Was I in the pub last night? Is that why my body aches and a black hole has eaten my memories? Please don't let me have had drunken sex with Mallory. I'm still pissed at him for yesterday's cave explosion.

The talking continues. At least two males and a female. The words flow over and around each other in a rich tapestry of sound. Beautiful and elemental.

Anann—the language of monsters.

How the hell did I get here? Verdanians just kill us, they don't take prisoners. Where is my squad? Did I hit my head during a battle?

I move my arms and legs a fraction. No resistance. No battlesuit, either. The arrogant bastards. I can't hurt them without my battlesuit and my weapons so they haven't bothered to restrain me. I'm more likely to hurt myself.

Well, the marble gods of Verdana are about to learn a valuable lesson.

I peek through my lashes. A male and a female sit with

their backs to me. Pink hair curls past the female's shoulders, tiny flowers woven among the strands. Her beaded top, little more than a bra though her species have no tits, leaves the smooth expanse of her back bare. The male has bright yellow hair to the nape of his neck. The pair block my view of the other male.

Three bloodstone rifles lie to their left on a bed of moss, the suns slanting double shadows through an overhanging fern. One is mine, my call sign inked on the barrel. Who did they slaughter for the other two?

Time to show them why I'm Godkiller. Three more kills will put me on fifteen and equal with First Minister Seabird.

What an honour. He's a legend.

I ease a breath in and out, my heartbeat steady. I'm pretty good at emulating the impassivity of our enemies.

Three, two, one...

"No, Axelle!" a voice yells.

My graceful leap happens only in my mind. My legs collapse, flopping me onto the guns instead of the roll and grab I planned.

How the hell does one of the creatures know my name?

I heave myself to my knees, the heavy familiarity of the gun in my hands.

Holy fuck, I'm in my underwear. What have the monsters done to me?

The pink-haired and yellow-haired Verdanians disappear into the trees. The final one stands alone. He's a breath-taking specimen—tall, the sweep of his shoulders narrowing to slim hips, his skin a milky swirl of rainbow colours. High cheekbones, emerald eyes, pale-green hair. A spike of fear clenches my gut.

But I'm not afraid.

I've been here before… No, not here. Somewhere darker. Rock dust and the drip of stalactites. The taste of something sweet.

And deadly.

I nock my gun to my shoulder and stare down the barrel. The Verdanian carefully spreads his hands. No weapon but an axe sticks up over his shoulder. I've seen the damage they can do.

My finger tightens on the trigger.

"You know who I am, Axelle," he says in perfect English.

My chest sings at his words. I wobble on my knees, and the gun wavers. There's something wrong with my heart. It's split into three and two are thud, thud, thudding to drown out the first.

"You do not want to hurt me."

My heart sings but my stomach twists. Have I been poisoned? He's my enemy, I have to kill him.

But… but…

Why does this all feel so damned familiar?

"Hurting you is all I want to do," I say, my conviction ruined by a bubble of doubt.

The Verdanian doesn't flinch. A lovely turquoise and violet stone hangs below the hollow of his throat. His trousers are calf-length and held up by a black belt, long fronds ending in beads dangling down one thigh.

I've seen it before. Played my fingers through the fronds. They're soft for bark.

I would never touch a Verdanian.

I've touched this one.

"Half-lie, half-truth," the male says.

His lips quirk. It's the most expression I've seen on one of them. They take stony-faced to the next level.

But that's not quite right, either.

Why am I so muddled? I am a squad leader. We are decisive. Confident. We do not get flustered by a Verdanian speaking in riddles.

"The real Axelle would never hurt me," he continues. "The Axelle they want you to be is trying to win. You have to fight her."

Fight who? Who am I if not Axelle?

He steps closer. Every muscle in my body jumps. The gun barrel jerks down, up, as if my arms can't decide what to do. Another step.

He's too close!

He's not close enough.

"Who am I, Axelle?" he says.

The ground shifts under my knees, the world unstable. I blink, and he's my enemy. Another blink, and recognition whispers to me. My gun droops. Confused tears blur my eyes.

I know things about him I can't possibly know—he has a scar on his upper thigh, his favourite colour is green, his feet are ticklish. When he was a child, he constantly exasperated his parents with his tendency to toddle off whenever their backs were turned.

He still exasperates his father.

I open my mouth to tell him he's no one to me but his name rushes along my tongue and spills from my lips.

"Zorian," I say.

I drop the gun on a wave of giddiness, and sit hard on my heels. The tightness in my chest is difficult to breathe past, the ghost heartbeats making it harder.

"You also know Fennanangullandolin and Dalrainenna."

Leaves rustle. Violet eyes watch me through gaps in the branches, an arrow notched in a bow but not pointed. Golden eyes stare from the next tree.

"No one will hurt you here," Zorian says.

My body sways. There's too much swirling around inside me to process. The shimmering rainbow of Zorian's skin dazzles me. Dizziness curls from my toes to the top of my head.

"I forget that dreams are safe," I whisper.

The jungle dissolves to tatters of black, a roar in my ears drowning the wind and hoots and howls. Strong hands catch me before my face meets the ground. Emerald eyes are the last to fade, filled with sadness.

"You are not dreaming," he says. "You have to keep fighting."

I try to conquer the dark but consciousness is a mist. It slips from my hands faster than I can grab it.

But I don't want to sleep.

What if the wrong Axelle wins?

* * *

"They use potions to confuse the senses and fill the mind with false images. It is like spikeweed but stronger."

I wonder when Fenna's English improved before I realise she's speaking Anann.

"When they wear off, we will see how much is left."

How much of what is left?

I catch snippets of conversations but can't keep my eyes open long enough to understand. I drift on the edge of consciousness, aware only that I'm missing something.

"Are you sure about this?" Fenna says.

It's always Fenna. Dalrainenna seems to be the silent type. Maybe he only talks in their dream space, though he was vocal enough from his cage in the basement of the dissection lab.

The dissection lab.

Horror-fury-fear rolls through my stomach before it recedes, leaving me shining and clean, like sand licked by a wave.

"No human has ever entered our cove. Perhaps your father will be more receptive if you wait for his return."

"She needs a proper place to rest. I am worried about her wounds."

Slim fingers cradle my wrist. I claw towards consciousness but my body is a prison. Something is unwrapped from my skin. If I concentrate, I can feel a slight pressure around my other wrist, my ankles, my forehead.

"She fought her restraints," Fenna says.

"Of course she did."

Pride burns in my chest. The sizzle is so strong, it resembles another emotion. One I've never felt. Not like this.

I want to talk to him. Touch him. Tell him I'm okay.

Am I okay?

Shivers wrack me. My teeth chatter, and I worry about biting off my tongue. It's impossible to be cold in the jungle but I'm frozen to the core.

"The effect of the potion is fading," Fenna says.

Zorian bathes me in hot water, and the shaking abates. Heat blazes from my skin. He cuddles me to the lovely coolness of his body, and I doze.

"Axelle," he says.

My eyes are open. I glimpse the pool, grey sand, then he scoops me in his arms, his face buried in my neck, my legs around his waist. He crushes me against him but there's no pain. He could keep squeezing until my spine snaps. I've seen it happen.

"Dreams are safe," I whisper for the millionth time.

His teeth graze my throat. I go from languid to throbbing in two nanoseconds. Zorian raises his face. My breath catches at the need in his eyes.

"Come back to me and we will do this in real life."

His kiss flutters in my belly and tingles where we're pressed together. It's frantic and full of promise. My fingers fist in his hair, his mouth hungry on mine. I've been numb for too long. The desire shocks my system and reminds me how good it is to feel.

There's a certain thing I'm desperate to feel. It's building already, teased by the kiss.

Can a woman get blue balls?

Zorian's hands grip my hips. Silky muscles tense and quiver. He slides himself against me, wonderfully slow, separated by thin layers of cloth. The kiss deepens, the stroke of his tongue mirroring his hips.

Fuck me, he's good.

I moan into his mouth, such eager little whimpering noises, and match his rhythm. Heat pools between my legs. The friction is amazing. Pleasure swells, aching to spill.

Oh god finally, I'm going to come. A dream one but I'm pretty sure it'll be spectacular.

Zorian pulls away. I strain to reach him—okay, to continue dry humping him—but he stops me easily.

"Only in real life, Axelle," he says, smirking. "Maybe I will use my mouth."

I gasp myself awake. The solidness of him curls around my back. My pulse thuds on my tongue, arousal shivering deep beneath his hand splayed on my belly.

Can he feel it?

"Axelle?" he whispers.

I swallow to get my voice under control. Speak too soon and it'll be all sorts of husky.

"I'm here," I say.

His lips curve against my hair. A flash of emotion tightens my chest—relief, joy, a tickle of nerves. A weight floats from my shoulders and leaves me light-headed.

It takes me two attempts to speak. "Were you worried about me, Zorian?"

"More than I have ever been."

"Is she going to try and kill us again?" comes a laconic voice in Anann.

It draws my gaze beyond the security of Zorian's arms. Opposite us, flanked by a spray of ferns, Fenna and Dalrainenna lie head to head, holding hands. Violet and golden eyes watch me side-on.

"Not today, Fenna," I say.

Zorian muffles a sound I'm fairly certain is a chuckle. Fenna blinks. The only sign of her discomfiture.

It's easy to forget how little they express. Zorian is the opposite of impassive.

"You did not speak Anann when first we met," she says.

"Zorianangullewell'yan taught me."

His hands clench.

God, he really likes me saying his full name. I should do it more often.

Fenna's gaze shifts higher. "Yes. It seems he has been doing many things with you."

Oh, so many things. Yet, still, I ache.

Zorian carefully props himself on one elbow. His eyes are filled with everything when he looks at me.

He feels so much. I feel so much.

My hand rises to touch the rainbow sparkle of his skin before I can think about whether it's a good idea in front of Fenna and the silent but watchful Dalrainenna. A frond bandage bracelets my wrist.

"But what is this word you used," she says, "Fenna?"

Zorian cuddles into my palm, his face soft. "It is your short name."

Fenna seems to take a second to process this.

"Zorianangullewell'yan," she says slowly, "what are you doing with your mouth?"

"Smiling. Axelle taught me."

I understand what Zorian meant when he said how he felt in the dream space. I want to take him far away and protect him. I want to show him to Home Base and say, "He is no monster. He is perfect and gentle and honourable. How can you hate him?" It's excitement, fear.

Things I can but shouldn't name.

We stare at each other and it's far too long for polite company.

"The way you're looking at me right now…" I whisper.

"I do not plan to stop."

Fenna manages a human-sounding throat-clearing. We both jump.

"May I be present when you introduce her to your father?"

My eyes widen. Zorian places his hand over mine where it's still attached to his cheek.

"Your father?" I yelp.

"I am taking you home, Axelle."

"That is a very, *very* bad idea."

I sit up but get no further than an inch off the ground, my muscles floppy and unresponsive. My body aches like I've hit the gym too hard, which usually happens when I try to run away from my loneliness or thoughts of the future.

I groan. "Why am I so weak?"

"They tortured you for more than twenty-one days," Zorian says. "It took me fifteen to reach you. You need to rest."

His slim hands pin me when I attempt another struggle upright. I'm wearing a vest and shorts. Shit. Am I in the dream space? No, it's not possible. There's too much of Zorian inside me to be anything other than real. Did he dress me? Did Fenna?

Best not to think about it.

"That reminds me—I told you not to risk yourself." I pinch his thigh and would get more response from pinching a rock.

Shame I can't reach his feet. He giggles and gets all squirmy. It's adorable.

But will he do it in real life? This is only the third time we've met outside of the dream space. I know his mind but not his body.

"If I had not, I would have lost too much," he says.

My heart skips under his hand. I command it to behave. It does it again at his tender smile.

Dammit. The blood connection was intriguing when we met every few weeks. Now, I'll be with him every day, completely vulnerable. Unable to hide. My emotions stripped bare for him. No wonder he didn't want anyone to feel what he feels. It's overwhelming.

Cock. Am I hyperventilating?

Stop panicking, he can feel it!

This makes it worse rather than better. My mouth is so dry, my throat clicks. My pulse thrums on my tongue like I've swallowed a skreeingbird.

"Breathe slowly, Axelle," Zorian says, his finger brushing the stone on my chest. "This will take some getting used to."

"I am surprised the blood connection worked with a human," Fenna says while I pretend I'm a squad leader and not a panting idiot.

I focus on the flow of humid air into my lungs. Breathe in, breathe out. I can do this. My heart settles into a normal rhythm. Zorian and Fenna debate the intricacies of blood connections with different species. What if you shared blood with a water-tiger, for example? Their voices wash over me. The panic ebbs.

Then I remember what Fenna said about Zorian's father.

I can't meet him. What am I supposed to say? Hello, Ballathus, I'm the reason your son reneged on your deal and caused your whole tribe to lose face. Instead of protection, you'll have to compensate the wasted journey of three thousand warriors. But I'm still going to shag your son as soon as we're alone. In fact, I'll have probably shagged him by the time you arrive home. Lovely to meet you.

My heart kicks, and Zorian shudders.

"What did you just think about?" he says.

"Your father."

"He will like you."

I shake my head but Zorian keeps talking.

"Even if he does not, I do not care." His finger strokes along my collarbone. "I have found what I want."

"Please, *please,* can I be there?"

"Shut up, Fenna," Zorian and I say together, though he uses her full name.

"I believe your father may already suspect," Dalrainenna says, and I manage not to flinch.

His silence makes it easy to forget he's there.

"Not the circumstances but you changed before you met your intended mate, though your reluctance for the journey did not. Therefore, it was not your intended. Having met her, I understand. She is… severe."

I fold my lips on a giggle but a hiccup slips out. Zorian presses his hand to his mouth as if he's pondering the statement.

"Some may comment," he says with absolute calm, "that she is not exactly cuddly."

I meet his eyes, and it's a mistake. Our laughter splutters past our defences and drowns out Dalrainenna saying, "What is cuddly?" I laugh until I'm weeping, my stomach sore. Zorian half-collapses over me, an arm braced on either side, his skin glowing. Fenna and Dalrainenna cast worried glances at each other, as if they fear for our mental health.

"This is an extreme example of what I am talking about," Dalrainenna continues despite our mirth. "Laughter is a human trait. As is smiling. You are not human, Zorianangull ewell'yan."

Zorian grins. "No, but some of them are not so bad."

We're doing googly eyes at each other. I'm so relaxed, I don't even care. The laughter has left me boneless. Heaviness creeps into my limbs, my eyes half-lidded.

It's been an exhausting few weeks, not to mention the emotional overload of Zorian's real-life presence.

But I just woke up, just started feeling like myself again. I don't want to sleep. I have too many questions.

"How did the three of you manage to get to me, anyway?" I say, failing to smother a yawn.

Zorian's grin softens to a smile. "I will tell you later. You need to rest."

"I'm not tired," I mumble. At his look, I say, "Right. I can't lie anymore."

"Did you lie to me before?"

I glance at Fenna and Dalrainenna. They are as still as marble statues.

"Only once," I say.

"I knew you did not mean it even before you told me."

"I'm still sorry I hurt you." Damn, I'm getting teary again. The thought of a sad Zorian tightens my chest. "I wanted to keep you safe. Home Base is not safe."

He gathers me in his arms, and I snuggle my face in his neck. He smells so good. My eyes close.

"Now we are both safe," he says.

38

The sound of trickling water teases me from a dream about Zorian. A normal dream. The slide of his skin, the blaze of his eyes above me, the thrust of him so deep—

Have I left the tap on?

I blink awake and stare at the ceiling. The rock ceiling. Threads of purple stone weave through. A heavy drape hangs from hooks drilled into it, sealing me into an alcove. Light sneaks around the gaps.

Where the hell am I?

I sit up, and a blanket of woven fibres folds into my lap. The mattress under my butt is springy. Both smell like mint.

Holy crap. Am I in Zorian's bed?

My pulse kicks but no ghost heartbeats echo alongside. I ease the drape far enough to peek. The room beyond is a domed space carved into the stone. Different-coloured seams glitter in the walls—blue, gold, a green like Zorian's eyes. The light itself comes from cracks in the ceiling, painting patterns on the floor. My bare feet slap on smooth stone, my legs still wobbly. I peer upwards and am blinded by a slice of silver. I blink the afterimages away and use my hand to shield the worst of it. A slab is wedged in the crack, angled to reflect light into the room.

What kind of cave system is this?

A curtain of moss parts on either side of a tiny alcove, a stream of water flowing into a hollow. I collect the liquid in my palm, and drink. Cool and sweet.

Cooled by layers of rock? Water in Ananngar is usually warm.

A wooden shelf holds four layers of bound scrolls. I run a finger along the intricate lines of the wood. The parchments contain neat, printed script. I scroll through poetry, a history of something called the Yullinngiyar Tribe and another where I don't recognise many words but the carefully drawn pictures capture plants of all shapes and sizes, the last few sections blank. I find a weeping nalwell near the end, the petals like a spill of fire. Next to the shelf, there's a puffy, round cushion. It rustles when I flop into it to survey the rest of the room, my legs already tired.

Other shelves line the walls all the way past a slimmer, curtained alcove, each with a variety of different objects— plants trailing from wooden or rock pots, shells, stones, little lantern things stuffed with balls of blue and green moss, a silver slab like the ones in the roof cracks, and—

"Ophrys!"

I leap from the cushion. Or try to. It hisses and shifts under my weight. My legs pedal at the air, and I'm glad I'm alone. I manage to heave myself free, stumbling to one of the shelves and its familiar glass tank. Water beads the inside and slicks the bottom. Ophrys perches on a mound of freshly picked leaves, munching happily. I open the net top and pluck him out to kiss his black shell with its purple- and green-shimmering highlights. He wiggles his fronds in greeting.

I clear my throat, pretending I'm not choked up over a snail.

"How did you get here?"

Ophrys, as usual, ignores me. I plop him into my hand and cuddle him to my chest. Who cares about the slime? I thought he'd starved or been crushed by Mallory.

God, is Mallory permanent squad leader now I'm properly AWOL? I can't let that slide. I need to find a way to talk to my squad.

Ophrys glares at me through four eyes. My turn to ignore him. The shelf his tank rests on is made of overlapping rib plates from a creature about the size of a water-tiger, as are the rest of the shelves in the room. Ophrys gets more impatient and flaps his fronds against my palm.

"All right, all right, go back to your food," I sigh. "I don't know why I keep you around."

I plonk him on his dinner pile but freeze before my fingers release his shell.

Ghost heartbeats.

I wipe my palm on my shorts and stop myself from fussing with my hair. It's gross and limp and patting at it isn't going to help. Zorian stands in an archway, the only door out, his skin rivalling the coloured walls of his room.

"Um, hi," I say with my usual eloquence.

Oh man, so many nerves squiggle around in my belly but I'm pretty sure some are his.

"Hello, Axelle," he says.

I cross the room and hug him before I can wonder whether I smell bad or look even worse.

When did I last brush my teeth?

"You rescued Ophrys," I mumble into his chest.

Zorian curls his slim body around me, his burst of happiness warming me to my toes.

"Of course I did," he says. "You care for him."

I squeeze Zorian harder. I could squeeze as hard as possible and still not hurt him.

He'll have to be a whole lot gentler with me. Why did I think kissing in real life would be a terrible idea? Something about losing my tongue.

His eyes are too intense to meet directly. I trace a finger across his chest and down the dip of his abdominal muscles.

God, he likes me touching him. *Really* likes me touching him.

I hesitate at the waistband of his trousers. Woven grasses form a belt, the strands dyed pink and gold and brown. A knot secures it at his hip.

He's holding his breath. His two hearts trip alongside mine. Longing clenches my gut and shivers lower. I stop breathing.

He said he got lonely but just how lonely was he? Am I really what he wants?

"Is there…" I lick my lips and try again. "Is there somewhere I can, um, wash up?"

Do Verdanians shower? This could quickly become a huge culture shock. And what am I going to eat? Bark will not go down well.

"Are you afraid, Axelle?"

I manage to meet his gaze for a nanosecond before I chicken out and focus on his mouth.

"Maybe," I say.

He cups my cheek, his lips curving in a smile.

"Half-truth," he says, and takes my hand. "Come, I will show you."

The archway leads into a larger space, more puffy cushions scattered around a bright, flower-patterned rug. Small wooden tables sit between the cushions. A painting of Zorian's favourite place hangs on the wall, the pool, waterfall, sand and jungle daubed in perfect colour.

"Did you do that?"

"Yes."

"It seems you've been holding out on how talented an artist *you* are."

"I am good with my hands," he says.

I trip on the edge of the rug. Zorian moves in a flash of white and catches me before I can face-plant into a cushion. He cradles my back to his chest, one hand on my belly, the other over my pendant, my heart thudding under his palm.

"You liked what I said about my hands," he says. "You got excited. Why?"

"Because I, ah, admire your creativity?"

Dammit. I shouldn't have phrased it as a question.

He nuzzles my hair. "Half-truth. Tell me the rest."

"And, um, being good with your hands could be taken as innuendo, ah, of a sexual nature."

For fuck's sake, I sound like an idiot.

His lips brush my ear. "Then I am *very* good with my hands."

All my blood pulses south. Zorian shudders and tucks his face into my neck, a growl in his throat. It doesn't help my throbbing one bit. My desire tangles with his to leave me aching. And wet.

"You feel the same as me," he whispers.

The beat of his emotions clenches my chest. They're so raw, so vulnerable. Hope and wonder. Joy. Anxiety.

I manage a husky, "I do," and he cuddles me on the border of rib-crushing. He lowers my feet to the floor but my knees wobble.

"You may have to carry me."

He grins, and the wobbling gets worse.

"I can do that," he says.

He scoops me into his arms. The silver light dances on his skin and pools shadows in his cheekbones. He starts walking towards another archway. I glimpse two more, one covered by another drape and the second into a room that could be a kitchen. I brush a flop of hair off his forehead. His eyes flit to me then away as he dodges around a cushion.

Screw it.

I throw my arm around his shoulders, and kiss him. He startles, nearly dropping me. I suck on his lip. Wood screeches on stone. He lurches and we fall.

Shit, this is going to sting…

He twists and hits the ground first, me on top, sprawled across him. He blinks at me.

"Are you okay—"

"Did I hurt you?" I say at the same time.

He shakes his head. "You surprised me."

"I noticed," I smirk.

We make it through the archway without further incident, mostly because we return to just holding hands.

No more kissing until I'm clean. With his emotions buzzing inside me, compounding mine, it's likely to lead to something much more intimate than kissing.

I ease a quiet breath in and out.

Sex with Zorian. Holy crap. It's going to happen.

He slides me a glance but stays silent. A smooth, stone corridor stretches past another couple of archways—"Toilet," Zorian says at one—and ends in a dim room. Stone steps lead to water bubbling in a pool. Wisps of steam curl from the surface, the air cooler in the cave. As cool as Zorian's skin. Yellow ferns with red veins grow around the edges of the space. Zorian picks some fronds and lays them in a rocky hollow on the edge of the pool.

"This is soap-fern," he says.

He picks up a stone next to the depression, and grinds the fronds. Orange lather stains his hands.

"Wait here. I also have some of your clothes. Not much but I can make you more."

His trousers hit him mid-calf, hugging his hips and slim legs.

I drag my gaze upwards. "I like how you dress. Did you grab anything else?"

"Your battlesuit, sketchpad, that thing you call a tablet."

My tablet! The stone will probably affect the signal but if I can get outside, I can call Loyanne. Talk to my squad.

The corpse of the *HMS Dòchas* has many uses.

"Thank you," I say, touching his arm as he moves past me. "You risked yourself to grab the important stuff. And me."

He gives me a shy smile. "You are important to me."

I struggle to swallow that for a minute but get myself under control by the time he returns with a forest-green t-shirt and trousers, plus underwear and a fluffy, almost feathery, towel. He turns to go.

"No one else will come in here, right? Your father, for instance."

Do I sound panicked? I definitely sound panicked.

"My father is not home yet. He will have another week to travel, I think, if he did not try to follow me."

"Your aunt? She's not going to barrel in demanding to know what you're doing?"

He flashes me a tender smile. "It is just you and me, Axelle. No one but my father can enter without permission."

"The perks of being the leader's son?"

"One of many," he says, leaving me alone with the burble of water and the fruity smell of soap-fern.

39

Zorian kneels between my legs. My butt sinks into the plushness of his bed, my bare feet nowhere near the smooth stone floor. He unwinds my fern bandages.

"You are right about our blood," he says, focused on his task. "Your wounds were raw and weeping a day ago."

He bites his thumb. An ache flares in my own, and I rub it against my thigh. Zorian peeks at me, a smile flitting across his face. Pearly beads well, and he dabs them on the scabs braceleting my wrists and ankles.

Verdanian teeth penetrate their skin better than any blood-stone. Imagine the damage blades or bullet tips could do, embedded with incisors and canines.

I guess I can't switch the soldier part off fully. One day, though. One day, I will be more than a killer.

Zorian shuffles closer, reaching up to swipe his blood along my forehead. His other hand drops to my thigh, probably for balance, his thumb brushing that sensitive, inner curve. The touch, conscious or not, sends a little pulse through me.

Just how horny am I?

Zorian goes very still.

I forgot I can't hide anything. Can't hide what the tiniest caress does to me. What being close to him does to me. I'm like a freaking water-tiger in heat.

But he can't hide, either.

I capture his hand where it hovers near my face. His eyes meet mine with a physical jolt. I force myself to hold his gaze and suck his thumb into my mouth, swirling my tongue around the pad to lap the blood. I remember sucking on another part of him and I feel it, a ghost mouth, searing hot, soft lips around a piece of anatomy I've never had. A drawing, pulling surge of pleasure…

It seems Zorian remembers, too.

I gasp and release his thumb. He sways bonelessly on his knees, blinking at me. His cheeks glow with a subtle rainbow glitter.

"Are you blushing, Zorian?"

He braces a hand on either side of me and shakes his head.

Nothing twists through my stomach.

So non-verbal gestures also avoid the whole truth/lie thing. Good to know.

I grin at his struggle to gather himself. I like it when he's the flustered one, though it flutters in my gut all the same. Time to get him *really* flustered.

"I've been wondering what the mouth stuff would be like in real life," I say, and move to slide off the mattress.

His hands catch my hips and clamp me in place. "You first."

The growl in his voice pools heat between my legs and twines with the nerves in my belly. My pulse splits into a million and puts the other ones to shame.

Zorian swallows hard. "All that from only the thought of it?"

"I told you anticipation was sexy."

I cup his face, my fingers splayed on his cheekbones, and

bend my head. I kiss him, properly, for the first time in real life. It's like in our dreams—firm, cool lips, ice and mint and hunger. His hearts kick in my chest. Need curls in my gut, building with the press of his mouth. I moan when his tongue glides against mine.

Snogging Zorian is awesome. Even if I have to be careful of his teeth.

His hands slip under my t-shirt to stroke up my back, playing along my ribs, my spine. Such talented hands. I throb everywhere I want him to touch.

He breaks the kiss and we pant at each other, my cheeks flushed, his skin sparkling rainbow colours.

So pretty.

I pop the button on my trousers. Nerves buzz in my stomach, mine and his. He helps me ease the material off and I snag my underwear with it instead of wimping out and keeping them on. It takes him a while to drag his gaze to my face. I guess I have more going on down there than a Verdanian female. More folds. More hair.

"You are very nervous now," he says softly. "But you want."

I clear my throat, though it still comes out husky. "I want."

His fingers curl around my thighs, and he spreads my legs wider. My whole body pulses. The tremor of his hearts echoes mine.

Fucking hell, I'm so wet.

"Axelle," he breathes.

"Sorry."

He shakes his head, his expression stunned. "Everything you feel is wonderful."

"It's about to get a lot better."

He flashes a shy smile. "I have never done this before. You

may be disappointed."

"I don't think that's possible with you, Zorian."

Joy expands in my chest and brings tears to my eyes.

How could I have ever believed he felt nothing?

He trails a finger up my thigh, hesitates, then swirls it through my pubic hair. He tugs gently, and we share a shiver. He leans close. Close enough for his breath to brush sensitive, swollen areas. Every part of me strains, aches, towards him.

"No teeth," I manage to gasp.

He grins, and my bones turn to water. His eyes stay on me, blinding emerald and gold. My heart flaps against my ribs.

"No teeth," he says, and places a soft kiss between my legs.

The sound that flies from my mouth is guttural and unfamiliar. Zorian's hands tremble on my thighs. He teases me with his lips—nibbling, sucking, pulling begging noises from my throat. The fork of his tongue explores each fold and dip and circles the throbbing bud at my apex.

He flops back on a groan, his eyes dazed. "Oh—"

"Fuck," I provide helpfully.

"—*fuck*, Axelle. Does it really feel that good?"

"God, yes," I sigh.

"This may be a problem."

"And by problem, you mean amazing, right?"

"Yes, amazing but also short."

"I don't care, as long as it's spectacular."

"I no longer doubt it will be."

"Look at you, all confident."

"Should I not be confident?"

His eyes pin me. He licks me in a long, cool, glorious line and I writhe on the edge of the bed, my response dissolving in a moan. His own moan vibrates between my legs as he presses his mouth against me. My spine bows, my head tossed back. A whimper of his name floats to the stone ceiling. His hands clamp me to him. Merciless. I struggle to breathe past the thud of my heart, his hearts. He slips his tongue inside me, and my orgasm explodes in a sizzling, muscle-quivering rush.

Aeons pass. Worlds are born then die. I return to myself, staring at the purple-veined rock above me, sprawled in sheets smelling of Zorian. Fresh and minty. His hearts play bouncy-ball with mine so he's still alive, though I can't see him. I roll, and peer over the edge of the bed.

He lies on his back on the floor, arms and legs akimbo, his eyes half-lidded. Rib plates heave under silky skin. He blinks and takes a few seconds to focus on me.

"I think I may also need to wash up," he says.

A dark stain covers the front of his trousers, which have slipped low enough to show his hipbones.

I slide from the bed and crawl to him, my legs too wobbly for walking. I straddle his hips, immediately worsening his wet patch, and give him a smirk.

"Or we could get dirtier *then* clean up."

"You need to rest," he says, though his need flares heat under my skin.

"You don't have the stamina?"

"I am a warrior—I have the stamina." He flexes beneath me and every part of him is stone. "But you are recovering."

I yank my t-shirt off, wearing only my bra. Leaning forward, I rub myself on his damp patch and splay my hands on his chest, my arms mounding my breasts together.

"Do you really want me to rest?"

He looks like I've rapped him between the eyes with a big

rock. His desire throbs in parts still wet from his mouth.

"You should," he manages, though his voice is strained.

"Half-truth." I straddle him on all fours to bring my lips close to his ear. "Feel this truth, Zorian—I want to fuck my alien. Right now."

He shudders underneath me. His swirl of emotion leaves me breathless.

"I am your alien?"

"Mine," I whisper, and kiss him.

I swallow his whimper and it tingles all the way down. He sits up, cradling me in his lap, grinding me to where he is so very hard. His trousers and my bra disappear. We stare at each other.

Really naked. Really doing this. A human and a Verdanian. Or am I half-Verdanian?

There are not many taboos left for me to break.

"What if I hurt you?" he says softly.

His hands flutter over me. His nerves and excitement flutter inside me. I'm on my knees, my palms on his shoulders, ready to lower myself into his lap. He aches for this, his need drowning me, yet his worry prickles on my shoulder blades.

"You'll feel it if you do. And you'll stop."

"You trust me that much?"

"I trust you."

"Axelle, I—"

I shush him with a kiss and slide myself onto him.

Holy mother of Verdana.

He is so deep, so cool, inside me but I feel the ghost of him buried in heat and tight, silken muscles. Pleasure swells, hot and cold. I ease him in and out, my body already quivering and close. Everything he's feeling throbs inside him and pulses into me.

"Oh, shit," I moan.

His fingers are gentle where they grip my hips but his eyes are half-crazed.

"Those are the first words you ever said to me."

"How different the context."

My laugh becomes a whimper as I drive myself harder, deeper. It's almost too much. Too much to take. Too much to hold.

And then it bursts.

I howl like a water-tiger after it's mounted its mate. I'd be embarrassed if Zorian's shout didn't also echo off the ceiling. We collapse into each other, his arms around me, my chin on his shoulder. Aftershocks make us squirm. His cool skin feels wonderful against mine.

"Perhaps it is just as well my species cannot have sex like this," he pants into my hair. "We would never get anything done."

"I'm not finished with you yet, buddy."

"Oh, shit," he says.

40

For the next three days, it's all we do, except eat and sleep. It's like I've never had sex before. There's not a surface we don't shag against. The floppy cushions are fun, as is the bathing pool. Zorian's ability to breathe underwater sure makes it memorable. He says the brush of my fingers in his gills is erotic. He likes when I kneel on the edge of the bed so he can take me from behind. He's in charge of the pace, the depth. On each hard thrust, he strokes me with his slim fingers.

We don't last long on that one. Or at all. As soon as the sex starts to feel good for either of us, it snowballs into one spectacular orgasm after another. Not that I'm complaining, though I've turned into the slobbering love-puppy I was afraid of.

He's just so damn curious.

He explores every part of my body with lips, tongue, hands. He discovers exactly what feels amazing. Teasing me. Teasing us both.

"You are a pulsing thing," he whispers.

His mouth nuzzles my neck, my body stretched on top of him, singing from the play of his fingers. His struggle not to tip us over the edge is fucking hot.

"Bite me," I sob.

320

He doesn't hesitate. He knows what I want and all I want is him.

Teeth pierce sensitive skin. He starts to suck, and slides himself inside me. It is our undoing.

His aunt yells at him to let her in from the front door—or drape—at least once a day but their culture forbids her from entering without his permission. Her tirades become increasingly frustrated. We only speak to Fenna. Dalrainenna disapproves but remains polite. He helped with my rescue since he owed me a debt for freeing him from his prison. No one knows I'm here apart from them. Zorian's father continues to communicate with his aunt on his journey home but he believes Zorian simply baulked from his chosen mate and is hiding in his room. He has no idea Zorian has chosen another.

Am I his mate? I can't imagine not having his hearts beating alongside mine. My life was empty before.

I like it when Zorian is on top, which is unusual for me, being a squad leader and all. We can't kiss in missionary position so he props himself on his hands. I love to watch the dance of his muscles and that long, white hardness gliding in and out of me.

He gasps my name like it's sacred.

We sleep wrapped in each other. In the dream space, we can be rougher. We last longer, though it's no less spectacular.

The exercise does wonders for my recovery, as does the Verdanian diet rich in fatty acids and protein from grains, berries, nuts and tubers. I decline to sample the bark.

Zorian grows food plants in pots carved from bone, wood and stone. It reminds me of my pod. He eats most of it raw but he can cook and heat water for tea.

"This is a sunstone," he says, smoothing his fingers along a slab of transparent yellow rock in the kitchen alcove. "Watch."

He plucks a scrap of material away from a cleft in the ceiling. A beam of light spears the sunstone. The yellow surface swirls, turning milky. He holds my hand above it.

"It's hot!" I say.

"It is very rare and hidden deep underground."

"Sacred?" I smirk.

He smiles and picks me up. I wrap my legs around his waist.

"Everything is sacred, Axelle," he says.

* * *

"They are the enemy!" Vail screams in my face. "They want to kill us all!"

I try to shake my head but the strap clamps me to the table. Vail unwinds the cord from his ponytail, his grey hair flopping to his wiry shoulders. The citrine gem thwacks against my collarbone, and I cry out.

"They are the enemy—"

"Axelle."

The voice calms my panicked struggles. My eyes dart around the cramped room but there's nothing except Vail and the familiar cupboards and sink. Vail swings the stone in a blur. I brace for the burst of pain.

"Axelle, come to me."

I open my mouth to yell, "I can't," and step off the table. My foot sinks into warm sand. Water burbles into a pool.

"I do not like that you have nightmares but this is better than the one with the eyes," Zorian says, cradling me in his arms.

322

"Yeah, I don't like that one, either."

"Who is he?"

Vail stands frozen, his mouth twisted in a snarl. The stone hangs suspended in its arc towards the empty table. A snail investigates the straps, its shell the size and colour of an Earth orange.

"Elderman Vail."

"Is he your leader?"

"Second in command." I magic Seabird with his tuft of white hair and his peridot eyes that could be gentle but are harder than a Verdanian's skin. "This is our leader—First Minister Seabird."

"Show me who else hurt you."

Carniss and Thorn join Vail and Seabird. Carniss holds her electric prod in her meaty hand. Thorn glares his disdain from black eyes.

"And this is Elderman McBurnie. He hurt me because he did nothing."

McBurnie towers over everyone except Zorian, though he's much broader. His ginger hair frizzes in all directions.

"You respected him," Zorian says, circling the still figures.

"I respected all of them. But the Elders are a barrier to peace. These are the people we have to stop. Maybe even kill."

Zorian cuddles me to his chest. "We will not kill unless we have to."

He bares his teeth at the gathered Elders, his expression feral and beautiful and all warrior.

"But that does not apply to the ones who touched you. Them, I could kill."

Funny. Me, too.

Loyanne bursts into tears as soon as she answers my sat call on her tablet. It worsens the guilt for neglecting my squad to have sex with my alien. He's just too damn good at it.

"Axe," Loyanne sobs, "we thought you were dead."

"The rumours have been greatly exaggerated."

Dante's face crowds in next to Loyanne's tear-streaked one. "Elderman Vail told us you were killed by the Verdanian insurgents a week ago. We thought they'd taken you in for reconditioning but they said they were training you for a special mission."

More lies to obscure the truth. Don't they ever get tired?

"Like I said—greatly exaggerated. Can you get the veterans together? We've a lot to talk about."

Loyanne swipes at her tears. "Where are you? We've missed you around here. Mallory is even more of a douche as squad leader."

"Of that, I have no doubt. I'll tell you everything once you're all together. How long?"

"Give us half an hour," Dante says.

"How's Marvyn?"

"On light duties, doing well. He struggled after your death but found purpose in goading Mallory about how terrible he compares to you."

I grin past the lump in my throat. "That's the spirit. Call me when you're together. Be careful."

I tap the screen and their faces disappear.

"You care about them," Zorian says, perched on the pink rock cradled by grey sand.

His favourite place is even more beautiful and serene in real life. The pool, the waterfall, the vibrant jungle.

"I love every goddamn one of them," I say.

"Do you think they will like me?"

He digs his toes into the sand. A sheen of sunlight glistens on his sheer top, the one he wore during our dream argument.

"We'll soon find out."

He gives me wide eyes, his bleat of panic in my chest.

"And this is how I feel about meeting your father," I say with a burn of satisfaction.

"Now you are the smug one."

I stand between his feet and brush a lock of pistachio hair off his forehead.

"If they can't learn to like you then they're not the people I thought they were."

His shy smile squiggles in my gut. "They call you Axe."

"It's my short name."

He grins and slides his hands up my legs to cup my butt. I climb into his lap. Desire flashes heat to my fingers and toes.

"We have half an hour to kill," I say.

He kisses my throat and his lips curve at my gasp.

"Plenty of time."

* * *

The news of my resurrection meets with such joy, I let my squad babble at me for a few minutes while I struggle to maintain my dispassionate persona.

Squad leaders do not bubble.

They're in an empty classroom, huddled together at the desks and staring towards me, Loyanne broadcasting her tablet to the large screen. I have to make do with their tiny faces but it's enough.

I missed them, too.

Zorian paddles along the edge of the water, still nervous about being introduced. He wants to cuddle me and soothe the happy-sadness of talking to my squad but he's afraid to get too close to the tablet.

My muscles have a pleasant ache from the previous thirty minutes. After the rock, we swam in the pool. I floated on my back, my arms pedalling to keep me from drowning, my stomach tight at the effort. Zorian cradled my thighs. The lap of his tongue in sync with the lap of the water. His—

Holy crap, this is not the time.

But he loves what I feel from just his mouth.

Thank god being flushed and wet is normal in the jungle.

"All right, guys, settle down," I say over my squad's excited voices, "before you attract attention."

Pride burns as they immediately fall silent. My squad is the fucking best.

"As you can see—my death was a lie, as was the shit about training me for a special mission. The Elders have lied to us from the beginning."

"Were you really in behavioural reconditioning, Axe?" Loyanne says, squashed on a chair next to Dante so they're almost in each other's laps.

"For three weeks."

Karine shivers. "You don't look or sound like Max."

"They didn't finish, otherwise I would."

"What was it like?" Lili says in her soft voice.

"Painful. Terrifying. Confusing."

Zorian meets my gaze, my truth ringing in his chest. He offers a burst of strength, and I have to stop myself from giving him a tender smile.

"Those bastards." Pacal slaps his hand on a desk. "We tried to get into the dissection lab after you went AWOL. We figured something went wrong at the hospital. Mallory was standing guard. He put us on a month of wall duty. The few hours of free time we had were on waste duty."

"You idiots. I ordered you not to attempt a rescue, no matter what."

"That was one order we couldn't abide, Axe," Glennis says, holding Nolana's hand on the table. "You're our squad leader. We don't want anyone else."

"And we thought you'd forgive us," Loyanne says with a sheepish grin. "You forgive us, right?"

I clear my throat. Once, twice.

It's the humidity.

"Of course I do. You're idiots but you're *my* idiots."

"How did you escape?" Marvyn says. He's pale, a little skinnier than I'd like but his brown eyes are bright. "Are you somewhere safe?"

"I'm safe, Marvyn. I hear you've been defending my honour to Mallory."

His cheeks pink. He traces a pattern on the desk with his fingernail.

"He can never be what you were—what you are—to us."

Damn. It takes more throat-clearings and swallows until my voice doesn't wobble.

"You guys are the best squad a leader could ask for."

Muffled sniffling and shuffling mix with the screech and hoot of the jungle.

"Dusty in here," Dante coughs, swiping at his eyes.

I give them another minute. Not because *I* need it.

No way.

"But I didn't escape, Marvyn," I say, and they all focus on me. "The Verdanian insurgency was my rescue."

The words drop into the room. They float around without registering for a millisecond, expressions flickering to puzzlement, then understanding sweeps across their faces. Their outburst startles a flock of ruby skreeingbirds that streak over the water, skreeing their fury and disappearing into the green.

I hold a hand up to dam the torrent of questions. "Remember a while ago, after the cave-in, when I said I hadn't been entirely truthful? Well…"

I walk towards Zorian. His attention snaps from his toes wriggling in the pool to me. He pretends to be stone but his hearts bounce around in my chest like two water-dragons fighting over a nut.

He's so cute when he's nervous.

"Guys"—I tap the screen to switch the camera and hold the tablet upright—"this is Zorian. Zorian is the Verdanian from the cave. His death may also have been exaggerated."

His eyes flick from the tablet to my face. "They can see me?"

I nod, and he gives a little wave. Chairs screech and my squad vanishes from the tablet, no doubt crowding around their screen, mouths agape.

What do they see? He's beautiful, the line of limbs and muscle carved from marble. I look at him and see everything I never knew I lacked. I see truth, freedom. Joy.

He touches his hand to his chest and smiles at me, flashing a hint of fang. A chorus of gasps ripples from off-camera but I'm somewhat distracted, struggling with the desire to wrap myself around that cool, solid body. The fact he wants the same, and it throbs inside me, makes it a million times harder to resist.

Pacal flops into a chair and huffs out a breath. "I think I speak for all of us when I say—what the actual fuck, Axe?"

My squad finds their seats, and I switch the camera back. I sit on the pink rock and tip my head for Zorian to join me. We squash together, my shoulder pressed to his arm, his leg against mine.

"What the actual fuck may take some explaining," I say.

Brindan keeps shaking his head, as if there's an insect dive-bombing his ear. Lili is so pale, her eyes are huge. Karine frowns at a desk, her fingernail picking at the surface. The others are harder to read, their expressions stunned but guarded. Except Dante and Loyanne. They appear to be joining the dots and content with the pattern.

Pacal waves his finger between Zorian and me. "Are you and he…?"

"I will not be taking questions on that aspect, Strife," I say.

He rocks in his chair but a smirk blooms and unfurls into a wide grin.

"You absolute dog," he says, his brown eyes glittering.

"Is that good?" Zorian mumbles out the side of his mouth.

"From Strife, it's the ultimate compliment."

"And Strife is…?"

"His codename. His real name is Pacal."

I point out the rest of the squad and they return a limp wave or two. Karine hunches her shoulders, refusing to look up. Brindan's gaze darts around as if he can't decide what to do with his eyeballs.

"Now that we've all been properly introduced," I say, "let's return to the WTAF question."

And I tell them everything. The blood connection, the dream space, the reinforcements bearing down on us, the real reason we're at war. Marvyn goes a little green on hearing what sped his recovery. Their eyes glaze towards the end but I can't blame them. It's a shock of information. More than they were ever expecting when we started our campaign in the hospital.

"Can I call you tomorrow, same time?"

"Of course, Axe but…" Loyanne blinks, as if waking from a deep sleep. "What can we do? How can we stop them?"

Practical Loyanne, always stabbing to the heart of the matter.

I take Zorian's hand. Squeeze hard. "We remove the cancer from Home Base."

<h1 style="text-align:center">42</h1>

Security lights bathe the walls of Home Base, banishing the dark and smothering the phosphorescent plants. It's why I've never noticed the phenomenon before, except in the cave.

Humanity—bringing pollution wherever we go.

I touch a fingertip to the radio on my collar. "Deltosaurus, Nails—what's your status?"

A monewt hoots sleepily in the depths of the whispering jungle. My skin itches beneath a layer of swamp mud, and I order myself not to scratch.

"Ten minutes," Glennis hisses. "They've upped their precautions. I wonder why."

"Can you still seal it once you have our guns?"

"Of course," she says.

I toggle the microphone off and settle into the warm dirt, stretching my muscles to ward off the stiffness. Leaves flutter in the breeze, the sky a glimpse of velvet black through the gaps. A snail climbs onto the barrel of my rifle and nibbles at the sights. Pale cones sprout from its shell in all directions.

"It is not too late to turn back. Chief Bruad'arach will return in four days. It is foolish not to consult him."

I strain my neck but can't see much beyond Zorian stretched out beside me, the shadow of Fenna over his shoulder, and the cloaking plants.

"Thank you, Dalrainenna," I say in Anann. "Your continued objection is noted."

"You are putting us all at risk. It is foolish to attack when reinforcements are days away."

"So you've said. And as I've said—we're not attacking, we're relieving them of command for their crimes against Verdana. You didn't have to come."

"My mate is here," he says stiffly, and I can picture the stony thrust of his jaw I've come to know as his mulish face.

I bite back my response and the swallowed words stutter on my heartbeat. Zorian shifts, the security lights reflecting in his eyes. Mud masks the gleam of his skin and clumps in his hair, the weight flopping it across his forehead worse than it usually does.

"So is mine," I want to say.

So is mine.

Oh, shit.

"Dalrainenna is not as curious as I," Zorian says, his lips curved.

Dalrainenna sniffs. "Recklessness is not curiosity."

Fenna murmurs something to him and they slide into one of their long, whispered conversations. As long as the gist is, "Quit complaining, we're risking us all to save us all," then I don't mind being excluded.

Zorian puts his hand over mine. "It will be all right."

"Maybe we *should* wait for your father."

He was due to arrive home tomorrow but a landslide swept away part of their route. Detouring around it gave us the extra days needed to plan.

I'm hoping his reaction to Zorian and me will be mellowed

if we present him with a proper peace treaty, one not sullied by the betrayal of the Elders. He should have a say in how they'll be punished for their crimes.

And I can't leave my squad vulnerable in Home Base any longer. What if Vail decides to recondition them all just in case?

"You were right—if we wait, it could take weeks of negotiation to agree on a plan. Or the Yullinngiyar withdraw their support and return north."

I huff out a breath. "I know. But I hate putting everyone I care about in the vicinity of Vail and Seabird. If they catch you…"

Nausea curls in my gut.

Vail would love to get his scalpel on Zorian. In Zorian.

Zorian squeezes my hand. "Are you worried about me, Axelle?"

"Always," I say.

He leans in for a kiss, and I meet him half-way. His lips taste of earth and mint.

I love kissing him in real life. His hearts jump every time and race alongside mine. He's careful with his teeth, his strength, even when his control slips and his hunger throbs in my stomach and lower places. Kissing in real life inevitably leads to sex.

I force myself to pull away before Dalrainenna gets all sniffy at our inter-species intimacy. Zorian's gaze drops, and I shiver at his pulse of desire.

He made me clothes and they're a little tighter than what I'm used to wearing. The shirt of finely woven material hugs my arms to my elbows and moulds to my breasts, giving more lift than any bra I've ever owned. Cord secures the plunging neckline and enhances my cleavage, the same cord that criss-crosses up the side of my trousers.

Zorian liked the new clothes. His need was too much to think past, too much to breathe past. I became a slick, pulsing thing, aching for his touch. It took me two hours to finally get dressed because he kept peeling the clothes off as soon as I put them on. He was insatiable.

It was bloody awesome.

"We're a go," Glennis says in my mic.

I jump but disguise it as a stretch, though Zorian knows exactly what's going on under my skin.

He loves it when I get all hot just thinking about him.

"Excellent," I say, only a little breathless. "We're moving in. Radio silence to the classroom."

The snail, having found nothing edible on my rifle, slithers onto my wrist and investigates the layer of drying swamp mud, six eye stalks waving gently. I pluck her off the pale trail she's left on my arm and place her on a waxy leaf. I crawl on my elbows through the last fringe of jungle and slip into the shade of the grass tunnel, the security lights turning the blades emerald and violet around me. Zorian follows, no louder than the breeze, then Fenna and Dalrainenna. The panel pops into my fingers, and I sigh out a breath when we're all crouched in the blackness of the wall space.

I worried the blood connection would be distracting in a combat situation. Feeling his anxiety and anticipation as well as my own. But Zorian is a comforting presence in the dark. Steady heartbeats and a burn of excitement.

Everything he's dreamed of is finally happening.

I ease the inner panel free. Home Base slumbers, the spaces and alleyways empty of people. A guard coughs atop the wall and footsteps clomp over our heads. They fade, and I climb through the hatch, sealing it behind us. Sticking to the shadows, I weave a circuitous path between the modules, avoiding the barracks, residencies and social areas, including the hospital.

Fenna and Dalrainenna must be sick of this barren place of concrete and alien-made buildings. I'll never forget they helped Zorian rescue me despite what they suffered here.

Even if Dalrainenna's attitude is a bit annoying.

I press my back to the side of a module and wave for them to copy me. Their tall figures slink into the shadows.

"Wait here," I say then touch my radio. "Squad, I'm coming in."

The classroom door hisses open and shut. I blink as my eyes adjust to the dark. A light clicks on, bathing a circle of desks in a warm, yellow glow. My heart swells into my throat.

The veterans of my squad stand to attention, fingers pressed to their chests. They've had a lot of shocks these past few days but their eyes still widen. Pacal grins at me.

"Axe, one question?"

"Does it have to do with what I'm wearing?"

His grin broadens. "Yes, it does."

I glimpse myself in the reflection of the screen. My hair is pinned but free enough to spill down my back and over my shoulders. Swamp mud streaks my face and bands my eyes. I look like a warrior. The rest, I'm still getting used to.

"It's camouflage," I say, and ignore the heat in my cheeks.

"Sure, the mud. Not so much the tit-hugging top and peek-a-boo trousers. Don't get me wrong—I like it."

Glennis joins him in the shit-eating grin competition. "Yeah, Axe, you're a real knockout."

"Fuck you all," I say.

They swallow me in a scrum of bodies. Loyanne crushes my ribs and sobs into my hair. Glennis pounds my shoulder to jelly. Lili is like cuddling a wisp of fog. I hug every last one of them until dirty tears drip from my chin and sniffles, some my own, fill the small space. Mud daubs their olive uniforms. Nine bloodstone rifles sit on the desks behind them.

"Where are the Verdanians?" Marvyn says, and his throat bobs. "Zorian and… Fenella? Dal-something?"

"I wanted to check how jumpy you were before I invited them inside."

Loyanne swipes a palm across her wet cheeks, her eyes red. "I'm nervous but mostly curious. I've never stood in a room with one; talked to one."

"It's time we changed that," I say.

Nolana douses the light and I usher Zorian, Fenna and Dalrainenna inside. Even though they're prepared for it, my squad tenses. Lili gasps. Brindan and Karine huddle at the back.

Blackness covers the white gleam of their skin but you wouldn't mistake them for human. For one, Fenna refused to put mud in her pink hair, though it's tied back. Their eyes blaze emerald and violet and gold from their dark, high-cheekboned faces. They seem huge in the tiny space of the classroom, though my squad are all a similar height. Zorian and Fenna have a rifle each, Dalrainenna a bow and arrows.

Loyanne shuffles forward and holds out a shaking hand. "Hello, Zorian. Nice to meet you. I'm—"

"Loyanne." He takes her hand and smiles, careful not to flash his teeth. "I remember. Nice to meet you."

She gazes at him, her eyes dazed, her scarred mouth slack.

Dante clears his throat. "Babe."

She jerks and snatches her hand away. "Right. Nice to meet you also, Fenna, Dalrainenna."

I translate to Anann, mostly for Dalrainenna's benefit, and Fenna inclines her head.

"Hello, human," she says in English, and I hide a smirk.

Dalrainenna maintains his stony expression and chooses to be mute. I wave everyone towards the seats. Zorian, Fenna and Dalrainenna struggle to get their long legs under the desks, unused to sitting behind them like we are. My squad slides glances their way every couple of seconds.

"So, first of all, let's just acknowledge this is weird as shit," I say, and my squad laughs, the tension slipping from their shoulders. "I'm officially dead, you lot are on probation and three of your enemies are sitting next to you. But what we do tonight could change the course of history on this planet."

Zorian sits straight in his chair, fingers clasped on the desk, his legs splayed underneath. His curiosity keeps getting the better of him, his eyes drinking in the room, though it's a pretty standard classroom module. Fenna and Dalrainenna watch the door, hands on their weapons, readiness carved into their muscles. They already know the plan since I told them earlier to save faffing around with translation. The risk of anyone wandering into the classroom is low but not impossible.

"Our mission is to capture and detain the Elders without alerting the Passengers and the generations. When they wake up tomorrow, they'll finally hear the truth." I pace in front of the blank screen. "Zorian, Fenna, Dalrainenna and I will take Seabird. Loyanne, Dante, Brindan—you're on Vail. Pacal, Lili and Marvyn take Thorn. Glennis, Nolana and Karine are on

Carniss."

"What about the other Elders?" Loyanne says, nibbling on a lock of blonde hair. "They all drank the blood didn't they?"

"They did but those four are the heart of it. The others follow, some reluctantly. McBurnie, for example."

"I can't believe they drink it," Karine says, and disgust ripples across her face. Zorian turns to look at her, and she ducks her head. "Um, no offence."

"I wish they did not drink it, either." He focuses on me. "Sharing blood is sacred."

His burn of tenderness threatens to bring tears to my eyes. I copy Karine's head bow and pretend to flick dirt off my trousers.

"Any other questions? Relevant to the mission," I add when Pacal opens his mouth.

The others shake their heads. I touch my fingers to my chest.

"Then, after tonight, may we never have to fight again," I say softly.

They startle at the words, their gazes flying from person to person. After a slight hesitation, nine hands return my salute.

"May we never fight again," my squad whispers.

<h1 style="text-align:center">43</h1>

The hull of the shuttle vessel curves from the dark, an alien egg in the midst of rectangular modules. The surface swallows the ambient spill from the security lights, dim now that we're deep in Home Base. I hunker next to the Passenger residencies, the Verdanians a silent weight at my back. I will my heart rate to slow and match Zorian's.

How is he so calm? Nerves prickle my skin and dance down my spine. This is different to the thousands of assaults I've completed, the orders I've followed. This time it's for the truth.

And I could lose everything.

"Squad—sound off," I say in my command voice.

"Angelface in position."

"Strife is ready to school this prickly motherfucker."

"Nails ready."

"Then let Operation Topple the Elders commence," I say.

"You really have to let us name the missions, Godkill—I mean Axe," Pacal snorts.

"Godkiller is fine. Turns out I've been focusing on the wrong gods." I flick two fingers towards Seabird's residence. "And let's hope there are no more missions after this."

I lope across the open space, and flatten myself in the

doorway. Zorian, Fenna and Dalrainenna crowd in and, suddenly, it's hard to breathe. Even when they're friendly, they're intimidating. Must be the height.

I slip my bloodstone knife from my forearm sheath and pry open a panel beneath the fingerprint scanner. Wires spill out like a ball of baby slivets. I palm the contraption Glennis made for each team and clip it to the wires that feed the main plate. My thumb presses on the slick surface. The door bleeps and slides open.

"Godkiller in," I whisper to the slice of darkness.

My squad confirms their successful entries as I creep into Seabird's receiving room through the short hallway. Hidden lights set to night level silhouette the long, padded seat where I sipped my wine under the veiled threats of my Elders. I skirt the tables and the pilot's chair, my boots louder than the pad of Verdanian feet. I signal Fenna and Dalrainenna to stay. Zorian trails me as I clear the kitchen, study and bathroom. We crouch on either side of the archway leading into the bedroom.

A pale patch of skin glimmers on Zorian's collarbone where he's missed it with the swamp mud. My fingers ache to touch it. I stroke the stone at my throat instead and he mirrors me, his soft smile almost lost to the darkness.

There's something I want to tell him. Should have told him ages ago. It should be easy since he feels the same as me.

I aim my rifle into the maw of Seabird's bedroom. The words 'HMS Dòchas' glow eerily from the wall above the bed. No lump mars the pristine sheets.

I frown at the empty mattress. "He's not here."

"Perhaps he is in the prison."

I shudder. "I don't want to go down there."

The dissection lab features heavily in my nightmares, though it's only a glimpse before Zorian banishes it for the dream space. Another advantage of the blood connection. He holds me until I stop shaking, takes me on walks to show me parts of Verdana I've never seen before. Distracts and flusters me as only he can.

He places a hand on my shoulder. "You will not be alone."

I allow myself a second to lean into him.

"Axe," Loyanne says, a curl of panic in her voice, "we've lost Brindan."

"What do you mean, you've lost Brindan?"

"He was bringing up the rear. We turned and he was gone. Vail's pod is empty."

I shake my head, Zorian very still and solid beside me. His bleat of unease joins mine in the pit of my stomach.

"Something's not right. Squad—abort. Regroup at rendezvous three." I glance up at Zorian. "Let's get out of here."

I jog for the receiving room, tamping down the urge to sprint as if a water-tiger is on my heels. The lights flare brighter than the main sun. I throw an arm up to shade my eyes.

"Good evening, Axelle of the first," says an awful, inflectionless voice.

Goosebumps erupt under the swamp mud. My rifle jerks up.

"I believe it would be prudent for you and your *friend* to drop your weapons," Seabird says, his crimson uniform a splash of blood against the darker walls.

He stands in the centre of the receiving room, unarmed between Carniss and Thorn, who cradle bloodstone rifles in their hands. Fenna and Dalrainenna lie sprawled on the floor, blinking at the ceiling, though there's no mark on them. Dalrainenna turns dazed, golden eyes on me and I don't need him to speak to hear the, "I told you so."

"Crawling in the dirt with the savages, I see," Thorn sneers, his gaze lingering below my chin.

A growl vibrates over my shoulder. The air smells of scorched turnip. Zorian steps in front of me before I can block him, and my heart leaps into my mouth. His hearts, which raced at the sight of my tormentors, start to slow. A strange numbness sweeps up my limbs.

"Axelle," Zorian says in Anann, his eyes wide, "I feel—"

"Funny," I whisper.

His gun clatters to the floor. He sways and drops to his knees then his hands. He shudders and flops onto his side. I stagger, wrestling with the lethargy.

Seabird drags his reptilian gaze from Zorian. "What did it say?"

"What have you done to them?"

Seabird nudges a metallic grey ball near his foot. It rolls and dinks softly against Fenna's forehead. She doesn't even twitch.

"Air-dispersed muscle relaxant. Effective only on Verdanians. Now drop the gun, Axelle of the first, or Carniss empties her rifle into this one's head." He nods at Zorian. "It'll waste the brain but there's plenty more meat for our needs."

"You fucking monster."

He grins but his eyes harden to chips of ice. My rifle slips from my fingers. I turn my forearm to hide the knife against my body, the sheath and straps masked by black mud.

"Did you really think you could waltz in here without us knowing?" Seabird says, pacing closer. "We suspected your plan but it was nice to have it confirmed."

"Confirmed by who?"

His smug smile carves my chest hollow.

"Dear Brindan of the seventh. A true soldier."

I'm shaking my head before Seabird finishes speaking. "You tortured it out of him."

"On the contrary—he needed no encouragement to expose your treachery."

"I don't believe you."

"Your trust in your little squad is truly touching but they are being caged as we speak. You'll join them soon." A pink tongue flicks over his cracked lips. "But not quite yet."

He stalks closer. I force myself to stay. Zorian's fingers flex on the floor, his knuckles white through the layer of mud. Anger and frustration nibble at my skin.

Did he get a lower dose? Can he move if I prolong Seabird's game?

I pull my gaze upwards before my attention gives him away.

"Vail went easy on you last time," Seabird says, drawing a knife from his uniform. "We couldn't risk damaging the merchandise, dwindling our precious stash. But thanks to your delivery of fresh specimens, we have enough to keep you fit and healthy. No matter how much we hurt you. And the more we hurt you, the more pieces we cut off your Verdanian friends."

He slashes for my face. I catch his bony wrist below his bracelet of tokens. The strength in his wiry arm forces me to use both hands. Something hard prods my ribs while my focus is on keeping the blade from scarring me worse than a Verdanian arrow. Electricity crackles. My muscles snap rigid. Zorian moans. I collapse on the floor, perpendicular with his feet.

"You were right, Melanie," Seabird says, tossing the electroshock weapon to Carniss. "This truly is a wonderful device."

"I'm glad you agree, First Minister. I'm hoping to get her to piss herself this time."

"It's good to have goals. Keeps one young."

The Elders share a laugh while I shiver on the floor. Seabird stomps over and aims a boot. I roll, his toe grazing my side instead of crunching into my ribs. Fury explodes in my chest, searing outward and burning more than the electricity. Zorian lunges, his slim fingers wrapping around Seabird's ankle. He tugs, and Seabird lands on his face with an, "Oof!" His knife flies under the long seat.

Zorian flops onto his back, his burst of energy swallowed by the effect of the drugs.

I shove to my knees, my knife in my hand. Seabird moves in sync and we face each other, his puff of white hair in disarray.

"Heal this," I say, and slide my blade into his chest.

<h1 style="text-align:center">44</h1>

I blink awake to a horribly familiar room, strapped to a table at wrist and ankle and forehead. Zorian struggles against his bonds on a table opposite mine, hard enough for the ghost of burning to circle my wrists. Swamp mud flakes to show the pristine skin beneath.

"Axelle," he says as soon as I focus on him. "Are you all right?"

I get the impression he's been calling my name for a while.

"What happened?" I say.

All I remember is the knife gliding easily into Seabird's chest. Then shrieking, pain and darkness. My temple throbs to the beat of my pulse and itches worse than my earthy camouflage.

"The thin man. He clubbed you with his weapon."

"Is Seabird dead?" I strain my eyes and catch a sliver of pink hair and black mud. "Where's Dalrainenna?"

"I do not know," Zorian says. "They bathed Seabird's wound in Dalrainenna's blood before carrying him away. Dalrainenna was put in a cage."

"I'm sorry, Fenna. Is he okay?"

Fenna's elbow jerks against the table. "The wound was deep in their panic but he is well. Angry. Worried for me."

I huff out a breath. "I guess I'm not his favourite person right now."

Though at least I don't have to deal with his accusatory stare.

"We had to try," Zorian says.

I forget and shake my head, sawing my eyebrows on the strap. "Your father was right. Dalrainenna was right. We should have waited."

"You could not leave your people in danger."

"They're in more danger now. You're in danger. You—" I suck in a breath to smooth my wobbling voice. "They're going to hurt you."

"I do not care, as long as I am with you."

My vision blurs, Zorian wavering to a slim, monochrome figure. His conviction sings in my chest, his hearts slower than the rapid, sickening thud of mine.

"I can't watch them hurt you, *feel* them hurt you. Treat you like Thommonn…" Bile somersaults in my gut and spurts into my throat. I squeeze my eyes shut and whisper, "I can't, I can't, I can't," over and over.

Zorian repeats my name until I look at him. His burst of calm soothes the spikes of my panic.

"I do not regret a single day since the cave."

"But we're going to die."

"Everything dies."

"How can you not hate me, my kind, even a little?"

His face softens, his smile cracking the mud over his cheekbones. "What do I feel, Axelle?"

"Too much. You feel too much."

"You feel the same as me."

"I love you," I sob.

Thank god my squad isn't here to see me fall apart. This squad leader is out of her depth.

"Same," Zorian says. "I am the same."

And I feel it, feel him. That intense, overwhelming need. I want to hold him so badly, it hurts. The ghost of his touch wraps its arms around me, strokes my hair, my face. Cradles my heart in its hands. I struggle to get myself under control. I definitely have tear tracks through the mud on my cheeks.

How embarrassing.

"I hate your kind a little," Fenna mutters as my crying jag abates. "Except you. You are an interesting human."

"Thank you, Fenna," I sniffle. "I like you, too."

The door slides open, and my settling heartbeat shudders into a gallop. Fenna and I watch Vail walk through, Zorian's back to the entrance in our triangle of torture tables. Mallory's oversized shoulders crowd the doorway, his slab of a face twisted in satisfaction. His olive uniform is still crumpled. Vail stomps over to me, his citrine gem shivering with each step. His slap cracks through my jaw and rings in my ears.

I forgot how much it hurt.

"I hope those are tears of shame, Axelle of the first generation," he spits. "You murdered a hero."

I touch my tongue to my lip and the familiar copper taste.

"I executed a war criminal," I say, my voice as bland as I can make it.

Vail's fists bunch but he spins away instead of striking me again. He plants himself in front of Fenna, and I strain my eyes to keep him in sight. Mallory hovers in the doorway, his burning gaze all for me.

"If it isn't our candy-haired runaway," Vail says then switches to Anann. "It is wonderful to see you again. We had little time to get acquainted, unlike your friend."

"May a water-tiger shit out your bones," she snarls.

She uses a more sedate word but my mind supplies the English expletive.

"And this must be Zorian," Vail says, pivoting on his heel.

Zorian bares his teeth, his eyes narrowed. The picture of a fierce Verdanian warrior.

"I hear you're the reason for this unholy alliance." Vail smiles his predator smile and turns to me. "How adept a liar you are, Axelle."

"I learned from the best."

Mallory bristles but Vail waves him off.

"I have also learned many things about you, Axelle of the first. Including how deep your treachery goes. Brindan of the seventh has been most forthcoming." Vail glides a fingertip on the stone at my throat, smirking at Zorian's growl. "It pained him to play along but he had no choice since you refused to share your plan until the eleventh hour."

"He wouldn't betray me or his squad."

Vail grins. "Step aside, Mallory of the fifth."

Mallory shifts his gloating bulk into the room and the already small space becomes claustrophobic. Brindan, exposed in the corridor, stares at his boots, his olive uniform immaculate. A flop of messy, brown hair hides his eyes. My stomach drops into my toes.

"Seems you're not such a great squad leader after all, hey, Axe?" Mallory says. "My influence saved Brindan from your bullshit."

Vail cocks a grey brow. "As Mallory of the fifth so eloquently puts it, we're fortunate your taint hasn't spread to your whole squad. Reconditioning the others will be work enough."

44

I ignore their triumphant expressions. Brindan continues to examine his footwear.

"Look at me, Brindan of the seventh," I say in my command voice.

He raises his eyes for a heartbeat. His cheeks flush dull red, and he hides behind Mallory.

"Tell her what you told us, Brindan," Vail says. "You don't need to suffer under her ego any longer."

"You don't deserve reconditioning," Brindan mumbles from behind his meaty barrier. "For betraying our trust, you deserve death."

"And what name did you call her? A name now befitting her station?"

Air whistles in and out. The silence after it seems to quiver.

"Verdanian slut," Brindan sneers.

45

"You are a traitor to your race, Axelle of the first. And I am looking forward to administering your punishment." Vail extends a knobbly finger and traces the cord criss-crossing my cleavage, eliciting another growl from Zorian. "Lovely outfit, by the way. Fitting to dress like the monsters now you're sleeping with the monsters."

I shake the echo of Brindan's words from my head but the pain lances deep.

"You're the only monster here," I say, my voice the same tinny echo after I saw Vail torture Thommonn.

Brindan must be bluffing. He can't—he *wouldn't*—betray his squad. I'm his leader. I've watched him grow up. Saved his life numerous times. I gave him his call sign after an overnight training exercise where Home Base turned into a big game of hide and seek. The kid sleeps with his arms and legs all over the place. I've never seen anything like it.

But the hatred packed into that insult…

Vail walks from my line of sight. A door squeaks. A package rustles, and metal clinks on metal. Zorian's gaze darts to me, a bleat of worry in my gut.

"The hour is late but I want to try something," Vail says. "A taster, if you will."

Vail slaps a silver mallet into his palm. The lights reflect off the sheen and spear my eyeballs. He halts in the centre of our triangle, hefting the tool in his hand. His gaze slides to me and something dark slithers behind his eyes.

The hammer swings. A thud of flesh. Pain claws at my ribs.

Zorian gives Vail his best blank face but I gasp before I can stop myself. Vail spins on his heel, his ponytail whipping his cheek, and brandishes the mallet at me.

"Oh, this will make the coming days interesting. Tell me, how long ago did you drink his blood?"

"I haven't," I say through gritted teeth, the pain fading to a throb to match the one in my temple.

The hammer cracks into my shoulder.

"Always with the lies, Axelle," Vail says over my shout.

Zorian roars loud enough to terrify a water-tiger. Long limbs strain against the bonds but even his strength can't break them.

Vail wags the mallet at him. "Did you feel that?"

"Leave her alone." Pistachio hair peeks through the streaks of black and flops into Zorian's eyes across the strap.

Vail presses the hammer into my throat. Mallory edges further into the room for a better look, his eyes fever-bright. Brindan, exposed again, turns his back without sparing me a glance. His face is as pale as a Verdanian's.

"Did you drink her blood?" Vail says to Zorian then leans close to breathe across my cheek, digging the hammer in until it hurts to swallow past it. "Did you offer your throat to the monster, Axelle?"

I glare at him. He disappears behind me, the mallet removed from my neck. A hand splays over my face. I jerk but don't move an inch. A fingertip pushes into my eyelid.

"One of you better start talking," Vail says.

The pressure increases, and pain blooms in my eye. Panic—mine and Zorian's—swirls in my stomach.

"I drank her blood," Zorian says quickly.

Vail pokes harder, and I clamp my lips on a whimper. Zorian winces, his eyelid fluttering shut. Vail laughs and strides into the centre of the triangle while I blink the blurriness from my vision.

"Fascinating," he says. "And the transference of emotion is the same?"

"Yes," Zorian hisses through his teeth.

"And you—do you share the same with the golden-eyed beast next door?"

Vail repeats his sentence in Anann when Fenna remains silent.

"I will skin you alive, human," she says.

Amusement smooths the wrinkles on Vail's face.

"Oh, yes, this will be very interesting indeed." He tosses the mallet out of sight and it rings on metal. "I can torture you both without damaging the precious merchandise."

Vail runs a finger across the scar on my cheek and down my throat, drawing a line all the way to my belly button. The light in his eyes tells me he's imagining a scalpel. My screams. Blood everywhere. Intestines if he cuts deep enough.

And Zorian, forced to watch, to *feel,* every slice while Vail slowly kills me.

Why didn't I stay in the caves, shagging Zorian into a coma? I've jeopardised everyone. I'm not a good squad leader. The only reason we're in this mess is because I'm their squad leader. If it weren't for me, they'd still be going to Earth lessons, getting drunk in the pub and shooting the occasional

Verdanian. Zorian would be mated to Calliyanna. And her army would obliterate Home Base.

They still might.

I struggle to squash the wave of despair. Zorian's bursts of calm vanish like pebbles tossed in an ocean. Vail steps away and gives me a pitying smile.

"Sweet dreams, Axelle of the first," he says.

My lip wobbles but lifts in a snarl. "Fuck you, Elderman Vail."

Mallory bristles, bunching his huge fists. Brindan attempts to melt into the wall.

Vail chuckles. "Such fighting spirit. We'll see how long that lasts this time. Are you coming, Mallory of the fifth, Brindan of the seventh?"

"With your permission, sir, I'd like to stay a little longer."

Half of Vail's mouth tilts in a cold smile. "Yes, I had a feeling you might. I advise caution, however. My plans do not include her breaking early."

Mallory turns empty blue eyes on me. "I'll show restraint, sir."

Oh, shit.

<h1 style="text-align:center">46</h1>

Fenna's elbow twitches at Vail's cheery whistle fading down the corridor, muffled by the door hissing shut.

The last time she heard it, it preceded Thommonn's screams. Now, it'll be mine.

Mallory unbuttons his olive shirt and spreads it open, the material framing his broad chest and ribbed stomach. His skin is too shiny, stretched tight, veins wriggling underneath. Nausea rolls in my gut.

"Don't even think about it, Mallory of the fifth," I say in my command voice. Strong and confident while the inside of me shrivels.

"You're not my squad leader anymore, Axe." His dimples flash in the parody of a grin that chills me to my toes.

"If you touch her, I will kill you."

Zorian's voice is as low and threatening as I've ever heard it. His fury nibbles my skin and chases the horror into a dark corner.

"And how're you going to do that strapped to a table?" Mallory circles Zorian, his expression a twist of disgust. "Him, Axe—really? Nice to know you'll let anything stick its dick in you. Well, alien, time to watch her get fucked by a real man."

The growl in Zorian's chest rumbles into mine. His muscles

strain, and fire bracelets my wrists. Beads of glimmering white slide from under his straps. Mallory spares him a smirk and focuses on me.

"I don't think your Verdanian sex toy is happy that I'll be the last thing you fuck before you die. Maybe try to hide how much you enjoy it. Oh, wait, you can't. He gets to feel it, too."

He directs a smug and savage smile at Zorian fighting vainly against the straps. I swallow hard, my tongue clicking in my dry mouth.

"Speaking from experience," I manage to say, "it's not much to write home about."

Mallory's turn to growl.

"Brindan!" he barks, and we both jump. "Bring me those scissors. Time to strip this cunt of any power she thinks she has."

Brindan scuttles from his position hugging the wall, his face alternating shades of white and green. He disappears towards where Vail got the mallet. More rustling and scraping metal.

Mallory strokes my cheek, his touch gentle. I clamp my lips on a surge of bile. Zorian's table rocks with the force of his struggles. Rage and anxiety war in my chest.

"Frankly, Axe, I don't give a shit if you enjoy it," Mallory says. "Because I will."

His hands drop to the waistband of his trousers and the bulge beneath the material. I glimpse a smudge of olive that must be Brindan but my eyes are fixed on Mallory, my stomach cramping dangerously.

I hope he likes vomit with his rape.

"Here, Barbie," Brindan whispers. "Enjoy this."

There's a streak of silver. A dull thud. Mallory's eyes roll and he thumps to the floor in a heap of bloated muscle.

The mallet follows to clink beside his head, a lump already forming on his thick skull. Brindan blinks at me, and I gape at him.

"Axe, I'm sorry!" he gasps, stumbling over Mallory's carcass. Shaking fingers fumble at my straps. Tears shimmer and fall unnoticed. "Mallory grabbed me outside Vail's pod. They already knew you were in Home Base, suspected your targets. I played along. They were seconds from capturing you. I thought if I stayed free, I could rescue you. I shouldn't have let it go so far but I didn't want to make them suspicious. I'm so sorry. I didn't mean any of it, I swear."

He's shivering, hiccuping, while I stare at him with my mouth open like a true, unruffled squad leader. He rips the straps free and I flop forward, my quivering legs just holding before I join Mallory on the floor. Brindan's hands flutter over me, not quite touching. I grab his shirt in both fists.

"You devious little bastard," I choke, and kiss him full on the mouth.

He blushes to the roots of his brown hair. I release him, and he sits hard on his butt right on top of Mallory. Zorian gives me a slow, beautiful smile, his shock and happiness exploding through my whole body.

"I am a little jealous," he says.

I leap Mallory's sprawled legs and collide with Zorian. His straps loosen under my desperate tugging then I'm hoisted in his arms, his mouth on mine, frantic enough to feel the press of his teeth. There's a small pain, the taste of copper, but I can't tell if it's from Zorian biting me or where Vail slapped me.

I don't much care.

I inhale Zorian instead of oxygen. He smells of mint and

swamp mud. A hint of burnt honey. I pull my mouth from his with a gasp. His ribs heave where my legs are wrapped around him and I'm not much better, panting into his face.

"Now *I'm* jealous," Brindan says.

We all grin stupidly at each other, and Fenna rolls her eyes.

"Not to interrupt but…" She jerks against the table.

Brindan scrambles to his feet. "Sorry, Fennanna… Fenno-golin… Fennangle—"

She steps from the table with a sniff and a shake of her pink hair.

"Fenna is fine, human," she says, and bends to kiss his cheek.

I giggle at his stunned expression, still a little giddy from our sudden rescue, though we're not safe yet. I cradle Zorian's wrist, the mud scraped away along with some skin, blood still weeping.

"Does it hurt?"

He smiles softly at me, and my heart flips.

"Can you not tell?" he says.

I kiss the raw wound on each wrist. Maybe lick him a little. He rewards me with a throb of pleasure that leaves me dizzy.

"What now, Axe?" Brindan says.

I gather myself back into squad leader mode.

"Now, we free the others and get the hell out of this prison," I say.

"It's been sealed," Marvyn says, slipping inside the jammed door of the above-ground dissection lab where we're all hunkered down.

I sigh. "I figured. Ah, well, Plan B—we go over the wall rather than through it."

Zorian squeezes my hand, crouched next to me and practically fused at the hip and shoulder. He hasn't let me get more than a couple of inches from him since we climbed out of the basement. Since I have no plan to stop touching him in the near future, I'm all for that.

He hoisted Mallory's limp carcass single-handed onto one of the torture tables and strapped him in before we left. His fingers left red marks on Mallory's skin but I said nothing. The anger burning my gut told me how much Zorian wanted to rearrange Mallory's limbs into an uncompleted Earth puzzle.

I was amazed by his restraint.

"I can give us a diversion," Brindan says, his hunched figure greyed by the murky dawn light bleeding through the blinds around the windows. "Give me a sec."

"What diversion?" I say but he's already scuttled out the door like a crab.

I feared for his life when the rest of the squad learned of his double-cross. They covered him in a scrum of bodies no human could possibly survive but he emerged flustered and dishevelled and grinning from ear to ear, his back no doubt pummelled to jelly. There wasn't a single dry eye in the room, except the Verdanians'.

A pre-emptive, "I know—you told me so," stopped Dalrainenna from making any remarks when I freed him from his cage. He crossed to Fenna and they held each other, touching foreheads and whispering in Anann. I admit, that got me a little teary, too.

It's been a long night.

Another plus, apart from us all being reunited, was our weapons left in a heap in the room of cages since Glennis messed with the armoury door. There's a knife on my hip, a gun in my hands, and my mate and my veterans are beside me.

I can do anything.

I thought about continuing our original mission. We have the upper hand, the Elders sleeping soundly in their beds, dreaming of torture and sweet, Verdanian flesh. But the generations and Passengers will soon be stirring and I can't risk them getting caught in the crossfire. It pains me to leave them living a lie but it'll only be for a little longer.

Soon, everyone will know the truth.

Brindan lollops into the room, cradling something against his chest. Something that looks suspiciously like a trigger fashioned into a box with wires and tape.

"Starfish, please tell me that's not what I think it is," I say.

"I learned something from Mallory." He gives a sheepish smile. "But I won't make any of his mistakes."

"Glad to hear it," I mutter. "Squad—move out."

We slip into the dawn hush of Home Base, the jungle awake with hoots and skreeing as the monewts and skreeingbirds welcome the day. We dodge between modules until we have a good view of the wall and the slumped figures pacing on top.

I hold up a fist. "Show me what you got, Starfish."

Brindan grins and mashes the button in his hand. The explosion shudders through my boots. Flames, smoke and twisted wreckage plume into the cobalt sky. Shouts follow a few seconds later. I turn wide eyes on Brindan, and he ducks his head.

"I didn't want them to ever use that place again," he whispers to his knees.

A fist squeezes my heart, and I blink back tears.

No self-respecting squad leader blubbers in front of her squad. Even if she loves every single one of them so fucking much.

"Hurly, please kiss Starfish for me," I say and my voice doesn't wobble. Not one bit.

She quirks a perfect, dark brow but leans in. Brindan's eyes pop out as she grabs his face and kisses him right on the mouth.

And keeps kissing him.

Brindan melts between her hands, his eyelids fluttering. His fingers cup her head and disappear into her silky hair. There's definitely a bit of tongue action.

I guess I'm no longer the person she's crushing on.

I clear my throat. "Okay, I wouldn't have done it quite like that but thorough job there, Hurly."

They break apart in a breathless rush, their cheeks tinged

pink. Brindan looks at Lili like he's never seen her before.

"Can I kiss Starfish next?" Pacal says.

"Strife, you can do whatever you want once we're over the wall." I aim a finger at his grin. "With consent."

We lope for the wall, Dalrainenna already unfurling the rope from around his shoulder. The weighted end flies true, looping around the handrail on our side and flopping back into Dalrainenna's waiting hand. He pulls it taught. Zorian goes first, as graceful as a water-tiger climbing a tree. He spools one end of the rope towards himself and rolls over the other side, Dalrainenna braced against the weight. I wave at my squad to follow, Fenna and Dalrainenna bringing up the rear. The whole process takes less than a minute, and the shouts remain concentrated on the merrily burning dissection lab.

I sprint into the jungle and my squad follows without hesitation, spacing into battle formation with the Verdanians easily keeping pace. When we're deep enough in, a whistle from Zorian brings Dacorna and two other falsielles belonging to Fenna and Dalrainenna, both of their names far too long for me to remember. Zorian smirked when I asked somewhat desperately for their short names and was told they had none.

I give my squad a few minutes to marvel at the new creatures. Dante and Loyanne pet Dacorna, laughing when she nibbles clumps of moss out of their hands. Karine seems fascinated by the crimson horns of Fenna's falsielle, the colour not far from her own bob of hair.

We walk further into the jungle, the rising suns casting shadows and spearing light through the leaves and fronds. Zorian stays beside me. Dante and Loyanne ride Dacorna, Lili and Brindan lost in each other. Nolana slings an arm around the much wider Glennis, a pink flower tucked behind her ear. Pacal, Karine and Marvyn scan the foliage with wary eyes and hustle to keep the rest of us in sight.

I take Zorian's hand. "Seems like you've adopted me and my squad."

He glances over his shoulder and slides me a smile.

"You are happy because they are safe. That makes me happy."

"Where will they all go?"

"We will find the space."

I cuddle into his side. "But we're locked out of Home Base. We need to get the people on the inside to rebel against the Elders. That could take ages."

"We will find a way," he says.

"Have you always been this optimistic?"

His grin flares bright in the dawn light. "Nothing has happened since we met to make me otherwise. We said we would stop the war together. Here are nine humans who are no longer fighting. Next, we get more. And more, until there is no war left."

I touch my head to his chest for a heartbeat.

"That sounds like a plan."

Fenna spurs her mount and pads along beside us, ferns brushing fur dappled grey and yellow. She twists to look behind her then focuses on Zorian, something glittering in her violet eyes though her expression is its usual blankness.

"Please, *please,* can I be there when you introduce them to your father?" she says.

"Shut up, Fenna," we say together.

A light rain starts to fall, misting between the leaves and forming rainbows.

It smells like home.

Let Me Know What You Think!

Thank you for reading my book! I love hearing from my readers so please leave me a review.

Can't wait to hear from you!

For exclusive free content and news on the next book in the *Verdana* series, join my mailing list at nadinelittle.com

About the Author

Nadine Little lives in Scotland and is an ecologist with an interest in botany, which came in handy for creating a whole planet's worth of flora and fauna. She writes science fiction and paranormal romance with sexy bits and swears. When she's not writing, she's making up different author biographies to put in the backs of her books. Oh, wait. That's writing. When she's not writing, she generally has her nose in her Kindle and can easily read a book a day. MM romance is her current favourite, much to the suspicion of her boyfriend.

For more on her books and a peek behind the scenes, sign up to her mailing list and follow her on social media.

You can connect with me on:

- https://nadinelittle.com
- https://twitter.com/Nadine_Little_
- https://www.facebook.com/nadinelittleauthor

www.ingramcontent.com/pod-product-compliance
Lightning Source LLC
Chambersburg PA
CBHW021237190726
48289CB00005B/1370